ADRIC'S HEART

A FADA NOVEL

REBECCA RIVARD

WILD HEARTS PRESS

Adric's Heart: A Fada Novel

The Fada Shapeshifter Series

Copyright ©2020 by Rebecca Rivard

Cover design by Laura Gordon/The Book Cover Machine

Editing by Katherine Teel

Adric's Heart/ Rebecca Rivard. — 1st ed.

ISBN 978-0-9985826-3-4

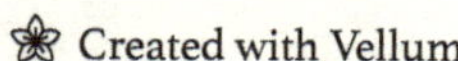 Created with Vellum

This one is for all the people who have helped shape the Fada Shapeshifter Series into six main books, a prequel, several shorter books...and counting!

Special thanks to my editor, Katherine Teel, whose insightful comments are always appreciated.

More thanks—and a warm hug—to my critique group, Julie, Cate, and Kalin, who push me to go that extra mile to make the books even better.

And a big, big thanks and lots of hugs to my awesome family, especially Nick and Ravenna, who read—and love—their mother's books. Your support means the world to me.

PROLOGUE

SEVEN YEARS EARLIER, IN THE LAST DAYS OF THE
DARKTIME

The kill was swift, silent...and without honor.

Honor was a luxury Adric Savonett couldn't afford.

He crouched on a dumpster in a dead-end alley. The alley was pitch-black, because he wanted it that way. While he'd acted as lookout, his sister Marjani had shimmied up the nearest streetlight and shattered the glass with the heavy handle of her dagger. Now she waited on the sidewalk while he squatted on top of the rusting metal container.

A human would've been nearly blind. But he was a fada. He picked up every detail. The dark pool of motor oil seeping into the cracked pavement. The sour-smelling garbage spilling out of the dumpster. The rumble of a late-night delivery truck barreling down the street.

And his uncle Leron as he stalked toward Marjani, brutal features displeased. "What the fuck are you doing here, girl? I ordered you to go to Jumar."

Adric's fingers clenched on his dagger. The blade was iron, honed to a razor-sharp edge. Inside, his cougar hissed.

Marjani lifted her chin. "And I said no."

They'd agreed to give Leron one last chance. If he rescinded his order that Marjani become his second's whore, Adric would let him live. For now, anyway.

Because everyone in the Baltimore clan, even their uncle, knew it was only a matter of time before Adric challenged him.

"I'm your alpha," Leron growled. "You don't tell me no." He backhanded Marjani across the face.

And sealed his fate.

She reeled backwards into the alley, their uncle following. Unlike them, he was a wolf shifter with his animal's big, powerful body even when he was a man. The S.O.B. was easily twice her weight.

Rage ripped through Adric, clouded his vision with red. He took a calming breath.

Come on, you fucker. Just a little closer.

"I won't whore for you," Marjani spat out. "Jumar can find his own damn woman."

Leron's eyes flashed wolf-gold. He showed his fangs. "You'll do whatever I fucking say. If I tell you to drop to your knees and suck off every single one of my lieutenants, then you will. Understand?"

Marjani snarled and backpedaled past the dumpster.

Leron prowled after.

Closer, closer. And...now.

Adric leapt, landing on Leron's back. His uncle cursed and tried to buck him off, but Adric got him in a headlock. Leron ran backwards, slamming him into a brick wall. Adric grunted and grimly hung on.

One hard stroke of the dagger across his uncle's throat, and it was over. Leron made a terrible sucking sound and clawed at his neck. The coppery scent of blood filled Adric's nostrils as the iron blade poisoned his uncle, hastening his end.

Adric met Marjani's eyes over Leron's head. Her irises glowed cougar-blue in the dark. A sharp dagger was clenched in her hand. He said a silent prayer of thanks that she hadn't had to use it. Better it be him who killed their father's only brother.

He released Leron, let him drop to the pavement.

The dying man managed to turn over. His eyes widened. "You," he gurgled as his blood pooled on the asphalt.

"Me," Adric confirmed.

"Too much of a coward...to challenge...me."

Adric leaned forward. "Everything I know about honor," he growled, "I learned from you. Burn. In. Hades."

Reaching into Leron's shirt, he grabbed his quartz pendant and jerked it over his head. His uncle's face contorted. His mouth opened and shut, and then he shuddered and went limp. His eyes filmed over.

Adric found a rock, smashed the quartz. Leron was powerful. Adric was taking no chances he'd somehow heal himself.

A quiver racked Marjani's lean frame, but the look she turned on Adric was triumphant. "You did it. You really did it."

"Yeah." He stared down at his monster of an uncle and wondered why he felt nothing, not even elation. The man who'd made both their lives a living hell was finally dead. Surely he should feel something?

Together, he and Marjani bundled the dead man into the trunk of their car. By dawn, Leron Savonett was buried deep in a western Maryland forest.

Within a week, Adric had fought off a challenge from first Jumar, then one of his own cousins, and been declared alpha of the Baltimore Earth Fada.

Adric and Marjani immediately set about saving the clan that his uncle had all but decimated. The Darktime, the clan had called it, although only behind Leron's back.

Adric's first order of business was to gather the clan in a secret corner of Druid Hill Park and appoint Marjani as his second-in-command. Then he looked around at his hungry, hollow-eyed people. In the last ten years, the clan had lost nearly half its members. The elders had been especially hard-hit, caught up in the bitter infighting of the Darktime. And he could count the number of cubs born during Leron's decade-long reign of terror on two hands—and still have a few fingers left over.

"As of today, the Darktime is over," he declared, hard-voiced. "You can leave, if you choose. But fight me, and die. Those who stay will follow my orders. In return, you and your cubs will be fed if I have to grow the damn food myself. The elders will be honored again, and you will be free to mate as you wish. We *will* become a strong, healthy clan once more. That, I promise on the souls of my mother and father."

The clan took a collective breath, and then one by one, they dropped to their knees, accepting him as the new alpha. It was spring. In a nearby tree, a single bird sang as the sun rose over the park, casting a pink glow on the kneeling crowd.

Adric allowed himself a thin smile. "Okay, then," he said, and watched as the clan rose back to their feet, some smiling, some—especially the clan's wolves—with set faces.

He hadn't asked for this, hadn't really wanted it. Hell, at twenty-six turns of the sun, he was barely an adult by fada standards. But he squared his shoulders and set to work rebuilding the clan, Marjani and a few trusted friends at his side, and he kept every damn promise he made.

Every promise but one, that is. The very first promise he'd ever made—to protect Marjani, no matter what. He'd saved her from Leron and Jumar, but five years later, she'd been lured into a trap by members of his own clan, who'd handed her over to a den of feral river fada.

And Adric hadn't known until it was too late.

Leron might be dead, but the Darktime hadn't ended with him. It still lived in the dark corners of the clan's souls.

Adric's included.

1

THE PRESENT DAY

*A*dric winced as a human female shrieked with laughter near his left ear.

The Full Moon Saloon was packed tighter than a can of sardines. Mainly with earth fada, but the mix included river fada as well as a handful of humans slumming with the shifters. The dank, poorly-lit saloon reeked of alcohol and lust, and the band had more enthusiasm than skill.

What in Hades was he doing in this crowded, noisy bar? But it was Saturday night, and he had nothing better to do. Which was fucking sad.

He glowered at his beer bottle.

Crowded around the table with him were two clanswomen and his friend Zuri. A big, smooth-talking wolf shifter with a shaved head and a soul patch beneath his lower lip, Zuri divided his attention between the women, and Dina and Cara flirted right back.

Then Zuri reeled Dina in for a leisurely kiss.

Cara just smiled and hitched her chair closer to Adric's. "Hey, babe." She set a hand on his knee. "Wanna take this back to your den?"

He hesitated. The gods knew, he'd gone too long without, and all Cara wanted was a night with the alpha. No harm, no foul, and both of them free to go their own way in the morning.

But he simply wasn't interested.

He removed her hand from his knee, kissed her fingers. "Not tonight, beautiful."

Cara wasn't so easily put off. She was a warm-hearted young deer, one of the few in the clan. She leaned in, a worried pucker between her liquid brown eyes.

"You sure? You seem—" She paused, choosing her words. "Edgy."

"I'm sure," he said in a voice designed to halt further questions.

Cara studied him another few seconds before nodding. She was low in the hierarchy. Just questioning him—her alpha—had clearly taken all her deer's courage.

Looping an arm around her shoulder, Adric nuzzled her cheek, offering reassurance in the way of their animals. She relaxed and turned back to Dina, who was now on Zuri's lap. The wolf shifter made a dry, Zuri-type comment and both women giggled.

Adric made himself listen, smile. But Cara was right. He *was* edgy, although he hadn't realized it was bleeding into his interactions with the clan.

He took a gulp of beer and forced his shoulders to relax.

One more drink, and he'd leave—or maybe check out the poker game in the back room. Because the only thing worse than this crowded bar was his solitary den.

The opening of the outer door sent a blast of icy air down the short hall into the bar. A long-legged beauty sauntered inside, her lush body poured into tight pants, a lipstick-red leather jacket, and ankle boots the same scarlet as her jacket. Wavy hair the blue-black of a raven's wings framed a heart-shaped face and curled over high, round breasts.

One wide smile and Benny, the hulking earth-fada bouncer who should've known better, fell over himself to wave her in.

Rosana do Rio. Adric's heart gave a hard knock.

What was *she* doing here?

And alone.

Inside, his cougar snapped to attention, eyeing her with a cat's intentness.

She headed towards the bar without bothering to remove her jacket or gloves. The woman didn't walk, she sauntered, hips swaying. All around the room, males pulled back their shoulders and puffed out their chests.

Zuri muttered a curse and set Dina back on her chair. Adric didn't even glance at him, his gaze glued to Rosana.

She hadn't even reached the long wooden bar when a human asked her to dance. A cocky blond college-type surrounded by three equally arrogant wingmen.

Adric's back teeth clamped together. *Not your business.*

Rosana smiled and allowed the blond human to take her gloved hand. He led her onto the microscopic dance floor and set his hands on her hips, drawing her closer.

A growl scraped Adric's throat. His claws slid out and he started to his feet.

No one touched Rosana but him.

"Easy now." Zuri's fingers clamped onto Adric's wrist. He wasn't just a good friend, but one of Adric's lieutenants. "Don't do anything you'll regret."

Adric snarled. *Back off.*

Zuri removed his hand but stared back steadily. Not challenging Adric, just reminding him of who and what he was.

He sank back onto his chair. His friend was right. Adric was drawing attention, especially from the other fada.

Rosana was a dolphin shifter, a river fada—and he was alpha of the Baltimore earth fada. Water and earth fada just didn't mix. And Rosana wasn't just any river fada, she was the sister of Lord Dion, alpha of Adric's clan's biggest rival.

Which meant he could look but not touch.

Rosana did one of those evasive twists women do, forcing the human to release her, and danced away.

Adric's claws retracted.

"Drink your beer," Zuri prompted.

He picked up his bottle but didn't bring it to his mouth.

The lieutenant fingered his soul patch. "You want me to boot her sexy ass out of here?"

"For what reason?"

"Disturbing the fucking peace."

The Full Moon Saloon was technically a neutral space owned by a Brazilian river fada named Claudio. But Baltimore was Adric's territory; if he gave the word, Rosana would be banned from the bar.

But then he wouldn't get even these occasional glimpses of her. The Rock Run Clan's base was an underground fortress protected by fae wards impossible for him to break. And he'd tried.

He brought the bottle to his lips. Swallowed. "Let her stay."

Zuri leveled a look at him. "Maybe you should just take her," he said in a voice pitched for Adric's ears only. "She wants you. Even her brothers know it—that's why they try to keep her up at Rock Run. Bang the woman already. Get her out of your system."

Adric's fingers tightened on the bottle. "I'll handle my own damn love life, thank you."

"But you haven't been handling it. When's the last time you had a good, hard—"

He sliced Zuri a look. "Enough."

The other man moved a big shoulder in a shrug and subsided.

Adric glanced around. In addition to Dina and Cara, there were five other unmated earth fada females in the bar, any of whom would be thrilled to take the alpha to bed for a night. And like with Cara, it would be no harm, no foul.

But he only wanted Rosana.

Who hadn't even glanced his way since entering the bar.

The music ended. With a nod at the cocky blond human, Rosana wended her way through the tables to the polished oak bar. The man followed, his gaze glued to her ass.

Fuck this.

Adric moved with fada-fast speed, cutting off the human to squeeze in next to Rosana.

"Hey!" The man's fingers dug into Adric's arm. "She's with me."

Adric turned. "No," he said, letting his cat into his eyes. "She's not."

The man's Adam's apple bobbed. He released Adric and backed away. "Right. I—" He fled back to the safety of his wingmen.

Adric turned to Rosana. "Hello, love." Her lips were a slick crimson the same shade as her jacket. "What're you drinking?"

"Adric." In her faint, sexy accent, his name came out as *Ah-dreek* instead of Aaa-dric. The two syllables shivered deliciously over his skin. He could almost ignore the way she inclined her head like she was a princess and he a slimy green frog.

So she was still pissed off at him. He supposed he deserved it. The gods knew, he'd been an ass the last time they'd met.

Her deep blue eyes flashed. "I can get my own drink, thank you." She reached for her wallet.

He slapped a hand onto hers over the glove. "I asked," he said between clenched teeth, "what are you drinking?"

"Fine." She jerked her hand out from beneath his. "Buy me a Dos Equis."

He raised two fingers at Sophie, the motherly Mediterranean Sea fada tending bar along with Claudio. "Two, please."

While they waited for their beers, he put an elbow on the bar and angled his body toward Rosana. She had the fresh, clean scent of a clear mountain pool. Beneath his T-shirt, his quartz warmed, like it always did when she was near—seeking to complete their connection, as if they were two mated earth fada.

But Rosana wasn't an earth fada, she was a river fada. And the two of them could never mate.

Inside, his cougar hissed in disagreement.

A corkscrew of black hair had fallen forward over her shoulder. He itched to finger it, see if it was as soft as he remembered. Instead, he fisted his hand and gave her a mocking smile.

"Didn't expect to see you in Baltimore again so soon. Decided you want to tangle with a cat, huh?"

The last time they'd met, he'd told her to stay out of his city if she knew what was good for her. Said that if she wasn't careful, "a big, bad cat would carry her off to his lair."

Her long-lidded blue eyes narrowed. "You know what?" she asked sweetly. "Sometimes you can be a real *cabrão*."

A *bastard*, a *motherfucker*. That was one Portuguese word he knew. She wasn't the first Rock Run fada who'd tossed it at him. But with Rosana, he deserved it.

His gaze slid from hers. "It was for your own good."

"Oh, yeah?" Her look should've fried him where he stood. "Well, maybe I'm tired of other people deciding what's good for me. Maybe I want to decide for myself."

He raised his beer to her. "Then go for it."

When she shot him an uncomprehending look, he shrugged. "Hey, I'm not your brother or even a member of your clan. You want something, go out and get it. Just don't come to *my* city and try to mess in *my* business."

She leaned closer, dropped her voice. "And if what I want is you?"

He gulped. Took a swig of beer. Replayed her question in his head. "*That's* why you're here?"

A tiny nod. She looked out over the crowd, seemingly unconcerned, her slim frame was taut with tension. "I want to take you up on your offer."

His heart slammed in his chest. Hard, disbelieving beats. "My offer?"

He'd practically begged her for one night, had even offered to meet her out of town so no one would know. But she'd turned him down.

He shifted closer and she turned her head to meet his eyes. The noisy bar faded away until it was just the two of them.

He swayed toward her, his gaze locked on her shiny red lips.

He could already taste them beneath his, feel their softness. Hear her gasp as he took her deeper...

"Here you go, *bibi*." Sophie's cheerful voice wrenched him to his senses. She set the beers on the bar behind them.

He dragged in a breath, handed the bartender a ten. "Keep the change."

"Thanks." Her gaze flicked between Rosana and him, and then she chuckled before moving on to the next customer.

Adric picked up both bottles and handed one to Rosana.

The other fada in the bar—both river and earth—were eyeing them.

He smoothed out his expression and lowered his voice to subvocal tones. "Just to be clear, you'll give me one night."

She dipped her chin in assent.

He rubbed a thumb over the bottle's two bright red X's. "And you changed your mind—why?"

Why the fuck was he arguing? She'd said yes, hadn't she? But he couldn't help being suspicious.

He'd wanted—no, craved—this woman for six and a half years. But it was like Romeo mooning over Juliet, and he wasn't the idiot Romeo had been. Besides, she'd been barely sixteen, too young and way too sweet for a cynical bastard like him. He'd contented himself with a dance the few times their clans had socialized— and a searing kiss or two. She was twenty-two now, and he was tired of pretending this thing between them didn't exist.

But he'd made a move—twice—and both times, she'd shut him down.

Then, a few weeks ago she'd come looking for him, said she'd had a "hunch" that he was planning something against the night fae, and she wanted to help.

He'd told her no fucking way.

They'd argued, and then he'd taken her hand. She'd gone stick-straight, her irises darkening to an eerie black. That was when he'd realized she had the Sight.

"The Darktime isn't over," she'd said in a Seer's toneless voice. "The prince will destroy your clan from the inside out."

A chill had run over his skin. *She was a Seer.* He hadn't known, and there wasn't much he didn't know about the do Rio family.

He'd shaken her, demanded to know what she'd Seen. There was a fraught silence, and then with a shudder, she'd come back to herself and whispered, "That's insane. You can't kill him. You'll set off something you can't stop."

But maddeningly, that had been all she could tell him.

His spine had iced. Nobody knew what he was planning. Not even his sister.

And Rosana didn't know. Not really. She'd Seen a possible future, that's all. So he'd sent her on her way, told her to stay the fuck out of Baltimore.

Now her fine dark brows scrunched together. "If you're not interested..."

He growled. "You know damn well I'm interested. I'm just wondering why now."

A shrug. "Maybe I'm curious."

Cat's balls.

His dick twitched, his dark side picturing all the things he could teach a curious virgin, because he *knew* she hadn't had another man. She was only twenty-two turns of the sun, and an alpha's pampered baby sister.

Unashamed, he reached down and adjusted his pants.

Her eyes tracked his movement. The tip of her tongue darted out to moisten her full lower lip. He stifled a groan as his dick went from half-hard to full, aching attention.

But the alpha in him was still suspicious. "Does this have something to do with that vision you had?" He lowered his voice even more. "Because I told you, there's no way I'm letting a river fada help in any way, shape, or form. Especially a Rock Run fada."

She blew out a breath. "*Deus*, Adric. I'm just looking for a little fun. But if you changed your mind, I get it."

And without giving him a chance to reply, she took her beer

and headed into the crowd. A few seconds later, she was dancing with another man, this one a river fada.

Adric's nostrils flared. *No. Hell no.*

So Rosana wanted some fun? Then she'd damn well have it with him.

Still, he hadn't become alpha of a murderous, warring clan by playing his cards for all to see. And the other river fada in the bar were glaring at him with fire in their eyes.

He lifted his beer to them in a mocking salute and headed to the back room and the poker game.

But when she left the bar, he was waiting.

2

———

*R*osana eyed the small bathroom window in the ladies' room, calculating she'd just fit. Locking the door—*Sorry, ladies*—she removed her jacket and gloves and eased up the window.

A hop and a slither got her upper body through the narrow opening, but her hips were stuck fast. She turned sideways, pushed hard against the frame and with a deep inhale and a little cursing, popped the rest of the way out. Twisting in mid-air, she landed on her feet in the tiny parking lot behind the saloon.

An icy January drizzle spattered her. She raised her face, drinking in the coolness against her heated skin, before pulling on her jacket and heading around the corner to her sportbike.

Built on the waterfront, Fell's Point dated to the time when Baltimore was a major port and shipbuilding center teeming with seamen and pirates. The road was paved in cobblestones, the streetlights an old-fashioned black metal. Trees pushed through miniscule squares of earth in the sidewalk to raise stunted branches to the moonless sky, and the buildings were a mix of shops, warehouses and brick rowhouses with gabled roofs.

Her hands were clammy. She wiped them on her pants and pulled on her gloves.

Elation filled her. She'd done it. Gone to Adric, the man she'd wanted since forever, it seemed.

But he didn't say yes.

Her steps slowed. Was he going to just let her leave?

He'd been so suspicious. She hadn't expected that. But then, that vision had shocked them both.

It had been last month, right before the winter solstice. She'd tracked him down because she'd been having maddening glimpses of the future. Her gut had told her he was planning something against the night fae, and she'd wanted to help.

He'd been suspicious then, too. But he'd taken her hand, kissed her wrist. His fingers had closed on hers, and...

Darkness. So much darkness.

Stomach churning, she pressed the heels of her hands to her eyes.

His touch had triggered her Sight. She'd Seen Adric crouched as his cougar in a tree, focused on a tall, black-haired man with pale skin and a fae's pointed ears.

Adric is slipping through the forest, a man now.

Something flashes in his hand—a dagger made of iron, the only metal that can kill a fae or a fada.

The black-haired fae turns around. It's Langdon, the night fae prince.

His gaze flicks in Adric's direction. A smile moves across his coldly beautiful face...and three night fae warriors converge on Adric.

The scene shifts to Baltimore, sometime in the near future. Adric's clan is hunkered down in their dens. The night fae are everywhere, and darkness slinks through his people like a feral wolf.

Cold. Relentless. Hungry.

And their alpha is nowhere to be seen.

She removed her hands from her eyes, stared at the gloved fingers.

Why had she let Adric touch her bare hand? She *knew* touching people could set off her Sight, and when she was in the grip of a vision, she wasn't in control. Things—prophecies—spilled out of her as if she were just a mouthpiece.

Her lips twisted. Wouldn't it be ironic if she'd scared off the man after he'd been chasing her for six years?

"Rosana." A thread of sound from a nearby alley, accompanied by Adric's scent, musky, a little earthy. The forest on a rainy day.

Her heart jumped.

The alley appeared empty until she looked up. The Baltimore alpha crouched on a warehouse roof like the cougar he was, blending into the shadows in dark jeans and a black leather jacket. She knew she'd only seen him because he'd let her.

Her mouth dried. Anticipation shivered up her spine.

A supple flex of his muscles, and he dropped soundlessly to the pavement.

He straightened, prowled nearer.

He wasn't as big as her brothers, but he was just as powerful, lean and hard-bodied. An alpha to the bone.

And gorgeous with tawny skin, spiked-up black hair bleached blond at the tips, and a face meant for sinning: long cheekbones, heavy-lidded eyes and a sensuous mouth just this side of mocking.

In the human world he'd have been a rock star. A badass, rule-breaking rock star.

He stopped so close she felt the heat of his body. Earth fada ran warmer than water fada; it was like standing next to a bonfire, hot and heady.

Her nipples pricked, pushed against her shirt. Her pussy clenched.

His nostrils flared, and she knew he scented her arousal. His odd bronze eyes darkened. "Tomorrow night. I'll book us a room on the Eastern Shore."

"And no one will know."

"No one," he confirmed. "There's a B&B on the beach. Owned by a human. He takes cash and he doesn't ask questions. Can you meet me on I-95?" He named a service plaza between Baltimore and Grace Harbor.

"What time?"

"Noon." His mouth edged up in a sardonic smile. "You sure this is okay with your brothers? I don't want to wake up with a knife to my throat—or..." He gestured at his crotch.

She shrugged, because it wouldn't be okay with them—if she told them. But Adric didn't need to know that. "No one followed me here, did they?"

A shake of his head.

"I'll be there," she told him. "Alone."

Fada had a hard time lying, but she didn't have to tell the whole truth, either. She'd explain to Dion and his mate, Cleia—who were more like parents to her—that she wanted to get away for a night or two. The Goddess knew, that was the truth. Sometimes she was so desperate to get away from the base and her well-meaning but overprotective family that she felt like screaming.

Adric stepped back. "Come here." He leaned against the brick wall and extended a hand.

Her stomach did a little flip. She moistened her lips.

I'm really doing this.

On the nearby sidewalk, several too-loud humans strolled past, but she barely heard them. Here in the alley, it was just her and Adric.

He cocked a mocking brow. "You in—or not?

She lifted her chin and took his hand. "I'm in."

He drew her closer and in one smooth move, had her crowded up against the wall. His eerie metallic irises were shot with blue now. His cougar was awake, intent on her like she was prey and it was starving.

He fisted his hands in her hair. His gaze went to her lips, and then his mouth was moving over hers. Softly, slowly. Teasing. Seducing.

The nerves in her belly fired up. Points of heat sizzled up and down her spine.

She moaned and opened her mouth, and his tongue slipped

in, curling around hers. She sucked it deeper. He gave a low, exciting groan from deep in his throat.

He tasted of beer and his own dark male flavor. His body pressed hers to the wall, his cock hard against her belly. Heat came off him in waves. Stoking her desire, scrambling her brain.

She forgot that anyone could stumble upon them, especially those Rock Run men in the saloon who'd watched, narrow-eyed, the whole time she was speaking to Adric. They'd be out here now if she hadn't escaped through the bathroom window.

Worse, she completely forgot that she shouldn't touch him.

She jerked off her gloves and slid her hands under his jacket. She dragged up his T-shirt, seeking skin. Sliding her hands over his hard, dangerous body.

His hands were busy as well. One gripped her hair, pulling her head back so he could nibble at her throat. With the other, he unzipped her jacket and palmed her breast through her shirt.

She twined a leg around his thigh, urging him closer, rubbing herself against his erection. His chest flattened her breasts, the pressure easing her aching nipples.

He sucked on the tender skin beneath her jaw. Sensation speared from her breasts to her womb.

She gasped and writhed against him. "Adric. I—"

"Shh. It's okay. Just a little more..."

He moved to another spot, murmuring how beautiful she was. Telling her how much he wanted her. That he'd make it good, so good for her.

"*Sim, sim.*" She slipped into Portuguese and then caught herself. "Yes. Anything."

Adric was the one who called a halt. He lifted his head, breathing hard, and she gave another moan and tried to pull him back, but he set her a little away from him.

"Tomorrow." He brushed his lips over hers. "Tomorrow. Noon."

"Okay. Yes." Her voice sounded hoarse to her ears.

"I want your promise. You'll be there, no matter what."

"I'll be there. I promise."

"Good." He nipped her earlobe and then faded back into the shadows, watching as she zipped her jacket with fingers that felt thick, awkward.

He waited until she'd picked up her gloves before turning toward the wall. She watched as he leapt ten feet straight up, catching onto a gutter and swinging himself back onto the roof.

The man was a freaking human cat. Literally.

He remained on the roof, watching over her as she walked the half block to her sportbike.

She touched her tingling lips. The man sure knew how to use that sexy mouth.

She turned and walked backward. "Tomorrow," she mouthed and blew him a kiss.

Adric's eyes flashed an electric blue. His growl was soft, but she heard it. A thrill shivered over her skin.

She grinned and turned back around. She was halfway up I-95 before her body stopped humming.

BACK IN GRACE HARBOR, she parked the sleek purple bike in the clan garage and wiped the rain off the body. She didn't own the sportbike—the clan shared most vehicles—but she used it enough that she thought of it as hers.

That done, she tossed the rag into the bin provided for that purpose and headed into the passage that tunneled under Rock Run Creek to the base on the other side. The caverns were quiet, most of the clan in bed. An aqua-blue fae light wafted over to light her way through the labyrinthine tunnels.

She nodded at the few people she met without adding the usual hug. Since coming into her Gift as a Seer, she'd learned to avoid casual touches so as not to set off the Sight. People thought it odd, but fortunately, she'd always followed her own quirky drum. The clan expected her to be different.

Only her family—and now Adric—knew about her Gift, and

she intended to keep it that way. She'd heard the stories of her Irish Seer mother. People might have liked Ula Gallagan, but they'd been wary of her, too. Everyone said they'd like to know the future, but when it came right down to it, no one wanted to be told their own death was barreling down at them like a great white shark, cold-eyed and relentless.

She turned a corner and stopped dead. She'd touched Adric without setting off her Sight. That was odd, especially after what had happened in December.

But not unexpected. One thing she'd learned was the Sight was erratic. It came and went at its own whim.

She continued walking until she reached the quarters she shared with Isa, her childhood nurse. Something else that had to change. She was too old to be living with her nurse, much as she loved the older woman. Everyone else her age had moved to the unmated warriors' quarters.

Easing open the door, she slipped off her boots and padded into the small *sala*.

"*Boa noite*," said a deep voice from the direction of Dion and Cleia's apartment.

Her alpha brother loomed in the doorway connecting their apartments, big hands gripping the doorjamb above him, his black hair loose around his shoulders, his only clothing a pair of cut-off sweats that bagged around his muscular thighs. Even fresh out of the bed, the man looked authoritative, in control.

She stifled a sigh as she set down the boots and stripped off her jacket and gloves. Yep, she definitely had to get her own place.

Dion was over one hundred turns of the sun, more like her dad than a brother. And like her *papai*, he'd been born and raised in Portugal with an old-world way of looking at things. He also had that whole alpha-protective-thing going on. He just didn't understand that at twenty-two, his little chick was ready to spread her wings and fly. And if she fell, well, that would be on her, not him.

"*Olá*, Dion. Sorry if I woke you up." She spoke in Portuguese, the language the clan used at home. She dropped onto the couch to take off her socks.

Dion sat next to her. "You didn't wake me. The little one was fussing."

"Brisa?" Rosana stopped in the act of removing a sock. Fada didn't often get sick, even the children. Their touch of fae blood fought off human viruses. "She okay?"

Brisa was the one thing Rosana and Dion agreed on. The tiny girl had them both wrapped around her plump little finger.

"She's fine. Just teething. Cleia gave her a shot of healing energy, and she went right back to sleep."

"*Bom.* I hate it when she's hurting."

Rosana pulled the sock the rest of the way off and wriggled her toes. *Deus*, she detested shoes, but even a shifter couldn't walk barefoot around Baltimore.

"Me, too." He exhaled. "I feel so fucking powerless."

She blinked. Her big brother had admitted there was something he couldn't fix? The man had balls of steel. Hell, he'd kidnapped the sun fae queen—one of the most powerful fae in the world—and not only had he survived, he'd mated the woman.

"She'll be fine." She awkwardly patted his leg over the cut-offs, careful not to touch his bare skin. "Kids have to go through these things, you know."

"I know." He gave her a lopsided smile. "I remember when you were teething—we all took turns walking with you at night."

"Yeah?"

"Oh, yeah. You were the cutest thing, and usually all smiles. But when you weren't happy, the whole family knew it."

She chuckled. "Sorry. At least Brisa has a mom who's a healer."

"*Sim.* And a full belly."

Their eyes met, and she knew they were both recalling the years when the clan was poor and hungry, the children too thin, sickly. Rosana might have been a pup, but she hadn't forgotten how hard Dion had worked to save the clan, even while their *papai* was still alpha.

And then their parents had gone missing, and Dion had had to step in and raise both Rosana and their brother Tiago while also leading the search for Nisio and Ula. Then, when it became clear their parents had either died or been ensnared by the fae, he'd taken over as the new alpha.

For the first time, she realized how hard it must have been on him. He'd become both a father and alpha, all within a few months.

"Brisa's a lucky girl," Rosana said. "She has you and Cleia for parents."

"You really think so?" A strange, almost diffident look crossed his face.

She gave an emphatic nod. "I know so."

"*Obrigado.*" Dion stifled a yawn.

"No need to thank me. It's the truth." She made to stand up. "But I should let you get to bed."

"Sit." A soft command.

She sank back onto the couch, spine stiff.

"You were in Baltimore."

She lifted her chin. "So?"

"Davi was here earlier. He said you were talking to Lord Adric. That the two of you looked...involved."

Her jaw tightened. On the way home from Baltimore, she'd toyed with the idea of telling Dion straight out about her and Adric. Now she was glad she'd kept her mouth shut.

"Davi should mind his own business." He was an ambitious young *tenente* who was only interested in her because she was the alpha's sister.

"He didn't have to tell me. I can smell Adric on you."

Her chin jutted. "So?"

"Rosana." Dion's tone made her feel like a pup again. "The man's a sneaky S.O.B. He wants Rock Run territory for his own clan. He tricked his way inside once—how do you know he's not trying to do it again?"

She stared down at her hands. They'd curled into fists. She straightened them out. She was *not* going to fight with Dion. He might have raised her from the time she was six, but she was an adult now.

"That was years ago. When was the last time you had any problems with him?"

"Doesn't mean he isn't planning something." Dion's mouth turned down. "The man doesn't have control of his own clan. In the last year alone, he and that sister of his have taken out two of his cousins."

She gritted her teeth. Dion was so certain he knew Adric, and sure, he'd done some bad things in the past. But Adric had changed. She knew he had.

"He's doing the best he can. It's not his fault he inherited a mess from that uncle of his. If he killed his cousins, then he had a good reason."

"And then there's his uncle. He didn't even have the balls to challenge him—Leron Savonett just disappeared. The man has no honor, and he wants Rock Run's territory. Don't forget Tiago. Adric played him like a fucking violin—and we almost lost the base because of it. The bastard will do anything to take me down, and you're my sister."

"So he can't want me for myself?" she asked evenly.

A muscle ticked in Dion's jaw. "That's not what I meant. You're a beautiful girl. You know that."

"I'm not a girl," she said between tight lips. "I'm a woman." Which was the whole problem. To Dion, she'd always be a girl, the little sister he'd raised from the time she was a pup.

"Rosana..."

She expelled a breath. "You were there for me after we lost Mama and *Papai* to King Sindre and the ice fae. I'll never forget that. But you're not my dad, Dion. Even if you were, I'm all grown up now. I love you, but you don't get to tell me who I—"

"And if he's just using you?"

The hurt nearly doubled her over. That the big brother she

admired more than anyone in the world thought she was so stupid Adric could use her to harm the clan.

She came to her feet. "We're both tired. I'm going to forget you said that. *Boa noite*."

"Rosana. Damn it, I—"

"No. Just...no." She walked into her bedroom and shut the door. Calm and controlled.

Then she fisted her hands, arched her back and let out a silent scream.

3

———

*A*dric tapped his quartz against the door to Jace Jones' den.

He'd been up since dawn, too antsy to sleep. After making the reservation at the B&B in Lewes, he'd headed across town to see Marjani, who, along with her mate Fane, roomed with Jace now.

The door opened—all the clan's dens were keyed to his quartz—and he slipped inside. Jace wasn't home. Another of Adric's lieutenants, the jaguar shifter was spending the winter in Grace Harbor with his human mate, Evie, and her brother Kyler while Kyler finished his senior year of high school.

Earth fada didn't gather in one base like water fada. Instead, the clan lived in underground dens scattered throughout the city. Everyone was still in bed, the living room empty except for the orange tomcat stretched along the couch's back. Tigger gave an ostentatious stretch—making sure Adric knew he'd interrupted his nap—and leapt to the floor. He butted his head against Adric's calf, one dominant feline to another.

Adric knelt to scratch Tigger behind the ears, his gaze taking in the homey clutter that spoke of the clan members who lived there. Jace, Evie, and Kyler when they were in town. Marjani and her mate, Fane Morningstar, an ice fae/human mix who was also Evie's father. Rounding out the group were three unmated males: a dreadlocked cougar named Horace; a burly tiger named Sam; and Beau, a big, slow-talking bear.

Sneakers and motorcycle boots were jumbled by the front door beneath the leather jackets and hoodies hanging from pegs on the wall. The couch was big and comfortable, and a sturdy coffee table held three empty beer bottles and a stack of cards. In the fireplace, chunks of amber quartz glowed cozily.

It made Adric's own den seem sterile. He frowned. Maybe he should invite someone to move into his sister's old bedroom. His den was too quiet these days, the two bedrooms more space than an unmated man needed.

But he was alpha. No one but his lieutenants and a few close friends were trusted with his address. And politics being what they were, he couldn't invite someone to live with him without appearing to be favoring one faction over the other. The cats would object if he invited a wolf, and the wolves would get pissed off if he invited a cat. And that didn't even take into account the dozen or so bears and deer. So for now, he lived alone.

The kitchen was large, welcoming. Jace had inherited the den from his parents, who'd always had an open door. Stop by for a meal or a few days, it was all the same to them. They'd never turned anyone away, even during the Darktime when they'd barely had enough food for their own small family. The stout plank table could seat twelve people, and the counter was tiled in a light green ceramic that Adric remembered from when he was a cub. A wood block held knives of various sizes, and pots and skillets hung over the elderly gas stove.

While he waited for Marjani, he boiled water for coffee. She would've heard the front door open, recognized his footsteps. Hell, she'd probably sensed him from a few blocks away. The two of them had grown up together, survived the Darktime and his uncle. She might be younger by a couple turns of the sun, but the two of them were more like twins, attuned to each other.

Which was the real reason he hadn't invited anyone else to take her room. He still hoped she'd move back in, even if it meant Fane came, too.

Still, he understood why she'd moved out. She was newly mated, and Adric and Fane weren't exactly good friends. The tall blond male was a little too slick, the kind of man who could charm your pants right off your ass. For his sister's sake, Adric had accepted Fane into the clan, but that didn't mean he trusted him.

Adric took out the French press, filled it with ground coffee. As he plunged the press into the glass carafe, Marjani padded into the kitchen in an oversized T-shirt that hung loosely on her spare frame.

"Ric. Whassup?" She smothered a yawn and stepped in for a hug.

"Morning." She'd gained weight, he noted with satisfaction, and stopped shaving her head. He gave her a hard squeeze and released her.

She really was better. He owed Fane for that.

Marjani got out two cups and he filled them with the coffee. She dosed both with half-and-half and handed one to him. "So. Why are you here?"

He took a gulp of coffee. It was perfect. Creamy, with a dark bite.

"I'm going to be out of town until late tomorrow." Gods, he hated having to inform someone every time he made a fucking move, but he was alpha. He couldn't just disappear for twenty-four hours.

"'Kay. Where?"

"Delaware. But unless the city catches fire, handle it. Anything else can wait until I get back."

"So this isn't business."

"No."

"You going to tell me what it's about?"

"No."

"Does it have anything to do with the little convo you and Rosana do Rio had at the Full Moon last night?"

He scowled. The clan grapevine had been working overtime. "And if it does?"

Marjani had told him straight up that this yen he had for the Rock Run alpha's little sister was insane. Hellfire, he knew that himself. But he couldn't let it go. His cougar insisted Rosana was his mate, but that *was* insane. Adric couldn't think of one single earth/water fada mating, anywhere.

What would their cubs be, anyway? Catfish?

"Because." Marjani set a hand on his arm. "If she's your mate, maybe you need to stop fighting it."

He almost choked on his coffee. He set down the cup. "Is this the same sister who's always telling me to forget about Rosana? That it will only fuck things up for me and the clan?"

Her dark eyes flickered. "I know, I know. It's the wrong thing for the clan, and we both know it. But Adric, this thing I have with Fane—I couldn't turn away from it if I tried. If either of us rejected the other, it would literally kill us both."

He wrapped his arms around her still-too-thin body. "That's because you accepted the bond. I haven't, and I never will. You know I can't. I'm alpha, and there are still people who are unhappy with that. I can't give them any more fuel for their fire."

She looped her arms around his waist and rested her head against his chest. "So you do feel the bond."

He stiffened. "No. Just the...possibility. And that's all it'll ever be. I promise."

"Oh, Ric. Don't make promises like that. Because if something changes..." She shook her head against his shoulder. "I just want you to be happy. You deserve it, more than anybody."

He pulled back and grinned. "Well, I intend to get very happy tonight."

Marjani chuckled, like he'd meant her to—and the sound went straight to his heart. These last few years, there'd been times when he'd wondered if she'd ever laugh again.

"Good." She gave him a squeeze and released him. "And don't worry, I'll cover for you. For the next twenty-four hours, forget you're alpha. Just be Ric."

4

osana waited until breakfast was almost over before making her announcement.

They were in the spacious cavern that served as the Rock Run Clan's dining hall. It was the second breakfast shift—the fishers and marine workers were already out on the river or at the marina, their children in the creche. Now the warriors took their turn before heading off to their duties.

Dion sat at the table's head with her brother Tiago on the opposite end. Lucky her—Tiago had stopped by with his dryad mate, so she had not one, but two big brothers to deal with.

Across from Rosana, Dion's mate Cleia fed strawberries to little Brisa, back to her usual cheerful, high-energy self. On the bench next to Rosana, Tiago's mate Alesia dug into a bowl of yogurt and berries. Perched beside her was Tiago's otter friend Fausto, greedily downing a heaping plate of raw mussels.

Rosana took a deep breath. "I just wanted to let everyone know that I'm going to the beach." She spoke in English for Alesia's benefit. The dryad only knew a smattering of Portuguese.

"I have a couple of days off and..." Rosana trailed off as Dion and Tiago turned identical frowns on her. The only two of her four brothers still at Rock Run, they could be scarily alike. Same wavy black hair tied back with a leather string. Same steel-blue eyes. Same disapproving scowls on their good-looking faces.

Fausto paused in the act of cracking open a mussel to dart a glance at Rosana. He might not understand English, but he could detect the abrupt change in atmosphere.

"Which beach?" Dion asked.

She hitched a shoulder. "I don't know. Somewhere on the Eastern Shore—Delaware, or maybe one of the Maryland beaches. I'll be back by tomorrow night."

"You're not going alone." That was Tiago.

She toyed with a piece of bread. She couldn't lie to them. Fada could scent a lie, and besides, it would make her violently ill. It had something to do with their fae blood, even though it was just a trace.

So instead, she went on the attack. "Look, I just want to get away, all right?"

"Not alone." Dion's stern look was spoiled by his tiny daughter wriggling away from her mama and onto the floor.

"Up, *Papai*." Brisa patted his thigh, a sprite in a pink-and-yellow striped dress, her fine gold hair caught up in two pigtails, her eyes the same warm amber as Cleia's.

His hard face softened. "Of course, *menina*." He cuddled her to his chest.

"You'll take a friend." Tiago again. "Davi would be happy to—"

"*Deus*." Rosana glared at him. "What part of getting away don't you understand? I'm going. *Alone*."

Most of the clan had cleared out by now, but those still in the dining hall glanced her way.

"Dion." Cleia spoke in her throaty voice. "It's only one day."

The sun fae queen was blindingly beautiful, with large tip-tilted eyes, shoulder-length hair in shimmering shades of gold, silver and copper, and a fae's pointed chin and ears. Rosana still wasn't sure how her hardheaded oldest brother had won Cleia's heart, but without the older woman to smooth things over, she just might've left the clan by now like her two middle brothers had.

Dion turned an irritated look on his mate. Their gazes locked, the two of them communing through their bond—not in words, but in some deeper way that only mated pairs could.

Alesia touched Rosana's back. "Take a breath, sweetheart."

Rosana sent her a guilty glance. The dryad was a solitary fae, more comfortable with plants than people, and she hated arguments.

"*Desculpe-me*," she muttered, and took a breath. Tiago's mate had that effect on people. Half-wild with an elfin face and mass of sun-streaked brown curls, the dryad radiated an earth-mama calm.

"Talk to them," Alesia added. "Please? Because they'll listen to you. Right, Tiago?" She reached across Rosana to squeeze his hand.

"*Sim, sim,*" he grumbled.

Rosana took another breath. Alesia was right. If she wanted Dion and Tiago to see her as an adult, then she had to show them she was calm. Mature.

And able to run her own fucking life.

Dion fingered a lock of his mate's sun-colored hair. "I'm her alpha," he told Cleia. "If I say she stays, then she stays."

"Of course," the queen agreed. "But it's just one day. And Rosana's a smart, capable woman. She's not a child anymore."

Dion shook his head.

Rosana gritted her teeth and helped herself to a slice of the thick peasant bread. She drizzled olive oil on it and tore off a piece to eat.

Calm. Mature. In control.

"I did you the courtesy of informing you where I'll be," she said. "But I'm not asking your permission. I'm an adult now. I don't need the alpha's okay to leave the base, as long as I fulfil my duties to the clan."

"Try it," Tiago invited, "and you'll find yourself with two body-guards on your ass everywhere you go."

"Since when did you become my dad?" she snarled back. She'd

expected better of him. Just five years older than her, they'd once been partners-in-crime, united against Isa and their three much older brothers when it came to childish pranks.

Dion raised a staying hand. "I just don't understand why you have to go alone."

"I'm twenty-two turns of the sun. When Tiago was my age, did you make him take a babysitter every time he left the base?"

"Of course not. He's a man."

Across the table, Cleia winced.

Rosana flung up her hands. "So this is because I'm a female? I made warrior with the rest of my cohort. You trained me yourself."

"No. Yes." Dion shook his head. "It's just..." He muttered a curse, then shot a contrite look at a wide-eyed Brisa. "If something happened to you, I'd never forgive myself."

"For *Deus*'s sake, I'm going to the beach, not a war zone."

"There are people out there who would love to get at me through you."

"Like Adric," Tiago muttered.

Rosana stopped tearing her bread into pieces and reached for her orange juice.

Calm, controlled.

She itched to defend Adric, but her brothers weren't stupid. It wouldn't take much for them to connect her conversation with him last night with this sudden desire to go away on her own.

Cleia set a hand on Dion's arm. "I can give her a protection charm. One that will deflect both physical and magical attacks."

A muscle jumped in his cheek. When he'd mated with the powerful fae queen, he'd made it clear she wasn't to interfere in his governing of Rock Run, however well-meaning. He hated asking her for anything. But to Dion, family was everything.

"*Bom*," he agreed. "But only if you wear the charm all the time. And one day only, understand? I want you back here by tomorrow night."

Rosana shot Cleia a grateful look. "Sure," she said calmly,

while inside, she was doing a full-out happy dance. "I'll be fine, you'll see."

"You'd better be," he returned, but his lips curved in a reluctant smile.

Cleia rose to her feet. "I'll be right back with that charm."

The air around her brightened and contorted so that it hurt your eyes to look straight at her. When Rosana glanced back, she'd 'ported out of the hall.

Brisa removed the chunk of bread she was gnawing on from her mouth and waved it at the spot where Cleia had just been. "Mama?" Her small brow knit uncertainly.

"She'll be right back." Dion set a cup of apple juice to her lips. "Here, drink."

Brisa took a sip and then wriggled off his lap to make her way around the table to Alesia and Rosana, one hand on the bench for balance. When she reached Alesia, she handed her the half-eaten piece of bread.

"Here, Tia Yesa."

"Thank you." The dryad gravely accepted it and set it on her plate. "I'll just keep it for you in case you want it back."

"Okay." Brisa continued to Rosana. "Up, Tia Wosa." She lifted her arms.

Rosa swung her up. "Well, hello, there."

Children were the one group she wasn't afraid to touch. She might get a glimpse of a possible future, but their lives had so many possibilities that it was like looking down a hall with a thousand doors.

"What's under here? A belly button?" She lifted her niece's striped skirt to blow on her stomach.

Brisa chortled with glee. Then Alesia tickled one of her tiny pointed ears, and she giggled even harder.

Cleia 'ported back with the charm, a silver Celtic knot inscribed on a plump heart. "It's not one-hundred-percent foolproof," she warned as she clasped the delicate chain around

Rosana's left wrist. "But it should at least buy you time to get away."

"I love it." Rosana turned her wrist from side to side, admiring the shiny charm. She beamed at Cleia. "It's beautiful—thank you."

"What if she has to shift?" asked Dion.

His mate's smile was smug. "I've had my people working on that. This is a new design that will magically adjust and attach itself to her tail fluke."

"No kidding? We may have to buy some of those from you."

"You know I'd give them to you for free."

"But we'll pay the same price as anyone else," Dion returned.

Cleia sighed. "Pigheaded, that's you." But her eyes laughed at him as she reached for Brisa and set her on her hip.

"Come here, you." Dion pulled the two of them down on his lap and gave her a hard kiss, while Brisa flung pudgy arms around both their necks.

Cleia nuzzled Dion's cheek contentedly. She wore a yellow top and a short pleated pink skirt the same colors as Brisa's stripes. The two of them could have posed for a mother-daughter photo in a fancy human catalog. Once, Rosana might've rolled her eyes at their matching outfits. But Cleia had waited a long time to have Brisa, and the look she turned on her daughter was so loving that instead, Rosana's heart constricted.

She dimly recalled her Irish mom looking at her like that. Before that summer when her parents had left—and never returned.

They're alive. That's something.

For a long time, they hadn't known if Ula and Nisio were alive or dead, although they'd suspected King Sindre of the ice fae was behind their disappearance. Then their brother Nic had confirmed it, but it was Adric's sister Marjani who, on a mission to Iceland, had seen them at the ice fae court. Ula and Nisio were under a *geas* that bound them to Sindre himself.

But Rosana still couldn't see them, because apparently each

time Dion or any of the do Rio brothers had come to court asking about Ula and Nisio, the king had punished their parents.

Rosana's throat worked.

She was lucky and she knew it. She'd had a brother who'd stepped in as a father, Isa to mother her, Tiago as a playmate. And then later, there'd been Cleia and now Alesia and little Brisa.

Ula and Nisio had never even seen their granddaughter.

But that didn't mean Rosana didn't feel an emptiness, a ragged hole in her soul that no one else could fill.

She rose to her feet. "I'd better get going."

Cleia smiled up at Rosana. "Have a good time, darling."

Their eyes met, and Rosana *knew* that the sun fae had guessed exactly where Rosana was going and with whom. But she also knew Cleia wouldn't tell Dion unless absolutely necessary.

"Thanks, I will." She blew a kiss at her niece, who puckered her small mouth back, and then strolled out of the dining hall.

Not hurrying, because that would make her brothers suspicious.

She waited until she was out of sight to speed up.

BACK IN HER ROOM, Rosana threw off her clothes. Fortunately, Isa had already left for the creche. Although officially retired, the former nurse still helped with the pups most mornings. With her round, comfortable body and graying hair, Isa might look like everyone's idea of a grandma, but she was nobody's fool.

Rosana shimmied into an ivory chemise and matching boy shorts, a birthday gift from Cleia. Soft and silky, the fae-made fabric magically molded itself to her body. Next were a black Henley, skinny jeans and the red kitten-heel boots, another gift from Cleia. She donned the matching leather jacket and headed to the clan garage.

The good news? There was a car available. The purple sportbike was too noticeable, and besides, she didn't want to leave it overnight at a busy rest area.

The bad news? The car was in for an oil change and wouldn't be ready for an hour.

By the time Rosana drove out of the garage, it was nearly noon, and she had no way to contact Adric, because she didn't have a cell phone. No one in the clan did. Something about a water fada's physiology shorted out small electronics.

He'll wait, she told herself as she raced the twenty minutes south to the rest area.

But she didn't relax until she saw him standing next to a sporty blue Mazda in a T-shirt, black jeans and combat boots, scanning the incoming cars. Their gazes met. His shoulders eased, and he gave her his trademark cocky smile.

But she'd seen that tense expression. He'd been worried she wouldn't show. She smiled to herself and pulled into a nearby parking space. Adric was right there, opening the door for her.

"Thanks for waiting," she said. "I'm sorry, I—"

"You're here." He stopped her apology with a kiss. "That's all that matters. This all you brought?"

He reached for her canvas overnight bag while she locked the car.

"That's it."

He set a hand on the small of her back and steered her to the Mazda. She dragged in a breath, released it.

"Trouble getting away?" His smile was knowing.

She lifted her chin. "Nothing I couldn't handle."

"Good." He dragged her to him for an open-mouth kiss, and while she was still catching her breath, helped her into his car.

He drove one-handed, wending his way through the Sunday afternoon traffic with ease. His mustard-colored T-shirt clung lovingly to hard, rounded deltoids. His forearms were dusted with soft dark hair, his hands strong, capable.

Anticipation churned in her. Those hands would be on her in just a couple of hours, and she could hardly wait.

But her stomach was jumping with nerves.

Her first time with a man. And she had the added worry of wondering if sex would set off her Gift.

Because sex was the most intimate touch there was.

She stared down at her gloved hands.

Adric reached across the console to brush the backs of his fingers over her cheek. A soft touch that shuddered through her like a promise.

She swallowed hard. *You want this*, she reminded herself.

Because she did want it, bad. If she had a vision, well, Adric would just have to deal with it.

She stripped off her gloves and shoved them into a pocket.

"Do you know Lewes?" he asked.

"Yeah. I go there with my—" She stopped, bit her lip. The last thing she wanted was to bring up Dion and Tiago. Adric didn't like her brothers any more than they liked him.

"So you like it?" Adric prompted as if he didn't know why she'd halted.

She nodded. "It's a pretty little town. But we go to swim in the ocean. Delaware has some of the cleanest beaches on the East Coast."

Some of her best memories were going to Lewes with her brothers and spending a few days cruising as their dolphins off the coast, following the currents and snacking on fish.

Adric took her bare hand, the one with the protection charm, and lifted it to his lips. "I like the beach this time of year. It's cold, but there's almost no one else out. You have it all to yourself."

She smiled at him. She hadn't expected tenderness, not from the hard-ass Baltimore alpha. But his lips were warm and soft as he pressed them to her skin, and his smile had a sweet, almost tentative edge.

He set her hand on his leg but kept hold of it. She tensed, but her Gift was quiet. Maybe, just maybe, she could get through the next twenty-four hours without freaking Adric out by going full Seer-mode on him.

Anticipation buzzed in her veins. She pressed her inner thighs together and concentrated on keeping her breathing even. But Adric was a fada. He could scent her arousal, spicing the small space.

His lips curved in a slow grin.

There. That was the Adric she knew. Sexy with an edge.

The kind of man your brothers warned you about—which only made you want him more.

She grinned back at him.

He responded with a hum that was almost a purr and released her to whip the little car around a semi.

Traffic was light. It wasn't long until they entered Delaware and turned south toward the beach. Adric fiddled with the radio while the flat terrain unspooled on either side of them, winter fields of tattered cornstalks and soybeans interspersed with shiny-new housing developments.

As they entered Lewes, the billboards and pizza places gave way to charming wood-shingled homes and hip little shops and restaurants. Crepe myrtle, bare for the winter, arched cinnamon-colored branches in front of painted Victorians with lacy trim. In the summer, she knew, the tiny yards would overflow with flowers and pots of fragrant herbs.

They took the drawbridge over the Lewes and Rehoboth Canal. The B&B was between the canal and the Delaware Bay. Three stories high and painted an eye-popping turquoise, blue and peach, it was as if a piece of Key West had levitated and flown north to Delaware.

Rosana slung her canvas bag over a shoulder while Adric took a leather jacket and a duffel bag from the backseat. The building was on stilts to protect against flooding. To reach the front door, they passed beneath an overhang guarded by a busty carved figurehead like the kind you saw on the prow of a ship, and wound their way through three kayaks, two surfboards and a stand of rusting beach bikes.

Inside, Adric led the way up a stairwell crammed with quirky art—an outsized pig in a red tutu, the head of a laughing cow, a seductive mermaid. They found the proprietor on the second floor in a small, open office, feet propped on his desk, watching a video on his computer.

He came unhurriedly to his feet. Solidly built with salt-and-pepper hair, he was dressed in pink board shorts and flip-flops despite the near-freezing temperature outside.

"Lord Adric," he said with an easy smile. "You're right on time. The room's all ready."

Adric inclined his head. "Mark. Peace to you and yours."

"And to you and yours." Mark turned his smile on Rosana. "Welcome to Lewes," he said as he took Adric's cash and noted something on the computer.

She smiled back. "Thank you. And peace to you."

"You've got the Hemingway Suite. Right down that hall." The innkeeper indicated the hallway to the left as he handed Adric the key. "There's only one other couple staying the night, and they're on the third floor. Other than me, you have the second floor to yourself."

Adric thanked him and, taking Rosana's hand, led the way down the hall to their room.

"He doesn't mind us being fada?" she murmured. Humans tended to be wary around shapeshifters, especially dominant ones like Adric.

"Nah. He says my money's as good as anyone's. I don't bother him and he doesn't bother me."

"So you've stayed here before."

"A couple of times. I mind my business, and he does the same."

Rosana quelled a twist of jealousy.

Who? she wanted to ask. *Who did you bring those other times?*

But she refused to go down that road. She'd known when she walked into the bar last night that Adric wasn't celibate.

Unlike her.

The Hemingway Suite was dominated by a king-sized bed covered with fake leopard-skin and flanked by two rattan lounge chairs. A photo of Ernest Hemingway presided over a hutch filled with copies of the author's books and an old-fashioned typewriter, and the sliding glass door was covered with blinds made of wood slats.

"Nice." Rosana set her bag on one of the rattan chairs and hung her leather jacket on a hook near the door. "I'm impressed."

She crossed the room, trying not to stare at the huge bed, to open the blinds on the sliding glass doors. Outside, a small terrace ran the length of the room, with steps leading down to a grassy strip behind the B&B.

"And private." Adric dropped his duffel bag by the door and hung his jacket next to hers.

She turned to face him. Picturing why they might need privacy made her shove her hands into her back pockets, and then take them out again.

Relax, damn it. You want this, remember?

Adric leaned against the door on the opposite side of the room, arms crossed, a small smile on his face. "Want a drink? Mark keeps wine and beer for the guests in the breakfast room."

"Water's good for now."

He nodded, and going to the small refrigerator near the door, removed two plastic bottles and held one out to her.

"Thanks." She forced her feet to unscrew from the floor. She took the bottle and gulped water, avoiding his eyes.

"Rosana."

She jerked her gaze to him. "Yeah?"

"It's okay." He set his water on an end table. "There's no rush."

"There isn't?" Oh, she was being such an idiot about this. But her insides were a big knot of tension.

"Of course not." He caressed her shoulders. "Are you hungry? We could go out for a late lunch."

"Not really. I had a big breakfast." Which was churning undigested in her stomach.

"Then why don't we go to the beach while the sun's still out?"

She sent him a relieved smile. "That would be nice."

"Okay." He brushed his lips over hers.

They walked the two blocks to the beach. It was a crisp, sunny day. A number of the houses were shut for the winter, but they passed a couple of humans out running, bundled up against the cold, and a woman pushing a baby in a stroller who took one look at Adric and made a wide circle around them. A pint-sized terrier barked at them from a covered porch, and a tomcat trotted across the road on its way to some important rendezvous.

They left their boots at the head of a path through the dunes and wended their way through the scrubby bushes and grasses to the water. They were on the Delaware Bay, a large estuary at the place where the Delaware River emptied into the Atlantic. An icy wind blew from the northwest, but the bay's winter-blue surface was calm. Long, low waves slid in, broke against the sand, and then slipped back out.

Adric took her hand. She tensed, and he brought her fingers to his mouth.

"Hey. I told you, there's no rush. I'm just happy to spend some time alone with you. If you've changed your mind, I'll live." He gave her a crooked grin. "I won't like it, but I'll live."

Her heart turned over. He was being so damn sweet. "It's not that. At least, it's not just"—she waved her free hand— "*that*."

"Then what's the matter?" he asked as they started walking barefoot along the bay's edge.

"You know I'm a Seer."

"I figured that out when your eyes went all scary black on me."

She nodded. "Well, I never know when touching someone will set off my Sight, especially someone's hand."

"Even someone you know?"

"Yeah. At home, they think I'm a little strange."

He frowned. "Your clan doesn't know you're a Seer?"

"Just my family and a few close friends—but no one else." She lifted her chin. "I'm going to tell them. Soon."

"Good. You shouldn't have to hide your Gift."

"That's what Isa says. She's the woman who helped raise me after the ice fae captured my mom and dad."

"She's right."

"You didn't tell anyone, did you?" Rosana asked.

"Just Marjani, but she can keep a secret. I'll make sure she knows to keep it quiet. And if you don't want to hold hands, that's okay."

She tightened her grip on his fingers. "No. I want to hold your hand." She took a deep breath. "I want to do everything."

"Good." His smile was wicked. "Because trying to be nice about this is fucking killing me."

She chuckled—and her tension eased. After all, he'd seen her in the grip of a vision, and it hadn't freaked him out. Much. He still wanted her.

They continued walking in a companionable silence, the wind ruffling their hair, the sand damp beneath their toes. Overhead, seagulls wheeled and shrieked.

She slid Adric a look. She'd never seen him so relaxed, almost boyish, his spiky hair tousled, a slight smile curling his sexy mouth.

She knew so little about him. Oh, she knew he was the bad-boy Baltimore alpha, the man who gleefully provoked Dion every chance he got.

That he hadn't won alpha in a challenge, as honor demanded. Instead, it had been a sneak attack. And worse, the alpha had been Adric's own uncle.

Some of the Rock Run men, like Davi, sneered that Adric was a coward with no respect for fada *tradição*, tradition. But Leron Savonett had dragged Baltimore into the Darktime, an internal war that ripped his clan apart. Even Dion said Adric's uncle had been a self-centered, sadistic *cabrão*.

As far as Rosana could tell, if Adric hadn't killed his uncle when he had, his clan would've been wiped out.

Adric angled his head in a very catlike way. "You're frowning."

"I am?" She smoothed out her forehead.

"No, don't hide. Tell me—what were you thinking?"

She hitched a shoulder. "That I don't really know you."

"You know the important things."

"But I want to know the unimportant things."

"Like what?"

"Like...do you bleach your hair tips?"

"Nah." He shook his head. "It happened the first time I shifted to cougar, and never changed back. It grows spiked-up like that, too. My dad had the same hair."

"Huh."

"Here's one for you. What's up with the claws? Your animal's a dolphin, isn't it?"

She let the short but sharp black claws slide out. "Otter. We can shift to other water animals, you know. We're not limited like you earth fada. I just prefer my dolphin."

"Limited, huh?" He grabbed her, tickling her until she was breathless with laughter.

"I'm sorry, I'm sorry."

"You should be." He kissed her on the mouth and then released her, keeping an arm around her shoulders as they resumed walking.

"I have more," she said. "What's your favorite color? The one dessert you can't pass up? What do you do for fun? I don't even know how old you are."

"Peach ice cream. Music—I don't play an instrument, but I like to dance. And thirty-three turns of the sun—eleven older than you."

Of course, he knew her age. The man probably kept files on everyone in her family.

"As for my favorite color"—he swung her to face him—"that would be blue. The deep blue of the ocean out there, where the color is so intense you can almost feel it." He nodded at the horizon. "The blue of your eyes." He cupped her face, his fingers warm against her chilled skin. "Sometimes I forget how incredibly blue they are."

She swallowed. "Yeah?"

His own irises were a brilliant golden-brown. She swayed toward him, entranced.

"I mean it." His voice was a low rasp that reverberated in her body. "I love your eyes. Almost as much as I love your face, your body. Your smile."

Her heart gave a hard thump. "My smile?"

"Um-hmm." His fingers curled around her waist. He reeled her in, slowly, deliberately, until her body was flush against his. The firm muscles of his chest pressed her breasts, his erection hard against her belly. "Your smile is so wide and happy. It makes me...want."

"Want what?"

"You." His mouth whispered over hers. A barely-there touch that made her catch her breath.

Excitement skittered up her spine. Her breasts felt full and heavy, the nipples pushing against the silky chemise.

His tongue teased the seam of her lips, coaxing her to open to him. When she did, he tunneled his fingers into her hair, holding her still as his tongue explored the soft cave of her mouth—the sides, the sensitive roof.

She rose on her toes and twined her arms around his neck, sucking his tongue deeper. His groan made everything female in her clench.

Her leg was around his hip now, her sex rubbing against his.

Somewhere nearby, a seagull screeched.

Adric lifted his head, his breath uneven. "Let's go back."

She swallowed. "Yes."

Adric's heart was thumping, his cock so hard it ached.

Rosana strolled beside him, her mouth swollen from his kisses, her bare feet dusted with sand, her hair a silky black waterfall down her back.

She was a pagan priestess in red leather and jeans. The kind of woman who dropped men to their knees.

He shoved a hand through his hair. The woman shredded his control. She'd all but melted in his arms, making those needy little noises, rubbing against him. Driving him insane with her unpracticed, uninhibited moves.

He shouldn't even be here with her. This could never go anywhere. But Rosana just had to crook a finger and he was there.

Her very innocence was a beacon to a man like him. A man who'd seen so much darkness, done so many dirty things that he'd never be truly clean.

He set an arm around her shoulders, pulled her closer. Because he could. He had one night with her, and he was going to enjoy it to the fullest.

She came readily. Their hips bumped, and she giggled, a young, happy sound.

His heart twisted. If only things were different...if only she were a member of his clan, a woman he could claim as his own.

You couldn't claim her even then.

He was basically a dead man walking.

A less selfish man would stop this before it began, but he'd waited six-and-a-half years for her. He was damned if he'd turn back now.

He nuzzled her hair, breathing her in. His hand went to her round ass.

"When I get you back to the room," he murmured in her ear, "I'm going to strip your jeans off you. But I won't take your panties off. Not right away. I'm going to tease you first. Make you hot and wet. Make you beg a little."

She moaned his name. The spice of her arousal teased his nostrils.

He smiled and ran his hand over the curve of her bottom. "Then, I'll peel your panties off—but not fast. We'll go slow, because it's your first time. And I want to drive you a little crazy. And you'll let me, won't you?"

Her pretty mouth formed an O. Her breath sped up, and she hunched her shoulders. She nodded rapidly.

Gods, she was so young, and so much less experienced. On some level she'd been his since age sixteen, when they'd first met at Cleia & Dion's mate ball.

And so, she'd waited for him.

He didn't know why he was so sure, but he was.

I'll be her first. His chest squeezed.

No other male had touched her. The primitive part of him reveled in that. He wanted to take her, long and hard. Imprint himself on her so that she'd always remember him.

But he also wanted to take care of her. Show her how special she was. Caress her. Love her.

He was a hard man, some would say a cold-blooded killer. But he'd done what he had to, survived when a softer man wouldn't have—and saved his clan besides. For Rosana, though, he'd dredge up whatever tenderness he could.

They exited the beach and stopped to put on their boots.

The wind had picked up. It whistled through the dunes, whipped Rosana's long black curls across her face. She captured them in one hand and beamed at him, her irises a deep sapphire in the fading light.

"Race you back to the B&B." She took off down the street, surprisingly agile in the high-heeled boots.

He blinked, and with a predatory grin, loped after her. His cougar loved a chase.

He stayed behind her until they were almost to the B&B, because hey, watching that ripe, pretty ass wasn't a hardship. Then he lunged, grabbing her waist and swinging her into the air.

She gave a shriek of laughter and grabbed his shoulders. Long legs wrapped around his hips.

"Beat you." He gently closed his teeth on her full lower lip and continued walking. "What do I win?" He nibbled his way down her neck.

"No fair." She angled her head so he could taste the tender underside of her jaw. "We didn't agree to anything for the winner."

He reached around her to open the door to the B&B. The stairwell was silent, his animal-enhanced senses telling him they were alone in the building. He headed up to the second floor with Rosana wrapped around him like a sexy vine.

He let his cat into his smile. "Where the fuck did you get the idea I play fair?"

5

—————

*A*dric set Rosana on the floor and reached behind him to lock the door. She had time for a single sharp inhale, and then he had a hand fisted in her hair. He tugged her head back, exposing her throat.

It was a very male, very dominant move. And damn, it turned her on.

Her pussy clenched. Her knees turned to jelly.

I'm going to tease you first... Make you beg a little.

Goddess, he'd almost made her come right then with those hot, dirty words rasped against her throat.

She set her hands on his chest. His face was still chilled from the cold, but the rest of him was all hot, tensile strength, his scent a mix of earth and the winter wind.

He fastened his mouth to her throat above the collarbone and sucked hard. Leaving a love-bite she'd have to hide, but right now, she just didn't care.

Heat shot from her breasts to her womb, pooled between her thighs. Her skin felt too tight. She moaned and gripped his shoulders.

Releasing her hair, he bent her over an arm and kissed his way down her neck to her breasts. Her nipples beaded against the thin barrier of her chemise and the cotton shirt. He pushed up the shirt and traced a finger down the V of the neckline to her cleavage.

"Pretty." He placed his mouth on the ivory material over one tightly furled bud and sucked.

Her lungs jerked. She dug her fingers into his shoulders and rasped his name.

"Mm." He swirled his tongue around her nipple through the silky cloth and then moved to her other breast. "I want to lick you all over."

Need twisted through her. "Right back at you."

That earned her a deep kiss. When he lifted his head, he pulled her shirt the rest of the way off so that she stood before him in just the chemise, jeans and boots.

His gaze locked on the wet fabric over her breasts. She glanced down to see her nipples dark against the pale material.

"Yeah," he said hoarsely, "I'm going to lick you all over. And maybe bite a little."

Anticipation coursed through her. She shivered and rubbed the goosebumps that popped up on her arms.

"Cold?" he asked.

"No. Just..." She shrugged a shoulder.

His smile was knowing. He dragged off his T-shirt.

Her breath jammed in her throat. In all the years she'd known him, she'd never seen him unclothed.

He was...perfect. Smooth, honey-brown skin stretched over firm muscles. Dark hair dusted his pecs, arrowed through washboard abs before disappearing beneath his waistband. Her gaze locked on the hard ridge beneath his zipper.

He didn't give her nearly enough time to look. Instead, his hands were on her waist, his mouth covering hers. He walked her backward until her thighs hit the mattress, then lifted her onto the bed and crouched at her feet.

Slipping off her boots and socks, he cradled one boot in his hand. "Later," he said with a wicked curve of his lips, "you'll wear these for me—and nothing else."

"I will?" She eyed the boot, intrigued. But it wasn't in her nature to submit easily. When you were the youngest child—and a girl—in a family with four large, hard-ass brothers, you either stood up for yourself or got crushed.

She moistened her lips. "Maybe if you ask nice." Her voice came out husky, seductive, in a tone she barely recognized as hers.

His smile increased. "You'll do it. That's my reward for winning the race."

She arched a brow. "What reward? I didn't agree to—"

"But you'll do it. Because I want you to." He set down the boot but remained where he was, crouched between her legs. Warm hands ran up her inner thighs. He rubbed a thumb over the seam of her jeans. "Won't you?"

She moaned, so sensitized that even that small pressure was almost too much.

Then he leaned forward and replaced his thumb with his mouth, and it got even better. He blew on the material, a hot, moist stream that nearly made her come out of her skin.

Gulping air, she dug her fingers into the fake leopard skin and arched her back. Pressing her pelvis toward him, unconsciously begging for more.

He undid the button of her jeans and eased down the zipper. Two long fingers slid inside. He worked them under the boy shorts so he could tease her clit.

"Say yes, angel. Say you'll wear the boots. To please me."

She studied him. His eyes glinted up at her, bright, devilish. Did he mean it, or was it a game? Either way, she wasn't ready to give in.

She smiled and twisted against his fingers. If he'd just apply a bit more pressure...

"More," she said in smoky tones that made him swallow. Hard.

He rose up to kiss her. His tongue swirled around hers, while inside her jeans, his fingers moved in a similar tantalizing pattern. Promising pleasure but holding it just out of reach.

"You're so wet." A low growl. "So ready for me. But I haven't heard a yes."

He withdrew his hand from her pants and brought his hand to his mouth, licking her juices from his first two fingers while he watched her from beneath his lids.

She blinked up at him. Somehow she'd ended flat on her back with him propped on an elbow next to her.

He peeled her out of the tight jeans, and then shucked his own pants. He crawled over her, heavily erect, his only adornment the big chunk of gray-and-orange quartz hanging from the leather thong around his neck.

His expression was hard with desire, his bronze irises shot with the blue of his cougar. They were gorgeous, mesmerizing, like cyan fireworks exploding against a dusk sky.

Both man and cat were making love to her.

A primitive thrill raced over her skin. She touched his cheek, letting her own animal into her eyes—and surrendered.

Because suddenly, she didn't want to play games. What mattered was that he wanted her, and that she wanted him back, clear to the wild, untamed heart of her.

"Yes," she rasped. "Make love to me. Any way you want."

His throat rumbled in a rough purr that vibrated in all her secret places. He tugged at the chemise's strap. "Take this off."

He helped her shimmy out of the sexy little top and then traced the edge of her jaw with his tongue before moving down to her neck. He pressed a damp kiss to the hollow of her throat and then continued licking and sucking his way to each breast. His hot tongue swirled around each nipple in turn, leaving them wet and aching.

Her body went taut with wanting, and maybe a touch of fear.

"Relax," he murmured.

She moved her head back and forth against the pillow. "I can't," she confessed.

He nuzzled her cleavage. "Maybe I can help with that."

He continued down her abdomen, leaving a trail of kisses in

his wake. And then he was between her legs, a hand on each thigh. He held her gaze, unsmiling—and blew on her clit through the silky panties.

Her hips rocked up. She rasped his name.

He pressed her back down to the mattress. "Slow and easy. Remember what I said?"

Belatedly, she recalled his promise to take things slowly. "No..."

"Shh. This will feel good." He hummed against her clit. The sound vibrated through her whole body.

A groan escaped her throat. The fada were easy about their sexuality. She might be a virgin, but she'd fooled around with a few of the men in her cohort, especially the year before she met Adric. And then later, when she realized that any man but Adric left her cold, she'd touched herself, learned what she liked.

But nothing had prepared her for this.

A man between her legs, his eyes burning into hers. The hot swipe of his tongue on her most sensitive flesh. The strong hands holding her open for him. The teasing heat of his mouth against her sex through the barely-there fabric.

"Please," she said. "Please..."

A sexy growl. "I like it when you beg. I just may keep you here for the next hour." He gently bit her clit through the panties.

Her breath stuttered. Her hands fisted in the sheets. "No..."

His eyes glittered at her. "You don't like it?"

"No. Yes. I do, but I need..."

But he kept her there for another ten minutes, licking and sucking her through the silky material. Keeping her on a knife's edge of need until her senses felt overloaded. Then he slid his hands into the boy shorts from beneath, squeezing and caressing her bottom.

And even as she begged him to stop teasing her, a part of her wanted it to go on forever. But then he was easing the shorts down, an inch at a time. Her chest heaved. Her muscles went tight with anticipation.

At last the shorts were off. He tossed them away and came back between her legs. His hands gripped her ass, lifting her up like a special dish for his delectation—and then he swiped his tongue through her slick, needy sex.

Sensation rushed through her like an out-of-control storm. Overwhelming and a little frightening. She was going to break apart, lose herself to him.

From far away, she heard her voice, high and needy. She was speaking in Portuguese now.

"*Meu querido. Meu amor.*" My darling. My love.

She reached for his head. To pull him closer, to push him away —she wasn't sure which.

He turned his head and kissed her palm, and then continued licking her.

Her lungs constricted. She couldn't get enough air into them. "Adric. I—"

"What, love?" A husky murmur against her clit. "Tell me."

She licked her lips, tried to form the words in English. "I can't. I need..."

"What?"

She released his head, dug her fingers into the mattress and gave in to it. She wanted this. Sometimes she thought she'd been born wanting Adric.

"More. Please."

A low chuckle. "Like this?" He closed his lips around her quivering flesh and sucked hard.

Her breath hissed out. Her hips rocked up, seeking more.

"Yes," he said against her clit. "Come for me, baby. And then I'm going to fuck you, so hard." He sucked harder.

The hot, dark words mixed with the sweet suction of his mouth sent pleasure rocketing through her. She sobbed out his name and let herself wallow in the sensations. Exhilaration filled her. It was like diving off a high cliff. Standing on the edge, you couldn't help being afraid, but the surge of adrenaline as you leapt made it worth it.

Her climax coiled in her belly, spread up her spine, unfurled through her nerve endings...and then erupted in a burst of heat and bright color.

He stayed with her but lightened his touch. Soft, sweet licks until even that was too much. Then he kissed her belly.

"Beautiful," he murmured, and rose from the bed.

She rolled onto her side and watched as he took a box of condoms from his duffel bag and set it onto the night table. She closed her eyes against a pang of sadness. He was right to be careful, but it still hurt.

Fada rarely had children even with their mates. Most fada didn't bother with birth control, since STDs were almost unheard of and they knew that any child would be welcomed by the clan.

Unless it was a child she'd made with Adric.

Together, they pushed down the covers. He pulled her into his arms and kissed the top of her head. "You're so beautiful when you come."

She tilted her head, summoned a teasing grin. If they had just this one night, she wouldn't ruin it by crying for something she'd never have. "You're so beautiful when you're making me come."

"Is that so?" He crawled on top of her with a wolfish smile. "I'll be even prettier when I'm inside you, fucking you." He dragged his cock over her stomach.

A hot ribbon of desire curled through her. Goddess, she ached to have him inside her, filling her. "Prove it."

His mouth came to her ear. She could smell herself on him, a warm, oceany scent.

"I will," he whispered as if it were a secret for her alone.

He left the bed to roll on the protection and then came down over her. Taking her hands, he pressed them to the bed on either side of her head. Her thighs instinctively bent up to cradle him.

His tip nudged her sex and she tensed.

He stilled. "I'm the first."

It wasn't a question, but she dipped her chin.

His eyes flashed, the blue blotting out the bronze. "I thought so." He pushed a little deeper. "I promise I'll be...easy."

She moistened her lips, nodded again. "I know. I want this."

"Oh, angel." His voice was tender.

His mouth touched hers. He kissed her, slowly, voluptuously, like she was a feast he'd waited for months to savor. She felt surrounded by him, his body...his heated, earthy scent...the strong hands pinning her to the bed. Against her breastbone, his quartz was warm, almost alive.

Something in her opened, like a flower unfurling, petal by petal. He gave another nudge, and his thick head slipped inside her.

It burned, but in a good way. Like he was marking her as his.

Excitement built in her. She needed this. She needed *him*.

"Rosana," he said on a sigh and pressed deeper.

He was thick, hot, wonderful. Stretching her until she had the brief, panicky fear that she couldn't stretch any more...and then he was inside her.

Her eyes widened. He held still, but she felt his cock pulsing. Or was that her? The small pain of his entrance receded, replaced by a sense of rightness.

This was her man. The one she'd always known would be her first.

Her and Adric, joined together. His flesh deep inside hers. Their two breaths mingling, their hearts beating in time.

"You okay?" His mouth whispered over hers.

"Oh, yeah." She interlaced her fingers with his, uncaring that it might set off her Sight. Just needing to touch him.

When nothing happened, elation raced through her. She tightened her fingers on his and gave an experimental lift of her hips.

"God's cat." His groan was low and raw, ripped from his chest. "You're so hot...so fucking tight. You're going to kill me."

She narrowed her eyes. "Not until you finish."

He gave a bark of laughter, and she raised up to give him an openmouthed kiss. Their mouths were still joined when he began to move, easy, unhurried strokes.

She tried to pull her hands from his—she wanted to wrap her

arms around him—but he tightened his grip and rose higher. Keeping her where she was, open beneath him, unable to do anything but accept his thrusts. Angling his body so that his cock massaged her clit with every stroke.

Heat radiated from him. He lowered his head and sucked each of her nipples in turn. Pleasure streaked through her, tightening her womb.

She was melting. She was burning up.

She dug her heels into the mattress and clenched her inner muscles around him. "Adric..."

His lips moved to her ear. He tongued the outer edge, slipped inside. It was warm and wet, and so sensual.

"Take it." His thrusts grew harder, more powerful. Dominating her in a way her animal craved.

She dragged in a breath. *"Ohgod, ohgod, ohgod..."*

"Come for me, love." A low command in her ear.

It was too much. "No," she rasped.

"Yes. Take it. Take *me*." He pushed into her. "All of me, angel."

Deep, so deep.

Then again, and again until she broke into a thousand shimmering fragments.

He groaned her name and propelled himself in and out of her, over and over, and then stilled. A growl that was more cat than man vibrated in his chest.

She tightened her thighs around his lean hips as he pulsed deep inside of her. He dropped his head forward, his cheek against hers.

Only then did he release her hands.

ADRIC HUNG OVER ROSANA, breath jerking in and out of his lungs.

He felt emptied out—and yet somehow filled as well. Complete in a way he was afraid to examine closely.

His quartz rested between her pretty breasts. Now that he

could think again, he realized it had heated as they'd approached their climax. He frowned down at it—and blinked.

The gray-and-orange crystals were lit deep within with a new color, a brilliant sea-green that spiraled through the center in a graceful twist. A green the same color as Rosana's dolphin's eyes.

What the hell? His brows drew together.

"Wow," she said. "Just...wow."

He shrugged mentally and decided to worry about his quartz later. He lifted up and she gave him a broad smile that warmed him clear to his toes.

He kissed her, wanting that smile against his lips. She was warm, her skin moist with exertion. She smelled like woman and sex—and him. He rubbed his cheek against hers, mingling their two scents even more. For this night, at least, she was his.

"Mm." She slid a languid hand down his neck, petting him in a way both man and cat craved. Fingering the gold stud in his earlobe. Tracing a finger over his jaw.

He licked her just beneath her ear. She tasted like the sea.

Inside her, his dick lengthened. He'd come hard. No, he'd fucking exploded—and still it hadn't been enough.

He had the sudden, sinking conviction that with Rosana, it would never be enough.

He wanted to thrust into her mindlessly. Imprint his body on hers so that she'd feel him all week. But she had to be tender, even though she'd been an eager, if innocent, partner.

Hell, he'd been too rough—at the end, his mind had blanked with pleasure and he'd forgotten he was fucking a virgin. But he was fully aware now, so he gritted his teeth and withdrew from her.

Her soft hiss told him she *was* hurting, at least a little. Guilt tightened his belly. "You okay?"

"Mm-hmm." She curled on her side, cheeks flushed, eyes half-closed, the picture of a well-pleasured woman.

His guilt eased. He kissed her cheek. "Be right back."

He made a trip to the bathroom to dispose of the rubber,

returning with a warm, wet washcloth. "Let me." He bent up her top leg and, pressing the cloth to her sex, gently cleaned her.

She winced at even a soft touch, and he grimaced in sympathy. "Sorry, love. I was too rough. I—"

"Was amazing." She grinned up at him. "It's fine. I'm just a little sore."

A wave of tenderness rolled through him. Unexpected and unwelcome—because he couldn't let this be anything more than it was.

Returning to the bathroom, he rinsed the cloth and tossed it over the towel rack, and then slid back into the bed. He pulled the sheet up over them both and reached for her, but she was already there, tucking herself into his side, one hand on his heart, as if they'd done this a hundred times.

Her hair spilled onto his chest in silky dark tendrils. He pressed a kiss to her temple.

The tenderness mixed with something basic. Primal.

Mine.

He wanted to keep her. Lure her back to his lonely den. He might even be able to convince her it was her idea. Just for the next few days, until he left...

He fingered his quartz, considering. He had a rare, little known Gift—he could hypnotize people with his quartz, compel them to obey him. He could induce Rosana to come back to Baltimore with him.

It wouldn't be that hard to get her to do something she wanted anyway. Just a nudge would probably work.

But even the cat, primitive beast though it was, knew that was wrong.

And the man admitted that having Rosana move into his den —even for a few days—would be hollow if she didn't do it with her full knowledge and consent. If she ever came to him, he wanted her whole heart and soul.

His lip curled. Gods, he was pathetic. Next he'd be lighting candles and scattering rose petals on the sheets.

He tightened his arm around her. "Last night—why did you come to me?"

She traced a finger over his heart. "It was time."

What the hell—? He pulled back so he could see her face. "Are you saying you Saw something? Something about the two of us?"

"Not a vision, no."

"Then what?"

She expelled a breath. "Look, I wanted you and you wanted me. Isn't that enough?"

She was evading a straight answer, but he let it slide. "If your brother finds out, he'll skin me alive."

Once, that would've made this little getaway all the more fun, but not these days. Maybe at the beginning he'd gone after Rosana partly to tweak the other alpha, but he'd long since admitted to himself that he'd want her no matter who she was.

"Don't worry. No one knows I'm here."

He played with the pretty silver charm on her wrist. "What if he asks you straight out?"

She moved a shoulder. "I love Dion. He pretty much raised me and Tiago after my mom and dad disappeared."

Adric nodded. There wasn't much he didn't know about the do Rio family, including that Rosana's parents had been captured by King Sindre when she was just six, leaving Dion to raise both her and Tiago. There were two middle brothers, but they'd left Rock Run rather than challenge their oldest brother for alpha.

"And he's my alpha," she continued, "but that makes him my boss, not my master. If he asks straight out, I won't lie, but otherwise, this is between you and me. It's none of his business."

"We're rival alphas, love. What I do will always be his business, and vice versa."

"So this is it?" She pulled away and sat up. "One night and nothing else?"

He stared up at her. "That was the agreement."

But fuck, he wished it were different.

Hurt flickered across her face.

"Hey." He touched her hand. "You know it can't be more than that."

Rosana's mouth twisted.

He swallowed against the desire to apologize, to somehow take the words back. He owed her honesty, at least.

"Right." She averted her face. "I understand."

"Rosana..."

She cut him off with a sharp shake of her head, then rose up on her knees.

His hand fisted. She was going to ask him to take her home, and he'd have to be a fucking gentleman about it. But instead, she straddled him, brought his hands to her high, full breasts. She looked down at him, cobalt eyes unreadable.

He held his breath, but he couldn't stop his thumbs from caressing her pretty nipples. They beaded under his touch, and his dick twitched in response.

The corner of her mouth edged up. She traced two fingers down his forearm, and every nerve in his body felt the shock wave.

"Then we'd better not waste any time."

6

Outside, the sun was setting. A hazy winter light slanted through the blinds, gilding Adric's skin a warm gold.

Rosana ran her hands down his rock-hard torso. Learning the shape of his muscles, absorbing the heat of his skin.

She hadn't lied to him. It wasn't worth it—it would make her sick, and besides, he'd scent the lie.

But she hadn't told him the whole truth, either. Because yeah, it was time.

Not time for them—she'd never Seen whether they'd eventually end up mates. That would be a glimpse into her own future as well as his, and she was as blind as anyone when it came to Seeing her own future. Still, you didn't have to be a Seer to guess that Adric was preparing to move against Langdon, and she didn't have another way of keeping him close.

She traced her fingers up and down his forearm. The hair covering it was soft, barely visible, the skin beneath warm. *Deus*, it felt good to touch someone, be touched back.

"I need you." She swallowed. "So bad."

But you need me, too. That's what I have to show you.

She hadn't Seen that, but her gut told her she was right, and Colm, the Irish Seer who was training her, had told her to trust her hunches. According to her Sight, Adric intended to assassinate Langdon, but instead, he'd be captured and executed.

She had to do *something*.

"Good." His smile was relieved—and a little devilish. "I like you all hot and needy." He cupped her breasts, squeezing and caressing.

Her breath hitched. She placed her hands over his and set her worries aside for the time being. These sensations were too new, too wonderful to ignore.

"More." She rubbed her breasts sensuously against his big palms. His hands were hard, calloused, with a couple of healing cuts. What did the Baltimore alpha do that gave him a laborer's hands?

"Like this?" He rolled her nipples between his thumbs. An electric pleasure stabbed to her womb.

"Yes..." She gripped his wrists. His eyes were dark with desire, his handsome face intent. Her core clenched. A hot, needful yearning slid through her veins. She wanted him so much it hurt.

Why you?

They'd met for the first time at Dion and Cleia's mate ball. To a teenager who'd grown up in Rock Run's rough-hewn, dimly lit caverns, the ball had been something out of a storybook. Outdoors on a bright summer day in two massive white tents overflowing with flowers, one tent for dancing, the other for dining. All seven of the sun fae clans had been present, their long, inhumanly perfect bodies clad in the finest fae couture, their hair all the fiery shades of sunshine: gold, silver, copper. One-of-a-kind jewels glittered in their ears and around their wrists and throats.

Rosana had been dancing with a tall blond sun fae when her nape had prickled. She'd glanced around, and there was Adric, lean and unsmiling and gorgeous in a colorful African-style tunic. Standing at the edge of the dance floor with his sister and watching her with a feline intensity.

Arousal had shivered over her skin, the first ever in her life. At sixteen, she was barely adolescent; a fada's life was measured in centuries. Too young to be thinking of love or finding a mate.

He'd sauntered across the polished wood floor, a cat on the prowl, and asked her to dance. She almost said no. His scent and quartz marked him as an earth fada, and she suspected he was just trying to piss off the Rock Run males.

Then he'd introduced himself, and she'd realized he was the new Baltimore alpha. The man who'd already managed to make an enemy of both Dion and Tiago.

"Well?" His expression was challenging.

A spark flashed between them—and she found herself saying yes.

He'd been polite, respectful, careful not to pull her too close, his hands light on her shoulder and waist. But for those few minutes, her nerves had tingled with excitement, her heart drumming crazily in her chest.

The moment the music stopped, two Rock Run men stepped in and suggested in hard voices that Adric find someone else to dance with. He'd left soon after.

Since then, she'd only seen him once a year or so. She'd told herself she wasn't interested, especially when she'd heard a group of warriors laughing a little enviously about what a horny dog the Baltimore alpha was. The man had a different woman every other week.

But the heat was always there, simmering between them.

Until Adric had changed the game. Stealing kisses whenever he had the chance. Making her want him. Daring her to come to him, when they both knew Dion would take it as a personal betrayal. And Adric didn't help. He seemed to take a special glee in seeing how far he could push Dion.

Well, she'd taken Adric's dare, and if it pissed off her brother, she'd just have to accept it. This wasn't some reckless, juvenile rebellion.

Adric was her mate, even if she'd resisted admitting it. How could he ever claim her? Their two clans barely tolerated each other. Mate with him, and the balance might tip, setting off a war or a series of challenges.

Hot tears stung her eyes. She inhaled, blinked them away.

Adric rubbed a thumb under her eye, confused and concerned. "You're crying?"

Her heart turned over. It was the uncertainty that got her. She guessed he didn't let many people see him looking anything but controlled, in charge.

She lifted a shoulder, let it drop. "It's just...so much." Which was the truth.

"Too much?" He curled up to cup her face, his gaze searching hers. "Just say the word and I'll stop. You want to go home?"

"No!" She clutched his shoulders. "I want this. So much."

He brushed his lips over hers, slow and sweet. "You sure?"

She gave a vigorous nod.

"Okay, then." His mouth nudged hers open, deepening the kiss. His tongue touched inside, teasing her, taking her deeper step by step until she was making low sounds of arousal in her throat.

He ended the kiss and lay back down, looking up at her with heated eyes while his hands played over her body, toying with her nipples, shaping her waist, her hips. Between their bodies, his cock pressed against her sex without entering her. She reached down and adjusted it so she could slide back and forth on its slick length.

His breath hissed in.

She felt an unfamiliar, very feminine sense of power. At least she wasn't alone in this neediness.

Setting her fingertips on his abdomen, she undulated her hips, pleasuring them both. He caught her hair in his hand, tugged her head back.

Craving contracted her womb, hot and liquid. "Adric."

"Ric." He rose up to kiss the side of her neck. "My friends call me Ric."

"Ric," she obediently repeated.

A sexy growl against her throat. "Lift up a little."

When she obeyed, he wet his thumb in her juices and then swirled it around her clit. The work-roughened pad made her suck in a breath. It aroused, and yet hurt.

And then the two mixed together, and she moaned.

His smile was feral, sharp-toothed. "That's it. Come for me, love."

He used the hand in her hair to control her, keeping her body stretched taut, her pussy rubbing against the edge of his cock and that erotically rough thumb on her clit. She had her own hands on her breasts now, both soothing her own ache and seducing him with an age-old instinct.

He muttered something dark and gave her hair a firm tug. Sensation rocketed down her spine.

"Come for me." A soft command.

She inhaled raggedly. He rolled her clit between his thumb and finger and the pleasure exploded through her. She moaned and let it take her, riding the waves as they crashed through her, over her, lifting her up and stealing her breath until she was wrung out and gasping.

She let out a slow exhale and hung over him, limp and satiated.

"Beautiful." He curled his hand around her nape, drew her close for a hard kiss.

Between their bodies, his erection pulsed. She slid a hand down to caress him.

His eyes sparked hotly into hers, but he set a hand on her wrist. "You're not too sore?"

Her heart constricted. He was being so considerate, even though he was hard as steel, his erection pulsating beneath her fingers.

"A little," she admitted, her gaze on his cock. It was smooth and a little sticky from her juices. She ran a thumb over the wide, flushed head, and he groaned.

But he continued, "If it's too much, we don't—"

She curved her fingers around him and squeezed, halting him

in mid-sentence. "I'm fine," she said, and lifted off him long enough to grab one of the little blue packets. She ripped it open with her teeth and worked the condom down over his erection.

When she was done, he lifted her by the hips so she was poised over him, and then paused. "You do it. Take me inside you."

Setting her hands on his chest, she eased herself down. He slipped inside and she stilled. "It feels...different." She slid down the rest of the way, and then sucked in a breath as he touched deep inside, where she still throbbed. "Deeper."

"Good," he said hoarsely as he grasped her hips and started to move. "It feels...good. So fucking good."

"*Sim...*" She slipped into Portuguese without realizing it. Telling him how beautiful he was, how good he made her feel.

She skated her palms over his chest. His skin was heated, a little sweaty. She fingered his nipples, and his breath hitched.

She leaned down to rub her breasts over his chest. The wiry hair abraded the sensitive tips. Electricity jolted through her.

She closed her eyes, drinking it in.

This. She hungered for this.

Not just the pleasure, but the closeness. She'd been so starved for touch.

Wonder filled her, a wonder touched with sorrow. How could she have found this beautiful, aching closeness only to let it go? Let *him* go?

She slid her arms beneath his hard shoulders, set her face against his.

Mine, she thought fiercely.

She *would* save him. And then somehow, she'd force both their clans to accept them as mates.

At that moment, it seemed not just possible, but inevitable.

He moved her so her breasts were over his face and latched his mouth onto her nipple. A single hard suck and she was lost, sobbing out his name.

"Take it." He thrust inside her, firm and deep. Moved his mouth to her other nipple to suck that, too.

Mine, she thought with each hard stroke. *Mine, mine, mine.*

Her blood heated, flushing her face, pounding in her ears. She dug her nails into his shoulders and with a helpless sigh, shot over the edge.

He released her nipple to capture her mouth. Devouring her while he thrust into her, over and over, until he pushed up hard in her and stilled. Tearing his mouth from hers, he buried his face in her hair.

"Rosana," he growled against her ear, and came.

7

———

*S*ometime after midnight, Adric jerked awake. He glanced around, shaking off a very pleasant dream. Rosana was sprawled on top of him, her breasts soft against his chest, her head tucked into the curve of his neck.

His mouth curved. So that part of the dream had been true.

After they'd made love the second time, they'd napped and then taken a hot shower together. Just a shower—he'd wanted to give her time to heal. But he'd never had such an erotic shower. They'd washed each other from head to toe, intermixed with slow, sensuous kisses, until the hot water ran out.

They'd toweled each other dry—and then she'd gone to her knees on the bathroom rug before him. Her mouth was warm and wet, and while a part of him registered her lack of experience, the rest of him muttered *who the fuck cares* and enjoyed.

Then it was his turn. He led her back to the bed and feasted on her, reveling in her sexy little sounds of pleasure and how she wriggled and bucked beneath his tongue and hands.

By then it was dinnertime. She put on her snug red jacket and those fuck-me boots, and he took her to a restaurant overlooking the canal. They had local beers and grilled rockfish as the stars appeared, one by one, over the canal's night-dark waters.

When they returned to the B&B, he had her strip and then helped her step back into the boots while she watched with those wide, ocean-blue eyes. They'd explored all the ways a man and woman could enjoy each other without full penetration before falling asleep, bodies entwined.

Now she snuggled closer, murmuring his name. He tightened his arms around her, nape tingling uneasily.

What had awoken him?

The outside door opened. Footsteps started up the stairs to the main floor. Three people, from the sound of it.

He lifted his head, straining to hear something. Anything. But they were dead silent. Yeah, it was late, but surely a group of three would speak at least a few words among themselves?

They reached the main floor and rapped on the door to Mark's private apartment.

"What the hell?" the innkeeper demanded in rough, just-woke-up tones.

"Where are they? The fada." A man's voice.

Adric tensed. Easing out from beneath Rosana, he crept to the door, setting his ear against the wood.

"I don't know what you're talking about," Mark returned.

"Yes," the man said in a cold voice, "you do."

"Get your hands off me," Mark snarled. "You've got five seconds to get out of here or I'm calling the cop—"

The thud of flesh against flesh was followed by an "oof."

"Talk," the man said.

The only sound was the harsh scrape of Mark's breathing.

Adric whirled into motion. "Rosana," he hissed.

She was already sitting up. Scrambling out of bed, she whispered, "What's the matter?"

He tossed her some clothes. "We're leaving," he replied in an equally soft voice. "Someone's asking about us."

She froze. "My brothers?"

He shook his head. The Rock Run men might be hard-assed

S.O.B.s, but they wouldn't beat a man just for renting the two of them a room. No, they'd kick Adric's ass instead.

"I don't think so. Now, *move*."

She hurriedly pulled on her jeans and shirt while he dragged on his own clothes. He shoved an iron dagger into his back pocket. Iron was the only sure way to kill a fae.

"No shoes," he told her. "We may have to run for it."

"Got it." She crammed her things into the canvas bag, leaving her barefoot in the Henley and jeans. He silently blessed the tight operation run by Dion. She'd clearly been trained how to respond in an emergency.

"This way." Rosana jerked her head at the sliding doors. "Down the back stairs."

He gave her a silent thumbs-up.

In the hall outside their room, footsteps could be heard. Another person ran lightly up to the third floor.

Apparently, Mark hadn't given up their location. Adric would owe him for that. He just hoped the human would be alive to collect.

Rosana slung her bag over a shoulder and eased open the sliding door. He grabbed his duffel bag and followed, quietly closing the door behind him. Hopefully, that would buy them a little time before their pursuers realized they were no longer in the B&B.

Rosana ignored the stairs to sling a long leg over the wood railing. She worked her way hand-over-hand down the outside of the stairs before dropping the last few feet to the grass. The entire descent took five seconds, tops.

Despite the danger, his mouth edged up as he swung over the railing and dropped to the grass beside her. Damn, he liked how the woman's mind worked.

They glided around the enclosed outdoor shower and halted against the far wall where they couldn't be seen from the B&B.

Rosana set her mouth to his ear. "They'll be watching the parking lot."

He nodded. Why the fuck hadn't he parked the rental car somewhere else? But he'd believed they were safe. No one knew his exact location, not even Marjani.

Had he'd been followed from Baltimore?

He peered around the corner. The lights in their room came on, visible through the cracks in the wood slats. His nostrils flared, but he couldn't pick up a scent from that far away.

If only he knew who, exactly, was after them—fada or fae? Because a fada could track the two of them even if they ran.

His neck crawled. The backyard was too small, nothing but a narrow strip of grass between the B&B and the tall fence surrounding it. They had to get out of here before the bastards came looking for them.

He jerked his chin in the direction of the beach. "We'll go over the fence," he whispered in Rosana's ear, "and stick to the back-yards. Make our way to the bay. You can go into the water, and I'll shift to my cougar and run along the beach. They won't be able to track us in the water."

Her mouth formed a shocked O. "You think they're fada? Not humans robbing the place?"

He shook his head grimly. "They asked Mark where the fada were."

And even if they hadn't, his itching nape told him he and Rosana were in danger. He trusted that itch. During the Darktime, it had saved his life more than once.

"Once you're in the water, head for Henlopen," he told her. "I'll meet you at the park."

The Cape Henlopen State Park was a good mile away, but in his cougar form, he could sprint as fast as fifty miles per hour. It would take Rosana a little longer to swim there, but unless one of their pursuers was a water fada, she'd be safer in the ocean than with him.

Not even a wolf could track her in the water.

She worried her lower lip with her teeth. "You want us to split up?" she whispered back.

"Just for a few minutes—maybe half an hour. I'll meet you at the Point. I'll be on the beach that faces the Breakwater Lighthouse. You know it?"

"Yeah, but—"

Footsteps on the balcony above made her snap shut her mouth. As one, they shrank deeper into the shadows.

Adric risked a look. The man was scanning the wetlands behind the B&B. Tall and dark-skinned, and dressed in a black leather jacket and pants, he would've blended into the shadows if not for his cropped silver hair. His pointed ears stood out in stark relief against his pale hair.

A fae, then. But Adric had been expecting a night fae, and the only fae with such light hair were ice fae.

His brow furrowed. What the fuck was an ice fae doing in Lewes, Delaware?

The fae turned his gaze on the backyard. Adric dropped his eyes so the fae wouldn't see them glowing in the dark.

"Ice fae," he mouthed at Rosana.

She gulped. Then she raised her left arm, the one with the silver bracelet. "Protection charm," she whispered back.

He nodded, relieved.

He fingered his quartz. A few months ago, he'd stumbled upon a new use for his Gift of hypnotism. He could somehow induce people to look right past him. It was similar to a cloaking spell, something the fae charged an arm and a leg for—if they'd even sell it to a fada.

But he'd never tried to cloak a second person as well. He wasn't even sure if he could. Plus, it drained energy at a rapid rate, energy he might need to shift.

Still, if it came down to it, he'd try. He was *not* letting that fae bastard get his hands on Rosana. At least she had that protection charm.

"See anything, Jon?" A woman's cool, aristocratic voice.

"No. But that doesn't mean they're not out here."

Adric risked another look as the woman joined Jon on the

balcony. She was tall and curvy with long hair the color of moonlight, her scent a mix of silver and something acrid.

Every hair on his nape rose. Only a night fae had that distinctive scent of metal and decay. His heart clenched with pure, unadulterated hate.

But she wasn't a pureblood. No, that silver-blond hair spoke of an ice-fae ancestor, and the only ice fae/night fae mix Adric knew was Lady Blaer.

The woman who'd put Marjani in a cage.

His upper lip peeled back in a silent snarl. He wanted badly to sneak another look, but night fae could see in the dark as well as cats.

Gods, he wished he were alone so he could shift to his cougar, rip both fae into tiny pieces. He'd lost too many good friends to the night fae, been hunted himself too many nights. And Blaer had not only attacked Marjani, she'd forced his friend Luc to accept her *geas*.

Rosana bumped her shoulder against his. "Calm down," she mouthed.

He gave a tight nod.

She was right. Night fae were energy vampires, with a creepy sixth sense that allowed them to home in on negative emotions—fear, anger, agitation. The only way to hide from them was to stay calm, slowing your heart and breath so they couldn't track you.

Breathe in, breath out.

Retracting his claws, he pulled out the dagger and held it against his side. He forced himself to relax, blanked his mind.

In, out.

Beside him, Rosana slowed her breath to almost nothing.

The two fae continued scanning the backyard. Power brushed over Adric's skin, cold and black. A night fae questing for prey.

He stilled, sinking deep into his animal.

Next to him, Rosana drew a barely perceptible breath and gripped his left wrist. He turned his palm over, threaded his fingers through hers and gave her an encouraging squeeze. She lowered an eyelid in a slow wink.

He managed a small smile back, although he'd never felt less amused.

Inside the B&B, doors slammed. From the third floor came the sound of frightened human voices. The bastards had rousted the couple upstairs.

Adric's fingers tightened on the dagger's handle, but he remained where he was. The fae wouldn't do anything but scare the crap out of the human couple. The humans hadn't even seen him and Rosana, so they'd be no help to the searchers.

Rosana's palm was damp with nerves. He squeezed her hand again.

Hold on, angel.

A minute ticked by. The tension wound tighter.

He took another deliberate breath.

Calm, cool, blank. A sheet of paper. A snow-covered field.

Serenity flowed from Rosana. Maybe it was her, and maybe it was the charm, but it helped.

At last the woman murmured in disgust. The dark tendrils withdrew.

"They could be miles away by now. All I know is they're not in this bloody inn."

The man murmured assent, and the two of them returned inside without bothering to close the sliding door.

Adric waited until their voices receded before jerking his chin at the fence separating the next yard from the B&B.

Rosana nodded, and together, they scaled the fence and sprinted behind the neighboring house. They continued that way down the street, sticking to backyards as they aimed for the water.

When they were almost to the beach, Adric pulled Rosana into the shadow of an empty cedar-shingled house.

"*Mãe de Deus.*" Her breath whooshed out. "What was that about?"

He shrugged, although he had his suspicions. "You were perfect." He gave her a hard kiss. "Cool as could be."

She shrugged, but he could tell she was pleased. "My training as a Seer includes meditation techniques."

"Well, it worked, but now we need to get the fuck out of here." He indicated the deck behind her. "We can stash the bags under there and come back for them later."

His quartz was engineered to be a smartphone. While Rosana stowed their bags beneath the deck, he notified the Lewes police about the break-in at the B&B.

"A man's hurt. Send an ambulance ASAP."

"Your name, sir?"

"That's not important," he said, and ended the connection.

He and Rosana peeled off their clothes and tucked them under the deck, and then he dragged her long, lush body up against his. Her skin was icy, and even though he knew river fada had naturally cool metabolisms, he hated that she'd been pulled out of a warm bed because of him.

"The Breakwater Light," he reminded her. "Stay in the water until I signal you. Three flashes with my quartz."

She wound an arm around his neck. "'Kay."

He brushed a strand of her hair back from her temple and then frowned. Rosana was a river dolphin, not an ocean-going dolphin like a bottlenose. "The salt water isn't a problem?"

She shook her head. "The bay is actually an estuary—a mix of fresh and salt water. And I can take salt water for short periods of time. My mom's a bottlenose."

"Okay, then." He kissed her nose. "Watch for a blue light—I'll flash it three times in a row, then pause and repeat it."

"Got it—three blue flashes." She touched his cheek. "Be careful, okay?"

He blinked, bemused. When was the last time anyone besides Marjani had told him to be careful? He was the strong one, the alpha. Even as a teenager, he'd been the one his friends looked to for direction.

"Yeah. Sure."

He watched as she glided across the deserted street to the beach, sticking to the shadows, silent as a ghost. She sprinted across the sand and dove into the shallow water. Shining bits of green and blue and purple glimmered beneath the surface, so beautiful he caught his breath. A slender torpedo-shaped body sketched an arc against the night sky and disappeared beneath the waves.

Adric waited another minute to make sure she got away safely. Then he shifted to his cougar—and headed back to the B&B.

8

———————

"What's the use of being a Seer," Rosana muttered as she jogged into the icy bay, "if you can't See your own freaking future?"

She hadn't had a hint the fae were coming. They could've been in the room before she'd known they were there. Why couldn't she have a useful Gift, like being a healer?

"You don't choose your Gift. It chooses you. Lucky us." She could almost see Colm's mouth twisting in a self-mocking smile. *"And you know Seers almost never See what lies ahead for themselves."*

"Yeah, yeah," she snarled. "Can't forget Rule 1." She dove into a wave.

Colm had drilled several truths about being a Seer into her. Colm's Rules, she called them.

Rule 1: A Seer almost never Sees his or her own future.

Rule 2: The Sight is unpredictable. You can train it, but it's like trying to ride a tiger. You never know when it will turn on you.

Rule 3: Belief is as important as skill. To free your Sight, you must believe in its essential truth.

Freaking rules. As far as she could tell, being a Seer was worthless. People were wary of you, and they didn't want to listen to you even when you *knew* you were right.

You couldn't even use your Gift to save yourself. If Ula had Seen that King Sindre was laying a trap for her and Nisio, they wouldn't have left on that trip across the ocean and Rosana wouldn't have grown up without her parents.

She gave a hard kick and let the change take her. Magic shimmered over her skin. For a timeless few moments, she was neither human nor dolphin, but colorful fragments of light and energy. Then her legs fused, became a tail. Her face elongated into a river dolphin's beak, and her arms became flippers.

She sucked air through her blowhole and with a powerful thrust of her tail, skimmed through the midnight sea. She was Rosana, and yet not Rosana.

Stronger, more supple. Wild. Free.

She remained beneath the surface for several minutes, not resurfacing until she was a few hundred yards out, the shoreline curving behind her in a giant C. Ahead, the flash of the Harbor of Refuge Light marked Cape Henlopen and the Delaware Bay's western boundary. The Breakwater Lighthouse was a little before it, but unlike its sister lighthouse, it was dark, having been decommissioned years ago.

She set out for the Point on a path parallel to the shore.

That had been a night fae on the balcony. Or maybe the woman was a mixed-blood, because Rosana had never heard of a pureblood night fae with blond hair.

Fear tripped up her spine.

Somehow, that woman was connected to her vision. Nothing else made sense. But how?

She knew Prince Langdon was out for blood. His only living son, Tyrus, had gone missing last June after attacking Adric's clan. The Baltimore fada had clammed up about what really happened, but everyone knew Tyrus was dead, with Adric the chief suspect.

But without proof, Langdon had done nothing. Yet.

Still, Adric wasn't the type to wait around for the prince to attack. If he thought Langdon was a threat, he'd strike first.

But when? And more importantly, how could she stop it?

If only she knew more.

She gave a frustrated swish of her tail. Helpless, and hating it.

If what she'd Seen was true—and she'd never had such a clear, detailed vision before—Adric was going after Langdon soon.

And he'd die.

THE SWIM to the Point took about fifteen minutes. Rosana navigated with sweeps of her sonar, emitting sound and interpreting the echoes: the curved shape of the shore line; the fishing pier that jutted into the water; a school of Atlantic croakers; a shipwreck dating to the 1700s.

A stack of huge granite slabs loomed before her, the half-mile-long breakwater that gave the lighthouse its name. She surfaced on the inner side of the breakwater a safe distance from the rugged slabs. The sky above was clear, the stars white pinpricks in its dark cloth.

She scanned the beach. No sign of Adric.

She slapped her tail against the water a couple of times. The breakwater blocked the Atlantic to form a calm, quiet harbor. If he was nearby, he'd hear her.

She waited a minute and then smacked the water with her tail again.

Still no Adric.

Her stomach clenched.

Stop worrying. The man's an alpha. A big cat with teeth and claws.

A pod of three wild female bottlenoses appeared, drawn by the commotion. They were larger than Rosana's six-foot length, but friendly. They greeted her with a mixture of squawks, whistles and clicks.

Rosana replied in their language, and they circled her.

Who, who who? whistled the eldest female, a motherly sort with small, wise eyes.

Visitor, Rosana replied. *I mean you no harm.*

Why, why why? the motherly bottlenose asked.

Meeting a friend. But he's not here. Worried.

Sorry... We wait.

Their bodies brushed hers, offering comfort.

For the next quarter hour, the four of them swam back and forth in front of the lighthouse until Rosana had to face facts. Either Adric had been captured, or he'd returned to the B&B to sniff around some more. It was what her brothers would've done.

The smart thing, the *safe* thing, would be to head farther out to sea. No one but another water fada could track her in the ocean, and with the head start she'd had, even a shark would have trouble scenting her.

But fuck being safe. If Adric had been captured, it was three against one, and at least two of the others were fae.

Not just any fae. A night fae.

Damn, damn, damn. She didn't want to go back. She wanted to get as far away as possible from that scary bitch and her henchmen.

But there really wasn't a choice. She wished the wild dolphins a polite farewell and whipped around to head back to Lewes.

9

———

*A*dric raced through the backyards, a shadow in the night.

He had a bad feeling about the second man with Lady Blaer, the one he hadn't seen. He couldn't leave without knowing for sure.

Sirens split the night. He gritted his teeth, the high wail excruciating to his shifter ears. At least it meant help was on its way to Mark.

The wood fence ran the length of the B&B's property. He peered through them into the parking lot. The two fae were just getting into the back of a glossy black limo. But it was their rangy, hard-faced driver who made Adric's lungs cinch tight.

His hunch had been correct. The second man was Luc, one of his lieutenants. No, make that former lieutenant.

Anger and guilt clogged his chest.

Late last summer, Luc had accepted a *geas* from Lady Blaer. For the next decade, the wolf fada was Blaer's man, not his. So Adric had been forced to expel him from the clan.

It didn't matter that Luc was an old friend, one of the small, close-knit group who'd helped Adric and Marjani take down Leron Savonett, their bastard of an uncle. It didn't matter that Luc had been imprisoned and tortured simply for being Adric's friend.

Adric had had no choice. As alpha, he was connected through his quartz to every man, woman and child in the clan. He couldn't allow a man under the control of a fae to remain part of that network.

"Get us out of here," the blond female ordered Luc.

Adric's lips peeled back in a silent snarl. He was sure now that she was Lady Blaer.

His muscles gathered, his whole body shaking with the need to attack.

Kill.

The woman had put his sister in a fucking iron cage. She'd forced Luc to accept her *geas*. And perhaps worst of all, Blaer had learned the secret of the earth fada's quartz. With the right words, a fae could control an earth fada through their quartz—and Blaer knew the incantation.

For so many reasons, Blaer needed to die. But attack now, and Luc would be forced to defend her. And while the two of them fought, Blaer would simply teleport herself and the ice fae male out of there.

"Where to?" Luc asked Blaer.

"Virginia—the New Moon Court."

Luc nodded and shut the limo door. His head swung to where Adric crouched, his eyes the amber of his wolf.

Adric froze, a sick feeling coating his stomach—because he wasn't one-hundred-percent sure that Luc wouldn't betray him.

The former lieutenant's face blanked. He opened the front door and slid behind the limo's steering wheel.

Adric released a breath.

The car purred to life and headed down the street. At the corner, Luc pulled over to allow two police cars and an ambulance pass by.

Adric waited until the limo was out of sight before racing back to the house where he and Rosana had left their things. There, he changed back to man and pulled on his pants and T-shirt, leaving the rest in the duffel bag for now.

Luc's face had been hard as stone, closed up tight. The man had always been grim, but now he looked like he'd been scrubbed clean of emotion.

Gods, it sliced at Adric, to leave a friend with the fae, especially Luc. During the Darktime, Adric had risked his own life to rescue Luc from Leron. If it would do any good, he'd do the same thing in a heartbeat.

But Luc had accepted Lady Blaer's *geas* of his own free will to save Marjani in Iceland. Now Luc was bound to her for the next decade, and Adric couldn't do a damn thing about it. Only Luc could break the *geas*, and his former lieutenant would never do that. The man would die before breaking his word.

Adric tightened his jaw. If only he hadn't sent Luc to Iceland after Marjani.

The clan needed you in Baltimore. And Luc insisted on going. You probably couldn't have stopped him if you tried.

But Adric was alpha. The final decision had been his—and because of it, he'd lost Luc to that fae bitch.

That's when it hit him. Luc was Blaer's man. He must have led the fae to Lewes—and Adric.

His lungs contracted. He pressed the heel of his hand to his chest, telling himself that it wasn't Luc's fault. He was under Blaer's control.

But it felt like Luc had shoved a knife into his heart.

He grimly set his hurt aside. Rosana was waiting for him. Rolling up his jeans, he jogged barefoot into the bay until it reached his calves before setting out for the Breakwater Light. If Luc did return, the water would erase Adric's tracks.

He hadn't gone far when he saw the river dolphin slipping through the waves, a sleek smudge against the lighter gray of the night sky. He should've known she'd come back for him.

He dropped the bags on the sand and signaled her with his quartz. She immediately headed in, shifting a few yards offshore. She rose from the bay, water streaming down her naked body, and everything in him stopped.

Breath, heart, even his mind.

All he could do was stare in helpless longing.

She strode through the waves toward him, all long legs and curves, wet hair snaking like seaweed over high, firm breasts. Water droplets shimmered on her skin, the charm a silver glint on her wrist.

She was a siren with ocean-colored eyes, come to land for one short night.

Sorrow squeezed his insides. She was so beautiful, so at home at the water.

So different from him.

They could never have more than these snatches of time.

But his feet were already moving, taking him to her.

10

───────

*A*dric was okay.

Rosana's knees went weak with relief at seeing him unharmed.

Their eyes locked, and her spine tingled at the need and heat in his. She walked toward him, a moth to his fire.

He met her halfway, hauling her up against his lean, sinewy frame. The water sucked at their ankles. The icy wind whipped around them.

She had time to draw a breath and then his mouth crashed onto hers. One kiss spun into the next, and the next. Hard, drugging kisses that took her deep and whipped her around until she clung to him as if he were the only solid thing in the world.

His hands gripped her hips, molding her to his body. His erection pressed against her belly through the placket of his jeans. She rubbed against it and he groaned.

The wind picked up, scouring her exposed skin. She shivered and pressed closer, tunneling her fingers under his T-shirt, seeking his warmth. She might be a river fada, adapted to cool streams and caverns, but even she got cold on a night like this.

He lifted his head, swore. "You need to put on some clothes."

"Clothes." Dazed, she rested her forehead against his chest. "Right."

As she got dressed, Adric suggested they camp out in Cape Henlopen for the night and get the car in the morning. "Otherwise," he added, "we'll spend half the night answering questions for the humans."

"Sounds good," she said as she rolled up her pants.

They set off at a jog down the beach, running through the surf to hide their scent. In the park, they continued off-road through the pine-covered dunes until they reached the Point, a sandy spit of land that hooked into the bay, dividing it from the Atlantic. There, they made camp in a hollow beneath a loblolly pine, zipping up their jackets and pulling on socks.

Leaning back on his forearms, Adric stared grim-faced into the pine trees. Whatever he was thinking, it wasn't pleasant.

She sifted a handful of sand and pine needles through her fingers. "You went back without me, didn't you?"

"Yeah. So?"

She rolled her eyes. Typical alpha. Send the female to safety so he could investigate alone. "So it was three against one. I could've helped you."

"Rosana." His voice was so reasonable, she ground her teeth. "It wasn't your problem. They were after me."

"What makes you so sure? Maybe it was me they were after. I *am* the Rock Run alpha's sister, you know."

He turned his head to look at her. His eyes had gone nightglow, the irises the same brilliant blue at the heart of a flame. "Oh, I know. I don't ever forget it. Not for a single second."

She swallowed. "But something made you go back."

He heaved a breath. "You're not going to let this rest, are you?"

"Nope."

He shook his head, but said, "The other man, the one we didn't see? He was an earth fada."

Oh. "He's working for the fae?"

"Yeah."

"From your clan?"

His mouth set. "Not exactly."

She rolled a loblolly needle between her fingers, releasing its sharp, piney scent. "This has to do with what happened last summer, doesn't it? When Lord Tyrus died."

He lifted a shoulder, dropped it. Not confirming, but not denying either—which told her she was right.

"His father wants revenge." She was careful not to say Prince Langdon's name. Speak a fae's name, and you risked drawing his attention. "But Tyrus attacked you, didn't he? Merry said he almost killed her uncle Jace."

Adric snorted. "He's a fae. He doesn't need a reason. No, I was supposed to lie down, belly up, while Tyrus picked off my lieutenants one by one."

"What about that blonde we saw? She's not a pureblood, is she?"

A pause. "That's what I can't figure out. She's not a member of the New Moon Court. She's an ice fae/night fae mix. So is she working for the prince—or on her own?"

Rosana frowned. "In my vision, three night fae warriors captured you. One of them could have been a woman, but none of them had blond hair."

A noncommittal grunt.

To the east, the surf boomed. Above, the wind growled and snapped at the treetops. Rosana shivered and hugged her knees. She'd known Adric was in danger, but seeing those fae at the B&B had rammed it home.

He was in a fight for his life.

The Darktime isn't over. The prince will destroy your clan from the inside out.

She gripped her knees harder.

"That earth fada," she said. "He's someone important to you, isn't he? A good friend."

Adric stiffened. "How the fuck do you know that?"

"I don't read minds, if that's what you're thinking, but I can tell he upset you."

Her Gift made her more sensitive to emotions than most people, although Adric had always been hard to read. But since they'd had sex, it was as if they'd connected on some deeper level. Right now, she *felt* the anger and hurt radiating from him.

She furrowed her brow. Was it always like that?

"You're right," Adric admitted. "He's not a clan member—not anymore—but the two of us go way back."

"He's *hunting* you for them?"

A curt nod. "He's under a *geas* to the fae lady. I know he doesn't have a choice, that he has to obey, but he is—was—one of my best friends, a lieutenant. It—" He shook his head. "He must've tracked me to Lewes for her. I had to expel him from the clan—I had no choice. The way our quartzes work, everyone in the clan is connected to me."

Her heart ached for Adric. She touched his leg. "He understands."

"Maybe." Adric's mouth twisted. "When I went back, he saw me. But he kept quiet. Just got in the car and drove off."

"So he *does* understand."

"I suppose so. I know he has to obey her, but—"

"I'm sorry."

He moved a shoulder. "Not your problem."

"But I'm the only one here." She lay down, gave him a tug. "C'mere. Keep me warm."

He let her pull him down so his head was cradled against her breasts. He set an arm on her waist and moved his head, finding a comfortable spot.

She stroked his nape, excruciatingly aware she was almost out of time. In a few hours, they'd be returning to Maryland. Who knew when she'd have him alone again?

But *Deus*, this was fucked up—the fae at the B&B, the earth fada tracking them. And she sensed there was more to the story, that Adric hadn't told her everything.

But then, she hadn't told him everything, either. Because that vision she'd had in December? A few days later, she'd taken out her scrying bowl, hoping to See a different fate for him. But she'd Seen the exact same thing—and this time, the scene had played out to its conclusion.

She swallowed sickly. Because she *knew* she was right.

Adric intended to assassinate Prince Langdon. And if he went alone, he'd die.

"What's wrong?" He lifted his head to scrutinize her.

She took a deep breath and blurted, "You need me. When you go after the prince, you have to take me, too."

He pulled away from her. "Rosana. Please."

She swallowed. "I know it sounds crazy. But I have this feeling."

"A feeling," he repeated flatly.

"That I can help."

"How? I'm not saying you're right, but what help could you be against the night fae? Or any fae, for that matter?"

She shut her eyes. Goddess, it did sound crazy. The fada might be physically equal to the fae, but the fae had magic to call on. They even healed more quickly.

She might be a warrior, but she'd never seen actual combat. What help could she give a man who'd spent half his life fighting a vicious civil war?

"You know I'm a Gifted Seer. The fae who's training me believes that someday I'll be one of the most powerful Seers in the world. And he says sometimes you don't See something, you *feel* it —a gut instinct. And my gut tells me I should go, too."

"Yeah?" he said in that same flat voice. "Well, my gut says you should stay home."

"Listen to me!" She gave him a shake. "There's more. After I left you that night, I Saw it in my scrying bowl. You—"

"Forget it." He rolled onto his back and dropped an arm over his eyes. "I don't care what you Saw, I'm not taking you with me."

She let out a breath through her teeth. "You know, Dion says you're smart. A bastard, yeah, but a smart bastard."

"I love him right back."

"Well, a smart man would listen to a Seer's warning."

A charged pause. Then he lifted his arm. "Okay, then. Talk."

She hesitated. How do you tell a man you foresaw his death?

That night in December, she'd Seen him going after Langdon. But later, there'd been more. Something so raw that just recalling it made her lungs lock.

The night fae capture Adric, drag him to a clearing in a dark woods. Stake him, spread-eagled, to the ground.

A black-haired priestess in a silver dress steps forward, a gleaming knife in her hand. She raises the knife above her head, brings it slashing down...

Rosana squeezed her eyes shut, but that just made it worse. The image was burned on her retinas. She opened them and stared fiercely up at the trees.

"Hey." He rolled over, touched her arm. "Take it easy. I *did* think about what you said, okay? But a vision is just one possible future."

She started, focused on him.

He was still free. There was still time to change his fate.

"I—I Saw your death. You go after the night fae, and you *die*. I Saw you on the ground. I smelled the freaking blood."

His swallow was loud in the clearing. When he spoke again, his voice was gentle. "I'm sorry, but my mind is made up. I'm going. Alone."

Her heart sank. "But *why*?"

He shook his head. "It's the only way."

"Adric. You have to listen. If you won't take me, take someone else—one of your men, or Marjani. Yeah, a vision is only one possible future, but it can only be the changed if you change the path you're on."

His face shuttered. "Enough, already. You had your say. Consider me warned."

She growled. "*Deus*, you're pigheaded—even more than Dion. And that's saying something."

Colm had warned her in his sardonic way that being a Seer was a thankless task, saying you might as well piss into the wind for all the notice most people will take of you.

But *Deus*, she hadn't realized how hard it was to have your warnings ignored.

Adric scrubbed a hand over his face, and then with a sigh, rolled over to face her. "Thank you, love." He took her hand, pressed a kiss to her knuckles.

"For what?" she snapped.

"For caring."

She looked down at the calloused fingers wrapped around hers. Sadness washed over her. "Oh, Adric. You don't have to thank someone for caring."

His mouth contorted. "Maybe not in your world." He reached for her. "Let me hold you. Okay?"

She shook her head but allowed him to pull her into his arms. Above, the wind whistled over the dunes, but here in the cozy hollow, they were snug and warm.

He nuzzled her hair. "It wouldn't work anyway. You know that, don't you?"

"Don't," she whispered, tears burning her throat. "Just don't. Please?"

He nodded and nudged her chin up so he could rub his lips over hers. They fell asleep like that, mouths still touching.

THE FIRST RAYS of dawn had pushed through the trees when Adric brushed Rosana's hair back from her face. "Time to go."

The two of them crept back to the B&B and peered through the fence. The parking lot was empty except for two cars—theirs, and a white truck that she assumed belonged to Mark. The human couple must've checked out.

Adric motioned for her to remain hidden behind the fence. "Wait here until I pull out of the parking lot. Just in case."

When she nodded, he slipped into the parking lot and strolled up to the Mazda. A press of the keyless remote, and the doors unlocked. He drove it a few yards up the street and then waited as she slid into the passenger seat.

The streets of Lewes were nearly empty, the houses still dark. Streetlights glowed against the slowly brightening sky as they pulled onto the highway.

Adric slanted her a look. "You hungry? We could stop somewhere."

She shook her head. "I'll eat when I get home."

"You sure?"

"Yeah."

They drove back to Maryland in silence. Rosana stared out the window, dully aware she'd failed.

So this was how it ended. One night was all they'd ever have.

In a few weeks—or maybe even a few days—Adric would leave for Virginia and the New Moon Court, and be captured by the night fae. Maybe he wouldn't die—maybe he'd somehow avoid that slashing knife. Like he'd said, that was just one possible future.

But even if he survived, what would become of the two of them?

It wouldn't work anyway. You know that, don't you?

They were almost at the rest area where she'd left the car when something in her snapped.

No.

She was *not* going to lose Adric because she was too afraid to speak up. If he didn't want her, he could tell her straight out.

She turned in the seat to face him. "*Why* wouldn't it work?"

"Rosana," he said in a hard, don't-question-me voice. "Don't do this."

"But it *meant* something. You felt it. I know you did." He'd touched her with such tenderness. Held her all night in the park. "You...thanked me for caring."

"And I meant it. But you and me?" He shook his head.

Her breath felt heavy in her lungs, as if she were trying to breathe underwater. Adric started to say something else and she threw up a staying hand.

"It's all right. Really. I get it. You don't want me that bad."

"Fuck." He swerved to the side of the highway and stomped on the brakes, throwing them both forward against their seatbelts.

A car zoomed past, horn blaring.

Rosana looked at the arm Adric had flung across her chest. "What the—?"

He unbuckled his seatbelt and hers with shifter-fast speed and dragged her toward him so that she lay half over the console.

"The hell I don't want you." His fingers dug into her shoulders. "If it was up to me, we'd be halfway across the country, looking for a place to make our own den away from both our clans. But I'm the alpha. The clan needs me. Before I took over, we almost lost everything. You know how many elders we have?"

She shook her head mutely. Hurting for him. Hurting for herself.

"Five—three women and two men. Other than them, no one older than forty survived the Darktime. I lost my mom and dad. Jace lost both his parents and his only sister. And the list goes on and on. That man I saw last night?" His throat worked. "He was captured and tortured for close to a year just for being my friend. So don't tell me I don't want you. It's not a question of what I fucking want."

He kissed her. A hard, fierce kiss, his arms clamped around her.

She brought her hands up, instinctively stroking, soothing.

He groaned and tore his mouth from hers. His grip on her loosened. He brought his forehead to hers.

"I can't turn my back on them," he rasped. "And they'd never accept you."

"It's okay," she managed to say, even though her heart had fractured into jagged shards. "I understand."

"The only way we can be together is if we keep sneaking around like this. Just say the word, and I'm there. But do you want a man who can never claim you? And what about your family, your clan? Do you really think Dion would accept me as your mate?" His laugh held zero humor. "God's cat. The man would probably try to carve off my balls if he found out we spent even one night together."

She shook her head, but in her heart, she knew he was right. A truck rumbled past, rattling their windows, but inside the car, the only sound was the harsh scrape of their breathing.

She pushed away from him. His hands tightened for a second as if he wanted to keep holding her, but then they opened, and she knew it really was over.

Adric regarded her moodily. "I'm not going to say I'm sorry. Last night was...special. I'll be damned if I regret it."

She pressed her lips together so he wouldn't see them trembling. Lifted her chin. "I didn't ask you for an apology." Returning to her seat, she fumbled blindly for the seat belt.

"I'll take you back."

She latched the belt and sat back. "Thank you."

Back at the rest stop, Adric turned off the engine. "One thing you can count on. I'm not going to die. He is. So stop worrying."

She just shook her head.

"So." He drummed his fingers on the steering wheel. "Take care of yourself—okay?"

"Yeah. Sure."

She reached for her canvas bag. Got out of the car. Shut the door.

Moving on automatic, because if she let herself think, the sobs locked in her chest might spill out.

Adric accompanied her to her car. After she unlocked the door, he reached around her and opened it. He didn't say goodbye, just touched her cheek and then closed the door for her. But he tailed her out of the rest area and up I-95. Making sure she got safely back to Grace Harbor, because that's who he was.

She watched through her rearview mirror as he followed her off the exit and then turned south toward Baltimore.

Her stomach was a hard, hurting knot. She pressed a fist to it and aimed the car for home.

ADRIC DROVE the thirty-five miles to Baltimore, foot heavy on the gas pedal, radio blasting. Just let the cops pull him over. Right now, he'd welcome the chance to pound on someone.

With every additional mile he traveled from Rosana, something inside him unraveled. Like his heart was attached to hers by some invisible thread, and with each mile, that wanting, needy organ was being shredded and left behind.

Mine.

His fingers tightened around the steering wheel. Her scent was still in the car, on him. Driving him insane.

He'd meant every word he'd said to her. The two of them together just wouldn't work.

Yeah, the clan had accepted Evie, Jace's mate, but everybody liked Evie. And she'd turned out to have a Gift that helped the healers, so she was an asset to the clan.

Marjani's mate, Fane, had been a harder sell, but Adric had made it clear the clan had better accept him or else. After what his sister had been through, she deserved to be happy.

But Adric was alpha. The clan needed him, and after the Darktime, they didn't trust easily. He'd worked his ass off to win over the doubters, convincing them that the only way forward was to work together. But choose a river fada as a mate—and worse, a Rock Run river fada—and that fragile accord could be blown sky-high.

Still, none of that mattered anyway. Because despite what he'd told Rosana, he didn't expect to get out of Virginia alive.

Inside his cougar lashed its tail, furious that he'd let Rosana just drive off. The cat was a simple beast. To it, Rosana was theirs and Adric was a fool for letting her go.

But he was a highly disciplined man, so he ruthlessly wrestled the cat under control, and then slowed enough to blend in with the human traffic.

11

Rosana returned home to find Rock Run on high alert. A Baltimore fada had been seen near the base, a wolf. A sentry had given chase, but the wolf had evaded capture.

Dion was coldly furious. In recent years, he'd made concessions to the Baltimore clan, accepting the clan's mining operation on sun fae lands and allowing Jace Jones to visit Merry near the Rock Run base. In return, Adric had agreed to stop trying to steal Rock Run's territory.

Now Dion felt betrayed. He and Rui do Mar, his second-in-command, were in the war room, discussing the situation with his *tenentes*.

At least they knew it couldn't be Adric. Unlike water fada, earth fada took only one form and everyone knew Adric was a cougar. Rosana took advantage of the confusion to sneak through the back tunnels to her quarters so she could wash off his scent before anyone noticed.

She and Isa had their own bathroom, carved out of the wall between their bedrooms. The counter was marbled granite, the toilet a solid black ceramic. Two shelves chiseled into the granite wall held her and Isa's toiletries, and the shower spilled out of the rough gray rock like a waterfall.

Rosana turned on the shower, stepped under it. She washed her hair, and then soaped up and leaned against the wall, letting the cool water wash over her.

She felt empty. Scooped out, one big hurt beneath her ribs where her heart should be.

What did you expect? One night with you and Adric would start to trust you?

She blew out a breath. Because yeah, she supposed she had expected it.

Not because they'd had sex—she might've been a virgin, but she wasn't an idiot—but because the two of them had finally had a chance to spend some time away from the disapproving eyes of their two clans.

She'd learned better. For him, it was just sex. End of story. There was nothing else between them.

Oh, he'd said he wanted more, just not enough to put her before his clan. Rosana respected that; for an alpha, the clan should come first. But if he really loved her, wouldn't he work out a way for them to be together?

Everybody leaves. Rosana had learned that early.

She'd begged her mom and dad to take her with them on that last trip, but they'd gently but firmly refused. Then her *papai* had handed her to Isa and told her to be a good girl.

And that was the last she'd seen of them.

She turned off the shower and reached for a towel.

The mirror over the sink had steamed up. She cleaned a circle in the center and stared at herself. Nothing had changed—and yet, everything had. She expected to look different, older. In the twenty-four hours she'd been gone, she felt like she'd aged at least a decade.

But she looked exactly the same. Same black hair hanging in wet curls around her face. Same full lips and slightly pointed chin. Same deep blue eyes that everyone said were just like her mom's. Even the love-bite Adric had left on her throat was almost gone.

Chest aching, she touched a finger to the small red mark.

Her shoulders slumped. She hung the towel on a peg, light-headed with exhaustion, and stumbled into the bedroom.

When she awoke a few hours later, Isa was bustling around in their little *sala*, or living room, humming to herself. Rosana pulled on a tank top and shorts and joined her.

Isa was wearing one of her usual simple dresses, this one dark blue. Her thick, graying hair was wound into a crown braid that framed her round face, and her sturdy feet were bare.

"*Boa tarde.*" She leveled Rosana a look. Isa might look like a kindly, cookie-pushing grandma, but not much got past her. "Are you hungry?"

"I guess." She listlessly eyed the fruit bowl in the kitchenette before helping herself to an apple.

"So," Isa said. "The beach, it was nice?"

"*Sim.* Hardly any humans. I even went for a swim." At night and to hide her tracks from the fae, but Isa didn't need to know that.

Isa set her hands on her ample hips. "And?"

Rosana took a bite of apple. "And what?"

"That's not all you did. You were with *him*, weren't you?"

"Yeah?" Rosana clenched the apple. "Well, if I was, that's my business, not yours, isn't it?"

The older woman's eyes flickered with hurt.

Rosana sighed. "I'm sorry. I didn't mean—"

Isa clucked disapprovingly—and then shocked her by saying, "You're a woman now, *bonita*. Your choices are your own. I just don't want you to be hurt."

A raw ache stung Rosana's throat. She set the half-eaten apple on the counter, hunger gone. "Isa." She reached out her arms, wanting a hug so bad, and then checked herself.

Isa crossed the room to gently rub Rosana's back over the tank top. She knew not to touch Rosana's bare skin. "Was it so bad? He was cruel to you?" Her dark brows snapped together. "I'll carve out his heart with a spoon."

"No, no. He was...sweet."

Isa snorted. "That one?"

"He was," Rosana insisted. "And it wasn't bad at all. It was...amazing."

Her cheeks heated, because after all, this was the woman who was like a second mother to her.

"Then perhaps I like him after all," Isa decided.

"It's just..." Rosana blinked back tears. "Me and him? It's never going to happen. He told me straight out."

"Sit." Isa's dark eyes were sympathetic. "I'll braid your hair. You went to bed with it wet, didn't you?"

Rosana ran a hand over her head. It felt like a bush had sprung up on her scalp.

"Thanks," she said with a sniff and allowed the other woman to guide her to the couch.

Isa shut the door between their apartment and Dion's, and then got a brush and sat on the couch next to Rosana. "Tell me," she said as she set to work on the tangles.

Rosana gave a small shake of her head. Once, she'd come running to Isa with every bruise and scrape, but this was one problem her former nurse couldn't solve.

"*Obrigada*, but I don't want to talk about it."

"It might help. And hold still." The tangles gone, Isa switched to long, soothing strokes.

Rosana let her head fall forward, eyes half-closed. How many times had Isa brushed her hair just like this? Nostalgia tugged at her, sharp and bittersweet, as if already, this was something she'd left behind along with her girlhood.

They fell silent, the older woman drawing the brush through her hair. When it was free of tangles, she began to plait one side into a braid. "Tell me," she repeated. "Perhaps I can help."

"I don't think so." Rosana's mouth twisted. "Unless you can turn me into an earth fada."

"Ah, *bonita*." Isa braided the other side. "Is that what you think it will take?"

"He won't have me any other way. And let's face it, Dion would disown me if I mated with a Baltimore fada. Especially Adric."

"Mated?" Isa joined the two smaller braids into a single plait at the back and wrapped a leather thong around the bottom. "You believe this is possible?" she asked as she tucked the end of the thong into the braid. "A river fada and an earth fada?"

Rosana turned to face her. "It must be. How could I feel like this if he wasn't my mate?" She pressed the heel of her hand to her heart. "I ache for him, Isa."

The old nurse's expression was troubled. "I've lived a long time, and I've never seen such a thing. I can tell you one thing, that one won't be tamed. He'll always be a little wild. Hard. You'll have to take him as he is."

Rosana lifted her chin. "He's hard because he had to be. He'd be dead by now if he hadn't been. And I don't want to tame him. I like him just the way he is." A smile tugged at her lips.

"It was good, *sim*?" Isa waved a hand. "No, don't answer that. There are some secrets a woman keeps close."

They shared a grin.

Isa tucked a stray hair behind Rosana's ear, serious again. "Your Adric is the alpha, not a man who can do as he pleases. The alpha is the leader of a clan, *sim*, but he's also bound by his duties, his responsibilities to the people he governs."

"That's what he said. And he's not *my* Adric."

"He hasn't mate-claimed you, then."

"No. And he won't."

"But if he did? You would accept his claim?"

Rosana opened her mouth, shut it. "I don't know," she admitted. "I'd have to leave Rock Run, my family, my friends. I—" She shook her head.

Adric's clan was so different from theirs. He seemed to be constantly fighting off challenges from his own people. Hell, just last summer, two of his own cousins had tried to kill him.

She heaved a breath. "It doesn't matter. He's never going to ask me."

"Then put him from your mind."

Rosana swallowed. Isa was right. Adric was an earth fada alpha, and she was a river fada from a rival clan. The two of them weren't going to have some fairytale ending.

But he needs me.

"You're right. I know you're right." She jumped up and paced across the *sala*.

"But I can't." She shot Isa a lopsided smile. "*Deus*, Dion would kill me if I mated with Adric."

"But it's not up to your brother, is it? Only you can choose the mate bond."

"You're right." Rosana stared at her, arrested, before shaking her head. "It doesn't matter. He told me straight out he'll never claim me."

"Bah." Isa clucked her tongue. "He's a man. What does he know? If you want him badly enough, you can convince him. But think about it. This is not a decision to be made lightly."

Rosana nodded slowly.

"Senhora Isa!" Brisa's voice piped from the other side of the closed door. "I-sa! Me here!"

"I'll get it." Rosana opened the door to find her niece standing wobbly-legged on the other side, one plump hand gripping the door jamb.

Her small face lit. "Tia Wosa!" She reached for Rosana with both hands and nearly overbalanced herself.

"Brisa!" Rosana swooped her up. "Just the girl I wanted to see."

She spun around in a circle as the toddler put her head back and squealed with glee. When she stopped, they were both laughing.

Rosana hugged her close, pressed a kiss to the little girl's sweet-smelling neck.

If she mated with Adric, she wouldn't get to see Brisa every day. Her smile faded. The thought made her a little sick.

She hugged Brisa closer until her niece squirmed to be put down.

Cleia appeared, Dion on her heels. Her brother had apparently been coached by his mate because he didn't ask a single question about her trip, just said, "I hope you had a good time." When Rosana said yes, he nodded, and with a glance at Cleia, turned the conversation to other matters.

So that was that, Rosana thought as she got ready for bed that night.

Even if Adric survived the night fae, he wasn't going to choose her over his clan. So it would be just like always. She'd see him maybe once or twice a year—at the Full Moon Saloon or one of the sun fae parties. Cleia usually invited Adric and his sister. She believed that if Adric and Dion just got to know each other, they'd realize they weren't so different after all.

Her mouth twisted sardonically. If she was lucky, she might even get to spend a few minutes alone with him without their respective clans breathing over their shoulders.

But Goddess, it hurt. A whole life stretching ahead of her without Adric.

12

---

*L*angdon woke at dusk as the black-out shades slid up to let in the last feeble rays of the setting sun. He pushed the silk duvet down to his waist and folded his arms behind his head. Above the four-poster bed, a handful of fae lights glowed on in iridescent shades of lavender and blue. The colors within spiraled around each other in a slow, hypnotic dance.

At his side, Fleur stirred. Her attentiveness to his moods was one of her most attractive qualities.

She propped herself on a forearm and trailed a glitter-tipped nail down his naked chest. The duvet sloped across her hips, leaving her upper body bare except for the black star medallion that marked her as a priestess of the night.

"Good evening, my lord." Her carmine lips curved, the dark eyes above watchful. One of her small, moon-pale breasts sported a nasty crescent where he'd bitten her earlier before taking her, hard and rough.

He'd been in a vile mood for months, dating to when his son Tyrus had disappeared, his body never found. But then, Fleur liked it rough. When he'd closed his teeth on her soft, delicate flesh, she'd merely sucked in a breath and, when he'd commanded her to beg, crawled in a most satisfactory way.

"Do you require anything?" Her hand slipped under the duvet to his half-hard cock.

A lock of shiny black hair had fallen over her shoulder. Looping it around his fingers, he tugged her closer. "You pleased me this morning, love." He sank his teeth into her lower lip hard enough to draw blood.

She made a small sound, and then her eyes drifted shut. He *felt* her excitement, knew she wanted him. In her own way, Fleur loved him.

But right now, he wanted her distress. Because he *was* a night fae.

He released her and left the bed, strolling to the bathroom without a backward glance. He knew by the time he returned, she'd have ordered his breakfast and then left for her own lair. After all, he'd trained her himself.

After showering, he donned a black silk bathrobe embroidered with silver moons and stars. His coffee, croissants and a bowl of hothouse peaches awaited him in the breakfast room, a small octagonal space off the living room. Taking a seat at the linen-covered table, he unfolded his napkin and set it on his lap.

A flick of a finger and the silver coffeepot floated off the table to pour coffee into an eggshell-thin cup, followed by a dollop of cream from a pitcher. His croissants were still warm. He broke off a buttery piece and put it in his mouth.

The Baltimore alpha was cannier than Langdon had expected. Adric had managed to dance around the fact that an earth fada had killed Tyrus. But they both knew the truth.

Langdon sipped his coffee. Frankly, his middle son had needed killing. He'd poisoned his older brother, and then sent assassins after Langdon's half-human son, Silver. Tyrus's men would've also slain Merry Jones, the daughter Silver had had with an earth fada, if Rui do Mar hadn't saved the child and taken her back to Rock Run.

Langdon had been furious with Tyrus. That he'd dare kill children of Langdon's own body. If it had been anyone but his son—

and only remaining heir—Langdon would've executed him on the spot. Instead, he'd banished Tyrus from New Moon, and set a protective spell on Merry's quartz.

But his son hadn't stopped there. He'd joined forces with an exiled Baltimore earth fada and tried to stir up trouble between Baltimore and the Rock Run Clan.

Which was why Tyrus was dead.

It had taken time for Langdon to unearth the truth. Adric had covered his tracks very, very well. But all trails led to Baltimore.

So Langdon had started to harry Adric, politely, relentlessly. The alpha hadn't broken, but a few months after Tyrus's disappearance, Langdon had finally Seen his son's death.

But not at Adric's hand, as he'd believed. No, it was Marjani Savonett who'd killed Tyrus.

Langdon knew damn well that his son had deserved it. Tyrus had come into Adric's territory, looking to stir up trouble. Sent assassins after Adric's people. Invaded Jace's den and kidnapped him and his mate.

Still, Langdon couldn't allow a fada to get away with murdering one of his sons.

Marjani Savonett had to die.

But Tyrus's death had left Langdon with a problem. He had no heir of his direct bloodline, and to the fae, blood was everything.

Blood, and tradition.

Picking up the slim silver knife, he cut a peach into six perfect slices and ate them before calling his butler to clear the table.

He stood before a window, hands clasped behind his back. Outside, his clan was emerging for the evening from their lairs. They glided among the winter-bare trees like elongated shadows, their tall bodies clad in black, their eyes dark holes in pale faces. The priests and priestesses wore shimmering silver—a dress, a shirt. A few of the more fashion-forward had added a splash of crimson—a scarf, high heels, a pair of gloves.

The New Moon Court was in a lush old-growth forest in Tidewater Virginia, spread across a peninsula that jutted into the mouth of the Potomac River. Each family or couple had their own home, built of granite or veined marble and set partly underground. The few feet that showed above ground were narrow structures with fanciful carvings at the apex—moons and stars, vining flowers, snarling wolves, bats with wings spread wide. English ivy ran rampant, crawling across the ground, over the roofs and up the towering trees.

To a human, it looked uncomfortably like a cemetery with above-ground tombs. To Langdon, it was home.

Tradition, he mused. His people had lived like this for thousands of years.

"Change is coming. The old traditions will be no more."

At the last full moon ritual, the Goddess had spoken through Fleur. The priestess had stared straight at Langdon as she channeled the prophecy, making it clear to whom the message was directed.

Langdon had inclined his head.

Later, when Quade, the captain of his guards, had asked what the prophecy meant, he'd replied, truthfully enough, "We must see what the Goddess has in store."

He glanced up at the immense oaks and tulip poplars that guarded the compound, their muscular branches stark against the dusky sky. The New Moon fae had established their court in this backwater country centuries ago, carving out a mile-square territory in the forest. It was dark, isolated, and yet easily accessible to the Chesapeake Bay and from there, the Atlantic Ocean. The indigenous peoples had been wise enough to give them a wide berth, and vice versa.

Langdon could still recall the arrival of the first European humans. His grandfather had been prince then, with Langdon's father the designated heir. The old prince had enforced their traditions with an iron hand. He'd arranged Langdon's mating with a high-born French fae, a beautiful, submissive woman. Langdon had been happy enough with her.

But she'd presented him with two sons and then died of a

sudden, mysterious illness. Langdon had suspected poison, but he had no proof. The fae had ways of making poisons that left no trace.

Langdon had still been a young man—a hundred-and-ten turns of the sun. Youthful enough to chafe at the restrictions put on him by his powerful family. He'd buried his French mate and then fought with his grandfather over some ridiculous thing.

Looking back, he'd been grieving, but he'd only known he was furious with both his grandfather and his father, who'd taken the old prince's side. So he'd left his sons with his parents and spent the next few decades traveling up and down the Americas disguised as a human folk healer. If he could heal the patient, he did—and if not, he fed on the family's misery.

It was in New Orleans that he'd encountered a dark-haired, golden-skinned human. Marie-Josana, a Creole singer who performed in the city's opera houses and theaters. He'd fallen hard. Within days, he'd bought a house in the Garden District and settled down with his beautiful Josana.

He hadn't mate-claimed her. The heir to the night fae throne couldn't have a human mate. But he'd loved Josana with all the passion in his dark heart.

With her, *he'd* been the needy one.

An uncomfortable sensation, one he'd taken care never to repeat.

In the end, he and Josana must have mated on some basic, primal level, because he'd gotten her with child. Langdon had named the boy Quicksilver, since he had the Gift of wayfaring. Silver, for short.

Then Langdon's father had died suddenly, and he'd been ordered home by the old prince to take his place as the heir. His grandfather knew about Josana and Silver, of course. Very little escaped the old man.

But he'd made it clear that no one else could know about Langdon's half-blood son.

To this day, very few people knew about Langdon's third son, and even fewer knew Silver had had a daughter with an earth fada. Langdon had kept Merry hidden. To the pureblood fae, she was a mongrel, an embarrassment. His grandfather had sneered at Langdon for letting his seed be diluted.

But Langdon had loved his youngest son, even if he was a half-blood. Silver had been educated at the best schools, and Langdon had set up a trust that made his son a rich man in the human world.

He scowled into the rapidly falling night.

Ironic, that of his three sons, the half-blood Silver had been the best. The oldest, Dorian, had been weak, and Tyrus a ruthless, power-hungry S.O.B.

Langdon had cursed the tradition that didn't allow him to claim a half-blood as his heir. And then it was too late. Silver was dead.

But Silver's mixed-blood daughter lived.

The table had been cleared. His butler Olivier waited until his assistant left with the dishes, and then appeared at his elbow in his usual perfectly pressed black pants, pristine white shirt and natty bow tie.

"Will you require anything else, my lord?"

"No." Langdon dismissed him with a wave of his hand.

Crossing to an antique mahogany hutch, he removed a scrying mirror wrapped in soft cotton. He unwrapped the mirror and sat down again, the mirror cupped in his hands. The mirror was carved of pure obsidian, the edges beveled, a flowing white frame around the stone's glossy black.

He gazed into the dark center. The shiny surface threw back his own reflection, his mouth a line of concentration.

He slowed his breath. The reflection blurred, transformed to dark-edged clouds that raced across the obsidian's surface like a fast-approaching storm.

Change is coming. The old traditions will be no more.

Both Cleia and Dion had let Langdon believe his grand-daughter was dead.

And Adric had told Langdon a flat-out lie, which must have made him deathly ill.

Langdon now knew differently. Merry was alive and still at Rock Run, as she'd been for the last seven turns of the sun. And soon, he'd bring her to Dark Moon to raise as his heir.

Centuries of tradition were about to be shattered. His grandfather would roll over in his grave.

Langdon's mouth edged up.

He tightened his fingers around the mirror, drew deeply on his Gift.

"Show me Merry Jones." He spoke her full name aloud to increase the power, his voice echoing in the small room.

On the mirror's shiny black surface, clouds swirled and piled upon each other into a towering thunderhead—and then parted to reveal his granddaughter.

13

———

"Have a good trip?" asked Zuri.

He and Adric exchanged a look. They were at the Full Moon Saloon again, standing near the long wooden bar. It was Monday evening and the tavern was nearly empty. No humans. No river fada, even—just a few of his own men and a couple of visiting earth fada. Claudio was serving as the only bartender, and instead of a band, the TVs on either side of the bar were tuned to the replay of a soccer game in Madrid.

"I did." Adric took a gulp of beer. "Anything happen that I should know about?"

"Other than my alpha going A.W.O.L. for a night—and then nearly being captured by the night fae?"

Adric's fingers tightened on his bottle. "Everyone's allowed a fucking night off, even me."

The lieutenant acknowledged that with a tight nod. "You are. But as your head of security, I should have been informed."

"Jani knew."

Another short nod. Then his friend sighed. "Did it work?"

"Did what work?"

"Did you get the woman out of your system?"

Adric's mind went to the sea-green swirl in the quartz tucked out of sight beneath his T-shirt.

Hell, no. I only want her more and my cat's insisting she's the mate. And I can't do a damn thing about it.

He took another swig of beer. "None of your fucking business."

"Hey, I'm the one who told you that if you wanted her, take her. But now you need to put her behind you. This thing with the night fae following you to Lewes? That's messed up."

"Yeah." Adric rubbed a thumb over the beer's glossy label.

He'd told his lieutenants about being tracked by the night fae. What he hadn't told them was that it had been Lady Blaer, and that Luc had been with her. Not even Marjani knew.

He just couldn't expose his old friend to the clan's condemnation. They might ask why Luc wasn't trying harder to fight Blaer's orders.

Adric wondered that himself. For instance, Luc could've taken his time tracking Adric so that by the time he and the fae arrived in Lewes, Adric and Rosana were gone. On the other hand, there was that moment in the parking lot when he could've given Adric away—and hadn't.

Zuri fingered his neat black soul patch. "Know what I think? Things are coming to a head. Something's about to happen. I can practically taste it."

Adric stilled. Had the lieutenant guessed his plans?

"And you think this, why?"

"Hell if I know. Things are quiet, but that's the problem. It's *too* quiet. For months, we've been seeing night fae every time we turned around. And then suddenly—nothing. Something's up. My wolf's so antsy I can barely sleep."

Adric relaxed. Zuri hadn't guessed.

"It's not just you. My cougar's antsy, too. Every time I'm out at night, my skin itches. I'm sure those bastards are still around, just hiding in the shadows."

"If only we had someone on the inside. If we had even a clue as to what they're planning, we could prepare a counterstrike." Zuri's lips peeled in a humorless smile. "A Seer, that's what we need. Although the old Seer wasn't much help. She didn't see her own death coming, did she? Or prevent the Darktime."

Adric blinked. "No," he said slowly. "She didn't. But she tried, remember? Except Leron didn't want to hear it."

A trickle of unease slid through his veins.

You need me.

What if Rosana was right?

Seers were rare. His own clan's Seer had met with an 'accident' during the Darktime when she'd refused to slant her prophecies to suit Leron's orders. Since then, no one else had shown signs of the Gift.

He reminded himself that no Seer was infallible. What Rosana had Seen was simply a strong possibility. She couldn't *know*. Not for sure.

The Darktime isn't over. The prince will destroy your clan from the inside out.

Adric's fangs pricked out. *The hell he would.*

"Step up patrols of the city," he ordered.

"Already did. But if a night fae doesn't want to be seen, we can run all the patrols we want and it won't do much good." Zuri shook his head. "Wish I knew how the motherfuckers slip in and out of the shadows like that. They can even hide their scent, which is just not possible."

"Except they do it."

"Yeah." Zuri took another slug of beer.

"Contact the alphas in each den, warn them that things are heating up. No one is to go outside without at least one other person. If they're younger than fifteen, they should have at least three people, including an adult. I'll make sure Jani knows to take extra care. It's her the prince really wants."

They shared a grim look. Langdon had somehow discovered it had been Marjani who'd killed his son, even though Adric had let everyone assume he'd been the one who knifed the prick.

His sister was a marked woman...unless someone took out Langdon first.

"I'm on it," Zuri assured him.

"Thanks, bro." Adric squeezed the other man's shoulder. "But watch your own back, okay? The prince knows you're one of my top men. If he can't get to me or Jani, he'll go after my closest people instead—and you and Jace will be at the top of the list."

Zuri's grin was all wolf. "He can try."

A commotion at the saloon's entrance made them both swing around. Dion do Rio stalked inside followed by his *tenente* Davi, both in black leather and jeans, their faces set in menacing lines.

The Full Moon went dead silent. Benny was on the door again. He moved to intercept them, but Dion snarled and the bouncer checked, his animal instinctively recognizing a dominant.

Dion's gaze swung to where Adric stood at the bar. His nostrils flared. He strode toward him, his eyes the pure silver of his animal.

"Uh-oh," muttered Zuri.

Benny recovered and stomped after Dion, but Adric shook his head. "Let them in." He set down his bottle, gave the Rock Run alpha a mocking little nod. "Peace."

"I'll give you fucking peace." Dion halted a foot away, Davi at his heels.

Zuri moved to block the *tenente*. The three other Baltimore fada present sprang up to form a semi-circle around them.

Dion didn't even bother to look at the other men.

Claudio moved out from behind the bar. Lean and charming, he had salt-and-pepper hair and the features of a Latin American aristocrat.

"*Senhores*," he said in his melodic Brazilian accent. "This is neutral territory. I must ask you gentlemen to take your dispute—"

Dion and Adric turned as one to bare their teeth at him, and he inclined his head and glided back behind the bar. "My apologies, *senhores*."

Dion's scent was hot with anger. His dark brows formed a

furious slash across his forehead, and the look he trained on Adric was pure murder.

"I've tolerated your mining in my mate's territory. I've let your people mix with my clan in Grace Harbor. And I was happy to allow your lieutenant, Jones, onto our land to visit his niece. But —" His lips peeled in a snarl.

Adric tensed. *Here it comes.*

"*Deus* if I'll let your people come and go on Rock Run territory as they please."

"What?" It took Adric a full three seconds to realize the other alpha wasn't here to beat the crap out of him over Rosana. "One of my people was on Rock Run territory?"

"A wolf."

Adric's stomach bottomed out. He straightened from the bar, conscious of their audience. If it was Luc, he didn't want the whole damn world to know.

"Let's take this to the back room."

He led the way down the hall without waiting to see if Dion agreed. A poker game was in progress, but at a nod from him, the four men tossed their cards on the table and vacated the room.

Adric entered and faced off with Dion. Davi stood at his alpha's shoulder, while Zuri shut the door and leaned against it, arms folded over his broad chest.

"What color was this wolf?"

"Dark brown." The other alpha's lip curled. "Are you saying you didn't know?"

Hellfire. It sounded like Luc, all right.

He willed his heart and breathing to remain steady. "Yes. No one in the clan has my permission to enter your territory without your say-so."

Dion inhaled, testing Adric's statement for truth. He leaned forward, his mouth a hard line.

"Then get control over your own damn people. Because that wolf was in my woods. If we see him again, he's fair game."

Adric went rigid. In the six years since he'd become alpha, he'd thrown his heart and soul into healing his fractured clan. However, as Dion knew, he still had trouble from time to time.

Davi smirked at him over Dion's shoulder. The *tenente* was Adric's height, with the dark eyes and Mediterranean features of his Portuguese ancestors. On Davi, those looks were poster-boy gorgeous.

Adric narrowed his eyes. He'd seen Davi hovering around Rosana. If the other man wasn't careful, he was going to find his pretty face rearranged.

From the door, Zuri growled lowly, his wolf pissed at his alpha being challenged.

Adric made himself give Dion a tight nod. "I'll make sure my people know."

"You do that," was the grim reply.

Zuri opened the door, but Dion stayed where he was after ordering Davi to wait in the hall. To Adric he said, "Tell your man to leave."

Adric nodded at Zuri. "Okay," he said when the door closed behind him. "Talk."

"The room is soundproof?"

"Yeah." He folded his arms over his chest, ignoring the sinking sensation in the pit of his stomach.

Dion took a step closer. "Stay the fuck away from my sister. She's not for you."

It was what Adric had told himself for years, but he bristled. "That's up to her, isn't it?"

A muscle jumped in Dion's jaw. He drew a breath through his teeth. When he spoke, his tone was irritatingly reasonable.

"She's young. I know you're not that much older than her, but you grew up in a whole different world than she did. She's sheltered." The corner of his mouth tipped up wryly. "A little spoiled. I did my best, but when my parents disappeared, she was only six. For months, she woke up crying for her mama. Begging me to let her help search for them. I...it broke something in me."

Adric pictured a small Rosana crying for her mama and swallowed. "I'm sorry."

"I know you wouldn't mean to hurt her. I've been watching you. You've done a good job with your clan, and *Deus* knows, that wasn't easy. Tiago tells me that quartz factory you're trying to get off the ground just might be genius."

Adric's mouth fell open. Praise from the Rock Run alpha? The world must be ending. For some damn reason, he got a lump in his throat.

"Get to the point," he said gruffly.

"Even if you could make a safe home for her here in Baltimore, it wouldn't work. River fada have to live near fresh water—a river, a lake. She needs to be able to shift, to swim as her dolphin. Yeah, you have the Inner Harbor, but that's a cesspool of human shit and trash. She couldn't stay in it long."

A dull ringing filled Adric's ears. He uncrossed his arms. "Got it. Stay away from Rosana."

"Thank you. And I mean it. I know there's...something between you. But this is for the best. You'll see."

Adric jerked his chin.

Dion gazed at him for another heartbeat, and then inclined his head. "Peace to you and yours."

"Yeah. Peace. But Dion?"

"*Sim?*"

"For the record, I was planning on staying away anyway."

The other alpha turned to leave, and then hesitated. "I'm sorry. But you know I'm right."

For answer, Adric reached past him to open the door.

Zuri was waiting to escort the men off the premises. Not causing trouble, just sending a message that they were in Baltimore fada territory.

Adric sank down on one of the metal chairs vacated by the poker players and waited for Zuri to return. The dull ringing was joined by a suffocating sensation in his chest. Like his heart was being wrung out. Crushed.

She's mine.

He dropped his head into his hands. *No. She's not yours, and she never will be.*

Rosana couldn't live with him, and there was no way in hell the Baltimore alpha could move to Rock Run. The very idea made his lips peel in a humorless smile.

Zuri returned, closing the door behind him. He set his hands on the table. "The wolf was Luc, wasn't it?"

Adric grimaced. *Right.* Luc was the problem here, not Rosana. And since Luc was being controlled by Blaer, things had just gone from bad to worse.

Somehow he pushed a response past the obstruction in his chest. "That's my guess."

Zuri's dark gaze narrowed. "And you're not surprised."

"No."

"Care to explain? Or is this something else your head of security doesn't need to know?"

Adric heaved a breath. "I'll explain. But tomorrow. We'll meet at the Factory. Jani and Jace need to hear this, too."

14

With the base on alert, Dion had ordered the sentries to double up, some to patrol the forests and vine-yards, some to patrol the water. Rosana reported to the marina for duty early Tuesday morning to find she'd been paired with Chico Nobrega, her brother Tiago's best friend, and assigned to the section of the Susquehanna River north of Rock Run Creek.

The two of them walked to the end of a dock and peeled off their clothes with the nonchalance of old friends. Chico was frankly gorgeous, with cropped brown curls and soulful dark eyes. More than a few hearts had been bruised when he'd mated with a human named Jenny. But to Rosana he was just a man she'd known since she was a pup, almost a fifth brother.

"Beat you into the water," he said and leapt, shifting to his dolphin in mid-air. She landed in the river a second after him. Just so he didn't get too cocky, she waited for him to surface and then slapped her tail on the surface, splashing his face..

Chico wanted to talk about the mysterious brown wolf, of course. Everyone did. Their orders were to capture the wolf if he set even a paw on their land. If he resisted, they were to kill him.

You hear anything else? he asked as they dodged between two fishing boats.

No, she returned shortly.

The endless speculation was driving her crazy. Adric wouldn't have sent a wolf to Rock Run. Not when he was in Lewes with her.

But if he hadn't sent the wolf, then why had it been on their territory?

She had a bad feeling it was the same earth fada who'd led the fae to the B&B—which opened up more questions, like why look for Adric at Rock Run?

Or had the wolf been looking for her, Rosana? Which made even less sense.

Davi says Adric didn't know one of his own men was on our land. Chico shook his head. *What's up with the Baltimore fada, anyway? They have no fucking discipline.*

She moved her body in the dolphin equivalent of a shrug. *Maybe they had their reasons.*

If they do attack, it won't be from the river. Chico's disappointment was clear. *Adric's not stupid. Water's our element, and he knows it.*

She released a forceful exhale through her blowhole. *They're not going to attack, period. Adric told Dion straight out he had nothing to do with it. If he was lying, Dion would've scented it.*

Okay, okay. Chico gave her the side-eye. *Hell, you still have a thing for him, don't you?*

That was the problem with people who'd known you since you were a pup. They knew you too well.

So what if I do? She circumvented another fishing boat. *It's not like it'll ever come to anything.* She tried to sound matter-of-fact, but her bitterness must've seeped through because Chico brushed his flank over hers.

Sorry, Rosie.

She body-checked him. *I told you not to call me Rosie.*

For once, he didn't tease her back, just nodded.

With a powerful pump of her tail, she shot forward. *Beat you to the dryads' islands.*

And she did beat him, because he let her win. She, in turn,

taunted him for being too slow because otherwise, he'd keep shooting her those concerned looks and she just might break down and embarrass them both.

As Chico had predicted, the river was quiet. They cruised around the trio of islands inhabited by Alesia and her two sisters. The trees were bare, their branches stark against the cloudy sky. Alesia waved at them from high up in an oak tree, but her sisters didn't leave the camouflage of their forests.

The rest of the day dragged on, the only excitement coming when they had to rescue a human fisherman who'd fallen into the icy river. Rosana steadied his boat while Chico shifted to human and heaved the half-frozen man back onto its shallow deck. They pushed him back to a Grace Harbor marina and then returned to Rock Run, where she left Chico at the operations room to make their report to the *tenente*.

As Rosana headed back to her quarters, Chico's mate Jenny waved from the other end of the stone corridor. "Hey, girl! I've been looking all over for you."

Rosana smiled and waved back. The two of them had become good friends in the year and a half since the human had moved into the base. "What's up?"

"I want to know what you think about that piece I'm making for Lady Olivia." Jenny's jewelry was rapidly becoming famous in both the human and magical worlds, but she'd been shocked— and flattered—when Lady Olivia, Cleia's intimidating older cousin, had commissioned a pendant.

"Sure." Rosana fell in beside the human. Anything to take her mind off Adric and the mysterious wolf fada.

"And you can tell me all about your trip to Lewes." Jenny's grin was knowing. "You met *him*, didn't you?"

"Yeah." Rosana grimaced. "Someday, I'll tell you all about it. But not today, okay?"

"That bad?"

"Worse."

Jenny shook her head, sending her long black braid dancing. "Men are asses. Except when they aren't."

"Yeah. The thing was, it was...incredible. Except when it wasn't."

They exchanged a look and burst out laughing. Maybe Rosana's laughter was edged with pain, but it still felt good.

"Just keep it quiet, okay? I'd rather not get into it with my brothers."

Jenny traced an X on her chest. "Cross my heart."

"Rosana, Jenny—wait for me!" It was Merry Jones. They halted as she loped down the hall toward them.

Rosana still recalled the night Rui do Mar had brought the orphaned earth fada back to Rock Run. She'd been all big eyes in a narrow, sharp-chinned face, her body too thin, her arms and legs brown sticks. At fourteen, she'd filled out some, but she was still skinny, with long legs and a lanky, boyish body.

Merry bumped her shoulder against Rosana's. "What'cha doin'?"

"Going to Jenny's."

"Can I come? Please?"

"Sure." Jenny slung an arm around the teen's slim shoulders. "I could use your opinion, too. You have an artist's eye." Jenny had been teaching Merry basic jewelry-making techniques.

"You think?" Her thin, mobile face lit up.

"Yep. In fact, I think you're ready to start that bracelet for your mama."

"Seriously? I can give it to her for her birthday."

Jenny's big gray tabby was waiting on a ledge near her apartment. He leapt off the ledge and brushed between Merry's legs, meowing in welcome. Merry's animal was a jaguar, and Max had apparently decided that as the only other feline at Rock Run, she was a kindred spirit.

"There's my sweetie." Merry scooped up the cat and rubbed her face against his. He butted his head into the space between her jaw and throat, purring loudly.

Jenny chuckled. "I swear that cat is crushing on you."

The teenager gave one of her rare, slow smiles. "Well, I love him, too. He's a handsome cat, aren't you, *meu querido*?" She cuddled the tabby closer, and his eyes slit in bliss.

Inside, Jenny prepared Max a small plate of sardines in her kitchenette and set it on the stone floor. While the cat made short work of his dinner, the three of them traipsed into the workroom that Chico and Tiago had built for Jenny off the *sala*.

A sturdy table had been installed along one wall, with shelves above for supplies. Every spare surface was cluttered: gemstones in all the colors of the rainbow, boxes of crystal beads, spools of wire, scraps of metal. Wire cutters in three different sizes lay next to pliers and calipers, and a ceramic brick held a jeweler's soldering torch. An idea board was covered with photos and sketches, and a slit in the cavern ceiling provided light and ventilation.

"Lady Olivia gave me a pink diamond to work with." Jenny took an object wrapped in cotton from a shelf.

"I didn't even know there was such a thing as a pink diamond," Rosana remarked.

"Right? She liked that necklace I made for Cleia, so she brought me this pink diamond, told me to see what I came up with." Jenny unfolded the cloth to reveal a thumbnail-size diamond set off-center in a hammered gold sun with wavy rays.

"Wow." Rosana's eyes widened. "Just wow."

"Genius," Merry breathed at the same time.

Jenny beamed. "I just hope Lady Olivia thinks so."

"She'll love it. Even Lady Olivia can't find any fault with *this*. May I?" Rosana stretched out a hand, and when Jenny nodded, fingered the pendant.

"You know," her friend said, "Cleia would give you a pink diamond—you just have to ask. Or any gemstone. And I'd make you a pendant for free. You'd just have to pay for the materials."

Rosana hesitated, tempted, and then resolutely shook her head. "I know she would, but I'm trying to be more independent, and that means earning my own way. But thank you—that's really sweet of you to offer."

Her friend nodded. "If you change your mind, let me know."

"You know I will."

Jenny rewrapped the pendant, and they returned to the *sala* for snacks and girl talk. It was exactly what Rosana needed. For the next hour she didn't even think about Adric—at least, not more than once every ten minutes or so.

Then Chico returned and pulled his mate into a kiss that made her heart constrict with envy.

She was happy for them, she was. Really.

She just wanted what they had.

Chico released Jenny, and they all chatted for a few more minutes until Rosana rose to her feet, saying she had to go. "I promised to meet Isa for dinner."

Merry jumped up as well. "I'll walk you to your quarters."

Rosana blinked. Her apartment was on the base's opposite side, while the do Mar's apartment was just a few minutes away.

But she waited until they were alone before slanting Merry a look. "Something wrong?"

"Not here," the teenager muttered. They were in a large, well-traveled hallway filled with people on their way to the dining room. Taking Rosana's hand, she pulled her into a side corridor. "I want to know what's up. Something's wrong, I know it is. They barely let me outside these days—and my *papai* won't tell me anything."

Rosana hesitated. "I'm sure they have their reasons."

Merry folded her arms over her narrow chest, but her lower lip trembled. "Don't you treat me like a baby, too. You're the only one I can ask. My mom and dad just tell me not to worry, they're handling it. Even Uncle Jace won't tell me anything."

"Oh, *querida*." Rosana's heart contracted. "You know it's for your own safety."

Merry had been born during the Darktime to an earth fada mother and Prince Langdon's half-human son. She'd spent her early life on the run from both the earth fada and the night fae. After her parents had died, she'd been adopted by Dion's second, Rui do Mar, and his mate Valeria—until Adric and her uncle Jace had discovered where she was and tried to kidnap her back. That had been sorted out, with the earth fada agreeing to let her remain with Rui and Valeria while Jace received visitation rights.

But now she had to hide again, this time from her own grandfather. It didn't make sense. Langdon had never formally acknowledged his mixed-blood granddaughter. No one had expected him to suddenly start asking about her.

"Well, I don't like it," Merry said. "All Mama will tell me is that it's better if the night fae believe I'm dead." She dropped her head, stared at her feet. "Why do they hate me so much?"

"They don't hate you, sweetheart." Rosana reached for her. Merry needed to be held. If she had a vision, so be it, although she was careful to touch only Merry's clothing.

Merry burrowed into her. "Yes, they do," she returned in a sad little voice. "Because I'm a mixed-blood. I don't really belong here. Or with the earth fada, either. And the night fae just want to kill me."

"Hey. You do belong here. Dion adopted you into the clan. Did someone say different?" Rosana pulled back, scowling. "Because if they did, I'll—"

"No." She hitched a shoulder. "Not really. But I'm a jaguar. I like to swim, but I can't spend hours in the water like the rest of you. I can't even enter through the water entrances—they're too deep for me."

"So? Neither can Jenny, and that doesn't mean she's not clan. And you have friends. What about Trina and Marco?"

"That's what Mama Ria says."

"And she's right."

"But Anabella says I'm just a freak. Not fae, not fada. Even my own clan doesn't want me." Her voice dropped to a ragged whisper.

Rosana's jaw worked. She was going to have a long talk with Anabella.

"That's not true," she told Merry. "Lord Adric *did* want you. He'd take you back into his clan in a heartbeat. And your uncle Jace wants you, doesn't he?"

A small nod. "But that's just them. There are others who think my mom should never have mated with a half-blood."

"You heard earth fada saying that? From Adric's clan?"

Another tiny, miserable nod. "Last year at the Midsummer Ball. They said"—she swallowed—"that I stink like a night fae."

Rosana's chest knotted with fury. "Well, fuck them. You have the scent of an earth fada, and maybe a little river fada, because you spend so much time with us. And you know what? It's their loss, because you're special. Any clan would love to have you as a member. Dion was saying just the other day how smart you are."

"Seriously?" Merry's hazel eyes were hopeful.

"Truth." Rosana touched her heart. "Cleia thinks so, too. And you're not only smart, you'll probably have a really cool Gift because you have so much fae in you." That fae blood had already made Merry one of the most beautiful teenagers in the clan.

"Yeah? You really think so?"

"I do. I really do." She ran a palm over the teen's electric black hair and was rewarded by a bashful smile.

"Thanks, Rosana."

"Anytime. You can ask me anything, all right? Because you're clan. And because I love you, just the way you are. Understand?"

She grasped Merry's hands—and stiffened at the vision that flashed across her retinas. A man's black eyes, and nothing else.

"Rosana? You okay?"

She squeezed her eyes shut, and when she opened them, all she saw was the younger girl's anxious face. "Yeah. It's...been a long day, that's all."

They continued walking. They were almost to Rosana's quarters when Merry asked, "Do you think my grandfather—the prince—could've found out I'm still alive?"

"I don't know. But Dion and your *papai* will keep you safe, no matter what—and Cleia wouldn't let him take you against your will."

Merry nodded, her expression troubled.

Rosana's skin prickled. "Why?"

"Because." Merry ran a hand over her nape. "Sometimes I could swear he's watching me."

ROSANA WAITED until she heard Isa's soft snores before easing her bedroom door shut. To ensure she wasn't interrupted, she propped a chair under the door handle before retrieving a small teak chest from beneath the bed. A bottlenose dolphin was carved on the lid. She traced its curving back, sadness pinching her heart.

The teak chest dated to when her parents had first come to America, a gift from her Irish granddad to his daughter Ula. The bottlenose carving was a reminder of her mom's sea fada roots. Dion had gifted the chest to Rosana on her sixteenth birthday, saying their mom would want her to have it.

Opening the lid, she took out a cobalt scrying bowl. As part of her training, she'd experimented with different modes of scrying —a mirror, polished lava, smoke, tarot cards, even a crystal ball— but not surprisingly, the best focus for her was a bowl of water.

Now she unwrapped the chamois cloth protecting the deep blue glass and set the bowl on a small table next to a pitcher of water.

She'd walked Merry to her own quarters, had waited while the teen told Rui and Valeria about Prince Langdon. But there wasn't much her parents could do beyond the close watch they were already keeping on their daughter. To protect Merry, Langdon had spelled her quartz so that no night fae could touch her without dying. Unfortunately, the prince had excluded himself from the spell.

But Rosana was a Seer. Maybe she could See something that

might help Merry. And what about those black eyes she'd glimpsed?

She poured the water into the shallow blue bowl, and then sat cross-legged on a sheepskin rug, the bowl in her hands. She took several slow breaths, calming and centering herself, and then let her gaze go soft.

At first, all she saw was the water. Then her vision shifted somehow so that she saw her reflection instead. She kept breathing, slowly, evenly.

She pictured Merry, adding details as she'd been trained. The teenager's sharp, lively face. Her serious hazel eyes and her rare but contagious giggle. The wiry, exuberant curls. Her lanky body and love of bright colors.

Rosana's mouth curved. Merry was adorable, the little sister she'd always wanted.

Minutes passed with nothing happening. Her mind wandered.

She dragged it back, focusing on Merry with a grim determination. But although she conjured up a photo-perfect picture of her friend that would've pleased even Colm, that's all it was—a picture conjured up by Rosana. Not a vision.

She expelled a breath and straightened up. Maybe scrying just wasn't her thing. Not every Seer could scry, right?

"Discipline, Rosana, it's all about discipline—and belief in yourself. If you think you can't, then you can't. Belief is as important as skill."

Her head snapped back. She cast a guilty look around. She could've sworn Colm had 'ported into her room to remind her of Rule 3. But it was empty except for her and the scrying bowl.

She set her back teeth and glared into the water. "I'm trying," she growled as if the sardonic Irish sun fae was actually present, shaking his mane of blond hair reprovingly.

She'd disturbed the surface. She waited for the ripples to smooth out and then focused again.

The water in the bowl grew dark and still as a deep-jungle pool, and then she saw Adric. On his motorcycle in a shadowy forest, his tires making a single track in the fresh snow.

Her eyes widened. She'd never had such a clear vision when scrying. She squeezed her eyes shut, re-opened them. Adric was still there, driving through the snow.

Her breath hitched. Snow was predicted for later that night.

Suddenly the water shivered as if touched by a finger, and she saw Adric-the-cougar slinking through the snow-covered forest. He reached the edge of the trees, stared at the fog-shrouded grounds beyond. At first, she thought he was looking at a grave-yard. But the tombstones were house-sized, with lush ivy vines snaking over fanciful gothic arches.

She'd never been to the New Moon Court, but she recognized it immediately.

And Adric was on his way to it.

Rosana's heart stuttered. The water shivered again, and she became part of the scene, slinking with Adric through the forest. She felt the frozen earth beneath his paws, heard an owl's mournful call, scented the musk of a deer herd huddled against the cold. The rising sun glimmered a pale gold, and then was hidden by a fast-moving cloud.

Once again, the water in the bowl lurched and swooped. When it cleared this time, a tall fae was strolling around a pond on a path of white pebbles, his black head bare to the falling snow, a duster swirling around his long legs.

Her bowels iced. It was Prince Langdon, exactly as he'd appeared in her vision in December.

His head swung to where the cougar crouched, and then his gaze flicked to her. He turned.

The scene shrank in on itself until his face filled the scrying bowl. It was a poet's face—narrow, dark-eyed, incredibly beautiful. Tiny diamonds outlined his pointed ears, glittered in his winged black brows.

She gulped. His eyes narrowed, looked straight into hers.

He can't see you, she told herself frantically.

Then he smiled.

15

The Factory was in an abandoned grocery on the west side. The sign outside still read Allen's Stop-and-Shop; it worked as camouflage, and suited Adric's sense of humor besides. After they'd gutted the place, there'd been plenty of space for the shop that Jace Jones had set up to test and manufacture the clan's quartz-based smartphones. When Adric entered Tuesday afternoon, the jaguar fada was already there, deep in conversation with his small team of quartz-crystal techs.

Jace turned to him. A tall, rawboned man, he had cropped black hair and the same serious hazel eyes as his niece Merry.

"Ric." A smile lit his face. "We have something to show you."

Jace and the three techs spent a few minutes bringing Adric up to date on their current projects, including the quartz mine on Rising Sun Fae land which was the clan's hope for turning the smartphone technology into a money-maker.

"We could have them in production by summer." Jace handed him a prototype made from the mine's high-quality quartz.

Adric fingered the smartphone. Durable and waterproof, one side of the quartz had been ground down to mirror-smoothness so the user could access the technology. "You'll be able to make enough for every adult in the clan?"

"Absolutely. With enough left over to start selling them to other clans."

"Impressive." Adric included the entire team in his nod of approval. "Keep up the good work."

Zuri and Marjani arrived as the meeting broke up. The four of them climbed down the ladder to the war room, a chamber carved out of the bedrock that had been magically soundproofed so they could speak freely, even refer to the fae by name.

They took seats around the round table that Adric had carved himself from a massive slab of granite. He looked around at his three remaining lieutenants. "You know why you're here. Dion do Rio came looking for me last night, seriously pissed off. A wolf trespassed on his territory—a large brown wolf."

"Luc." Marjani's face remained expressionless, but Adric scented her distress. She'd probably always feel guilty that Luc had accepted Blaer's *geas* to save her.

The wolf had loved her since they were both teenagers. The problem was, she'd never felt the same way.

Adric nodded grimly. "That's my guess. And if he's here, then so's Lady Blaer."

"But why would she send him to Rock Run?" his sister asked.

Zuri's jaw hardened. "To piss off both clans, of course. If she's really lucky, she'll set off a war between us and Rock Run."

"Wouldn't be the first time a night fae tried that," Jace muttered.

Adric exhaled and came to his feet. He felt like he was banishing Luc all over again, but Zuri was right. His lieutenants needed to know the full story about what had happened in Delaware.

"What I say next doesn't leave this room." He waited until the other three nodded before continuing, "It was Luc who tracked me to Lewes. He brought Blaer and another fae—a male—straight to the B&B. They came in after midnight and tore the place apart. It was sheer luck that I got out of there with my hide intact. And Rosana do Rio, too. You may as well know she was with me."

Marjani drew a sharp breath.

"Yeah," Adric said. "He's not to be trusted. He's completely under that fae bitch's control. We have to consider him one of them."

Zuri's dark brows lowered. "Fuck, Ric. You should've told us this immediately."

"Maybe. But there was a minute, right at the end. Luc and the fae were in the parking lot, and I was on the other side of the fence. I know Luc scented me. He could've fingered me then, but he didn't." Adric lifted his shoulders, let them drop. "I didn't want the whole clan to know."

Zuri swore. "He knows everything we do. The location of our dens, the Factory. Our secret tunnels. He even knows about this room."

"He can't get through the ward," Adric said. "Any of our wards. I made sure of that when I expelled him from the clan. But—"

"—he could bring Blaer to the Factory," Marjani said. "Or even your den. He might not be able to bring her inside, but all they have to do is wait outside for you to show up. And Blaer knows the secret incantation. If she gets close enough, she doesn't even have to force you to accept her *geas*. She can control you through your quartz."

Adric growled. "Let her fucking try. I was this close to her." He held up his index finger and thumb, the pads almost touching. "*This* close. But I had to let her go. Luc would've fought me and given her time to 'port out. And I would've had to kill him."

"Plus, you had Rosana to think about," said Marjani. "You did the only thing you could. But you can't let Blaer get that close again." She toyed with the smooth ivory handle of one of her daggers.

None of them paid it any mind. Marjani's blades were as much a part of her as her claws.

She scowled. "I don't like this. You have to increase your security."

"Jani. I can take care of myself."

By tomorrow, it wouldn't matter anyway. He'd be on his way to Virginia. But no one—especially his sister—could know that.

A small whetstone appeared in Marjani's other hand. She began sharpening the already keen-edged iron blade. "We could buy you a protection charm."

"We don't have the money, and you know it."

"But—"

"No. The best defense is to eliminate the threat."

Marjani compressed her lips and swiped the blade viciously over the whetstone.

Adric set his hands on the table. "Lady Blaer is up to something, and thanks to my asshole cousin Corban, she knows the secret of our quartz. It's time to take her out."

Zuri's smile was all teeth. He and Luc had been close friends. "I'm your man."

"Agreed. But take your time, assemble a team—the woman's powerful, and she's smart. I'll be damned if I lose anyone else to her. And before you do anything, ramp up our defenses. You and Jani both."

Marjani jerked her chin in assent.

"I'll let the clan know that the cubs aren't to go out alone, and that even the adults need to take care." His jaw set, because Gods, he hated to do this. "I'll also warn them that Luc can't be trusted. Anyone seen talking to him will answer to me."

Zuri fingered his soul-patch. "The wolves aren't going to like it. One day Luc's a hero for saving Jani, the next, he's bad news. If you don't tell people about Lewes, they'll say it's just another example of how the cats have taken over since you became alpha."

Jace scowled. "Ric appointed two wolves as lieutenants. What more do they want?"

"Hey, don't shoot the messenger. I'm just saying it looks bad. And then there are your cousins," Zuri said to Adric. "Two out of three of them are dead."

"Thanks to me and Jani." Adric blew out a breath. "I know. It's damn convenient that out of Leron's immediate family, only Nash is left. A suspicious man might think we planned it that way."

And everyone knew Marjani's Gift was strategy.

Zuri moved a big shoulder. "Nash says himself that it's Corban and Kane's own fault they're dead. But you gotta admit it looks shaky."

"He's right," his sister chimed in. "And I have an idea. You need a new lieutenant—why not Nash?"

Adric sank back onto his chair. "Nash Savonett?" he asked, as if she could mean anyone else. "I don't know, Jani."

"He's a Gifted tracker," she returned, "one of our best, and he's backed you since day one. If he wasn't Leron's son, you probably would've considered him before now. And he's a wolf. It keeps the balance."

"She's right," said Zuri. "The lupines appreciate that you appointed me and Luc as lieutenants. After the way Leron treated you, you could've turned on the wolves, but you didn't. You brought us into your inner circle. But these last couple of years have set some of them off again—too many wolves have died."

"Because they attacked me and mine," Adric shot back. "Every damn one of them would be alive today if they'd accepted that *I'm* the alpha now. Not Leron, and not any of his sons."

Zuri spread his large hands. "I know that. Even they know that. But..."

Jace had been sitting back in his chair, silently observing. Now he leaned forward. "Nash has my vote. Keeping the balance is important, and the man is smart. Plus, he doesn't have the prejudices his brothers had. Take Evie's brother, Kyler. Nash has gone out of his way to be a friend to him—a human. He's been working with Kyler, showing him how to defend himself."

"So it's unanimous," said Adric. The clan wasn't a democracy —the final decision was his—but these three were his lieutenants precisely because he trusted their judgment. "I'll inform Nash that he's my newest lieutenant. But he's on probation for the next six months. If it works out, we'll make it official."

"Fair enough," said Zuri.

"Anything else?" Adric glanced around the table.

When the other three replied in the negative, he adjourned the meeting.

Marjani fell in beside him as they left the Factory. "I keep telling myself that Luc's not responsible, that he doesn't have a choice, but he *knows* what that bitch is capable of. If she'd captured you..." She shook her head. "It's like I don't even know him anymore."

He set an arm around her narrow shoulders. "It hurts."

Her chest heaved. "Yeah."

"You sure you're okay with Nash making lieutenant?"

"I wouldn't have brought it up otherwise."

"Even though his own brother was behind your—" He halted.

They didn't discuss the attack on her. At first, it had been because she wasn't talking to anyone but Suha, the clan's head healer. Then, as the months passed, he'd let it go. Some things were better left buried.

"You can say it—I won't break. Corban Savonett was behind my kidnapping. And—" she swallowed, then lifted her chin—"it was because of him I was raped by those bastards."

Dragging in a breath, he forced the words past the hot ball in his throat. "I'm sorry. So fucking sorry."

"Damn it, Ric." She jerked away to glare at him. "You've got nothing to be sorry for. It. Wasn't. Your. Fault."

He kept his gaze on where they were going so he wouldn't have to meet her eyes. Heavy gray clouds had blotted out the sun, bleaching color from the Formstone rowhouses that marched up either side of the street. It was going to snow later.

"I'm alpha. I should've known what was going down."

"Stop it." Marjani punched his shoulder. Hard. "Just stop, already. They fooled me, too. I thought Shania was my friend. I agreed to meet her at that bar. I was stupid enough to get drugged."

"You would never have been attacked if not for me. Corban

targeted you because I was alpha. That's the only reason." He drew a breath between clenched teeth. "And I didn't even know until the next morning."

By then, she'd been given by Corban and his people to a den of sick river fada. They'd smashed her quartz, leaving her hurting and defenseless, and then proceeded to gang-rape her. She might have disappeared forever if not for Tiago do Rio, who'd been kidnapped along with her. Somehow do Rio had resisted the drug enough to fight back.

And Adric hadn't known until it was too late.

"It's over." She gave him a shake. "I need you to accept that. It's hard, I know." Her throat worked. She closed her eyes, took a deep breath. "But it's over, and I'm okay. And I'm working on putting it behind me. Because I will *not* let those motherfuckers ruin my life. But I can't if you're still beating yourself up about it."

"I'm sorry." He smoothed his palms up and down her arms. "I'll try, okay?"

"You do that." She opened her arms and he came into them.

And then they had their arms wrapped tight around each other, rocking back and forth. Adric's throat ached with unshed tears. He gulped them down. For the first time in forever, he let himself take comfort from his sister instead of giving it.

When she released him, her cheeks were wet. She wiped them away with the sleeve of her hoodie. She sniffed. "They're happy tears."

He eyed her doubtfully. "Yeah?"

"Yeah." She gave a watery chuckle. "Come to dinner tonight? Beau's cooking."

He managed to smile back, because that's what she needed from him. "In that case, I'm there." The bear shifter loved to cook, and his Louisianan mama had taught him well.

She gave him another hard hug and then they separated—her to meet up with Fane, him to inform Nash of his promotion to lieutenant.

His cousin could barely contain his excitement. Like Corban, he was tall and good-looking with close-cut black hair. But the resemblance ended there. Corban had been a tight-lipped, calculating man, while Nash had warm brown eyes and a ready smile.

"You won't regret it. You'll see." Nash stepped toward Adric, arms outstretched, and then hesitated, head cocked to one side to expose his throat. His wolf demonstrating its complete loyalty and trust.

Adric pulled him into a hug and gently bit the offered throat, acknowledging and accepting that trust. "You have to pass the trial period first."

"Don't worry." Nash nuzzled Adric's cheek, marking him and being marked. "I will."

Adric gave Nash's head a rub, just like when they were kids and Nash was the little cousin who idolized him. "You know what? I think you will, too. Report to Jani tomorrow. She'll bring you up to speed."

After that, Adric crisscrossed Baltimore. Checking in with the various dens. Spreading the word about Luc and the night fae. Reassuring the cubs, who'd picked up on the adults' tension. At least he could throw in the good news about Nash, too.

Doing what an alpha did, because his conscience wouldn't let him leave without making sure everyone and everything was as ready as possible.

~

DINNER WAS A ROWDY AFFAIR. A dozen clan members squeezed around Jace's big plank table. They laughed and talked over one another, drank beer, passed bread and salad. Gorged themselves on Beau's truly excellent shrimp étouffée.

Beneath the table, Tigger bumped his head against Adric's leg. He scratched the cat behind his ears and watched approvingly as his sister devoured a good-sized helping of the shrimp étouffée.

Fane had taken the seat by Adric. He glanced over to see the other man watching Marjani, too, a smile on his narrow, good-looking face.

Fane turned his head toward Adric, and their eyes met.

Adric drew a breath. He'd accepted the other man into the clan for Jani's sake, but that didn't mean he was happy about it. Not only was Fane a quarter fae, he'd been one of King Sindre's envoys, a trusted member of the ice fae court. The blond mixed-blood was as wily as they came.

But Fane was proving useful. His wayfaring Gift meant he could slip in and out of places as well as the night fae, and as an envoy, he'd been inside all of the major fae courts—sun fae, ice fae, and most importantly, the night fae. As a sign of good faith, he'd drawn Adric maps of all three courts, with key buildings and rooms marked.

Fane leaned forward, letting his long blond hair curtain his face from Marjani. "I'll take care of her," he murmured. "Lady B will have to go through me to get her."

Adric kept his expression blank. "Oh?"

"Don't worry—Jani doesn't know for sure. She just suspects. She *is* a Gifted strategist, after all."

Fuck. "She can't know. No one can. I want your word on that."

"I won't lie to her."

"I'm not asking you to. Just keep your mouth shut."

Fane inclined his shiny blond head. "Then you have my word."

Adric took a gulp of beer. "Thank you. And not just for keeping your mouth shut, but for being the mate she needs."

From the other end of the table, Marjani regarded them with narrowed eyes. Fane winked at her.

"I'm the one who's thankful," he murmured, and then asked Horace to pass the hot sauce.

Adric blinked. The thick stew was already spicy enough to burn a hole in a man's stomach.

An evil grin split Horace's broad face. "You sure?"

Fane stuck out a hand and the cougar fada placed the bottle in it.

While Fane recklessly risked his stomach lining, Adric took a thoughtful bite of shrimp.

Good thing he'd already decided that tonight was the night.

If Marjani suspected something was up, then he had even less time than he thought. Because he was going alone. His sister had a mate now, a chance at real happiness.

No way would he let her risk that.

He'd failed her once, let those river fada get ahold of her. He wasn't going to fail her again.

Fane got up and took Marjani's plate, filling it with another helping of étouffée before Adric could.

Something tightened in his chest. He had to admit Fane had turned out to be a good, caring mate. His sister was a lucky woman.

Their brother-sister bond would never be the same...and that was how it should be.

But it was a bittersweet feeling, knowing that it was now Fane she turned to, not him.

BY THE TIME Adric left for his den, an icy rain was falling. Cursing under his breath, he headed across town with a ground-eating lope. He didn't scent Luc or Blaer—or any fae at all—but just in case, he intermittently used his quartz to cloak himself. The energy drain was too great to use it constantly unless absolutely necessary.

He zigzagged through the concrete and granite towers of the business district, circled the Inner Harbor. As he left the harbor behind, the streets emptied, becoming an industrial wasteland of warehouses and parking lots.

To the south was the Seagirt Marine Terminal, its hulking cranes like metal giants backlit against the night. There'd been a time right after he made alpha when the clan had been so poor that some of his men had hired themselves out loading coal at the nearby CSX railyard.

Adric himself had worked for the fae. He was a Gifted tracker. Smart, dogged and with that magical something that meant if he wanted to find you, you couldn't run far or fast enough. The fae were willing to pay stupid sums for his services. He'd poured the money back into his hungry, impoverished clan, making sure everyone was fed and clothed. The remainder had gone to developing the quartz smartphones.

He could leave for Virginia with a clear conscience, knowing the clan was in a much better place than when he'd taken over as alpha. That his sister was healing.

His only regret was Rosana. He slowed, pressed the heel of his hand to his heart, which literally hurt for her...a constant, low-level ache.

Shaking his head at himself, he shoved the hand in a pocket and picked up his pace again. A few minutes later, he entered a neighborhood of shabby rowhomes with worn marble stoops. A couple more turns and he was on his own street of small detached houses, half of them boarded up with the rest locked up tight for the night.

His neck itched. He rubbed it, looked around, inhaled deeply.

Nothing unusual. Still, that eerie feeling someone was watching tripped up his spine. Luc? Blaer? Or just one of Langdon's warriors, here to harass Adric?

He peered into the shadows. But if it was a night fae, he or she remained concealed. Just in case, Adric bared his teeth at the darkest corner.

Footsteps sounded behind him. He whipped around, hand going to the switchblade in his pocket.

A wild-eyed human kid aimed a handgun at his head.

Cat's balls. He really needed to clean up his neighborhood like Jace had.

He let go of his switchblade, raised his palms. "Easy, now."

"Your wallet." The kid's throat worked. He clutched the gun in two shaking hands. "Give me your w-wallet and ph-phone, and you won't get hurt."

"I don't think so." Adric didn't bother going clawed, just aimed a booted foot at the fool's solar plexus.

The kid wheezed and folded in on himself, dropping the gun.

Adric snatched it from the air before it hit the sidewalk. He opened the chamber and shoved the bullets into a pocket.

The human was on the ground, sucking air like a beached fish. Adric shoved his fangs into the would-be robber's face. The kid's eyes went flashbulb. Terror scented the air.

"Yeah." His mouth curved. "You messed with the wrong dude. Next time you rob someone, make sure he's not a fada. This is my territory, asshole. I see you around here again, and you're dead. Understand?"

The kid's head bobbed. He tried to speak, couldn't.

Adric nodded at the gun. "And I'll be keeping this."

The kid's breath finally whooshed in. "Yes, sir." Tears filled his eyes. "I...just needed something to eat. I—I'm hungry. P-please don't hurt me."

Adric hesitated. The kid didn't smell of alcohol or drugs. He was just a skinny teenager scared out of his mind. His quilted puffer jacket was a size too large and his sneakers a size too small.

And Adric could scent the truth in his words. The kid was hungry.

He shoved the gun into the pocket of his jacket. "What's your name?"

"Shawn."

"Well, Shawn." Adric picked him up by the scruff of his coat and set him on his feet. "You know Bruce's Creole Kitchen?"

"Yes, sir."

"Tell the cook that Lord Adric sent you. He'll let you work for food. If you're a hard worker, he might even give you a job."

The kid's thin face lit. Then his eyes narrowed. "You're not shitting me?"

Adric growled.

"S-sorry, sir. Okay. I will. Thank you, sir." The kid bobbed his head several times. Then he gulped. "*Lord* Adric? Fuck. I'm really sorry. I—"

"Get going," Adric suggested.

"Yes, sir." Shawn scurried back the way he'd come. When he reached the corner, he shot a look at Adric over his shoulder and then broke into a run.

Adric continued down the street. He was almost to his house when his nape prickled again. He heaved a breath.

Maybe he should've slept at Marjani's den after all.

Without breaking stride, he scanned the shadows. A human wouldn't have seen the woman leaning against the side of his house, but his cat detected her just fine. She wore a baggy hoodie and a knit cap pulled low over her forehead. But he'd know that long, curvy body anywhere.

16

---

*A*dric's heart kicked into gear. Hard, slow, and damn it, needy.

Rosana's back was to the brick wall, one leg bent and her foot on the bricks as if she'd been there a while. A small backpack was on the grass beside her.

What was she doing in Baltimore? And how the hell had she known which house was his? His den was two stories underground and warded against intruders, its location on a need-to-know basis only.

Slipping into an alley, he circled through the neighborhood so that he came out in the backyard behind his. He vaulted the chain link fence, landing behind his shed, and peered around the corner. Rosana had her head turned toward the street.

He gathered his muscles...and leapt.

By the time she swung around, he was on her. He pushed her face-first into the bricks and touched a claw to the soft underside of her jaw.

"What are you doing here?" he growled against her ear.

She turned her head sideways and tried to shove off the wall, but he thrust a thigh between her legs, pinning her in place with his body. Her fingers curled against the bricks, but her answer was as calm as if they were having a friendly cup of coffee.

"Not out here."

Her ponytail was against his cheek. The fresh meadow scent of it tangled his thoughts. Below, his pelvis pressed against her firm ass, her inner thighs warm around his leg.

The gods knew he was no saint. He couldn't help reacting to the suggestive position. Her breath hitched, and he knew she felt him hardening against her.

He scowled and increased the pressure of the claw, careful not to break the skin. He'd cut off his own hand before hurting her, but she didn't need to know that.

"How did you find out where I live?"

Her mouth twitched. "Nice to see you, too."

"Don't mess with me, love." He pressed her a little harder into the bricks. "I'm not in a good mood. Now, how did you find this house?"

She expelled a breath. "I'm a Seer, remember?"

"You had a vision that showed you where I live?" he asked, incredulous.

A jerk of her chin. "I saw the street name, anyway. And then I followed your scent to this house. I can't find the entrance to your den, though."

"It's protected by a *look-away* spell." He let out a breath, thinking. "Does anyone else know you're here? Your brothers?"

A short laugh. "You think they'd let me come down here alone?"

She had a point. Especially after Dion had gone out of his way to warn him away from her.

"Fine. Swear you won't give the location of my den to anyone else, and I'll let you in."

"I swear it," she replied without hesitation. "I'm not your enemy, Adric."

He retracted the claw and released her. She spun around, the sharp point of an iron stiletto aimed at his balls.

He raised a brow, impressed. Not many people could get close enough to pull a weapon on him. "Careful, love. You might damage my junk, and then neither of us will be happy."

A pissed-off snarl. "Threaten me again, cat, and I'll make you into a rug."

A rug?

He let out a startled chuckle—and grabbed her wrist, lightning-quick. He dug his thumb into a pressure point until she opened her fingers and released the knife. They both lunged for it, but he snatched it by the blade just before it hit the grass.

The iron seared his palm and fingers. His breath hissed in. It was like grabbing a hot poker. He quickly transferred the knife to his other hand, this time careful to touch only the mother-of-pearl handle.

He straightened, and they stared at each other.

Rosana's chest heaved. Blue eyes seared into his.

He forgot about his burned hand. He forgot that a river fada shouldn't be able to locate his den so easily, Seer or not. He forgot that in the morning he was leaving for Virginia.

And most of all, he forgot that Dion had warned him away from her.

All he knew was that Rosana was here, and he craved her with a hunger that ate at his insides. It felt like it had been two months, not two days, since he'd had her.

His jaw set. Because he did *not* need a distraction, tonight of all nights.

He shoved the stiletto at her, handle first. "Stay away from my den, and I won't have to threaten you."

She snatched it from his hand and slid it into her back pocket. "So." She reached for her backpack. "Where's your den?"

"This way." He closed his fingers around her upper arm and marched her around the back to the small brick hut that concealed his den's entrance. He'd never actually lived in the house, preferring instead to rent it out to the locals as a smokescreen. No one expected the Baltimore alpha to have a couple of drug dealers living above him.

He muttered an incantation, and the *look-away* spell lifted, revealing the heavy oak door that led down to his den. As he tapped his quartz to the door lock, Rosana jerked her head at the purple sportbike propped against his shed.

"What about my bike?"

"I'll put it in the shed." No one around here would touch it—they knew better, Shawn excepted—but there was no sense advertising she was here. "Don't move," he added as he crossed to the bike.

"I asked to come in, remember?"

But she obeyed, arms crossed over her chest and a scowl on her pretty face, while he locked the sportbike in the shed with his own motorcycle and then opened the heavy steel door to his den.

"After you," he said with a mocking wave of his hand. He reset the spell and followed her in.

They were on the landing at the top of the steps his dad had cut out of rock. Set into the rise of every other stair were quartz-powered amber lights. As they started down, the tiny lights glowed on, illuminating the carvings that his dad had chiseled into each step—a leaping manticore, a fierce griffin, a soaring dragon. After his dad's death, Adric had doggedly continued, working the stone with a combination of chisels and magic, until only the bottom few steps were still unadorned.

"Wow." Rosana shot him a look over her shoulder. "Who's the artist?"

He shrugged. "Me. And my dad."

"You're kidding." She crouched to trace the raised outline of a phoenix bursting into flames.

"My dad did the first four, and we did the next few together. Then things...changed, and he was always gone. He was a soldier, although he really wanted to be a stoneworker."

"You must miss him." Her voice was sympathetic.

He gave a hard swallow. "Yeah." His father had been one of the first slain, executed by his own brother, Leron, over some trumped-up charge. Adric and Marjani had been forced to watch.

"And your mom, too. I'm so sorry."

"It was a long time ago."

"Not that long. And you never really get over it."

"No," he agreed.

They exchanged a look. He recalled that until a few months ago, she hadn't known herself if her own parents were alive or dead.

And she was right, you never really got over the death of a parent. The wound scabbed over, but it never really healed. You just tried your damnedest to live your life the way they'd have wanted.

"I guess you know how it is."

She gave a jerky nod. "Sometimes I wonder if it's even true. It's hard to believe they're really alive, since I can't see or talk to them."

"It's true." He crouched to squeeze her shoulder. "Marjani spoke to your mom herself. She was fine, and so was your dad. They just have to serve out the terms of their *geas* and then they'll be home."

"I know." She grimaced and touched his arm. "But hey, I know I shouldn't complain. At least I'll see them again someday."

"Yeah." He glanced away.

She fingered the carving. "These are really beautiful. I don't know anyone who can work stone like this." She stood back up, and he rose with her. They were crowded together on the same step. She met his eyes. "You're not what I expected."

"It's just a hobby," he muttered. He set a hand on her lower back, urging her to continue down the stairs. "Now, get going. I still want to know what the fuck you're doing here."

But he'd lost control of the situation, if he'd ever had it.

Rosana acted as if she were an invited guest instead of a not-so-welcome trespasser, exclaiming over each carving as they continued down the two flights to his den. He had to admit, he enjoyed showing his carvings to her. They even discussed possible designs for the last few steps.

And when they entered his apartment she didn't feel like a trespasser. She felt right. Like she belonged there.

Her eyes widened as the amber sconces in the foyer glowed on. "Those are powered by quartz?"

He nodded.

"Cool."

He guided her into the living room and tossed his jacket on a chair. The gun clattered to the stone floor. Rosana didn't even blink, but his cheeks heated.

"It's not mine." He set it on the mantelpiece. "I took it off a human kid before he hurt himself."

"I saw. And I heard you send him to that restaurant for food. That was nice of you."

"Yeah, I'm a real philanthropist. So. Why are you here?"

A secretive little smile. "Maybe I just couldn't stay away."

Setting her backpack on the floor, she peeled off her gloves, then removed her knit hat and hoodie and dropped them on his jacket. She was all in black. No high-heeled boots this time; instead, she wore short moto boots. He couldn't help noticing how good her ass looked in the tight black jeans. Almost as good as her breasts in the ribbed sweater.

He swallowed. Hard.

She turned back and caught him looking. Their gazes snagged. It was her turn to swallow.

"I'm sorry about your hand." She reached for it and turned it over to view the damage, and for some reason he didn't shake her off. She clucked her tongue at the blisters forming on his palm and first three fingers. "You should soak it in salt water."

He pulled his hand from hers. "It's okay. The blade didn't even break the skin." If it had, the iron would already be poisoning his blood.

She rolled her eyes and muttered something about hard-headed men. "Come on. I'll prepare a salt water soak for you."

Bemused, he followed her into his kitchen and watched as she prepared a solution of salt and warm water. She set the bowl on the table and ordered him to sit. "Put your hand in the bowl."

Why not? He shrugged and obeyed, and then sucked in a breath as the salt bit into the wound. But within a few seconds, the pain eased. To help it along, he pulsed some energy from his quartz to the injury. He wasn't a healer, but he had a minor ability to heal. The blisters began to recede.

"Better?" She took the seat across from his.

He nodded and reluctantly tacked on a thanks. "Now, about why you're here—"

She gave him a sunny smile. "Aren't you going to offer me a drink?"

"Would you like a drink?" he said between his teeth.

"Yes, please. But don't get up," she said airily when he started to remove his hand from the bowl. "I can get it." She opened the quartz-powered cooling unit and peered at the nearly empty shelves. "You don't entertain much, do you?"

He set his jaw. "I wasn't expecting company. There should be a couple of beers, though. Or I can make coffee."

"I'd rather have juice."

He winced. "I'm not sure how fresh it is."

She pulled out a carton of orange juice, took a sniff and poured it down the drain. "I'll stick with water. What about you?"

"Water's good. The glasses are to the right of the sink."

She found two mismatched glasses, filled them with tap water and set one on the table before him. But instead of retaking her seat, she moved back into the living room, glass in hand, examining the amber quartz sconces, taking in his thrift-shop furniture. A second-hand couch. A coffee table he'd scavenged from a dumpster and repaired. The only newish item was the soft orange shag rug in front of the fireplace, purchased because his cat liked to warm itself at the fire.

He felt a curl of shame. He and Jani had furnished the apartment right after he first made alpha, back when the clan could barely manage to feed the women and cubs. Things had improved enough that he could've bought some new furniture, but why bother? Plus, it sent a message that, unlike his uncle, he wasn't enriching himself at his people's expense.

But compared with what Rosana was used to, his den must seem cramped, shabby. The Rock Run Clan was three times the size of his, with a huge base and hundreds of acres on the outskirts of Grace Harbor. Not only that, they were allied with Queen Cleia and her powerful Rising Sun Fae Clan.

Still, Rosana didn't seem disdainful, just curious.

Taking his hand from the water, he tentatively worked the fingers. The blisters had almost disappeared. He set the bowl in the sink and joined her in the living room.

She was examining the foot-high geode on his mantelpiece. On the outside, it appeared to be an ordinary gray rock, but he'd split it open to reveal the amethyst crystals inside.

She ran a finger over the reddish-purple crystals. "Amethyst is a type of quartz, isn't it?"

"Yeah." Not many laypeople knew that, though. "You work with crystals?"

"A little. I study with a fae Seer. He had me try different crystals to see if any of them amp up my Gift. Amethyst, especially. He says it helps promote balance, calm, peace." Her mouth curved in a wry grin. "In my opinion, he's the one who needs it. The man's an arrogant pain-in-my-ass. But he knows his stuff—I'm already getting better at controlling and directing my visions."

"Did the crystals work?"

"Not really."

She moved to a basket of quartz crystals on the mantel that he kept as an emergency stash for the clan and fingered another amethyst, a six-sided chunk of purple that faded to almost white at its points. "Pretty." She held it up to the light.

"Keep it."

"Really?" A smile lit her elfin features.

"Yeah." He moved forward, closed her fingers around it. "I

found it myself—it's a special, high-quality quartz with a strong internal energy. Maybe you've just been working with the wrong crystals."

"Thank you." She carefully pocketed it.

He remained close to her. Breathing her in. Taking in every detail from the jet-black lashes fringing her eyes to her lush lower lip to her slightly pointed chin.

A strand of hair had escaped her ponytail. He brushed it back behind her ear. "That must be a tough Gift to have. My clan had a Seer, but my uncle ordered her to remain silent when she didn't See what he wanted her to."

Her pretty mouth twisted. "Everybody thinks they want to know the future, but they don't—not really. And even when you tell them what you See, they do what they wanted anyway."

"Like me."

"Like you." She met his eyes, and he knew they were both thinking of her prophecy.

"We always have free will," he reminded her.

"I know." She sighed and moved away. "It's okay? Your hand?"

He blinked. "My hand?" He glanced at his injured limb. "It's fine."

"Good. Because you'll need it when you leave."

His heart thumped. "When I leave?" he repeated neutrally.

"For Virginia," she said, as if she was inside his head. Those ocean-colored eyes narrowed thoughtfully. "And soon, I think. Maybe even tonight."

17

———

he stare that Adric turned on Rosana made her go very still.

Time had run out. A terrible urgency vibrated in her body, banded around her chest. She was convinced he was leaving for New Moon—soon.

And Langdon *knew*.

He prowled closer. *Deus*, he was beautiful, even with his face dark with suspicion. His gold-tipped hair was damp from the rain, his jaw shadowed with stubble. His long-sleeved T-shirt clung like paint to his body, and cargo pants hung low on his hips.

But it wasn't just his looks. It was the way he moved, the sexy growl of his voice, his aura of power.

"What do you know?"

She moistened her lips. This man had killed his own uncle for the good of the clan. She needed to remember that. "Nothing for sure. But I Saw something new."

"What?"

"You, alone in a forest. On your motorcycle." She closed her eyes to better picture it. "There was fresh snow on the ground. And then suddenly, you weren't on your motorcycle, you were a cougar instead. Staring at the night fae court. And Adric, the prince Saw you. He *knew* you were there."

"Did you tell anyone?" He was a foot away, his metallic brown eyes boring into hers.

That he'd even ask hurt. But she shrugged like she didn't care. "Who would I tell?"

"So you're here to try and stop me." He exhaled. "God's cat, Rosana. Enough already. Nothing you can say will change my mind."

"I'm not here to change your mind."

His eyes narrowed. "No?"

"No." She took a deep breath. "I'm here because I'm going with you."

He fingered her ponytail, so close the heat of his body licked at hers. "Are you?"

"Yes." She lifted her chin. "You need my help."

"What did I say in December when you told me that? And again last Sunday? Oh, yeah." He leaned closer, his breath hot against her face. "I said, 'No. Fucking. Way.'"

She gazed back steadily. She'd expected this. Colm had even warned her. It was the Seer's Dilemma: You could plead, argue, demand, but if someone was determined to stick to their chosen path, there was nothing you could do short of locking them up.

But damn, it was hard.

Because Adric *had* to take her. Everything in her screamed that she was right. Not just her Gift, not just a gut feeling, but her whole self.

She set a hand on his chest. Maybe she was going about this all wrong. The man was an alpha to his core, and when it came down to it, an alpha always put the cubs first.

"There's something you don't know—we just found out ourselves. The prince has been watching Merry. He has the farsight."

His head angled in that feline way. "You're sure?"

She nodded. "She feels like he's watching her, and we believe her."

Adric swore. "So he knows she's still alive?"

"He must. Dion tried to put him off, but he must've found out somehow."

Adric stepped back, shook his head. "Maybe she's imagining it. Jace told me she's been edgy, worried that the prince might kidnap her—or simply demand that Dion hand her over."

"He can demand all he wants. Dion would never give her to the night fae. And she's not imagining it—I Saw the prince myself." Rosana gulped and rubbed her upper arms. "And I'm pretty sure he Saw me."

Adric tensed. "What do you mean, the prince Saw you?"

"In my scrying bowl. I thought maybe I could See something to help Merry, and suddenly he was there in the bowl."

"You're sure it was him?"

She nodded. "I've seen him a few times at Rising Sun. Never up close—Cleia made sure of that. But he's not a man you forget—tall, with black hair and pointed ears, and diamonds outlining his brows and ears." She traced her outer ear with a fingertip. "Beautiful, the way a cobra is, so that you can't look away, even though you know it thinks you're prey."

"That's him, all right." Adric raked a hand through his hair, leaving the spikes sticking every which way like a furious cat. "Gods. How could you let him See you?"

She scowled back. "I didn't mean to."

"And you want to come with me? The night fae are happy enough to play with a fada. But a fada Seer? A young, beautiful fada Seer? The bastard must be salivating like a wolf over a fawn. If he captures you, you're fucked."

"So I won't let him know I'm with you." Because yes, Colm had warned her that the night fae got a special charge from tormenting a Seer, but it was a risk she was willing to take. "I'll stay out of sight, disguise myself somehow."

"What if he Sees you? You just told me the man has the farsight."

"I'll take my chances. He can't be looking all the time—no one can. And what about Merry?"

"She's safe enough as long as she stays inside Rock Run's wards. Hell, you have a fae queen on your side. Can't she do something?"

"I just found out tonight, and the queen wasn't at Rock Run. But Rui and Valeria know. Still, from what I've heard, it's almost impossible to block someone with the farsight from viewing you. There's nothing *to* block. The person isn't really there—it's like trying to stop a ghost from walking through a wall."

"Fuck." Adric clenched his fists. "So Merry has to put up with that prick watching her without her permission?"

"Unless we stop him."

"Rosana." Her heart sank at his hard tone. He was going to say no.

"Thanks for the intel," he continued, "but I can't take you with me."

"So you are going."

He lifted a shoulder, let it drop.

"But why do you have to go alone? That's the part I don't understand. Take me—or some of your people."

Adric's face closed up like he'd slammed a door. "Trust me, I've figured every angle, and this is the only way. And before you ask— I've tried to lure the prince to Baltimore. It doesn't work. He never comes without at least two bodyguards. No, I have to go to him— catch him alone."

She grabbed his shoulders. "But don't you see? That's just what he wants. He *knew* you were in the forest. You're heading straight into a trap."

He gently set her away from him. "I'll follow you until you're back in Rock Run territory. You shouldn't be down here after dark —not alone. Here." He thrust her hat and hoodie at her.

She batted the clothes away. "Will you listen to me? He. Knows.

You're. Coming. If he has the farsight, then maybe Merry isn't the only one he's been watching. Maybe he's been watching you, too."

He just sighed and pushed the hat and hoodie at her again.

She snatched them and stared at him, hands fisted in the material, angry and defeated.

She took a calming breath. Time to switch tactics.

"What's the hurry?" She dropped the clothes on the chair and stepped closer. "No one knows I'm here."

By the time she'd decided to go to Baltimore, Isa had been fast asleep. Rosana had scrawled a note of explanation and then slipped out of the base. By the time anyone knew she was gone, she'd be on her way to Virginia with Adric.

Or at least, that had been the plan.

Adric's throat worked. "It's late, Rosana. I'm going to bed." But he didn't move away.

"Okay." She unwrapped the leather tie around her ponytail, tossed it onto the hoodie. Her damp hair tumbled around her shoulders.

His gaze tracked her movements. "Alone." It was more a growl than a word.

She slid her hands up his chest and out to his shoulders. Beneath the cotton shirt, he was all hot, smooth muscle. "You said yourself, it's not safe for me to go back tonight."

A muscle jerked in his jaw. "Did I say that?

"More or less." She lifted onto her toes to nibble his earlobe.

His breath hitched, but his arms stayed at his sides. "Fine. You can sleep in Marjani's old room."

"I'd rather be in your bed." She tongued the outside edge of his ear.

He groaned. "Your brother should've turned you over his knee when you were a cub."

Her mouth twitched. "How do you know he didn't?"

"I know."

"Adric?" She trailed kisses down his jaw, traced his full lower lip with the tip of her tongue. "Kiss me, you stubborn ass."

His body went taut, and then with a muttered curse, he hauled her up against him, his lean, powerful frame pressed to hers from breast to thighs. She had time to draw a breath and then his mouth was on hers.

Need jolted through her. She eagerly opened to him. His tongue swept inside, tasting every corner. She sucked on it, rocking her pelvis against his. He was hard, so hard, and she felt a thrill of triumph.

Until he dragged his mouth from hers and set her a foot away. "I'll show you your room."

"My...room?" She blinked rapidly, a little stupid from that kiss.

He guided her down the hall. "Bathroom's here, and you can sleep there." He pointed across the hall to a cozy bedroom with warm amber lighting and a colorful quilt on the bed.

She glanced around, dazed. "But I thought—we're not going to...?"

"No."

She swallowed her hurt. "You said that if I wanted you, I could have you. That we'd just have to sneak around. Well, here I am." She spread her arms wide. "Ready to sneak."

A shake of his head. "Not tonight, Rosana."

She brought her arms back to her sides, tilted her head. "I scare you, don't I?"

"Scare me?" A mocking smile curled his mouth.

"Yeah. You're afraid because you want me too much. I make you lose control, and you don't like that."

His eyes sparked blue. His primal growl set her spine tingling.

She took a step back before she realized it.

"You want this?" His body crowded hers, backing her to the wall next to the bathroom. "Fine. I hate to leave my women... unsatisfied." He slapped his hands to the stone on either side of her head.

She slit her eyes at him. "Your *women*? You *filho da puta*—"

"Shut up," he said gently, and captured her outraged gasp with his mouth.

His kiss this time was rough, demanding. Arousal jolted through her. He kept his mouth on hers, pressing her into the unforgiving stone. His heat surrounded her, his earthy male scent filled her nostrils. He didn't let up until she was clinging to him, knees weak.

He tore his mouth from hers, pressing hot kisses to her face, her neck, while she gulped in oxygen.

"Is that what you want?" he ground out. "A hard fuck?"

Somehow, she found the energy to straighten her legs and push him away. "Go. To. Hades. I am not just one of your women."

He grabbed her wrists and pressed them to the wall above her head. His burned hand was barely marked. She had time to think that he healed awfully fast, even for a fada, and then he was kissing her again.

Slow, sweet kisses that slid through her blood like wine.

She was lost. She could fight him when he was rough—maybe —but how do you fight tenderness from the man you want with everything you are?

She sucked on his tongue, drawing him deeper. His cock was a hard bar against her lower belly. She rubbed her mound against it, desperate to ease the ache between her thighs.

He tore his mouth from hers, took a jagged breath. "You're right."

"I am?"

"You're not just one of my women."

"Oh." She remembered that she was still pissed off and curled her lip. "Well, fuck you anyway."

She tried to wrench her hands free, but he easily kept them where they were, stretched above her head. And damn if that didn't make her hot, which just made her fury increase.

"Let me go." Her glare should've reduced him to a smoking pile of ashes. "*Now.*"

He nipped her lower lip. "I'm sorry, okay? It was an asshole thing to say."

"Yeah, it was."

"Forgive me?" A sheepish smile, but she caught the glint in his eyes.

Her lips twitched, but she continued glaring.

"I'd go down on my knees and beg," he murmured, "but I think you'd rather I did this…" Transferring her wrists to one hand, he jerked her shirt up. Strong fingers cupped her through her purple exercise bra, sending another bolt shooting through her.

She arched her back against the wall and bared her teeth. Daring him. Challenging him. Somehow, this had become a game, and she was more than happy to play.

"You'll have to do better than that. And I'd love to see you on your knees. Begging."

A dark chuckle. He squeezed her nipple, a little too hard. "But I'd rather hear *you* beg. Tell me, Rosana." He pinched her nipple. "Tell me you want a good, hard fuck."

Her smile was slow, knowing. If he thought he could scare her off, he was mistaken. She was a fada female. Her animal reveled in the rough play, understood it meant her male's need matched hers.

She lifted onto her toes to lick the seam of his lips, enjoying how he went taut. How his heart kicked into a pounding rhythm that matched her own.

"Yeah," she said against his mouth. "That's exactly what I want."

18

———

*A*dric's vision hazed.

That's exactly what I want.

He crowded Rosana against the wall. Drowning in her. The breast filling his hand. Her scent in his nostrils, fresh and clean as rain. The needy moans she made when he rocked his pelvis against hers.

He'd tried to be good. Tried to send her away. If she refused to go, well, he wasn't a fucking saint.

Besides, it wasn't safe for her to be out alone. Not tonight. The hours between dusk and dawn were when the night fae hunted. Better she stay with him until morning.

And yeah, he was grasping at straws, but tough shit.

Her tongue flicked at his closed mouth. He dragged in a breath, picturing what else she could do with that hot little appendage.

For an almost-virgin, she was sure catching on fast. He loved that she felt comfortable enough to challenge him. His cat adored a good game.

"*Ah-dreek.*" A husky murmur against his lips. "Kiss me back."

"Rosana..." He squeezed his eyes shut, struggling to remember why this was a bad idea. Why he should boot her sexy ass out of his den.

But he could barely recall his own name, and somehow his hand was on her other breast now, pinching that nipple into hardness beneath the purple stretchy-thing she wore.

She nipped his lips. "Kiss me."

Hunger crashed through him. He wanted, no *needed*, to spend this one last night with her.

Langdon had to be taken out. Marjani would never be safe otherwise. And he'd be damned if he'd let the prince tear Merry from the only family she remembered to raise her in the dark, twisted world of the New Moon Court.

When he left this time, not even his sister would know. Because she'd never let him go alone, and the plan called for one man—a quick, surgical strike. The problem was getting back out again after he'd made the kill. Frankly, he didn't expect to return.

Then here came Rosana, offering herself to him. And gods, he wanted her. Craved her more than life itself.

She wasn't just one of his women.

She was the only woman.

He released her to strip off her shirt and bra. The silver charm bracelet got tangled in the shirt sleeve and gave him a slight shock, so she removed it and pulled off the shirt and bra herself, shoving the bracelet into her pants pocket.

Meanwhile, he dragged off his own shirt, and then pressed her to the wall again. Her nipples were hard and aroused against his bare chest.

The knit cap had protected her hair from the rain. Only the ends were damp, curling wildly around her face. He filled his hands with her glossy tresses and brought his mouth to hers.

She made a sexy sound low in her throat and gripped his head. Heat leapt between their bodies, like they were kindling and someone had set a match to them.

They kissed each other, hungry and unrestrained, both their animals awake, greedy. Devouring each other's mouths. Raining kisses over each other's faces. Grinding their hips against each other.

His fangs pricked out of his gums. He drew back, wary of hurting her, but she just smiled and pulled him back to run her tongue over the tips.

Her hands were on his waistband, undoing the button and streaking inside. He'd gone commando, and she gave a hum of satisfaction before closing cool fingers around his cock.

His eyes rolled back in his head. He groaned and reveled in the squeeze and slide of her fingers.

She was right, he was a little afraid of how he was with her. Only with Rosana did he forget he was Lord Adric, an alpha with an entire clan depending on him. With her, he was just Ric Savonett. A man with his woman.

Grabbing for the last shreds of his control, he caught her wrist, stopping her.

For the first time, she looked unsure. "You don't like that?"

"I like it fine." He crouched to unbuckle her moto boots, tapped the right boot. "Lift your foot." When she obeyed, he removed first that boot, then the other one, slipping off her socks as well. Rising back up, he swung her into his arms. "But I want to get horizontal with you."

"Oh." Wrapping an arm around his neck, she smiled into his eyes. "So now you're asking."

"I'm not asking."

Her chuckle drew an answering smile from him. He realized he did a lot of that around her—smiling. They were still grinning at each other when he set her on her feet in the bedroom.

Their smiles faded, and they stared at each other. He didn't know what Rosana saw, but he saw a woman coming into her full beauty. Wavy blue-black hair tumbled around a heart-shaped face. Her nipples were a dusky rose, her waist a taut indentation above softly curved hips, and her skin the color of rich, warm cream.

Her chest heaved. "Adric?"

He traced a fingertip around each high, flawless breast. "I like how you say my name. *Ah-dreek*."

Her mouth edged up. "*Aa-dric*," she said with perfect American pronunciation. "I just like how it sounds in Portuguese better."

He huffed a laugh. "You're such a bad girl."

"Bad girls have more fun."

"Do they? Let's see..." Bending his head, he gave each of her nipples a hard suck. Her arms came around him, one on his back, one holding his head to her breasts.

For a few heartbeats, he allowed himself to remain there, cradled against her body. Just breathing her in.

His shifter senses picked up her pounding heart, but that was only fair, because his heart was beating just as hard.

"Definitely more fun," he managed to murmur.

He undid the button of her jeans, slipped a finger inside. She opened her legs a little as he teased the edge of her panties.

A fine quiver raced over her skin—and something inside him melted. Something so hard and tight and hidden, he hadn't even known it existed.

He felt sad and angry at the same time, that this was probably the last night they'd ever share. But it was one more night than he'd expected, and he was determined to make it good for her.

The amber sconces had glowed on when they entered the bedroom. He snapped his fingers and they dimmed to a warm, candlelight yellow.

Guiding Rosana to the bed, he pulled down the quilt. She sat on the mattress and he drew off her jeans. Her panties were the same purple as her bra, and damp with her excitement. Sliding them over her hips and down her legs, he dropped them on her jeans and then knelt on the floor before her.

He nudged her thighs apart. Her sex was a slick, rosy pink. Using his thumbs to open her, he swiped his tongue up the center.

Her breath hitched. She gripped the edge of the bed.

He raised a brow. "More?"

A jerky nod.

"Like this?" He licked her again, and again. Swirling his tongue around her clit, then sucking it into his mouth. Feasting on her. Inhaling the wild, musky fragrance that was Rosana.

When she fell back on the quilt, eyes closed and thighs clenching around him, he lifted her feet onto his shoulders and slipped a finger inside her.

"Yes..." Tiny muscles tightened around him. "Oh, Goddess..."

"That's it," he said against her clit. "Come for me, bad girl."

He ruthlessly sucked and tongued her until she was begging and pleading with him to come inside her. "Not yet," he said against her sex. "I want you to come for me first."

"Please," she rasped—and then arched her back and came with a low, animal sound.

He crawled up her body. Her eyes were closed, the lashes thick ebony crescents, her mouth turned up in a replete curve.

"I think I like being bad."

"You're very good at it," he returned, straight-faced.

Her smile increased. "I am, aren't I?"

Amusement rumbled in his chest. "But I bet you could get even better with practice." Rolling on a condom, he set his mouth to the tender underside of her throat.

"Oh, yeah," she said on a moan. "Lots and lots of practice..."

Her arms came around him. Their scents mingled, hot and aroused. She widened her thighs, making space for him.

He settled into that warm, welcoming place. Not entering her, but it still felt like coming home.

Be mine. I want you. Always.

He didn't say it. Fada mated for life. If he mate-claimed Rosana and then died in Virginia, she'd likely never mate again.

He'd seen how his mom had been after his dad's death. She'd tried to keep it together for him and Marjani, but she'd stopped caring whether she lived or died.

Rosana was too young to spend the rest of her life alone. At least this way, she had a chance at happiness. Kids.

Even if the thought of her with another male made him want to smash something.

Rosana smiled up at him, her eyes midnight-blue stars, her full lips kiss-swollen.

His throat constricted. "You're so fucking beautiful."

Her smile increased. "Yeah?"

"Yeah. Beautiful...and hot." Holding her gaze, he reached down and opened her, and then entered her in a slow slide, groaning as she closed around him like a hot fist.

He gave her an openmouthed kiss, and then rested his cheek against hers and began to move.

"Yes. *Deus*, yes." She wrapped her limbs around him.

Gods, he loved her. It wasn't just that she was his mate. He loved how she smelled, how she moved. How she was so damn open to him, in a way that had nothing to do with sex. He even loved her stubborn insistence on doing what she thought best.

"More." Her heels dug into the backs of his thighs, urging him on. "I need more."

He slowed even more, and she whimpered. "*Adric.*"

"Trust me," he murmured against her ear. "This way is better. We don't want to rush things."

"No..." Her head moved from side to side against the pillow.

He pulled out.

"No!" Her hands came to his hips, urging him back to her. "Stay. Don't leave me."

He nipped her plush lower lip. "You'll like this, you'll see."

He turned her over, helped her up onto her knees. She blinked at him in surprise over her shoulder, so damn cute his heart contracted. Then understanding dawned and she came down on her forearms, her wild raven locks spilling over one silky shoulder.

He smoothed his hands over her ass. It was perfect: round and smooth, a luscious fruit that he wanted to lick, bite.

Own.

He played with her ass for a while, giving her light smacks, slipping his fingers into the slick, warm cove beneath to tease her. He even scraped his teeth over her soft skin until she was begging and pleading with him to come back inside her.

He took her by the hips and entered her with a firm thrust that made her moan his name.

"That's it," he told her. "Take it, bad girl. *My* bad girl."

He reached around her to play with her heavy breasts as he slid his cock in and out of her. Pleasure gripped him by the scruff of the neck. His nerves were heated, sensitized.

"Touch yourself."

"Oh." She gave him another adorably startled look.

He gently bit the turn of her neck. "You heard me."

Her hand slid down between her thighs. The fingertips grazed the root of his dick and he hissed with the pain/pleasure of it. He put his hand over hers, guided her to tease her plump little clit.

She groaned and pressed her ass into him.

"That's it. Make yourself come, angel. I want to feel that hot pussy squeezing around me."

The cougar surfaced, reveling in this most primal of mating positions.

So tight. So wet. So fucking hot.

He wanted to pound into Rosana, lose himself in her slick heat, but he also wanted this to last. For minutes, hours...as long as it took. Until she knew exactly to whom she belonged.

So he gritted his teeth and grasped her hips, setting a firm, steady rhythm until she keened out his name and constricted around him.

"Please, please, please..."

Flames streaked up his spine. His balls drew up, tight and hard.

At some point, she'd stopped touching herself. Reaching around her, he circled her clit with two fingers until she arched her back and with a little scream, went the rest of the way over.

He gave a few hard thrusts and followed her into the fire. Emptying himself into her until he had nothing left.

For a long minute, he stayed inside her, chest heaving, and then he somehow summoned the energy to withdraw from her. Flopping onto his back, he pulled her into his arms. She nestled against him, head on his shoulder. He dragged the quilt over them both and dozed for a few minutes before rousing himself for a quick trip to the bathroom.

After that, he didn't remember anything else until she left the bed an hour later to use the bathroom herself. When she rejoined him under the covers, she cuddled close, combing her fingers through the crisp dark hair on his chest.

His larynx vibrated in contentment.

She chuckled. "You're purring."

His mouth curved. "I'm a cat, love."

"I like it." She propped herself on an elbow to smile down at him. "You'll have to show me your cougar. I'll bet he's beautiful."

The purr increased in volume. Inside, the cat preened itself.

"He thinks so," Adric said dryly and tucked her into the crook of his elbow. "And yeah, he'd love to show himself to you."

He didn't add that it would probably never happen. For these few hours, he didn't want to think about what lay ahead, just enjoy being with her.

She resumed petting him, and his eyes closed. He hadn't expected to get much sleep his last night in Baltimore, but the sex had wrung him out in a good way.

He was drifting in that warm, comfortable place between waking and sleep when she murmured his name.

"Mm?" he replied without opening his eyes.

"There's something I've been wondering."

"Yeah?" he asked warily.

She traced a finger down his sternum. "You don't have to answer."

His wariness increased. He opened his eyes. "Just ask."

"Why did you kill your uncle?"

He went motionless. Even after all these years, the thought of Leron Savonett could still fill him with a murderous rage.

The hand on his chest stilled. "It's okay if you don't want to tell me."

He *didn't* want to tell her, but he wasn't surprised she'd asked—only that she'd waited this long.

"Because he needed killing," he said in a hard voice.

"I see."

"But what you really want to know is why I didn't challenge him for alpha in a fair fight."

A short silence. "Yeah. I guess I do wonder about that."

His teeth clenched. He put her away from him and sat up. "I know what your brother says. That I have no honor, no respect for tradition. That I murdered my own uncle in cold blood. Well, Dion knows *nothing*."

She sat up, too, the quilt clutched to her breasts. "But I'm not my brother. Tell me. Make me understand."

He eyed her. It occurred to him that this was his chance to push her away for good. To make her leave and never look back.

"Well, everything you heard was true. I lured my uncle Leron into a back alley and slit his throat because I wasn't sure that if I challenged him, I'd win."

She flinched. He waited for her to throw off the quilt, announce she would sleep in the other room after all.

But instead, she took his hands. "Oh, Ric. I know that. But that doesn't tell me why. Because I know you had a good reason. You *are* honorable, and your clan is so much better off ever since you became alpha."

He looked down at their clasped hands. So much for scaring her off.

The woman fucking *believed* in him.

And he found himself explaining further, something he never did.

"He...went after people I loved. He guessed that I'd grow up to challenge him, so he was especially hard on my friends. It got so I was afraid to even talk to someone, because they might end up locked in a cell—or dead. And it wasn't an easy death."

She squeezed his fingers. "Oh, Adric. I'm so sorry."

"So fuck honor. The man needed to die, and I was the only one who could take him out."

"You did the right thing."

"Not according to most of the world."

"Then they're wrong," she said fiercely.

"Maybe. But right or wrong, I'd do it again in a heartbeat."

He reached for her. He was done talking about his uncle. She had a red abrasion on her jaw—whisker burn.

"I hurt you." He lightly touched the mark. "If I'd known you were coming, I would've shaved."

"I don't mind." She captured his hand, held it against her face. "I kind of like it."

He leaned in to brush a kiss over the reddened skin. She turned her face so that he kissed her full on the lips instead, her mouth open, welcoming, as if he hadn't just admitted to breaking one of the fada's most sacred traditions.

"Me, too," he said. "I like seeing my mark on you, having you carry my scent." And that gave him an idea. He got out of bed and removed the amethyst quartz from her jeans. "I'll be right back."

He returned with the amethyst secured by a leather cord. The quilt had slipped lower, exposing her breasts. He dropped the cord over her head and settled the purple chunk of quartz between her cleavage.

"Thank you." She clutched the pendant with a starry-eyed look that made his heart clenching uncomfortably. "I love it."

"It's not much." Still, he liked seeing his amethyst there, over her heart.

"It is to me." She tugged on his hand. "C'mere."

"Is this where you show your gratitude?" He traced those pretty globes with a finger, teased the nipples into points.

A huff of laughter. "I thought it was a gift."

"Everything has a price." He crawled over her, pressing her back onto the pillows.

"And if I don't want to pay?" Sapphire eyes dared him.

He dipped his head to suckle a dusky nipple. "Then I'll just have to convince you it's worth it."

19

Marjani unlaced her combat boots and set them on the floor, frowning.

What was up with Adric? He'd acted odd all day. Calling meetings, visiting all the dens. At supper, he'd been almost sentimental, telling stories about when they were children, and then later, he'd actually pulled her aside to say how happy he was to see things with Fane were working out.

And when she'd boxed up some shrimp étouffée for him, he'd turned it down. Her brother never turned down food. The man hated to cook.

If she didn't know better, she'd think he was leaving town. But he wouldn't go anywhere without informing his second, would he?

Fane wrapped his arms around her from behind and kissed her nape. The jagged gold half-heart that hung from his neck pressed against her spine. She wore the other half—his mate gift to her—on a leather cord along with her quartz.

Long, clever fingers teased her nipples. "Did I tell you how hot you look in this tight little shirt?"

Pleasure slid down her spine. She told herself that Adric wouldn't do anything in the next few hours, and turned in Fane's arms.

"I don't believe you did." She threaded her fingers into his silky blond hair and heaved a sigh. "Mate with a man, and he starts taking you for granted."

He had the most gorgeous summer-blue eyes, made even more stunning by the dark brows and lashes framing them. Now the blue heated. "Oh, I'll take you all right."

Swinging her into his arms, he tossed her on the bed and followed her down. The T-shirt was deftly removed along with the rest of her clothes. She was still chuckling when his mouth covered her sex.

But she passed an uneasy night, gut churning, her Gift for strategy working overtime. Sometimes she knew what someone was going to do almost before they did.

Just before dawn, she bolted upright in the bed. "That *ass*. He's going after the prince."

Fane rolled over, his corn-silk hair tumbling around his bare shoulders. "Adric?" he mumbled sleepily.

"Who else?" She tapped her quartz, tried to raise him.

No response.

Which was suspicious in itself. Her brother *always* answered her calls.

"I'll kill him," she growled. "I swear to the Mother Goddess herself, I'll stick a knife in his big, fat ego."

She shoved off the cloud-soft feather comforter—Fane's purchase, not hers, although her cat was rapidly getting used to such creature comforts—and stalked down the hall to the bathroom.

She was back in under a minute. As she jerked on her clothes, Fane rose naked from the bed and headed to the bathroom himself. For once, she barely noticed his lean, beautiful body, just sent him a distracted glance as she slid an iron dagger into a sheathe in her boot.

When he returned, he reached for a pair of slim black jeans. "I'm coming with you."

Damn, she loved him. The man had her back—always. But she shook her head. "It's better if I talk to him alone."

"Then I'll wait for you outside." He pulled on a cashmere sweater. "I'm not letting you out there alone. The night fae have you in their sights."

She sheathed a second dagger in her other boot—her mate-gift from Fane—and laced the boot. Her custom-made iron switchblade was already in her pocket.

"They haven't caught me yet." She rose on her toes to kiss him. "And the sun will be up soon."

He caught her arm. "I'm not asking your permission, Jani. You're not going without me."

She narrowed her eyes. Her easy-going mate rarely put his foot down, but when he did, he was as immovable as a boulder. A large, house-sized boulder.

However, she was the Baltimore second and Fane was now a clan member. Which meant she outranked him, although his place in the hierarchy was...fluid. On the other hand, was it worth a fight? She hadn't been mated long, but she was learning compromise was key, especially with two people as different as her and Fane.

"I'll only follow you anyway," he added.

She expelled a breath. "I'm leaving in two minutes."

The corner of his mouth lifted. "I'm a wayfarer, love. I'll be waiting on the surface." There was a blur of motion, and then their bedroom door opened and she was alone in the room.

Her lips twitched. Sometimes she forgot how fast he was.

She grabbed her leather jacket. Time to stop her brother before he did something stupid.

20

———

When Adric awoke just before dawn, Rosana was curled up in his arms, their bodies spooned together. He watched over her shoulder as she turned the amethyst pendant in her fingers, examining it like it was a fucking diamond.

He nuzzled her temple. "You really like it."

"Well, yeah." She rolled over to face him. "You gave it to me."

She had that soft, open expression that hit him like a fist to the chest. Didn't the woman know how to protect herself?

He swallowed and touched the pendant so that he didn't have to look at her face. "You're not what I expected either."

She circled his nipple with a fingertip. Petting him again. Like she couldn't get enough of him.

"What did you expect?"

He shrugged. "A brat. You're the alpha's baby sister." He only just stopped himself from saying *spoiled* baby sister.

The hand on his chest stilled. "Doesn't mean I got a free pass. I worked my ass off in the training cave, and I made warrior with the rest of my cohort."

"I know." He captured her fingers, kissed her knuckles. "That's what I'm trying to say. There's more to you than I expected. You're smart, tough. Good in a crisis. And sexy as hell."

A roll of her eyes. "Thanks." But she resumed petting him.

Tracing his collarbones, teasing his nipples, bumping a fingertip down each rib. He closed his eyes, drifting in a satiated haze, until she touched his pendant.

"Your quartz—there's a swirl of green inside."

His whole body jerked—an instinctive reaction. He yanked it away from her.

"Oh, gods." She clapped a hand to her mouth. "I'm so sorry. I wasn't thinking."

He gave a taut nod. Only another earth fada could know how bad it hurt—worse than a knee to the balls.

"It's all right. But nobody touches our quartz except family."

Or a mate.

Because Rosana's touch hadn't hurt. It had felt good, like she'd reached inside and caressed his heart.

His breath tangled in his chest.

No fucking way. We are not *mated.*

Both members of a pair had to agree to a mating. Words had to be spoken, a commitment made before the gods and the clan. But that sea-green thread was the same color as her dolphin's eyes.

She touched his arm. "You *are* hurt. I should've know better. Merry *told* me..."

He jolted, jumped out of bed.

"Ric?" She sat up, the quilt gripped to her breasts. "You sure you're okay?"

"Yeah, yeah." He shoved his fingers through his hair. "Sorry— I'm just....on edge. But don't touch it again, all right?"

"I won't. I promise. But I didn't know your quartz could change color. Merry's doesn't."

He wrapped his fingers protectively around the pendant. "It's...unusual."

In fact, he'd never heard of anything like it. Fada mates shared a special, mystical bond. Earth fada pairs connected through their quartzes—that warmth he'd noticed when Rosana was near—but he'd never heard of it appearing as a twist of color.

But then, he didn't know any water/earth fada pairs.

If only his parents were still alive. He needed to ask someone about this, someone he trusted. So few of the clan's elders had survived the Darktime.

Rosana was staring at him. Releasing the quartz, he got back into bed and pulled her back into his arms.

She rested her head on his shoulder, her hand carefully on his waist, far from his quartz. "You sure you're all right?"

"I'm fine. Really." He kissed her temple. "Go back to sleep."

She twisted her head so she could examine his face and then relaxed back against him again. Her breath sighed out, and a short time later she was asleep.

The fae lights dimmed to a muted peach. They floated above the bed like the last, glowing embers of a dying fire, painting Rosana's creamy skin a warm gold. Her inky hair tumbled over them both. He stroked it away from her face. Her mouth was slightly ajar, the full lips lax with sleep. Her eyelids fluttered but didn't open.

She looked so damn young, sweet...in a way he'd never been.

Mate.

His chest tightened, as the man recognized what his cougar already knew. The mate bond had already formed. A few fine-spun, hopeful strands, connecting his heart to Rosana's.

His stomach sank.

He couldn't let it happen, couldn't leave her behind to suffer as his mom had. He had to cut the link. He just prayed it wasn't already too late.

He slid out from under Rosana and rolled her onto her side facing away from him. She gave a discontented murmur, and he froze until she settled again, head pillowed on her hand.

He waited another few minutes. Then he set his jaw and rejected the bond. It resisted, more than he expected for such a tenuous connection. But the few strands were already intertwined, his a shimmering blue, hers aqua-green.

Behind him, Rosana mumbled unhappily. "*Não, meu querido, não ...*"

Sweat broke out on his brow. He pulled harder at his blue strands, but they just elongated as if they could stretch infinitely long. Without realizing it, his hand closed on his quartz, seeking strength, energy.

Rosana's strands wavered, tried to move around the barrier of his fist. And with that, he knew what to do.

He called on the power of his quartz. His cat clawed at him from inside.

Mate, it hissed. *Ours.*

He ignored it to ruthlessly throw up a barrier between his heart and Rosana's. There was an almost audible snap as the strands broke, severing the link.

He jolted. It hurt—bad. Like a crater had opened in his chest. The sheer emptiness made the breath whoosh from his lungs.

Rosana whimpered and flung out an arm as if warding off a blow.

He reached out a hand and then curled his fingers into his palm. He ached to touch her, to tell her it would be okay, but he'd lost that right.

He waited another few minutes before slipping out of bed. When he picked up his quartz, the sea-colored spiral had vanished. Sadness swamped him, bone-deep and grim, like the sun setting on his dreams.

He dropped the pendant over his head and glided soundlessly out of the room.

21

*R*osana woke in time to hear the outside door shut. She blinked groggily—then sprang out of bed, snatching up her clothes.

Everybody leaves.

But Adric hadn't just left, he'd cut the connection to her. She'd felt the mate bond last night—a few fragile, delicate strands—but now it was gone.

Pain slashed her. She curled into herself, arms wrapped around her waist.

She was six again, begging her mama and *papai* to take her with them.

Ula had taken Rosana's face between her hands. "I'm sorry, love. We're traveling as our dolphins. You're too young—you couldn't keep up with us."

Her lower lip had trembled. "Please, Mama. I'm fast. I swear I am. I'm the fastest girl in the creche. See?" She dashed from one side of the *sala* to the other, then grinned up at her mom, triumphant.

"Oh, *alanna*. I love you. But not this time." Ula's eyes swam with tears.

"No!" Rosana hollered and clamped onto her mom's leg like a limpet.

Her father had had to pry her off. "Hey, now, *bonita*. We need you to be a brave girl, okay? No crying. I want your promise."

He waited until Rosana gave a tearful nod, then handed her to a grim-faced Isa, ignoring her panicked attempts to scramble out of the nurse's arms back to Ula.

"Keep her here," he commanded.

"*Sim*, Senhor Nisio." Isa held the sobbing girl in a gentle but unbreakable grip. Ula cast her a last, sorrowful look, and then the door shut behind the alpha couple.

"Mama!" Rosana let out a heartbroken wail and then shoved her fist in her mouth, because she'd promised not to cry. It had been months before she'd spoken again.

Now she hugged herself harder. Biting her lip so hard it bled.

She'd been left behind. Again.

She dragged the amethyst pendant off her head. Goddess, she was an idiot. She'd actually thought it was Adric's way of saying he loved her. Or at least, that he wanted her, wished things were different.

Hot tears stung her eyes. She went to fling the pendant across the bedroom—and then hesitated, unable to do it.

Everybody leaves.

Her fingers tightened around the chunk of purple quartz. *Not this time.*

Dropping the pendant back over her head, she hurriedly donned a fresh shirt and pants and shoved everything else into her backpack before sprinting barefoot up the stairs.

A wet snow covered the grass with more flakes drifting down. She peered around the side of the house as Adric wheeled a black motorcycle down the short driveway.

She dashed to the shed, jerked on the quartz handle.

Locked.

With a muttered curse, she dragged a boot from her backpack and hammered the handle with the heel.

Adric sent a startled glance over his shoulder. For a long moment, they stared at each other.

She took a step toward him. "Take me. *Please*."

He shook his head, donned his helmet. "The lock will open for you in an hour." He snapped down a dark visor.

She gave the handle one last thump before looking around for a better tool. Her gaze lit on a rock. She dropped her stuff and lunged for it, but it was larger than it appeared, the bottom two-thirds lodged in the semi-frozen ground.

Adric zoomed off.

Her breath sobbed in. "No, no, no. You can't leave without me."

She was never going to catch him, but she clawed at the dirt until the rock loosened. She snatched it up and started to her feet.

Something slammed into her from behind, knocking her to her knees on the snow-covered grass. The rock flew out of her hands.

A man's rough fingers closed around her throat. A knee shoved into her spine.

She tried to buck him off, but he was bigger, heavier. He easily controlled her.

The blunt fingers tightened. She scrabbled frantically at them but the steady pressure didn't let up. Squeezing the breath from her.

Black edged her vision. Her hands felt strangely numb.

"*Adric*," she rasped.

A small, broken sound.

But in her head, it was a scream.

The fingers squeezed harder. The blackness rose up like a rogue wave and sucked her under.

22

_L_uc had waited outside Adric's den most of the night. He'd noted Rosana's scent, of course. Fresh, as if she'd been there recently.

His mouth flattened. First Lewes, now Baltimore. Adric had finally gotten lucky.

Luc had never approved of his friend's obsession with the do Rio female. Adric was the alpha; he should know better. Earth and water fada didn't mix. Adric could never mate with the woman, and fucking her was asking for trouble. Dion would love an excuse to come down hard on Adric and the clan.

The rain changed to a wet snow. It clung to Luc's hair, melted on his face. His pants were soaked through, his feet blocks of ice in his boots. He started to shiver but didn't shift to his wolf.

He'd need his hands for what came next.

Still, snow was good. It would cover his scent.

He stationed himself upwind anyway. No one knew better than one of Adric's former lieutenants how sharp the alpha's senses were.

Dawn came late in January. The sun was just a glimmer on the horizon when Adric emerged from his den, a duffel bag in hand. He sniffed, glanced around.

On the opposite side of the house, Luc plastered his back to the bricks. Inside, the part of him that Blaer could never touch implored his alpha: *See me. Kill me.*

Death was preferable to being enslaved to a fae.

But his friend seemed distracted. Getting his motorcycle from the shed, he donned his helmet, shoved the duffel bag into a saddle bag and pushed the bike down the snow-covered driveway.

The *geas* pulled at Luc. *"Bring Adric Savonett to me."*

No. He resisted Blaer's order, shaking and sweating like a goddamn addict needing a fix.

Blaer would be furious, especially since it was at his suggestion they'd gone to Rock Run first. "Adric will take the river fada straight home," he'd told her. "We can capture him there."

But of course, Adric had never showed—which was what Luc had been counting on. Disgusted, Blaer had left Luc the car and 'ported herself and Jon back to their hotel, with instructions for him to meet her in Virginia—with Adric.

If he didn't return with the alpha, Blaer would want to know why. And she had ways to drag the truth from him.

Then the woman came out—a river fada.

Luc did a doubletake. But yeah, it was Rosana do Rio, with Adric's scent all over her. Not hard to guess what the two of them had been doing last night.

Even though he'd known she'd visited recently, he was shocked that the alpha had taken a river fada into his den—the same den that was a closely guarded secret from most of Adric's own clan.

The man was in deep. Way deeper than Luc had realized.

He eyed Rosana. A river fada, and the Rock Run alpha's sister. For Blaer's purposes, Rosana do Rio was just as good as Adric. In fact, she might even be better.

And Adric would be safe.

His gaze swung to the do Rio female. Better her than his friend.

Luc might no longer be a member of the Baltimore clan, but

Adric would always have his loyalty. The man had rescued him from a living hell. That year Luc had been Leron's prisoner, he'd been tortured by not only Leron and his lieutenants, but his night-fae allies. He'd barely escaped with his sanity intact.

On the other side of the house, Adric started his bike. Luc took a step toward the street, the *geas* dragging at him.

No.

Crouching down, he dug his fingers into his scalp and resisted with everything he had until the motorcycle's engine faded into the other city sounds.

Behind him, Rosana was still in Adric's backyard. Apparently, her transportation was locked in Adric's shed.

He rose to his feet.

A female, argued his conscience. *A young, innocent female.*

Slapping it down like an irritating fly, he loped soundlessly across the lawn—and pounced.

Rosana groaned.

Her throat *hurt*, both inside and out.

She moved her hand to touch it, and then jolted when she realized her wrists were bound together in front of her. She popped her eyes open.

She was in the backseat of a car. A moving car.

She swung her feet to the floor and struggled upright.

Fuck. Her ankles were bound, too.

The world swung queasily around her. Bile coated the back of her sore throat. She squeezed her eyelids shut and tried not to vomit.

When the world righted itself, a long-limbed, dark-skinned man was regarding her in the rearview mirror with fierce gold eyes. A leather jacket and hoodie lay on the seat beside him, leaving him in a maroon T-shirt that exposed lean, ropey muscles —and the chunk of quartz hanging from his neck.

"Who are you?" The question came out as a rasp. She swallowed and tried again. "And where the fuck are you taking me?"

"There's water in the pocket in front of you," he replied, ignoring her questions.

She threw a wild-eyed glance around her. They were on a highway she didn't recognize, and according to the dashboard clock, it was a little after nine a.m., which meant she'd been out a couple of hours.

They could be almost anywhere, and she was trussed up like a pig on a spit.

Her lungs seized. Drawing up her knees, she slammed her bare heels into the back of his seat.

"I want to know what's going on. *Now*."

A rough growl. "You'll find out soon enough."

"Do you know wh—?" She clamped her mouth shut. She'd been about to threaten him with Dion, but if the earth fada didn't know who she was, it might be smarter to keep it that way.

She surreptitiously tested her bonds, but the rope was bespelled. The more she struggled to get free, the tighter it got, biting painfully into her wrists and ankles until she gave up, exhausted. Bile burned her throat again.

Water.

She worked the bottle from the seat pocket with her bound hands, awkwardly removing the cap and bringing it to her mouth.

Her throat felt too swollen to swallow. But she craved fluids. Water fada needed hydration more than other species.

She took a small, painful sip. The cool water slid down her throat. She took a few more careful sips before returning the bottle to the seat pocket.

Now that she was calmer, her internal GPS told her they were heading south, with the Chesapeake Bay ten or twenty miles to her left. So they were on their way to southern Maryland, or possibly Virginia. Not on I-95, though—this was a narrower highway with only two lanes in each direction. They passed through a small town and she tested the door, but her captor had removed the inside handles.

If only Adric would ride up on that black motorcycle of his... But he'd been gone before the earth fada had attacked her—or had he?

Her fingers curled into her palms. For a breath-stealing instant, she wondered if Adric was behind this.

No. He might be a hard, take-no-crap kind of guy, but he'd always been straight with her. He wouldn't kidnap her in this underhanded way.

Hell, he'd left her sleeping in his bed, which hurt, big time. Still, it wasn't the action of a man who intended to kidnap her.

She inhaled slowly, sifting the air for the driver's scent. Definitely an earth fada, but his scent had an unusual overlay of silver, like he was mated to a fae...or under a fae's power.

Fear scrabbled up her spine. She gripped her hands in her lap.

Nobody knew where she was. That note she'd left for Dion and Cleia? All she'd said was that she was going to Baltimore to be with Adric, and that they shouldn't worry about her.

She glanced at her left wrist and groaned. Cleia's protection charm was in the pocket of the jeans that she'd shoved into the backpack along with her boots and other clothes.

The backpack she'd dropped outside the shed.

She briefly closed her eyes, and then opened them to kick the backseat again. "Your alpha won't like this," she snarled. "I was in his den with his permission."

The driver's jaw worked. The pungent scent of anger filled the small space.

"He's not my alpha—not anymore. And some river fada bitch doesn't belong in his den anyway." His mouth turned down contemptuously. "Especially the Rock Run alpha's sister."

So he did know who she was.

She frowned. "You're not a Baltimore fada?"

"I am. But—" His fingers clenched on the steering wheel. He

shot her a single, burning look in the rearview mirror and then shook his head, tight-lipped.

"Cleia won't like this, either." She spoke the sun fae's name clearly and distinctly. "If you know who I am, then you know Queen Cleia is my brother's mate."

They were out in the countryside again, with farmland on either side of them. The earth fada swerved onto the grassy berm, slammed on the brakes. "Don't say her name."

She lifted her chin. "Cleia! Help!"

"Shut the fuck up." He lunged over the seat, catching her jaw in powerful hands.

She glared back. "Cleia," she said indistinctly from behind his covering palms.

"You want to play with me?" He shook her—hard. Her head snapped back and forth and her teeth clacked together. "I could break your neck right here."

Her heart raced. He meant it.

But what did she have to lose?

Her preferred animal might be a dolphin, but river fada could shift to any river-based animal—and some of them had teeth and claws. Now she brought her bound hands up and sliced her claws down the inside of his arm. The metallic scent of blood filled the air.

His face hardened. "*Bitch.*"

He surged the rest of the way into the backseat and flipped her onto her stomach. Pushing her face down into the vinyl, he shoved a knee into her spine between her shoulder blades. She was trapped, her hands caught beneath her chest, her nose and mouth squashed against the seat.

She couldn't breathe. Spots swam before her eyes. She tried to buck him off, but he pressed her deeper into the seat.

Strong fingers closed around her bruised throat. A strange calm descended on her.

She was going to die. But at least she'd gone out fighting.

But as she started to black out, he lifted her enough to take a gulp of air—and then pressed her face down again.

"Listen, you crazy bitch." A harsh growl against her ear. "I took you instead of Adric. You make me kill you, I'll have to go looking for him. I'm under a *geas*."

She stilled.

This was the earth fada lieutenant Adric had told her about. The man who'd broken into the B&B along with the fae.

"Yeah," he said grimly. "I thought that might change your mind. His scent is all over you. The choice is yours. Come with me willingly—and that means no tricks. Or I'll slit your throat and leave you here for a farmer to find, and then go after Adric."

"Mmph."

"Say it." He lifted her off the vinyl. "I want to hear the words. You'll come with me willingly. No tricks, including calling the queen's name."

She sucked in a breath. "Yes," she said as clearly as she could, although it came out as a rasp.

"Yes, what? And use your name. Your full name."

It would bind her to keep her promise. But she wasn't going to try and escape now anyway.

"Yes." She pushed the words out as best she could through her abused throat. "I, Rosana Marie do Rio"—she sucked in another breath—"will go with you willingly. No trying to escape or calling Cl—I mean the queen's—name."

"Okay, then." He released her. "I'll just take this, too."

Sliding her stiletto from her back pocket, he returned to the front seat with a fluid twist of his body. As he pulled back onto the highway, Rosana rolled onto her side and lay there, lungs heaving. A tear trickled down her cheek. She knuckled it away and then pushed herself back up to sitting again.

With shaking fingers, she reached for the water, took a few gulps. She put it back in the seat pocket and then leaned back.

During their struggle, the leather cord of her pendant had

twined around her throat. She unwound it and tucked the amethyst back into her shirt.

Too bad it wasn't one of those quartz smartphones. She could use it to contact Adric. But the six-sided stone was a comforting weight over her heart.

The earth fada eyed her in the mirror. "Ric gave you that?"

She moistened her lips. Would knowing the truth help her, or piss him off even more? But a lie would exact a cost, too.

"Yeah."

The earth fada shook his head in disgust. "The clan will never accept you. You can't be anything to him but a piece of ass."

That hurt. But she was damned if she'd let this *cabrão* see it. "Go to Hades," she said wearily and closed her eyes.

She must've drifted off again, because when the car stopped again, she jerked awake. They were deep in the forest on a narrow dirt track.

The earth fada rounded the car to open her door. "Out."

She grabbed the water bottle and downed the rest of it before swinging out her legs.

"Hold still." Flicking open a switchblade, he cut the rope around her ankles but left her hands bound. He grabbed her arm and helped her from the car. Not gently, but not roughly, either.

She stumbled forward, stiff and aching from their two clashes. As he righted her, his hand slid into her back pocket and she tensed.

Really? He was going to grope her—now?

Then she felt the stiletto he'd slipped back into her pocket.

Her heart bumped. She slid a sidelong glance at him, but he marched her into a small clearing and halted.

A tall blond female emerged from the shadows between a pair of towering maples. It was her. The mixed-blood fae from Lewes.

Rosana's right hand twitched, itching to go for the stiletto, but she forced herself to remain still. Adric's life might depend on it.

The earth fada inclined his head. "My lady."

The fae sauntered out of the trees on strappy high heels, long legs bare under a short silver dress, hands in the pockets of her black leather jacket. She was model-thin with a fine-boned face and a sharp chin. Pointed ears poked from pale shoulder-length hair and coffee-colored brows arched over large eyes so unnervingly dark you couldn't tell where the pupils ended and the irises began.

"What's this, Luc?" She eyed Rosana as if she were a piece of day-old fish. "Your orders were to bring me Adric."

"Yes, my lady. But this is Rosana do Rio. I believe you'll find her even more useful."

"The Rock Run alpha's sister?" A single dark brow flicked up.

The earth fada—Luc—nodded.

The fae pursed her full pink lips. "And you brought her instead of your alpha because—?"

Luc held himself soldier-stiff, but Rosana scented his uneasiness.

"Adric has escaped me. Twice. But his scent is all over this woman. Take her to the prince, and chances are, Adric will walk right into New Moon." Luc's mouth twisted. "I know him, you see."

Rosana's fingernails dug into her palms. *Devious fucking bastard.*

"Ah." The woman's mouth curved in a cold smile. "A man who thinks for himself."

He gazed steadily back without saying anything.

The fae lady paced forward, circled the two of them. "But your orders were to bring me Adric Savonett." Her voice was icy. "Weren't they, Luc?"

He released Rosana, took a step away. "Yes, my lady."

The fae homed in on him. Dark magic crackled in the air.

Rosana gave a hard swallow.

Luc clenched his fists at his sides and stared stonily at his fae mistress. She grabbed his quartz, and he jolted. She murmured a few words and a cold white energy crackled around it. Luc jolted again, sinking to his knees with an agonized groan. The blond fae bent with him, the pendant held tightly in her hand.

Rosana gasped as frost covered his torso, spread out to his limbs. Only his face was left untouched.

His claws slid out. He glared up at the fae, chest heaving.

She gazed back, a smile on her lips. Darkness slithered around the two of them as if the very shadows had come alive.

Rosana growled and took a step forward. "Are you *feeding* on him?"

The woman pinned her with an icy midnight gaze. "Come any closer, and I'll freeze you, too."

Rosana stilled until the fae turned her attention back to Luc. Then she twisted her arms around her body, trying to reach the stiletto in her back pocket. Luc might be a *cabrão*, but she was damned if she'd stand by while the woman tortured him.

But before she could work the stiletto free, the fae released the pendant and straightened up. Luc's head dropped to his chest. His breath sawed in and out, the sound harsh in the quiet clearing, as the frost slowly receded.

Rosana brought her hands back in front of her body.

"You *will* bring me Adric Savonett," his mistress said. "That's an order, Luc."

The earth fada's head came up, eyes blazing with hatred.

The fae lady only smiled before turning to Rosana. "The Rock Run alpha's sister, hm?"

Rosana swallowed queasily. Then she pulled back her shoulders.

"That's me. And if you're smart, you'll let me go, because my brother will come after you with everything he has. Hang on to me, and you're a dead woman."

"I'll let the prince worry about that. Come." She held out an imperious hand.

Rosana found her feet moving. Long fingers clamped around her arm, cold even through her hoodie.

Ice fae, Rosana realized. The woman was an ice fae/night fae mix, her scent a swirl of snow and decay.

"Go," the fae told the still-kneeling man. "Find Adric and bring him to me. And this time, don't fail me."

He rose slowly, painfully, to his feet as if every bone in his body ached. "To New Moon?"

"Yes. I'll instruct the wards to allow you both to enter."

Rosana swallowed. If only she could warn Adric somehow. But she could do nothing but stand by helplessly as Luc trudged back to the car.

Blaer murmured something in fae and the air around them *bent* in a dizzying way. Rosana braced herself to be teleported, and then the bottom dropped out of the forest. For a vertiginous moment, everything went black, and then the two of them reappeared inside a large, dimly lit room.

Rosana's eyes went night glow.

They were in a large, quietly elegant library. The walls were lined with books, the floor a cold white marble veined with black. The tall, narrow windows were covered with dark shades, the only illumination a few fae lights the color of black opals floating near the ceiling.

At one end of the room was a graceful Art Nouveau sofa and two chairs in a blue burnout velvet, and at the other end, a wide mahogany desk gleamed. Museum-quality statues of smooth black stone were scattered on pedestals around the room—a snarling panther, a feathered raven, a winged woman with flowers spilling from her hands. A table near the window held a silver vase with a single red rose.

Rosana's heart jittered. She could've sworn the room was empty—she hadn't even scented him—but now a man was seated at the table near the window. Like Blaer in the forest earlier, it was as if he'd coalesced from the shadows themselves.

A night fae, casually dressed in a loose white shirt and black pants, his pale, elegant feet bare. One long-fingered hand toyed with a pair of black dice.

Prince Langdon.

He tossed the dice on the table. She watched, stunned, as they transformed into two iridescent blue butterflies and flew away to perch on the snarling panther's head.

The prince rose to his feet. Onyx eyes examined Rosana.

Power emanated from him. Cold. Dark. And so strong she could literally feel it, like an icy black ocean sucking at her.

"Lady Blaer," he murmured without taking his gaze from Rosana. "What have you brought me?"

23

———

A few tardy snowflakes sifted down as Cleia and Dion slipped out the back door of her mansion for a morning stroll, leaving Brisa to eat breakfast under her nanny's watchful eye. Cleia loved Rising Sun in the summer, when the gardens were a mass of colorful blooms, fruit swelled in the trees and the surrounding meadows were a soft, fecund green. But the overnight snowfall had touched the grounds with a sparkling wand, turning the gardens into a sugared wonderland.

Dion steered her onto a little-used path and pressed her up against a tree. His mouth took hers in a lazy kiss. She slid her hands under his leather jacket and kissed him back. Even with a nanny to help, a busy toddler meant they didn't have much time alone.

A low, sexy growl. "I could take you right here," he said against her throat, "if it wasn't so cold."

"Who's cold?" Her hands went to the zipper of her own jacket...and then fell away.

Rosana's in trouble.

Cleia clutched Dion's shoulders, ears straining.

His hands tightened on her waist. "What's the matter?"

She held up a hand, silently asking him to wait. A full thirty seconds ticked by before she gave up.

"It's Rosana." She swallowed hard. "Something's wrong. She called my name—four times."

"Where?" he bit out.

"Not close by." She scrunched her brows, focusing. "Somewhere south of here. Virginia, or maybe southern Maryland. It was quick—a brief touch, and then nothing."

Their eyes met. They'd spent the night at Rising Sun. Neither of them had seen Rosana since yesterday afternoon.

Dion muttered a nasty Portuguese curse. "She's supposed to be at the base."

"I'll 'port to her."

"Take me."

She nodded and took Dion's hand and teleported to the approximate location she'd sensed Rosana.

They were on a narrow country road, although that didn't stop cars from hurtling past. A field of dormant winter wheat stretched along one side of the road, and on the other, stubbled cornstalks marched off to the horizon.

Dion turned in a circle, scanning the area. "We're still in Maryland, about five miles from the Potomac River. What in Hades is she doing down here?"

"I don't know," Cleia said. "But she hasn't tried to contact me again."

His nostrils flared. "I can't pick up her scent. But if she was in a car, she wouldn't leave one."

Cleia narrowed her eyes to the south, as if she could somehow see where Rosana was now. "New Moon is right across the river in Virginia."

"I know." Dion glared in the same direction. "If that fucking *cabrão* thinks he can use my sister as a bargaining chip..."

Cleia's stomach hollowed. It was exactly what a night fae would do.

"We'll go after him with everything we have. Rosana isn't just your family, she's mine."

"I know. And I'm grateful, *querida*." Dion squeezed her hand. "But first, let's make sure that's where she is. Take me back to Rock Run. I need Rui—his shark can track anything."

"At least she has my protection charm. It'll give her an edge."

He nodded, expression grim. Humoring her.

Because they both knew Rosana might not be wearing the charm.

They found Rui in the training cave. The shark fada had once been Rock Run's top assassin until the job had taken its toll. These days Rui spent his time training the younger warriors, a position to which the hard-faced, taciturn man had taken like a duck to water.

"Be right there," Rui called over his shoulder, his gaze on the two young males he was sparring with. Another seven young men and women stood in a circle, observing.

The man on the left lunged. In a few swift, scarily efficient moves, Rui dropped him by hooking a heel behind his knee and then spun around to kick the other in the chest. The man flew backwards.

Cleia winced, but the two males bounded back to their feet.

"Good work," Rui said with a nod. The younger men beamed as he turned to the observers. "The rest of you, form groups of three and practice the sequence I just showed you."

He strode across the cavern to Dion and Cleia, big body naked except for a pair of shorts. "What's up?" he asked as he pulled on a T-shirt.

Dion tipped his head at the exit. "In the ops room."

"*Sim.*"

The operations room was in its own private corridor near the base's center. A couple of warriors were always on duty to sift through communications and respond to emergencies. Like most of the base, it was a utilitarian space with a handful of chairs and a sturdy plank table, the only lighting a handful of watery blue and green fae lights.

By the time they arrived, Dion had brought Rui up to date. Dion jerked his chin at the pair manning the room. "Wait outside."

They nodded and exited, but before they could close the door, Isa bustled down the corridor, her round face anxious.

"My lord, my lady. I need to see you, *por favor*."

Dion nodded for the men to let her pass and then shut the door behind her.

Isa thrust a folded piece of paper at him. "I found this on Rosana's pillow."

Cleia read the note over his shoulder.

Dion, Cleia, Isa—

I'm on my way to Baltimore. But don't worry. You might as well know, I'm with Adric. I'm tired of hiding it. I love him, and he loves me (even if he hasn't told me yet).

More, he needs me. I'll be back in a few days—please, don't worry. Hugs and kisses, Rosana

"I'll kill him," Dion said calmly. "I'll wring his goddamn neck."

Cleia eyed her mate warily as he passed the note to Rui.

"If he's hurt her," Dion continued. "Forced her to go with him against her will—he's dead."

She set a hand on his arm. The bicep was balled tight. "Let's not jump to conclusions," she murmured.

"No?" The eyes he turned on her were the cold silver of his animal. "She goes to Baltimore and somehow ends up in a car a hundred-fifty miles south of here. She calls on you for help— which she's never done in her life? Tell me, what am I supposed to think?"

"I agree it looks bad, but I've seen how Adric looks at her. We've all seen it."

Dion snarled. "Like a fucking cat stares at prey."

"No. Like a man who wants a woman with everything he has— but knows he can never have her. He's stayed away from her for her own good. And she feels the same. If he'd wanted, he could've lured her away years ago."

Beside her, Isa murmured agreement.

"Then why is he taking her to Virginia?" Dion demanded.

"We don't know it's him."

"Who else could it be?"

"I'm just saying, keep an open mind."

"Of course," he surprised her by saying, and then spoiled it by adding, "as long as you keep an open mind when I tear his lying, cheating throat out."

He turned to Rui. "I'm leaving ASAP. Who's available?"

"Three men plus the two of us?"

"*Sim.*"

"Then Ed and Jaxon can come." Ed was an older, canny *tenente*, and Jaxon a young, hard-driving warrior. "And Tiago—he's at the marina right now."

"That works. Tiago would want to come anyway. I'll tell Davi he's the *tenente* in charge."

Cleia chewed her lip, wishing she could help. But she wasn't strong enough to teleport even Dion and his motorcycle to Virginia, let alone four other men. They'd have to get themselves to southern Maryland.

Dion nodded at Isa. "Thank you. You did the right thing, bringing this straight to me."

His former nurse inclined her graying head, fingers twined tightly in front of her waist. "I don't know when she left. I didn't even know she was gone until after breakfast. For that, I beg your pardon."

"Senhora." Dion gently took her hands. "You have nothing to apologize for. You're not Rosána's keeper. Now, go back to whatever you were doing, but let's keep this between us, okay? Until we know exactly what we're up against, I'd rather the whole base didn't know."

"Of course," the woman said, and with a dignified nod to all of them, left the room.

"If that's it, then?" Dion asked, clearly impatient to be off, but Rui held up a staying hand.

"I'm afraid we've got another problem."

"It can't wait?"

"No," Rui said bluntly. He closed the door behind Isa. "Merry believes her grandfather's been watching her."

"The hell you say. Is that possible?"

Both men looked at Cleia.

She spread her hands. "Anything is possible. Our wards can block him from entering the base physically, but if he has the farsight, that wouldn't stop him from keeping a watch on her."

"Valeria knows?" Dion asked.

"*Sim*," said Rui. "She'll keep her inside the wards."

Dion squeezed his nape. "So the prince knows she's alive."

Rui nodded, his strong, sculpted face set in grim lines.

Dion swore. "I don't like this. There is no way to keep him out?"

"He can't do it constantly," Cleia said. "Only intermittently. Using any kind of Sight requires your whole attention. But I'll talk to Olivia, see if there's anything she can do to block him." Her cousin was a spell-worker and ward-maker. "Maybe a *look-away* spell would work."

"Good." Dion wrapped a hand around her nape and gave her a hard kiss. "Go home. Stay close to Brisa. Just in case."

Cleia's breath snagged. "He wouldn't dare."

"I don't think so, no. But I don't want to take any chances." He turned to Rui. "Have the men at the garage in fifteen minutes."

"Will do."

Cleia waited until Rui left before telling Dion, "Let me know the minute you find out anything. And if there's anything I can do, you'll call on me."

His black brows lowered, but he nodded reluctantly. "Fine. If it will make you happy."

"It will. And I want your promise that when you do catch up to Adric and Rosana, you'll hear them both out before you do anything. If she's his mate, and you hurt him…"

His chin jerked back like she'd hit him. "She's not his mate. That—it's not possible."

"But if she is, and you hurt him, she'll never forgive you."

"I can handle my own sister," he growled, and stalked after Rui.

Cleia pinched the bridge of her nose—and 'ported back to Rising Sun and her baby girl.

There was only so much a woman—even a powerful fae queen—could do. Some things her mate had to work out for himself.

24

———

The New Moon Court was in a densely forested state park near the mouth of the Potomac. A powerful *look-away* spell meant the local humans didn't even know they had a night fae compound in their midst. The court didn't appear on maps or satellite scans, and if hikers somehow managed to bumble too close, they couldn't penetrate the court's wards.

Adric downed a plate of sausage and eggs at a local diner without tasting them. His chest still felt like a black hole had opened where his heart used to be. He ground the heel of his hand into his breastbone, trying to rub the ache away.

He kept seeing Rosana's face when she'd realized he was leaving without her. Anguished. Betrayed.

You did the right thing.

He couldn't mate with her, not when he might be dead before the week was out.

He forked up a bite of egg and stared at it. *She's back at Rock Run by now. Safe.*

So why did he feel like he'd left something vital behind?

Don't think about it. Do the job. You can make it up to her afterwards.

If there *was* an afterwards...

He grimly shoveled down the rest of his meal. Ten minutes later, he was checking into a cheap motel a few miles from New Moon, paying cash and requesting a room facing the strip of trees at the back. He wheeled his bike around back and went inside.

The room was a beige box. A king-sized bed vied for space with a flimsy armoire and a desk with one chair. Dropping his helmet and duffel bag on the bed, he stripped to the skin and then sheathed his iron dagger in a leather case with its own cord before dropping it over his head next to his quartz.

He cracked open the door. Other than his motorcycle, the only vehicle in the back lot was a dirty white sedan, and the sole sign of life was the humming of a vacuum cleaner two rooms down.

He locked the door and jogged into the trees behind the motel. He'd researched the area around New Moon until he could've navigated it blindfolded. The narrow strip of trees connected with other wooded patches, enough to provide cover for his cougar until he could disappear into the state park.

On the deserted country road, a truck rumbled past, accompanied by a belch of oily fumes. From the fenced-in yard of a nearby house, a dog barked, its scent a tart mix of bravado and fear.

Adric snarled, and the dog gave a startled yip before cowering next to the back steps.

He tucked the key card into the crook of a crepe myrtle, then closed his eyes and opened himself to the change. Hot sparks danced over his skin. Power surged through him, obliterating his human form. For a time, he was both Adric and not-Adric; pure, formless energy. And then he was on all fours, the wet brown leaves cool beneath his tawny paws, his senses a hundred times sharper.

He gave himself a shake, settling his fur into place, then set out for New Moon, intermittently cloaking himself. He hadn't forgotten Rosana's warning that Langdon had Seen he was coming to the court. The bastard might know Adric was on his way, but he couldn't know the exact moment. No Seer was that powerful.

A half hour later, he entered the state park. He was in a stand of sharp-scented longleaf pines, the sun high in the pale blue sky. He aimed for the park's center.

As he neared the New Moon compound, gray clouds blotted the sun, and the pines changed to menacing hardwoods that loomed over him like grim soldiers. His fur bristled. He crept forward, scanning the dark spaces between the trees.

Gradually, he became aware of the *look-away* spell pressing at him.

Turn away. There's nothing here.

When he continued, shadows gathered, and the warnings grew more foreboding.

Danger. Run...while you still can.

He closed his eyes, drew on his tracking Gift. The compulsion to look away passed. When he opened his eyes, the shadows parted to reveal a shimmering trail winding through the trees, the kind of path only a fae—or a fada with their touch of fae blood —could see.

Gotcha.

He avoided the shimmering fae path. The *look-away* spell was just the first layer of security around the court. The trail would be watched, possibly even booby-trapped. Instead, he ducked deeper into the woods, taking a parallel course to the trail.

A gravel road barely wide enough for a single car intersected the trail. He dropped to his belly and slunk forward to investigate.

The scent of rainwater and woman.

His nostrils flared. *Rosana?*

No fucking way. She was in Baltimore, or more likely, safely back at Rock Run.

Unless she'd followed him.

He shook his head. Impossible—he'd have noticed her and her motorcycle.

But she could've come straight to Virginia. After all, she'd guessed he was going after Langdon.

He inhaled, sifting through the forest scents. There, to the west. It was Rosana, all right.

He clenched his jaw so hard his molars hurt. He should've known she wouldn't return tamely home.

He muttered a cougar's equivalent of a curse and faded back into the trees, following the gravel road to the west.

Rosana's scent grew stronger, entwined with the scents of two others—Luc and a fae.

His heart stuttered. His curses changed to a low, continuous growl.

He entered a clearing. In the leaves and mud were the tell-tale prints of three people. The sharp indentation of a woman's high heels. A man's lug soles. And a single imprint of a long, narrow bare foot.

He sniffed. It was Rosana, all right, her pores leaking fear.

His body went taut as a stretched wire. He already knew the man was Luc, and he suspected the high heels belonged to Lady Blaer.

He could think of only one reason Rosana would be with them.

Luc had captured Rosana for Blaer. The fae who put fada in cages.

Rage blasted through Adric, a fury edged with panic. His claws dug into the mud. But the rest of him remained icy-calm, cat and man fusing into a single cold-eyed predator.

First, he'd rescue Rosana. Then he'd take revenge on those who'd dared to abduct her.

He scrutinized the foot prints. The story they told was clear. Luc had returned to a nearby car, but the women's tracks ended in the clearing. The only explanation was that the fae lady had 'ported out with Rosana.

He stilled, drew on his quartz. Tracking Rosana with every ounce of power he possessed.

But it was as if the earth had opened up and swallowed her whole. Still, that in itself was a clue. If she was at New Moon, the wards would shield her from him.

He raced back along the gravel road to the shimmering fae

path and then turned north again, following the trail as closely as he dared, torn between the need for speed and concealment. He was closer than he'd realized. Within a few minutes, the half-buried, vine-covered buildings of the New Moon Court were visible through the trees.

He took to the treetops, leaping from branch to branch. Even another fada would have trouble tracking him high in the forest canopy. A few yards from the perimeter, he halted in a sturdy oak and crouched on a branch, a shadow in the trees.

The clouds dissipated, allowing the sun to melt the last patches of snow. The compound was arranged as Fane's map had depicted, with Langdon's lair near the center. Fog snaked around the eerie, cryptlike building. Walking paths of smooth white pebbles meandered through a lush landscape of azaleas, crepe myrtle and southern magnolia, and huge willows wept over the still black pond.

Adric's gaze returned to Langdon's lair. The tallest building at one-and-half stories, it was draped in the same ivy as the others, with vines and flowers chiseled into the creamy granite beneath. At its apex, a giant bat flew past a crescent moon.

He narrowed his eyes at the windows. If only he could see in...

At this hour, the prince was probably asleep, but Adric couldn't be sure. The powerful old fae was one of the few night fae who could tolerate the noonday sun.

And was Rosana with him, or elsewhere, with Blaer?

His stomach twisted into icy knots.

There was no choice but to hunker down on the branch to wait for someone to open a portal into the court. If possible, he'd slip inside before it closed, using his Gift to cloak his presence from the guards. But if not, he'd use his quartz to compel the person to allow him to pass through the portal.

Long minutes ticked by with nobody entering or leaving. In fact, it had been at least an hour since he'd seen anyone at all, even a human servant. Adric frowned. It was as if the shadows had thickened to conceal the court's inhabitants. Could the wards have sensed him and reacted accordingly?

If only he knew more. But the night fae were the most secretive of the fae. He was lucky to have Fane's intel; without it, he'd be going in completely blind.

He settled deeper into his cougar, drawing on its patience. Only his twitching tail betrayed his growing agitation.

More time passed. He'd been on the branch an hour now.

How long had Rosana been inside?

A fist squeezed his bowels. He knew—too well—what the night fae did to their prisoners. And it wouldn't be quick. The motherfuckers liked to toy with their prey.

Don't think about it. She's smart—she'll play for time.

Something rustled in the forest below.

Very slowly, he turned his head, scanning the undergrowth.

The big brown wolf was almost as good as Adric at concealing himself. But he couldn't hide his musky scent...or his gleaming amber eyes.

25

In person, Prince Langdon was even more beautiful.

Tall and lean, with silky black hair framing his narrow poet's face. Against his pale skin, his lips were a dark, sensuous red, and the diamonds that outlined his ears and brows sparkled like tiny stars.

Rosana realized she was gaping. She closed her mouth with a snap.

"My lord." Blaer dipped her shining blond head. "Peace to you and yours."

"Peace, Lady Blaer," the prince returned in a low, rich voice.

He paced forward, quiet as death, his gaze on Rosana. Distantly, she noted a night fae's unpleasant scent, but against his unearthly beauty, it somehow didn't matter.

He inclined his head to her. "And to you, Senhorita do Rio."

So he knew who she was. She jerked her chin in acknowledgement. "Peace."

"I offer her as a gift," Blaer said.

"Do you?" The prince lifted a winged black brow.

A gift? Rosana forgot how gorgeous he was and narrowed her eyes. There were rules about these things. The fae couldn't just snatch you without your permission.

"I agree to nothing," she said. "I'm here against my will, and I demand to be returned to Rock Run immediately. My lord."

Blaer just smiled.

Langdon stopped in front of Rosana. He was at least a foot taller. She had to tip her head back to meet his eyes.

He stared back, growing more beautiful by the second. Power enfolded her, as if he'd sprouted black wings and embraced her.

Her gaze snagged on his full mouth. She could almost feel his lips against hers, soft, caressing.

The dark wings tightened around her like a warm cocoon.

Her breath sighed out.

The prince's mouth curved in a faint smile.

Uneasiness skipped up her spine. She dragged her gaze from his mouth, pulled back her shoulders. "My lord? I repeat, I'm here against my will."

"She speaks the truth, Blaer?" Langdon asked, his gaze still on Rosana. "She didn't enter my court willingly?"

The fae lady's smile faded. She shot Rosana a dark look. "Yes, my lord."

"A miscalculation, no doubt," the prince returned silkily. "But perhaps I can convince her to stay." He smiled into Rosana's eyes. "What do you think, my dear? Would you like to spend a few days with me?"

That unearthly beauty tugged at her again. Was he using a glamour on her?

She scowled and wrenched her gaze from his. "I already gave you my answer," she said to his chest. "I want to leave. *Now.*"

"Is there nothing I can do to change your answer to a yes?" He fingered one of her curls. The dark power constricted.

Tighter, tighter.

Her heart sped up. She took short, rapid breaths, unable to fill her lungs. She fought the urge to thrash wildly at the invisible cocoon. He'd only use her fear to ensnare her further.

Instead, she stared stonily at the V of his shirt. "No, my lord."

Langdon *knew* she was afraid. So did Blaer. They had both stilled, their bodies vibrating with a greedy hunger.

But the prince nodded and to her surprise, released her hair and stepped back.

Her breath whooshed out.

Blaer glanced between the two of them, frowning. Rosana edged away from her.

"You're hungry." Langdon waved his hand and a steaming bowl of fish stew appeared on the table with the silver vase. "I've had my cook prepare something." Another flick of his fingers and a basket of crusty brown bread settled beside the stew, along with a bowl of fruit and a plate of small, perfect chocolates.

Rosana eyed the food, her mouth watering. He was right. She hadn't eaten since dinner last night.

It could be a trick. Eat his food, and you'll end up "owing" him.

She swallowed and looked away. "No, thank you."

"Then perhaps some wine?" A crystal glass appeared in her hand.

She stared down at the pale gold liquid. *Maybe just a sip?* She moistened her lips. It looked so good, and her throat still ached from Luc's attack.

Her fingers tightened on the stem. She set the wine on the table. "Not right now."

The prince shrugged a shoulder. "As you wish. But please, sit." He indicated a black burned-velvet couch on the other side of the room.

Rosana fingered the stiletto in her back pocket. For courage.

Because using it was a last resort. Even if she managed to escape this room, she'd still have to evade any guards and somehow open the portal to the outside world.

"With respect, Lady Blaer brought me here against my will. She admitted it herself. Now, either let me leave or I'll call on Queen Cleia." She spoke the sun fae woman's name loud and clear.

Langdon picked up the wine she'd refused, sipped it. "I should tell you that the queen can't get through our wards. In fact, it's unlikely she can even trace you to the court."

"She might surprise you," Rosana returned, but her heart sank. She was on her own, then. Even if Cleia had heard her earlier cry for help, she had no reason to suspect that Rosana had been taken to New Moon. And Dion might have a hunter's Gift, but Luc had made sure she couldn't leave a trail. She'd been closed up in his car until they'd reached the forest.

Blaer shifted impatiently on her sky-high heels. "My lord?"

"You did well," Langdon replied. "I accept your gift."

Rosana glared at them both. "I am *not* a fucking gift."

The two fae ignored her. "So I've won a place at your court?" Blaer asked.

The prince inclined his head. "Olivier will assign you an apartment. You will, of course, refrain from any attempts to influence my court. You'll find I'm not as forgiving as King Sindre."

Blaer's face set into a pleasant mask. And it *was* a mask. Rosana scented her anger, mixed with a cold determination.

"I understand, my lord." She sketched a small bow.

The prince studied the tall blond mixed-blood for a moment. "Do you?" he murmured, and then turned to Rosana, effectively dismissing Blaer.

Behind him, the fae lady's eyes blazed, twin red fires flaring to life inside obsidian pupils. But she meekly murmured, "Peace to you and yours," and strode to the door, silver heels clicking on the marble floor.

A portly human with deep brown skin and a shiny bald head appeared in the doorway. "If you'll come with me, my lady. I believe we have an empty apartment near the north gardens."

Rosana eyed Langdon, tight-jawed. "You won't get away with this."

"You're angry," he said—and smiled. But of course, to a night fae, anger was like catnip.

Her hands balled at her sides. "You know who I am," she said evenly. "Keep me here against my will, and my brother will come after you with everything he has."

"You're the woman I saw in the scrying glass," he said as if she hadn't spoken.

She stilled. "Am I?"

"Oh, yes." A tilt of his gorgeous head as he examined her, a wolf with an intriguing—and very tasty—rabbit. "Which brings me to an interesting question: why were you looking for me?"

Oh, Lord. She did *not* want to bring Merry into this—or Adric, for that matter.

She spread her hands. "It just...happened." Which was true enough. "Is that what this is about? You're pissed off that I accidently spied on you?"

"Pissed off?" he repeated. "No, merely curious. I assure you, I had nothing to do with Lady Blaer bringing you here."

Somehow, he was just a foot away again, that dark, seductive power licking at her. And gods, it was tempting to give in to it.

No. I love Adric.

But Adric doesn't want you. Not enough anyway. He cut the mate bond, and then he left you. You begged him to take you along, told him if he didn't, he'd die—and he still left.

Her heart squeezed.

"You're distressed," the prince murmured. "But there's no need. As you say, you've agreed to nothing." He paused. "Yet."

She shook her head and slipped around him. Putting some distance between herself and that seductive aura.

She picked up the wine glass, toyed with the stem without drinking.

Stall for time. Think about Dion, not Adric.

Because Dion would come for her. That she knew, as surely as she knew the sun rose in the east and set in the west.

Just picturing her large, very capable brother heartened her.

"It's you who was spying on Rock Run," she said. "If I happened to See you, that's not my fault. We just—intersected somehow."

Langdon nodded without confirming or denying that he'd been spying on her clan, or at least, on Merry.

"So you're a Seer."

Rosana's spine prickled. "I didn't say that."

"No," he agreed. His black eyes scrutinized her like she was an insect under a microscope. "I seem to recall your mother is, too. But then, her mother was a quarter fae."

Rosana swallowed. She didn't like that this dark prince knew so much about her family. But that was the fae; they collected information like dragons did treasure, hoarding it on the chance it might be useful.

"The question is, why were you scrying for me?"

She couldn't tell Langdon about Merry. Rock Run had never officially confirmed that the teenager was still alive. It didn't matter that he knew differently. Admit it straight out, and the night fae would have grounds to retaliate, resulting in open war between New Moon and her clan.

She saw only one option—admit she was a Seer.

"I was curious." She threw his own words back at him. It was the truth, after all. "I didn't expect to See anything."

Least of all, Prince Langdon himself. The most she'd hoped for was some clue that might help Merry.

"You're quite Gifted for one so young. You're being trained?"

"Yes." She set down the wine glass, nerves shrieking at all these questions. But he was a powerful fae, and she was in his territory. Answer his questions, and maybe he'd be satisfied, let her leave.

Yeah, right. And jellyfish can fly. But she had no choice but to play along.

"Odd, that I haven't heard of you before now." He sank gracefully onto the burned-velvet couch, crossed one long leg over the other. "I could work with you. It's been many turns of the sun since I encountered a Seer with such a strong natural Gift."

Oh, no. Hell, no.

"It's good of you to offer," she returned smoothly, "but the sun fae are overseeing my training."

"With me, you wouldn't have to hide who you are."

She flinched. What did he know?

A tiny nod. "I thought as much. Others so rarely understand what it is to be a Seer. They fear us, ridicule our Gift. Or worse, ignore our warnings."

Like Adric.

"Yes," he said with a commiserating smile. "That's the hardest of all, isn't it? When the people we love simply won't listen."

Rosana moved to the panther statue. The butterflies were still perched on its snarling black head, their fragile blue wings opening and closing.

She stared at them unseeingly. *Don't agree to anything.*

But, a sly voice countered, *Langdon's an old, powerful fae. He's probably forgotten more than Colm ever knew.*

"My people would honor a Seer with your Gift," the prince purred from the couch. "You could name your price. You'd be a wealthy woman—you could buy and sell your own brothers. But more, you'd have their respect. They don't see you how you really are, do they?" Soft, seductive tones. "They think you're still a child who doesn't know her own mind."

Her hand fisted.

"I'm right, aren't I?"

She shook her head, not because he was wrong, but because it hurt to admit he was right.

"Think about it. That's all I ask."

Temptation tugged at her. She swallowed around the constriction in her throat. "No," she rasped.

On the couch behind her, Langdon made a sharp, irritable movement. "Consider what you're turning down. Imagine the power you'd wield as an honored Seer."

She closed her eyes. Because she *could* picture it.

She fingered Adric's amethyst through the shirt. If she stayed at the court, she'd lose him.

Her mouth twisted. *So? He doesn't want you. Even your own clan doesn't know who you really are. Here, you could be yourself.*

Her fingers tightened around the pendant.

No. That's Langdon's darkness talking.

Beneath her shirt, the pendant warmed, almost as if Adric had infused it with a spark of his own energy.

Adric had given the pendant to her, attached it to a leather thong so she could always wear it. In that instant, she saw something very clearly—with her heart, not her Sight. The warmth expanded to fill her chest.

Adric did want her. He just didn't *want* to want her.

And suddenly, she wasn't tempted at all.

She turned around. "And if I say no? Will you let me leave?"

The prince moved an elegant shoulder. "Perhaps."

Anger balled in her stomach. "You can't keep me here."

"No? Try to leave without my permission and the portals will slam shut. I'm told it's like running full speed into a stone wall."

"You think you're safe behind your wards?" She stalked toward him. "Keep me here against my will and my brothers will carve out your fucking liver and feed it to the fish."

The prince's mouth curved. "You're a bloodthirsty little thing, aren't you?"

"Yeah." She smiled back, drew the stiletto—and leapt over the couch. She instinctively avoided touching his skin with her bare hands. Instead, she grabbed his long black hair, jerked his head back and touched the needle-like point to the hollow of his throat. His flesh sizzled, the acrid scent stinging her nostrils.

Langdon stilled—and then he raised a diamond-studded brow, that irritating half-smile on his lips again. "Now what?"

She pressed the blade a little deeper. "This isn't a joke, asshole," she said in her animal's guttural voice.

His hand shot out, quick as a striking snake, to grip her jaw.

"Careful," he gritted. "Right now the fact that you amuse me is all that's keeping me from returning you to Blaer. She's rather primitive in how she treats fada. She seems to consider you animals to be kept in cages. Perhaps you heard what happened to the Baltimore alpha's sister?"

"Marjani Savonett?" She sucked in a horrified breath. *Adric's sister had been shut in a cage?*

But she'd gone too far to back down now. "Go to Hades. I'm not here to fucking amuse you." She pushed the stiletto deeper, piercing the skin.

Blood slid down Langdon's throat, soaking the V of his pristine white shirt.

Cold fingers dug into her jaw. "That, my pretty little fada, was a mistake."

A red flame flared to life deep in his pupils.

She swallowed and tried to wrench her gaze away. But she was caught. The dark power that had been pulling at her surged to life. Tentacles wrapped around her like an invisible octopus, latching on to her skin with eager, mindless mouths.

Terror swamped her. "Stop it!"

She knocked Langdon's hand from her jaw and slapped at the writhing tentacles. But her hands slipped through them as if they weren't there.

Langdon rose from the couch without taking his gaze from hers. Her lungs seized. Her fingers opened and the stiletto clattered to the floor as she stared helplessly into his fire-touched pupils.

Yesss. The mindless tentacles drank up her fear, *enjoying* it.

She shook her head from side to side. Her knees felt like jelly.

Look away.

But she couldn't. She was ensnared, helpless as a trout in a net.

Breathe in. Breathe out.

A sharp rock of fear lodged in her throat.

I can't. Hopelessness welled up inside her.

Yes, you can. This isn't you—it's him. He's making you feel this way.

Somehow, she managed to drag her gaze from Langdon's. Her breath shuddered in. She stared at the floor, chest heaving, and stopped her useless slapping at the tentacles.

"Get them off me," she said. She tried to make it a command, but it came out more like a plea.

He stalked toward her. "I want you." A cold statement, spoken through set lips.

She blinked. "What? No."

"You still think to fight me?" His brows bunched in a baffled frown, and the sucking sensation receded.

She took a deep breath and lifted her chin. "I won't bargain with a man who's attacking me."

A considering pause. Then he nodded. "Very well." As suddenly as the tentacles had appeared, they disappeared.

She backpedaled, getting as far from him as she could. When her back hit a bookcase she halted, sucking in oxygen, skin crawling.

Langdon picked up her stiletto, tossed it into the air. It transformed into a small brown bat and with a high-pitched squeal, shot across the room straight toward Rosana.

She stilled. What kind of Gift did Langdon have, that he could bring inanimate objects to life?

The bat circled her head, its tiny face inquisitive, its scent wild, earthy, and then flapped away, curiosity satisfied, to perch on a window valence.

The prince stalked toward her, hand outstretched. "Come."

She forced herself to take it. His fingers were cool, firm.

He drew her toward the table. "Sit," he said, and it wasn't a request. "Eat my food. Drink my wine. And then we'll talk."

She moistened her lips. The best thing was to buy some time. Dion would come for her, and Cleia.

And then there was Adric. He'd left before her.

Which meant he was probably already in Virginia.

Ice sheeted down her spine. What if her being at the court somehow set off the timeline that led to his death?

The prince pulled out a chair for her. She sank numbly into it. As he took the seat beside her, an ornate silver spoon appeared on the table next to the fish stew.

"Eat." Langdon nudged the bowl in her direction.

26

*D*ion practically flew south, Rui and the others fanning out to either side so that their motorcycles formed a five-man arrow with him at the point. Just let the humans try and stop him.

Fortunately, it was a Wednesday morning in January. Even I-95 wasn't that crowded.

He clenched the handlebars, white-knuckled, trying not to picture all the ways a young female could be hurt. If he was going to save his sister, he needed to stay calm, in control.

But this was Rosana. The pup who'd owned his heart from the day Nisio do Rio had emerged beaming from the bedroom he shared with Dion's mom and announced that after four boys, Ula had finally blessed them with a girl. Dion and his three brothers had eyed the tiny bundle with awe.

Nisio had passed her to Dion first. "We're calling her Rosana Marie."

"Rosana Marie," he'd breathed. She was so light, like a handful of flowers. He'd held her so carefully, terrified of somehow hurting her, and cautiously touched his lips to her petal-soft brow. She'd scrunched up her little nose, scenting him, and they'd all chuckled.

"You'll take care of her," Nisio had stated. "If anything happens to her mama or me."

He'd met his *papai's* silver eyes. "Of course."

She's smart, he told himself now. *And she knows how to handle herself.*

Cleia was always telling him not to underestimate his sister.

As they neared the exit for downtown Baltimore, Rui moved up beside him. "I vote we get off here," he called above the roar of the motors. "Check out Savonett's den." They both knew its approximate location, even though a spell kept it hidden.

Dion frowned, not wanting to stop for even a few minutes. "Why?"

Rui rolled a big shoulder. "A hunch. But we're flying blind here."

Dion hesitated. He'd grown up with Rui, the two of them brothers in all but blood. He trusted the shark fada's instincts.

The Baltimore exit loomed ahead. "Let's do it," he called back, and veered right, Tiago and the other two men following. They rumbled through the eastside until they came to Adric's street.

Leaving the bikes in a vacant lot that smelled of garbage and piss, they strode down the sidewalk, Dion and Rui in the lead. The few people they encountered took one look at their faces and moved aside. One man did an about-face and walked rapidly in the opposite direction.

Rui stalked forward, nostrils flared. The shark fada could pick out a single person's scent in a crowd of hundreds.

"There." He indicated a run-down brick house with three concrete steps leading to a faded green door. The bushes needed a trim, and a rusted porch swing took up most of the narrow porch.

"You scent Rosana?"

"*Sim,*" was the terse reply. "And Savonett, both recent."

Behind him, Tiago cursed.

They strode down the driveway. The first thing Dion saw was Rosana's backpack on the ground near the shed. Crumpled nearby were her hoodie and a knit hat, and a single black boot lay a few yards away.

He gave a hard swallow. He'd known something was wrong, but seeing her belongings scattered forlornly on the grass brought it home in vivid, terrifying color.

Rui touched his arm. "It doesn't mean anything. We already know she's not here."

"But it proves she didn't go with that bastard willingly." Dion pawed through the backpack, Tiago at his side, hoping for some clue, but all it held was the other boot, a pair of socks, a change of clothes—and the silver charm bracelet.

Hades. His fingers tightened on the charm. He and Tiago exchanged an apprehensive look.

Rui jerked a dagger from a hip sheath and leapt in front of Dion. "Up there." He indicated the shed roof.

Dion let go of the backpack and grabbed his own dagger. Tiago and the other two men ranged themselves at his back, knives ready.

Marjani Savonett dropped lightly to the ground in front of them. She took a fighter's crouch, a knife in each hand, lips peeled to reveal lethal canines.

"What the fuck are you doing in my brother's backyard?"

Dion pushed in front of Rui. "Looking for my sister."

Marjani's gaze flicked to the backpack, and he knew she scented Rosana. "She was here? With Adric?"

He nodded. "She left a note saying she was coming to him. That was last night. But this morning, she called on Cleia for help. We traced her to southern Maryland and then lost her."

"That's a good two hours from here. Even if she was with Adric last night—and I'm not saying she was—why would he take her that far from Baltimore?"

"That's what I'm trying to find out."

"Look somewhere else, then. Adric would never hurt her."

"Then why leave her backpack here? And her boots?"

A bewildered look crossed Marjani's catlike face. "I don't know," she admitted.

Rui sheathed his knife to sniff the grass. "The scent—" He shook his head. "Adric's scent on her is strong, but there's another, more recent scent. And Rosana was afraid. There was a fight, I think."

Dion pushed past Marjani to crouch beside him. "An earth fada."

"The brown wolf," Rui confirmed. He looked up at Marjani. "One of your brother's lieutenants—Luc."

She sheathed her knives and dropped to all fours, scrutinizing the slight depression the backpack had left in the wet grass. She inhaled deeply. They all heard her breath catch.

Dion grabbed her arm. "What is it?"

She shook her head. "I have to think," she said, tight-lipped.

"Damn it." He gave her a shake. "If you know something, tell us."

Her eyes flashed with the blue of her cougar. "Get your goddamn hands off me."

Suddenly, a tall blond male appeared out of nowhere—Fane Morningstar, Marjani's quarter-fae mate. He shoved his face into Dion's. "You heard the woman. Let her go."

Rui clamped a hand on Morningstar's shoulder, but Dion shook his head, and he let the other man go.

Dion released Marjani. "My apologies," he told her as he and Rui came to their feet. "You understand, I'm worried about my sister."

Marjani and her mate rose as well. Tiago and the other men closed in, and she bared her teeth. "Back off."

Dion raised a hand. "Let her talk." To Marjani, he said, "I would consider any help you can give me a personal favor. Rui is correct—my sister is with this wolf?"

She exchanged a glance with her mate.

They know something.

Fear for Rosana chewed at Dion's insides, but he forced

himself to wait calmly. Adric's sister wasn't a woman you could push.

"Do Mar is right," she said. "It was Luc. But he's not a lieutenant—not anymore."

"He was demoted?"

She gave an unhappy shake of her head. "Not really. He accepted a fae's *geas*. Adric had to expel him from the clan, at least until he serves out his term. But Luc shouldn't be in Baltimore. We've been looking for him ourselves."

"So you're saying that if he took Rosana, it wasn't with your brother's permission."

"That's right. But—" The cougar fada scraped a hand over her wiry black hair.

"Tell me. Please."

"You say you traced her to southern Maryland?"

He nodded. "A few miles from the state line."

"Fuck." She dropped her hand back to her side. "Adric's gone, too. And I'm pretty sure he's on his way to Virginia. To the New Moon Court."

"He didn't tell his second where he was going?" That was Rui.

"No." Her mouth flattened. "He knew I'd never let him go alone."

Dion frowned. What was the Baltimore alpha mixed up in now? "But why go to New Moon in the first place?"

"To protect me, damn it."

"Jani," warned her mate.

She hitched a shoulder. "What does it matter if they know?" she said. "In fact, maybe it could help." She turned back to Dion. "It's me the prince really wants."

Rui made a small sound.

They knew, of course, that someone in the Baltimore clan had slain Langdon's only surviving son, but they'd assumed it was Adric. Now, the pieces of the puzzle rearranged themselves in a way that made perfect sense.

Dion lowered his voice to a sub-vocal level. "It was you who killed Tyrus."

She jerked her chin in assent.

"To save Jace Jones and my daughter Evie," Morningstar added in equally low tones. "And it was Adric who made the bastard's body disappear."

"Doing all of us a huge favor," muttered Rui. He'd argued for years that Merry would be safer with Tyrus dead.

"But what the fuck does this have to do with Rosana?" Tiago demanded.

"Nothing," Marjani said. "Unless..."

"What?" Dion said. "Please, tell us. Even the smallest piece of information could help."

The cougar fada met his eyes. "Unless the prince knows how Adric feels about her."

"And that is—?"

"She's his mate."

No. Deus, *no.* "Not if I have anything to do with it," he grated.

Beside him, Tiago shook his head, although he seemed unsurprised.

"Take it easy." Marjani glowered back. "He hasn't claimed her. He doesn't want this any more than you do."

Rui set a hand on Dion's arm. "Whether he's claimed her isn't important. What's important is what the prince believes." To Marjani, he said, "You think the wolf took her to New Moon?"

"I don't know. He's not under a *geas* to the prince, he's under a *geas* to a fae lady. But she's half night fae—she might be at New Moon."

Dion's stomach tightened. He had a bad feeling about this fae lady. "What's her name—this half night fae?"

"Lady B," Morningstar said, confirming Dion's suspicions. "I believe you've had some trouble with her yourself."

"We did," Dion replied grimly. Blaer had tried to kidnap his brother Nic's young daughter for some sick purpose of her own.

Morningstar spread his hands. "I'm afraid that's all we know."

"My thanks," Dion said. "I won't forget this."

Fear beat in his blood. If Adric's sister was right, then Rosana was at the night fae court...or worse, Blaer's captive.

The fae who amused herself by capturing fada and forcing them to live out their lives in iron cages.

He spun on his heel, rapping out, "Let's go," in Portuguese to his men.

"*Sim.*" Rui was right with him. "I know a way inside New Moon."

"Wait." Marjani raced after him. "Take me, too."

"No." He kept moving. Adric's sister was an unknown quantity —who knew what she'd do once they were in Virginia?

She kept pace with him. "My bike's on the next block. It will only take me a minute to get it." She grabbed his arm. "You owe me, my lord. Remember?"

His stride checked. The den of river fada who'd kidnapped her had included two former Rock Run men, and Dion would always wonder if he could've somehow prevented the attack. He'd promised then that if Marjani ever needed anything, she had only to ask.

"Come, then," he growled. "But you'll be under my command, understand? You'll do nothing without my express permission."

"Understood." She hurried down an alley, her mate following.

"I'm coming, too," he declared, and a low-voiced argument ensued.

Dion didn't wait to hear the outcome. He broke into a jog for the motorcycles, the other men at his heels. Let Marjani keep up if she could.

But as they turned onto the I-95 ramp, she zoomed up on a slim black bike built for speed, her long-limbed mate's arms wrapped around her waist, and with a terse nod at Dion, fell in behind him and his men.

27

She was in.

Blaer's mouth curved as she followed Olivier down the wide staircase to the starkly elegant foyer.

No windows, but the fae lights had been shaped into disembodied torches. They floated near black marble walls, their imitation flames flickering purple and blue. The floor was a white-and-black checkerboard marble, and in a far corner, a lush arrangement of creamy flowers and vinca spilled from an onyx bowl on a stainless steel stand.

A lean, black-haired woman with a face like a fox's—all high cheekbones and pointed chin—stepped out of the shadows. "Welcome home, daughter."

Blaer's smile warped into something dangerous as the butler faded discreetly into the background. Now, Fleur claimed her. The woman who'd sent her to live with the ice fae when she was just a child, tearing her from everything she knew with no warning.

"Mother." Blaer descended the last step to the foyer and they air-kissed.

Fleur wore heels and a chic silver shift that showed off her long legs. Funny. Blaer had never realized that she'd unconsciously emulated her mother's signature style.

Unlike Blaer, though, Fleur wore the high priestess's black star around her neck. So her mother's scheming had paid off.

"How kind of you to greet me," Blaer murmured as she stepped back.

A shrug of her mother's bare shoulder. They both knew kindness had little to do with it.

Fleur tipped her head to one side. "How is your father, anyway?"

It was Blaer's turn to shrug. "Sindre suggested I...leave." As her mother surely knew. "So here I am. And you?" Her gaze raked over her mother's slight body, taking in the bite mark just above the silver dress's low neckline. "How is the prince?"

As a ten-year-old child, she'd clung to Fleur, begged to be allowed to stay. But her mother had been adamant that she leave. It hadn't been until Blaer was an adult that she'd understood why she'd been sent to Iceland. Her mother had caught the eye of Prince Langdon, and she wanted no reminder of her half ice-fae child at the court.

Especially a child sired by the ice fae king himself.

The ice fae hadn't known what to do with Blaer, and her father had taken only a slight interest in her. When she'd tried one too many times to feed on the other fae at his court, Sindre had forced her into a tower with only goblins and the occasional elf for company. The fae governess he'd provided to educate her had only 'ported in for a short period each day.

For a decade, she'd only been let out of the tower for occasional visits, until she'd grown old enough to play Sindre's games and he'd decided it amused him to let her rejoin his court.

Fleur brushed a cool finger down Blaer's cheek.

Blaer stiffened. Even as a child, her mother had rarely touched her. She hadn't needed to. A night fae could inflict a world of pain without any physical contact.

"You've grown," Fleur murmured. "Become a beautiful young woman...and a powerful one."

So that's what this was about. Blaer's mouth twisted. But she'd play along, see what her mother wanted.

"And I see you've been appointed high priestess. You must have...pleased the prince."

Fleur's full lips lifted in a catlike smile. "He seems satisfied." She glanced at Olivier, standing at attention by the front door. The butler was doing his best to resemble a blank-faced statue, but they both knew he was listening.

"Langdon has granted you a place at the court?"

"He has."

"Good." Her mother nodded at Olivier, indicating he should precede them out the door. "Come, I'll walk you to your new lair."

"As you wish."

Outside, the temperature was just above freezing, but to a woman who'd spent two decades in Iceland, it was practically balmy. Her mother, though, concealed a shiver. She must have rushed to Langdon's lair the instant she heard Blaer had arrived.

And how *had* she heard so quickly?

Blaer eyed Olivier. No, the elderly butler wouldn't risk his well-paying position to spy for Fleur. But that didn't mean someone else in Langdon's household wasn't a spy. She filed that away for possible future use.

More interesting was that her mother appeared unaffected by the noon sun. She donned a pair of sunglasses but didn't seem concerned that the skin on her face and arms was exposed. Blaer recalled a time when her mother wouldn't have been able to face even the weak winter sunlight except at dusk or dawn.

Blaer wasn't the only one who'd increased in power in the years she'd been away.

"You came from France?" Fleur asked.

"Paris," Blaer confirmed, unsurprised at this evidence that her mother had had her watched.

"Such a lovely city, especially this time of year. Short days and lights everywhere. Did you pick up that dress there?" Some of the world's top fae design houses were located in the French capital.

"I did."

"It suits you."

Olivier took a path through a grove of towering oaks. They followed, discussing fashion as if they'd been separated for only a few days instead of two decades.

Blaer's new home was located on the compound's outskirts, Langdon's way of letting her know she was here on sufferance.

Fleur looked on as Olivier showed Blaer around. Her new lair was smaller than the tower she'd had at Sindre's court, with just two bedrooms, a living room and a small kitchen, but it would do. She didn't plan to remain on New Moon's outer edges for long.

"You may decorate how you wish, of course," the butler murmured as they returned to the living room.

Blaer glanced around. Like the prince's lair, the walls were black Italian marble with narrow windows covered by black-out shades. The furniture was Art Nouveau, all sinuous lines and plush burn-out velvet, and the rug was a dramatic swirl of black and white. The rest of the apartment was decorated in a similar style.

"This will do." The twins would have to sleep in the second bedroom, but Jon was often gone on assignments anyway. He was her eyes and ears in the fae world, while Krysten stayed close.

And Luc would sleep in her bed—or on the marble floor. The choice was his.

Her mother eyed her thoughtfully. Then her mouth curved. "I'll see you at dinner. Introduce you around. They'll be dying to see how you turned out."

They shared their first genuine smile.

"I look forward to it," Blaer returned.

28

____

*A*dric *knew*, even as he fought admitting it. He'd have taken a blade to the heart rather than believe Luc would betray him like this.

But the wolf fada knew the location of Adric's den, even if the *look-away* spell prevented him from finding the entrance. If Luc had been outside when Rosana emerged...

Adric was moving before he realized it. He dropped from the tree, shifting in mid-air to land directly in front of Luc.

The wolf fada was much larger than an ordinary lupine. His head reached Adric's chest, and his canines were a good two inches long. But Adric was the dominant and they both knew it.

He grabbed Luc by the scruff of the neck, shook him. "What the fuck have you done?"

Orange tinged with gold glittered over the wolf's coat, and then Luc stood before Adric. He was thinner, all bone and sinew, his eyes burning holes in his craggy face.

His chin jutted out. "I gave that do Rio female to Blaer."

"Rosana?" Adric gaped at him. Even in the face of the evidence, he'd hoped it wasn't true. That Luc would have an explanation.

A black fury filled his head. His heart exploded into frenzied beats.

The cat clawed to be free. *Stole the mate.*

Blood.

Kill.

Adric's hands shot out, wrapped around Luc's throat. "You thrice-damned bastard."

Luc stared back proudly, not even trying to fight. "Did it...for you," he gasped out. "Lady B...ordered me to...capture you. When I saw Rosana...took her instead."

"For me?" Blood pounded in Adric's temples. He gave Luc a hard shake. "You traded an innocent female for *me*. What kind of a goddamned excuse for a man are you?"

Luc's eyes flared. "A man...under a *geas*."

He didn't add that he'd accepted the *geas* to save Marjani. He didn't have to.

Adric forced his fingers to unpeel from Luc's neck. Killing the other man might satisfy his blood lust, but it wouldn't help Rosana, and the wolf had intel that he needed. With a frustrated growl, he shoved Luc away from him.

The wolf stumbled back a few feet before catching himself. He brought a hand to his throat and eyed Adric, breath sawing in and out.

"Where is she?" Adric rapped out.

"Inside." Luc jerked his head in the direction of New Moon. "Lady B took her to the prince. An offering. She's trying to buy her way into the court."

Adric's lip curled. "I don't fucking believe it. You gave Rosana to that fae bitch after what she did to Jani. To *you*."

Blaer had caged not only Marjani, but Luc. And then she'd enslaved him.

"I did it for the clan, too," the wolf retorted. "If the fae get hold of you, the clan would never recover. We—they need you."

Adric's fingers flexed. Gods, he wanted to wrap them around Luc's throat again.

"Fuck what the clan needs. There are some lines you don't cross. Ever."

Luc's gaze slid from his, but he didn't apologize. He clearly believed he'd done the right thing.

Adric shook his head in disgust. He'd known Luc since they were both cubs, but now he wondered if he'd ever truly known the other man at all.

Inside, his cat crouched, a concentrated ball of rage. Aching to sink its teeth into Luc's throat, to drench the earth with his blood.

Easy. We need to find out what he knows.

"Why?" he ground out. "Why would the prince want Rosana?"

"He's a fae." The wolf shrugged a shoulder. "Since when do they need a reason to be S.O.B.s?"

It wasn't a lie, but Adric recognized evasion when he heard it. He scraped a hand over his spiky hair. Luc wasn't telling him everything, but maybe he couldn't.

"You say Lady B wants to join the New Moon court?"

A shrug. "She can't return to Iceland—the ice fae king banished her from his court for a fae year-and-a-day."

Adric nodded. "Jani told me."

"The night fae are her mother's people, but they don't want her, either. They pawned her off on the ice fae when she was still a kid."

"Figures." Adric snorted. The night fae would devour their own young if they didn't need them to pass on their precious bloodlines. "But that doesn't explain why the prince would want Rosana. Me, I can understand. Take me, and Jani will come running."

Their eyes met. They both knew the prince would do just about anything to get his hands on Marjani.

"But Rosana?" Adric shook his head. "He must know it will bring Rock Run down on him. They're a powerful clan, and everyone knows the sun fae queen has a soft spot for Rosana."

Luc gave a noncommittal grunt. He seemed distracted. A drop of sweat trickled down his face. At his sides, his fingers twitched.

Suddenly, he lunged. Adric flung himself to the side, but Luc's fingers closed on his quartz.

Adric jerked. It was like Luc had plunged his hand into his chest and wrapped his fingers around his beating heart. He couldn't think, couldn't breathe, his whole being consumed with a deep, visceral agony.

He shoved at Luc, but the other man held on grimly.

"Sorry." His old friend's face was a stony mask. "She gave me a direct order. I can't disobey." He gave the quartz a hard squeeze.

Adric bit down on a scream as more pain jolted through him. His eyes locked on Luc's own quartz, just inches from his face.

He scrabbled for it, missed. Tried again.

Claws slid out on Luc's free hand. He slashed at Adric's forearm, ripping him to the bone, but Adric was in too much pain to register it.

There.

His fingers closed on Luc's quartz. He glared into the wolf's eyes, using all the dominance at his command. Praying it would be enough to overcome the *geas*, at least temporarily.

"Release my quartz. *Now*."

Luc shuddered. Sweat poured down his face. But he gripped the pendant even tighter.

Pain lashed at Adric like a fiery whip. Scorching through his veins in an unending shriek of agony.

His body jerked, but he kept up the pressure. "Let. It. Go."

Luc's gaze slid sideways—and then he released the pendant and stumbled back.

The absence of pain was stunning. Adric sucked in a breath. Another breath, and then he realized he'd let go of Luc's quartz.

Fortunately, the other man was in no shape to fight. He bent forward, hands on his thighs, chest heaving.

Adric didn't wait for him to recover. Jerking his dagger from its sheath, he slammed Luc to the forest floor. Straddling his abdomen, he touched the sharp iron edge to the soft place beneath the jaw where Luc's right carotid pulsed.

"Don't move. Don't even *breathe*. Understand?"

Luc hissed as the poisonous metal seared his skin. He stilled, resignation sketched on his face.

"Speak." Adric pressed the sharp edge a little deeper. "Tell me you understand. You won't move until I say so."

"Yes." Luc swallowed. "My lord."

Adric sheathed the dagger and dragged off his quartz, dangling it from his fingers. Blood ran down his arm. He ignored it to swing the stone back and forth on its leather cord. Deep within, a fiery bronze mixed with blue flared to life.

"Look at my quartz."

"No." Luc squeezed his eyes shut.

Adric growled. "Look at it, you son of a bitch. *Now*."

Luc shook his head, but Adric was still his alpha, even if he was technically no longer a member of the clan. His wolf wouldn't let him fight too hard, especially now, when Adric's command didn't interfere with Blaer's *geas*.

He opened his eyes. They were dull gold. Flat, hopeless.

Adric gave a hard swallow. For a few desolate seconds, he was back in the abandoned den where his uncle had imprisoned Luc for twelve long months.

By then, Adric and Marjani were on the run from their uncle. Leron Savonett had tortured and starved Luc for months, but he'd never given up their hidey-holes. Adric knew he'd have died rather than betray them.

When Adric and Marjani had finally tracked Luc down, they found him manacled to the wall with an iron cuff around one wrist. The constant exposure to iron had weakened him, making it impossible for him to heal. He lay curled up on the stone floor, his body a rack of bones on which to hang his skin. Open sores on his manacled wrist. His back bloody from a recent beating.

The eyes Luc had lifted to Adric and Marjani had held that same bleak hopelessness. Even as a teenager, the wolf fada had rarely smiled.

But at the sight of them, a corner of his mouth had lifted. "About time you showed up."

"Don't do this," Luc rasped now. "Just kill me."

Adric's throat worked. "I can't," he whispered.

Back and forth.

Luc might hate Adric for hypnotizing him, but at least he'd be alive.

"Damn you to Hades." The wolf's gaze locked on the quartz swaying, pendulum-like, above his nose.

Adric pumped energy into the crystals. Inside, the flames flared brighter until they were reflected in Luc's pupils, eerie blue flames in the glistening black circles.

"You'll take me to Lady B."

"Yes," Luc said in a flat voice.

"Can you get me through New Moon's wards?" He'd planned to use his Gift of hypnotism to trick a guard into sneaking him inside, but entering with Luc was even better. The wards would open for Luc, and Adric could slip inside with him.

"Yes."

"I want your promise on your honor as a wolf."

"Yes. On my honor as a wolf, I will get you through the wards."

Gotcha. Adric's mouth curved in a feral smile. "Where are your clothes?"

"There." Luc's arm swung up, pointed into the trees.

"Take me to them."

Luc immediately started to his feet. Adric had to scramble out of his way.

The wolf fada walked in the direction he'd pointed, halting in front of an oak tree, where his clothes were bundled into a leather jacket and wedged into a crook of the tree. He stood at attention, awaiting instructions.

Adric was surprised at how easy Luc was to control; it was as if he'd surrendered completely to Adric's will. But then, he was Luc's alpha, whether or not he'd been expelled from the clan. When a man like Luc gave you his loyalty, he'd walk through hell or high water for you.

"Give me the clothes," he told Luc, "and then shift to your wolf."

While the other man obeyed, Adric used his quartz to heal the slashes on his arm. After they'd scabbed over, he dropped the leather cord over his head and took the clothes from Luc.

They were a little big, but they'd do. He tucked the sheathed dagger beneath the T-shirt and laced on the lug-sole boots. If a fada came across their tracks, they'd see Luc's prints, not his. Lastly, he put on the black hoodie, pulling up the hood to hide his distinctive hair. The leather jacket he returned to the crook of the oak. It would only be in the way if he had to shift—or fight.

Weak as he was, Luc took a long time to shift. Too long.

Adric stood helplessly by as his old friend wavered between man and wolf, sparkles flickering anemically over his skin. If Luc couldn't complete the shift, he'd die, his body a grotesque mass of incompatible organs.

He growled. "Focus, damn you. You can do this."

A weak glimmer of orange, and at last Luc's huge brown wolf appeared. He was too thin in this form as well, his fur dull, patchy. At this rate, he'd never survive his decade with Blaer.

"Fuck, I'm sorry." He touched Luc's head. "When this is over, I promise I'll do what I can. There's got to be a way to break the damn *geas*."

The wolf's breath sighed out. Then he gave Adric's hand a firm nip. The message was clear: *Stay out of this.*

Adric scowled down at him. "I'm the alpha, remember?"

Luc growled lowly.

It was Adric's turn to sigh. "At least let me give you a shot of healing energy."

At Luc's nod of assent, he ran his quartz over the wolf's body. He was still thin—there wasn't much Adric could do about that, but his fur grew shinier, the patches closing over until he had a thick coat again.

Luc nuzzled his chest in gratitude.

Adric grimaced. "Don't thank me yet."

He lifted his quartz, dangling it in front of the wolf's face.

He paused, sorting his thoughts. He had to get the command just right. Once they were inside, and especially if Blaer caught sight of them, he had to make sure the compulsion to obey him, Adric, was stronger than the power her *geas* exerted on Luc.

When he was ready, he infused his voice with dominance. "Take me to Rosana do Rio. *Now*. No detours, except whatever's necessary to keep the night fae from detecting me. Understood?"

The wolf whined...and then turned and trotted out of the trees. Adric dropped his quartz back over his head, tucking it into the T-shirt along with the dagger, and strode after him.

Luc didn't take the shimmering fae path, confirming Adric's suspicion it was booby-trapped, or maybe even an illusion. Instead, he veered right.

They circled the compound, Luc padding stiffly beside him, his will under Adric's command. Adric swallowed something acrid. He'd promised himself he'd never compel any of his lieutenants or close friends.

The Darktime isn't over. The prince will destroy your clan from the inside out.

Was this how it started? With Adric himself?

As they passed through two longleaf pines, a small circle shimmered into being, widening into a wolf-sized portal. Luc stepped through it, Adric glued to his side.

His spine tingled. He pulled back his shoulders, his stance tough, as if he were a fada bodyguard. Someone who belonged. Meanwhile, his gaze roamed the compound, his body poised for anything.

A second ticked past, then another and another. From a nearby oak, a raven studied Adric with beady brown eyes. Finally, the portal behind them contracted shut.

He was in.

He blew out a breath, took a cautious step forward. It was darker in here—too dark—the weak sunlight barely penetrating the forest canopy. Something rustled behind him. He spun around, but nothing was there. Then it was in front of him, although he still couldn't see anything.

Until he realized the shadows themselves had come alive.

They blotted out the sky, slithered over the vine-covered buildings, morphed into nightmarish creatures that grew larger until they loomed over him and Luc before dissolving, only to reappear somewhere else. The worst were the faces, their eyes wide, their mouths stretched into predatory howls—or worse, smiles.

It was the Darktime amped up ten times over.

Breathe. Stay calm. Think of something good, something that makes you happy. Making love to Rosana, or playing soccer with the cubs.

Then it got worse. Magic shivered over Adric's skin...black, cold magic.

His nape tightened. Memories pricked his skin like sharp, painful darts.

Luc hadn't been the only one tortured to feed the night fae's craving for negative emotions. After he and Marjani had sprung Luc, Leron had finally captured them. They'd been lucky, though. His uncle had only let the beatings and torture go on for a few days, because he still had a use for them.

Marjani, he hadn't touched at all. No, she'd been chained to the wall, forced to watch as Adric took the beatings for them both.

When he'd deemed them sufficiently broken, he'd had them brought to him. Adric had been told he was leaving the country to fight as a mercenary for the fae, and Marjani had been ordered to whore herself to Jumar.

It was Leron Savonett's final mistake.

Adric's knees locked. Caught in the dark memories, he couldn't make himself continue moving forward.

Beside him, Luc seemed unaffected, probably because unlike Adric, he had permission to be here. He continued forward alone until he realized Adric was no longer following. Turning his head, he yipped a question.

"Right behind you." Adric steeled himself to walk into the nightmarish shadows. For Rosana, he'd enter Hades itself.

Luc sniffed the air and then aimed for Langdon's lair.

The shadows sucked at Adric, but the darkness lessened. His whole body slumped in relief.

Time to hide.

Adric removed Luc's boots and hid them under a bush. Then he touched his quartz, drawing energy from the tiny crystals to cloak himself. But he'd have to be careful—the energy drain was tremendous. He had fifteen minutes, maybe less, before the crystals ran out of power.

Luc swung his head from side to side, nostrils flared, clearly wondering where Adric had gone. Then he must've picked up Adric's scent because he gave a wolfy shrug and turned down a path of smooth white pebbles.

This time, when the darkness sucked at him, Adric twisted his fingers through Luc's ruff, and as he'd hoped, whatever protected the wolf spread to him as well. Together, they followed the path through the trees and around the still black pond.

The entrance to Langdon's lair was down a short flight of granite steps. Ivy spilled down either side of the tall door, a dark, polished wood with a triple moon carved into the top.

He stilled, inhaled. Lady Blaer had come this way.

And even though he couldn't scent Rosana, she was also nearby. He knew it with the same certainty that he knew the location of each of his clan members at any given moment.

"You go first," he told Luc in an undertone. "Distract the prince so I can get Rosana out. And Luc? If someone asks, you'll say you never saw me. That's an order."

The wolf's head swung up and down.

Adric tried the door handle. He wasn't surprised when it moved—Langdon had little to fear in his own compound. But as the door swung open on silent hinges, uneasiness crept up his spine.

This had been too damn easy.

Rosana's warning played in his head. Was he walking into a trap?

He can't see you. He doesn't know you're here.

The foyer stretched two stories up, and was completely empty except for an extravagant arrangement of white flowers in a large black bowl.

He hesitated, his uneasiness increasing, as Luc stepped across the threshold.

Then he scented Rosana. Faint but distinctive, and with an underlying tang of fear that made his chest clench.

His lips drew back in a silent snarl.

Thrice-damned, fucking fae.

He followed Luc into the foyer. Behind him, the wood door thudded shut.

29

On the level below, a door opened and closed. Claws clicked on a marble floor.

Rosana's gaze flew to Langdon, but he didn't seem to have noticed. Instead, he set cool fingers on her wrist and urged the spoon toward her mouth.

"Eat." So soft, almost gentle, but steel edged his tone.

The portly butler appeared in the door. "My lord."

"Yes, Olivier?"

"There's a fada in the foyer."

No. Rosana froze, the spoon clenched in her hand. *You stubborn ass.*

Langdon's mouth turned down. "Deal with him."

Olivier inclined his shiny bald head. "As you wish. However, I believe he is one of Blaer's people. A wolf."

Not Adric, then. Rosana let out a breath.

The prince flicked her a look, no doubt detecting her agitation with those eerie senses of his. He rose to his feet.

"Alone?" he asked his butler. "You saw no one else?"

"No, my lord."

"I see. Well, let the wolf upstairs, and then inform Captain Quade that our wards have been breached."

Olivier gave a discreet cough. "The wolf has permission to pass through the wards."

"But the man with him does not."

The butler's eyes widened slightly. Then he nodded. "Very good, my lord." He made his stately way out of the room.

Rosana was still holding the spoon. She set it back on the linen napkin and stared unseeingly at the table.

The man had to be Adric. But why hadn't Olivier seen him?

Langdon pushed his chair in but remained behind it, his long, elegant fingers curled around the seatback. She felt him eyeing her downturned head.

When she glanced up, he arched a single diamond-studded brow. "Nothing to say? Perhaps you know why Lord Adric is here?"

She blanked her face. She couldn't let him know what she'd Seen. It could be the very information that tipped the balance and led to Adric's death.

"I don't speak for Lord Adric," she parried. "But I can tell you his animal isn't a wolf."

Langdon sighed. "I'm aware of that. And I didn't say Adric *was* a wolf. He's the man who entered with the wolf."

Rosana spread her hands in genuine confusion. "I'm sorry, but I don't know anything about a wolf."

Or did she? She stilled.

The wolf had to be Luc. And more, she'd bet a month's pay that he was Adric's former lieutenant, the fada who'd been with Blaer in Lewes. In fact, it was probably Luc who'd been seen at Rock Run earlier this week. The question was, why was Adric with him?

The wolf was outside the door now. Langdon strolled across the room to a bookcase and removed a small packet from an inlaid ebony-and-ivory box.

Rosana came to her feet as the wolf entered the library. She'd never seen Luc as his animal, but the scent fit. And damn, he was big. His head was almost level with hers, his eyes a deep amber just a few shades away from the gold of his man-form.

Her nostrils twitched. Adric *was* here. But why couldn't she see him?

Langdon's mouth turned down. "Does Blaer know you're here?" he asked Luc.

The wolf peeled his upper lip in a tooth-baring snarl.

"And you, Adric," the prince added. "Did you think I wouldn't know the instant you crossed through the portal?"

No reply.

But in the silence that fell, Rosana detected slow, almost-imperceptible breathing to Luc's left. Without moving her head, she slid a look in its direction. There was an odd, man-size disturbance in the air that made it difficult to see the bookshelf behind it.

Her heart jumped—and then sank. She smoothly turned back to Langdon. "All I see is a wolf, and I told you, Adric's not a wolf."

"Yes," the prince returned with a chilly little smile. "You did tell me that." He tore open the packet and tossed an acrid-smelling gray powder right at the man-sized disturbance.

Luc surged forward, aiming for Langdon's throat, but the prince threw up an arm to block him. The two fell to the floor, Luc on top, his teeth sunk into Langdon's forearm.

The gray powder outlined Adric and the dagger in his right hand. Swiping the powder off his face, he stalked across the library floor. Langdon was on top now, his hands wrapped around Luc's muzzle, the gash on his arm spattering blood everywhere.

"*Go,*" Adric growled at Rosana as he circled the two combatants, searching for an opening.

"I don't think so," she muttered. She shot a longing glance at the brown bat that had once been her stiletto and then grabbed the raven statue from its pedestal instead. It made a nice, solid weight in her hands.

She eyed the fighters. Adric was completely visible now, his body coated in the bad-smelling gray powder. He sliced at Langdon with his dagger, but the night fae rolled, shoving Luc in front of him. The blade slashed through the heavy muscles of the wolf's left shoulder.

Luc turned and snapped at Adric, and then froze.

A horrorstruck look crossed Adric's face. "Fuck. I'm sorry, bro."

He eased the knife out just as the prince grabbed Luc's ruff and slammed him headfirst onto the floor. The wolf made a final, jerky movement before collapsing, motionless.

Langdon flowed to his feet and faced Adric, taking a martial arts stance, arms raised and knees bent with one leg forward.

Adric prowled forward, the dagger loose and ready in his hand. His eyes were a cougar-blue, his expression hard, predatory. Rosana could almost see the big cat overlaying the human.

Langdon stepped backwards. He was at his desk now. Reaching behind him, he grabbed a paperweight and flung it at Adric. It turned in mid-air into a thick, hissing snake with a copperhead's distinctive hourglass markings. With a growled curse, Adric slapped it away. The snake landed on the floor, and he bent and chopped off its head with a single stroke of his knife.

Langdon's eyes flickered red and Rosana growled.

Oh no, you don't.

She regripped the raven, palms sweaty, and moved to the prince's left.

Adric indicated her with his chin. "Let Rosana go. This has nothing to do with her. She's not even a member of my clan."

Langdon tilted his head. "A trade?"

"What kind of trade?"

"Your sister for Rosana."

Her head jerked back. "No!"

Neither man looked at her.

"And if I say yes," Adric asked, "what would happen to Marjani?"

"That's between me and her. But I swear, she'll have a chance. More than she gave my son."

What were they talking about? Rosana clenched the raven, her gaze darting between the two men.

Adric's jaw clenched. "No fucking way. You get me, not my sister. And no matter what, Rosana goes free. That's non-negotiable."

Rosana had heard enough. She lunged, swinging the statue like a club at Langdon's head, but he ducked and flowed sideways so the blow glanced off his shoulder instead. A long leg swept out, knocking her own legs from beneath her.

She landed on her ass, the raven clattering to the marble next to her. But she'd given Adric an opening, and he pounced, dagger aimed at Langdon's throat.

The prince threw up an arm to block him, and with an agile twist of his body, used Adric's own momentum to throw him into a bookcase. Rosana scuttled backward as books showered down around her.

Catlike, Adric turned in mid-air so that his shoulder hit the bookcase instead of his head and landed on his feet, still holding the dagger. He stalked back toward Langdon, and the two men started circling each other again.

Rosana scrambled back to her feet.

Adric jerked his head at her without taking his gaze from the prince. "Get out of here already." To Langdon, he said, "You're dead. Nobody touches my sister. Nobody."

The prince went whiter, if that were possible for such a pale man. "Olivier!" he called.

Adric lunged, slashing the dagger through Langdon's shirt, drawing the poisonous iron across his torso.

Langdon sucked in a breath and danced backward. His eyes narrowed. "Kill me, and you'll never get out of here alive."

"You think I fucking care?" Adric shook his head. "You fae just don't get it, do you?"

The prince took another step back until he could reach his desk again. This time, he grabbed a handful of pens to fling at Adric. They turned into hornets and swarmed his head. Shoving the dagger into his pocket, Adric caught and crushed them with shifter-fast speed, one after another.

Meanwhile, Langdon had circled around Adric. He aimed a kick at Adric's knee cap from the side, which Adric only just evaded. Catching the prince's arm, he jerked him forward and down. His hand chopped down on the back of Langdon's neck. The night fae rolled with it, coming smoothly back to his feet.

The two men turned in a tight circle. Langdon flicked his fingers at the dagger and it turned into another bat that dove for Adric's head. He grabbed it in mid-air, flinging it to the hard floor where it lay, dead.

Adric let his claws and fangs slide out. With a guttural growl, he backed the prince into a corner.

Langdon's eyes narrowed. Shadows gathered at the room's edges.

Despair crawled over Rosana's skin. Hopelessness descended on her in a suffocating cloud. *You can't escape. Why even try?*

Adric gave a hard swallow.

Rosana clenched her fists. "Breathe," she whispered, speaking for herself as much as Adric. "It's him, not us. Don't let him win."

The shadows receded. She sidled along the bookcases, watching for a chance to help Adric. Her foot slipped and she looked down to find the hornets had changed back into pens.

Olivier rapped on the door. "My lord? Is everything okay?"

"Send for the guards!" Langdon called back.

"Pardon me?" The elderly butler opened the door, blinked.

"Send for my guards," Langdon gritted.

"Immediately, my lord." The door closed with a decided click.

Oh, no, you don't.

Rosana sprinted across the room, throwing open the door. She caught Oliver right before he reached the stairs and shoved him face-first against the wall.

"Don't move." She wrenched his arm up, ignoring the pinch of guilt at manhandling an elder. "I don't want to hurt you, but I will if I have to."

Beneath the natty yellow bow tie, the butler's throat worked. "Yes, miss."

"This way." She urged him back down the hall. "What's in there?" She jerked her head at the door opposite the library.

"The prince's bedroom."

Behind her, she heard grunts and a crash. She shot a glance over her shoulder, but all she could see was the still unconscious wolf. If Langdon managed to get a message out to his guards, they were fucked.

"Open the door," she snapped at Olivier, then waited impatiently as he turned the knob with agonizing slowness. "Inside." She punctuated the order with a small shove. As she kicked the door shut behind them, her gaze lit on the sturdy four-poster bed. Perfect.

"Take off your belt."

Olivier undid the buckle, slid the belt from its loops and handed it to her.

"Hands together."

A pained expression crossed the butler's broad face. "Is this necessary, miss?"

"Yes," she snapped. "Now do it."

His mouth thinned, but he presented his hands, palms together. Quickly, she wound the belt around his wrists a couple of times and then looped the rest around one of the bed's thick black posts.

"It's better this way," she told him as she cinched the belt. "You can tell the prince you had no choice."

His mouth lifted in a wry arc. "Next you'll be saying I should thank you."

Their eyes met. So the man had a sense of humor hidden behind that stone face.

"Sorry," she said with a shrug and shot out the door.

Downstairs, the front door crashed open. She darted down the hall long enough to see what looked like an entire cadre of warriors pouring inside.

Langdon had gotten a message out.

She sprinted back to the library, slamming the door shut and turning the key.

The entire room was roiling with shadows. Luc was still unconscious, but Adric and Langdon were in another corner now. Langdon was bleeding from the torso and favoring the arm the wolf had savaged, but he looked better than Adric, who wavered drunkenly from side to side.

He had the dagger again. A quick glance at the floor told her the bat had disappeared.

Unfortunately, the dagger wasn't doing Adric any good. He had it gripped in both hands but could barely keep the point turned up. Blood dripped from a gash in his temple, mixing with the gray powder streaking his face. He looked like a crazed clown.

He glanced at her, scowled. "You're s'pposed…to be gone."

She snatched the dagger from him. "Someone has to save your ass, cat."

She advanced on Langdon. He faded back into the darkest shadow—and disappeared.

With a frustrated growl, she shoved the dagger into her pocket and ran her hands over the wall, just in case Langdon was still there. But the bastard was gone.

The warriors banged on the locked door, demanding entrance.

"Now what?" Adric asked Rosana with a lopsided smile.

"We get the hell out of here."

"Sounds…like a…plan." He walked several unsteady feet and sat down hard next to the wolf. He stroked his friend's fur. "Luc?" When the other shifter didn't move, Adric looked up at Rosana, a perplexed line between his eyes. "He's hurt."

"So are you."

"Oh." He touched his head and then stared at the blood on his fingers.

From across the hall, Olivier was shouting for help.

She gripped Adric's shoulder. "We have to get out of here. The window."

"'Kay." He came onto his hands and knees and then just stayed there, staring at the floor as if he'd never seen marble before.

Outside the door, she heard Olivier explaining the situation to Langdon's guards. There was short silence, and then a loud explosion shook the library.

Hellfire. They were using fae balls.

The door shuddered on its hinges, but the thick wood held. For now.

Rosana crouched next to Adric, trying to lift him up. But he was heavy, with a fada's extra solid bones. She stifled a sob.

"Adric." She tugged on his arm. "Get up, damn it. If they find us here, we're dead."

"Yeah." He nodded sagely—and collapsed. She barely managed to catch him before his head hit the marble. She eased him the rest of the way down onto his stomach. He lay still, head turned to the side, blood seeping out of the wound.

"*No.*" She pressed a fist to her mouth. What was she going to do now?

Next to him, Luc's eyes fluttered open. He whined and nuzzled Adric's shoulder.

The door shuddered with a second explosion, and then another.

Bang. Bang.

The hinges shrieked as they started to give.

She lurched into action, grabbing Adric's wrists and dragged him toward the nearest window. Jerking the blind open, she ran her hands around the sash, frantically searching for a way to open it. But the window was one long oblong of glass with no latch that she could detect.

Giving up, she snatched up the poor, abused raven one last time and swung it as hard as she could at the center of the window. The glass didn't even crack. Instead, she watched, incredulous, as the statue broke instead, its stone head careening sideways and almost landing on Adric.

The door broke from the wall and crashed to the floor. She

tossed the raven's body aside and whipped out Adric's dagger. Five night fae stormed into the library. One set a foot on Luc's neck, stilling his weak, half-conscious movements, while the others surrounded her and the still-unconscious Adric.

She moved in front of him, dagger out. "Stay where you are."

The man who'd led the charge regarded her with icy eyes. "Where's the prince?"

"He 'ported out of here. Or whatever you call that disappearing-into-the-shadows thing he does."

The warrior jerked his head at one of his men. "Find Prince Langdon. The rest of you, take these two."

"Yes, Captain." The three remaining men closed in on her and Adric.

She bared her teeth. "Come any closer, and I'll rip your goddamned hearts out." She knew she wasn't being rational—she was surrounded, with no way out—but her animal wouldn't let them get any closer to Adric. Not while he was injured.

The captain swirled his hand, magician-like, and held it, palm up, fingers spread wide. A purple spark appeared in his palm, expanding into an orb of dark, pulsating light.

A fae ball, night-fae style.

She swallowed sickly. One of those could burn a hole right through you.

"Surrender," he said, "or I'll throw this at your mate, there."

"He's not my mate," she returned dully. But she brought the dagger to her side.

They swarmed around her. The knife was wrenched from her hand. The captain took her arm in a firm grip while two others lifted Adric like a sack of potatoes and carried him toward the door.

Langdon appeared in the doorway.

"My lord." The captain inclined his head respectfully.

"I see you finally realized there were intruders."

The tall warrior's spine went ramrod straight. "My apologies, sir. We didn't detect him when he came through the portal."

Langdon gave a cold nod. "We'll discuss your failure later, Quade. For now, confine the earth fada below. The woman you can leave here."

"No!" She jerked against the captain's confining hand. "You're not taking Adric anywhere without me."

Langdon tilted his head to the side. "You prefer to go with him?"

She raised her chin. "Yes. In fact, I insist on it."

The prince's lips stretched in a chilling smile. Too late, she realized she'd given him permission to imprison her.

"Then we'll be happy to accommodate you both."

30

———

Captain Quade marched Rosana out of the library and down the marble stairs. The two warriors followed with Adric.

It was the first she'd seen the foyer. She had a brief impression of a large, dimly lit space, and then the captain urged her through an open door and down another flight of stairs.

They were in an underground warren with rooms and halls spearing off in multiple directions. As with the foyer, the only lighting came from a few torch-shaped fae lights. She glimpsed a cavernous wine cellar with hundreds of dusty bottles, and a room with an ancient brick hearth that she guessed had once been a kitchen.

Their destination was a short hall with just three doors, all constructed of a thick wood reinforced with iron straps. The men carrying Adric opened the door at the end and tossed him inside.

She flinched as his body thumped against the stone floor.

The captain gestured her after Adric with a mocking smile. "Be my guest, senhorita."

Her throat constricted. The three steps into that small, windowless room were the most difficult of her life, but the need to protect Adric drove her forward.

She had time to see a long wood bench against the far wall and that to her left, there was a rough toilet alongside a metal spout with a thin stream of water flowing into a narrow trough before disappearing down a drain. Then the door thudded shut behind her.

A key turned in the lock, and she was alone in the dark with Adric. The only light came from a slit at the top of the door.

Her eyes went night-glow, but all she could make out were dim gray shapes—Adric, the bench. Her chest tightened.

It felt like a tomb. Small. Airless.

She stumbled to the door, lungs pumping. Not sure what she was going to do, just knowing she had to get out. *Now.*

This side of the door had no handle. She ran her hands over the wood anyway, hissing when her fingertips brushed one of the iron bands.

Behind her, Adric groaned.

She leaned her forehead against the wood.

Calm the fuck down. He's hurt—bad. He needs *you.*

She took a deep breath.

Okay, then.

She'd make Adric as comfortable as possible and then trust that his natural healing ability would take over.

She made her way to the trough, rinsed her burned fingers. The water was ice-cold, fresh from an underground stream. She splashed it on her face and then stuck her head under the thin trickle, gulping water until the dryness in her throat eased.

She was pretty sure she'd glimpsed a cup near the trough. Calmer now, she felt around until her fingers closed on the cool metal. She filled the cup and took it back to Adric. Using a combination of touch and sight, she cleaned the gash on his head before returning to the trough for more water, which she used to rinse the gray powder from his face and hands. She was afraid the powder's bitter smell meant it was poisonous.

Adric moved restlessly, and she touched his cheek. "Adric? You okay?"

He mumbled something and then went limp again.

"That's it, *meu amor.*" She rubbed his shoulder. "Rest. Let your-self heal."

His lips moved, but all that came out was a croak.

"You must be thirsty. Hang on—I'll be right back." She made another trip for water, and then wet a finger and moistened his lips. He tried to suck her finger, so she trickled water into his mouth, but he murmured fretfully and turned his head away.

"Just a little," she said, and kept at him until he took a few sips. Setting the cup down, she sat next to him and eased his head onto her lap. "Rest." She stroked his cheek. "Everything is going to be all right."

It didn't matter that he probably couldn't hear her. Just saying it aloud made her feel better.

She was silent for a time, but that made the darkness creep closer, almost like it was a living being. Like when Blaer had tried to feed on them in Lewes—or Langdon just now.

She shuddered.

It's just your imagination.

At least, she hoped it was. She pulled Adric closer.

"Know something?" She nuzzled his hair. "I love that I can touch you without setting off my Sight. Although right now, I wouldn't mind Seeing how to break us out of here. Because I have to tell you, I just *knew* that I had to be here with you." She grimaced. "Just don't ask me why, because I haven't been much help so far."

She stilled. Not only had she not helped, she was probably why he'd been captured. Because she had the bad feeling that if not for her, Adric wouldn't have rushed into the library like that. He'd have waited to catch Langdon off-guard.

"No." A sick feeling seeped into her belly. "My being here does *not* set off the timeline leading to your death."

In her vision, Adric had been alone. She had to believe that somehow her presence changed things, although that didn't mean she could sit by and let things play out. She had to *do* something. But what?

She resumed stroking him. *Think, Rosana.*

But she was fresh out of ideas. Her only hope was that Cleia had heard her cry for help, and that she and Dion would realize Rosana had been taken to New Moon. If they didn't find her note and blame Adric for her disappearance...

She blew out a breath. *Deus*, what a mess.

She rested the back of her head against the wall. The rush of adrenaline that had carried her through the fight had worn off, leaving her feeling like a deflated balloon. Her eyelashes fluttered down. She forced them open, afraid to go to sleep.

The cell smelled musty, the floor covered with a layer of dust as if no one had been here for a long time. How long would Langdon leave them down here in the dark?

And what if Adric got worse? She was no healer. She could scream herself raw and no one would hear.

Fear clogged her throat. Her breath shortened. Were the walls closing in?

Stop it. That's just what Langdon wants. If you freak out, he wins.

Her chest heaved, shifting the pendant Adric had given her. She pulled it from her shirt, fingered it. As in the prince's library, the amethyst was oddly warm.

Her jaw set. "You do love me. You're just afraid to admit it."

"Mmph."

She glanced down. Adric looked back at her, eyes gleaming a brilliant blue in the gloom.

31

From far off, Adric heard Rosana arguing with Langdon. Was aware of other people in the room, too, all men.

Get the fuck away from her.

His vocal cords vibrated in a growl that only he heard. He tried to rise but couldn't.

Rough hands lifted him, conveyed him down first one flight of stairs, then another. Pain jolted through his head, down his spine. He gritted his teeth and bore it. He would *not* give them the satisfaction of hearing him groaning.

The movement halted. The hands released him and he fell to the floor. His head bounced. A white light exploded behind his eyes. The pain reached a screaming pitch and he passed out.

For a time, everything was blissfully dark. But gradually, sensation returned, and with it the knowledge that Rosana needed him.

He clawed his way back to consciousness.

Cold. Dank.

Hard stone beneath his body.

The musical trickle of water.

Rosana's scent, and the murmur of her voice.

A soft thigh beneath his head...and his head pounding like a moth-erfucker.

"You do love me," she said. "You're just afraid to admit it."

"Mmph." He wasn't sure if he was agreeing or disagreeing, but he did know that he needed to see her.

He forced his eyes open. He was on his back with his head on Rosana's lap. The room was so dark he could barely see a foot in front of his face. His eyes went night-glow.

Rosana gave a tremulous smile, her own irises a luminous aquamarine in the shadowy light. "You're awake."

He grunted, the only sound he could manage right then.

He hurt everywhere. His muscles. His bones. His fingers. His face. Even his toes twinged when he gave them an experimental flex.

But the worst was his head. He fingered his right temple. He vaguely recalled Langdon slamming him face-first into the desk. The blow had reverberated through his skull and down his verte-brae. He was lucky the prick hadn't broken his neck. Thankfully, the wound had already scabbed over, his body drawing on his quartz to speed his healing.

But after that, he didn't recall much. In fact, he couldn't remember exactly how Rosana had come to be involved.

"How long...was I out?"

"About fifteen minutes."

"Fuck." He tried to lift his head off her lap and froze as the dull throbbing in his brain spiked.

"Shh. Don't move." Rosana guided him back onto her thigh. "Rest."

She smoothed a palm over his eyes and nose, down to his chin. The pain eased. His eyelids drifted shut. He nuzzled her hand, both man and cat wanting nothing but to drift off again.

He forced his eyes to open. "Where?" he asked through swollen lips.

"Still in Langdon's lair—a level below the foyer. A prison cell. The door is solid wood reinforced with iron, and there are no windows, just a slot at the top of the door. They didn't bother with a bed, either. Or heat."

His throat worked. "Sorry."

It was coming back to him now. Discovering that Rosana was the night fae's prisoner, rushing to her rescue. He'd have pulled it off if the prince hadn't tossed that damn powder at him. Its bitter scent still clung to his skin.

How the fuck had Langdon known he was there? He'd been careful to stick close to Luc. But he'd been angry with Luc and terrified for Rosana. He must've been leaking emotion, especially when he found Rosana alone with the bastard.

And now they were locked in an underground cell. His heart punched at his rib cage. A cold sweat prickled his skin.

The Darktime.

A dank cell concealed beneath Leron's den. The clanmates who disappeared below never to be seen again. The pervasive scent of fear, as if it had soaked into the very stones.

And the growing conviction that it was only a matter of time before Leron found an excuse to throw him in the cell...or worse, Marjani.

The teenage Adric had tried to appease his uncle, but Leron had seen how the younger clan members turned to his nephew. Hell, he'd known before Adric that he was alpha material.

So Leron had set out to break him.

One by one, everyone Adric loved had been stolen from him. His dad. His mom. Jace's sister. Until the only ones left were a few stubbornly loyal friends like Zuri, Jace, Luc—and Marjani.

That was when his uncle had made his fatal mistake. Go after Adric, and he would've endured it until he was strong enough to challenge for alpha.

But go after Marjani, and all bets were off.

"It's not your fault." Rosana's voice yanked him back to the present. "You've got nothing to be sorry for."

He unclenched his jaw, forced himself to inhale.

"Yes, I do. Luc...was ordered...take me, not you. But when he saw you...figured he'd save me...give you to Blaer instead. Last night...should've made you...go home."

The caresses stopped. "So you knew Luc was outside your den."

"What?" His brow lowered. "No."

"Then this is on Luc, not you. You didn't tell him to take me instead of you, did you?"

"Of course not."

"Then how is it your fault?"

He set a hand to his head. He *knew* he was right. Rosana wouldn't be here if not for him. "You...my guest, in my territory... and...I'm alpha."

"Which makes you the leader, not a god. Luc isn't even a member of your clan anymore."

He blinked. Nobody but Marjani took that no-nonsense tone with him.

"Now shut up and rest." Rosana touched her lips to his forehead. "Concentrate on healing. Because we need you better if we're going to get out of here—and we *are* getting out of here."

His mouth quirked despite the swelling. "Yes, ma'am."

She was right. Beating up on himself wasn't helping anything.

He drew more deeply on his quartz to increase the rate of healing. It would drain the crystals, rendering them useless for a few hours, but it couldn't be helped. In this condition, he was no use to anyone.

He dozed, catlike, relaxed yet aware of his surroundings. Rosana was quiet, too, her hand resting on his shoulder.

An hour or two passed before he opened his eyes, cautiously lifted his head. This time, the pain wasn't so bad.

"Luc?" His gaze skimmed the cell, confirming what he already knew. The wolf fada wasn't with them.

"He's okay," Rosana assured him. "When they took us away, he was just coming around. But I don't know what they did with him."

"Probably sent him back to Blaer."

"Oh." She grimaced. "I'm sorry."

"Yeah. Woman's not right in the head." Still—"Not right to drag you into this. When I found out...could've hurt him myself."

Rosana resumed stroking his face. He let out a grateful sigh. It felt so good.

"It's okay," she said. "If I was under a *geas* to Blaer, I might've done the same thing. I saw how she treats him. She grabbed his quartz and it *hurt*. And she just smiled. She was feeding on his pain."

"Fuck." His stomach clenched. Gods, he hated feeling so damn powerless. "If I could break the *geas* for him, I would."

But Luc had given his word. He'd serve out his time, or die. That's how he was.

Rosana squeezed his shoulder. "I'm sorry," she said again.

Taking her hand, he brought her fingers to his lips in silent thanks.

She leaned down to brush her lips over his. "Thirsty?" When he dipped his chin in assent, she eased his head from her lap and reached for the cup. "Be right back."

Just moving that tiny amount sent another jolt through his skull. But he made himself turn over, then pushed himself up to sitting, slowly, painfully. Halfway up, his stomach rebelled at the change in position, and he had to pause to ride the nausea out. He set his teeth and breathed through it.

By the time Rosana returned, he had his back against the wall, legs stretched in front of him. That was better. He felt more clear-headed. Less vulnerable.

Taking the cup from her, he drained it with small, careful sips. "Thank you," he said, handing it back.

"Let's see how that goes down," she replied. "Then you can have more if you want."

When he nodded, Rosana got herself a drink and then sat beside him, arms hugging her bent legs. Outwardly calm, but her scent was sour with fear.

He turned toward her, set a hand on her arm. That's when he noticed the finger-sized bruises on her throat.

He touched one of them. "Who did this?" he growled.

She shook her head. "Doesn't matter."

"It was Luc, wasn't it?"

She jerked a shoulder.

A dark rage balled his stomach.

Rosana shot him an uneasy look. "They're already better. If I could've shifted, the bruises would be almost gone by now."

He swallowed his anger, nodded. This was between him and Luc. But the man was going to pay for every mark he'd put on Rosana.

For now, they had other worries, like the fact that Rosana was a river fada who'd been forcibly removed from her home waters. And on top of that, she couldn't shift in this cramped, underground cell.

"You need your river. How long—?"

"I'm fine. The Chesapeake Bay isn't far from here, and we're right by the Potomac River. And this water"—she indicated the trickle coming from metal spout—"is spring water. Just splashing it on my face helped."

He frowned. She wasn't lying, but he recognized a half-truth when he heard it. "Why not shift to your otter?"

"If it comes to that, I guess I'll try. But the dolphin is my preferred animal. I haven't shifted to otter since I was a pup."

"So how long?"

She groaned. "You're like a pit bull sometimes, you know that?"

"Rosana."

"Okay, okay. I need to immerse myself in fresh water, and even if I shifted to otter, I'd still be too large for that little trickle to do any good."

His stomach knotted. "How long?" he gritted. "One day? Two?"

"I honestly don't know." She gave a half laugh. "It's not like I've ever been locked up before. But I'm not going to shrivel up overnight. I have at least a few days, maybe longer, although I'll start to feel it in a day or two." She opened her mouth, shut it.

"What aren't you telling me?"

"I have a feeling we've been in here longer than we realize—maybe even a day already. You know how time runs differently in a fae court."

He swore. "So you're already feeling it?"

Another jerk of her shoulder.

"Just hang on, okay?" He gathered her to him. "Your brothers will come for you."

Dion and Tiago would tear apart heaven and earth to save Rosana.

Like Adric would have for his sister—if he'd known those bastards had kidnapped her. But they'd smashed her quartz so she couldn't call for help. By the time Adric had found out, it was too late. They'd had a whole night with her.

He swallowed.

Let it go. Jani's okay, getting better all the time.

A silence. Then Rosana said, "About that..."

An icy finger traced down his spine. "What did you do?"

She lifted her chin. "I told the prince I wanted to stay with you."

"You did *what*?" He winced as pain squeezed his head. "Why the hell would you do that?"

"Because. I wasn't sure how hurt you were, and—" She swallowed audibly. "I didn't know what else to do."

"You should've demanded to leave. This is between him and me. Having you here just fucks things up."

"Maybe. And maybe not. In my vision, you came to the court alone—and you died, damn it." Her voice broke. She took a jagged breath. "You *need* me, Adric Savonett. Why won't you believe me?" Tears glimmered on her face.

Hell, now he'd made her cry. "Rosana..." He touched her wet cheek, but she growled and buried her head in her knees.

"Hey." He set a tentative hand on her back. "I'm sorry, okay? Just...don't cry."

"For your information," she said to her legs, "I did demand to leave—more than once. The prince wouldn't give me a straight answer. He was playing with me. Then you got here and you got hurt—bad. You were out cold, for *Deus*'s sake. And you think I should've just left you with them?"

He heaved a breath. "C'mere."

She scowled but allowed him to guide her back to his shoulder.

"I'm sorry, love." He kissed her temple. "I just hate like hell that you got dragged into this."

She gave a tight nod. "There is something," she said, low-voiced. "On the way here, I called on Cleia for help, and I'm pretty sure she heard me. We were still in southern Maryland, so they may not realize Luc was bringing me here. But at least they'll know I'm not in Baltimore."

"That's good. But why would they think you're in Baltimore?"

"I left Dion and Cleia a note saying I was coming to you."

His brows flew up. "You *told* Dion? About us?"

"Yep." Her full mouth set in stubborn lines. "I'm not going to sneak around to be with you."

"Rosana..."

"I mean it. If you want me, it's got to be out in the open."

"But I told you—"

"You want me. You're not going to tell me last night didn't mean something."

"No." He tightened his arms around her. He just couldn't do it. It would be a lie, and besides, he couldn't hurt her like that. Not when she was locked in this fucking cell because of him. "You know it did."

"Okay, then." He hadn't realized how stiff she was holding herself until she relaxed and curled closer, one arm resting on his stomach, the other around his back in a loose hug. He sucked in a breath when she pressed a tender spot on his lower abdomen.

"Sorry." She tried to pull away, but he kept her where she was.

"No, stay. I like you close."

"Me too." A pause, and then she added in a small voice. "It makes me less scared."

His heart lurched. "Don't be scared. You'll get out of here—soon. I promise."

"Not without you."

He tugged a long black curl. "Are you this much trouble to Dion?"

He felt her grin against his shoulder. "More."

"Never thought I'd feel sorry for the man."

She chuckled, and then laughed aloud when her stomach rumbled immediately after. "Sorry."

"You're hungry." He stroked his palm down the delicate knobs of her spine. "Why didn't you grab something this morning? There was cereal in the cabinet."

"I didn't have time," she said sweetly. Too sweetly.

"Oh."

"Yeah. You snuck out on me, asshole."

He moved uncomfortably. "You were asleep. I figured we'd said our goodbyes."

"Yeah, right. You were afraid I'd talk you into taking me with you."

"Not because I don't want you. It's because *I don't want you hurt.*"

A low growl. "Stop trying to protect me. I can take care of myself."

"Against another fada, maybe. But these are fae. You saw the kind of power the prince has."

"So what makes you think *you* can beat him? You're a fada, too."

"Because, damn it, I don't care about me." He gripped her shoulders, gave her shake. "But if something happened to you, I'd fucking break. I've lost too many people. I can't lose you. I *won't* lose you."

Her eyes widened. "You *do* love me."

His gaze slid from hers. His mouth opened, closed. Because he couldn't bring himself to deny it. What else could this hot ache crowding his chest be?

"That's okay." She snuggled closer again. "I can wait for you to say it."

AFTER THAT, they fell asleep, spooned on the bench together, his front to her back. But sometime in their dreams, they turned to each other. Adric woke with his hand on Rosana's breast, his tongue deep in her mouth. He was much better, his battered body nearly healed.

Rosana's eyes were closed but she was sucking on his tongue.

"Angel?" He nuzzled her neck. "You awake?"

"Mm-hmm." She tugged at the hem of the borrowed shirt.

He dragged it off and removed his pants while she wriggled out of her own clothes. He made a rough bed of their clothing on the stone floor and laid her down on it before coming over her. She moaned and bent her legs up. But even with their clothes as a cushion, he was conscious of the hard rock beneath her. He rolled onto his side, taking her with him.

She bent up a leg, rested it on his thigh. His cock brushed against her warm nest of hair, and he closed his eyes in pleasure.

"You're better?" She touched the bump on his temple.

He nodded. "I have a small healing Gift. I had to draw on my quartz, though, so I won't be able to shift for a few hours."

She traced the scruff on his jaw. "You know, I still haven't seen your cougar."

"He's here." And wide awake.

"He is?" She looked deep into his eyes before giving a satisfied nod. "So's my dolphin."

"Did I tell you how pretty she is?" He turned his head, sucked her wandering finger into his mouth.

Her breath hitched. "Uh-uh."

He rolled his tongue around her finger before releasing it to wrap his arms around her. "She's strong, graceful. Like you."

"You think?" She scooted closer, plastering that long, curvy body against his.

"Yeah." He smoothed a hand down her ass. Damn, she had a fine butt, round and firm, the skin like satin.

She nibbled on his earlobe, teasing the gold stud with her tongue. "In the summer," she said, as if there was no doubt whatsoever that they'd both escape the night fae, "we have to go for a swim together. My dolphin's skin is very sensitive—she'll want to rub all over you. You wouldn't mind, would you?"

His dick jumped. *Mind?* The thought of a wet, naked Rosana rubbing all over him sounded like his idea of paradise.

"No," he managed to say. "I wouldn't mind at all. As long as you promise to swim with me as a human, too."

"It's a deal."

"Naked."

A throaty chuckle. "Oh, I will be. I love to feel the water flowing over my bare skin."

He swore. "Have mercy, woman."

She gave a gleeful laugh—and pressed her mouth to his. When his lips parted, her tongue slid in, just a bit, sending a hot shiver down his spine.

She teased him with small tastes and nips until he groaned and sucked her tongue deeper. Kissing the breath out of her—and himself as well. Even in the dank, musty cell, her scent had a hint of fresh water.

When he finally came up for oxygen, she drew a serrated breath. Her eyes seared into his, the deep blue streaked with sea-green. "I love you."

His heart stumbled. "Rosana. I can't—"

"I'm not asking you to mate-claim me. But I wanted you to know. In case—" She moved a shoulder.

His stomach fisted. "Nothing's going to happen to you," he bit out. "You'll be out of here in a day, maybe two. I'll *make* it happen."

He speared his fingers into her hair, drawing back her head to press love-bites to her throat. She moaned and angled her head to give him better access. One hand came up to his nape, urging him closer. Her back arched, pressing her pelvis into his.

Electricity danced over his skin. He felt feverish, needy.

"Come into me," she murmured. "Now."

His throat worked. "Can't. No protection."

"Adric. I love you. And I would love any pup—or cub—we made."

She reached down and guided his cock into her, and the gods help him, he didn't stop her.

Because he felt the same way.

She was slick, hot. She gasped and clenched her inner muscles around him. Pleasure rocketed to his balls.

He clamped his teeth together, resisting the urge to pound into her. Instead, he dragged her bent leg higher on his hip so that he was rubbing right against her clit and rocked slowly in and out.

Drawing out the pleasure. Teasing them both.

Her arms tightened around him. "I love you," she repeated in a fierce whisper.

He faltered, swallowed.

Never had he heard those words from a lover.

While Leron was still alive, he'd stuck to casual, no-strings-attached hook-ups. He couldn't risk anything more—Leron would've used any woman he cared for against him.

After he'd become alpha, he'd been too busy, his hold on the clan too shaky. Especially that first year, when he'd not only been working day and night to heal his fractured people, he'd had to fight off multiple challenges.

And then he'd seen Rosana at the sun fae ball, a vision in a sexy little dress the brilliant blues and greens of a peacock's feathers, her shiny black curls tumbling down her back...

Her eyelids drifted down. Her soft lips parted as she sank deeper into pleasure.

His cat bristled restively, hungry to lay its wild heart at her feet.

My woman.

My mate.

Mine.

He swallowed the words, although it *hurt* not to let them out. He was a killer, a man who'd cornered his own uncle in a dark alley and slit his throat. So what if he'd done it to save Marjani? It still shadowed his soul.

Someone like Rosana deserved so much better than him.

But too fucking bad.

Deep inside him, something moved, opened. In that moment, he understood what the cat had known for years. Some things were meant to happen. A man could only fight fate for so long.

If they got out of this alive, he was mate-claiming Rosana do Rio.

Whether her brother liked it or not. Whether his clan agreed or not.

Sinking his fingers into her hair, he tugged her head back and set his mouth to the silken skin of her throat.

"Mine," he rasped. "I'm not claiming you—yet—but when I do, you'll say yes."

Her full lips curved. "Haven't you figured it out? I already have."

32

The Rock Run men rode fast and hard. Marjani grimly kept up, fear for her brother a live creature gnawing at her insides.

Behind her, Fane maintained a loose grip on her hips. She was thankful now he'd insisted on coming. She'd never needed his calm, steadying presence more.

As they pulled onto I-95, she tapped her quartz, calling Jace.

"Hey, Jani." He raised his voice to be heard over the sound of drilling. He must be at the quartz mine. "Whassup?"

"It's Ric. He's not at his den. I think he's going to New Moon."

"Alone?"

"Yeah. I tried to get ahold of him, but he's cut off all communication. And it's deliberate. I can tell."

"He didn't give you a heads-up?"

She ground her teeth. "No."

"Fuck." They both knew that if Adric hadn't told Marjani he was leaving, it was because he'd wanted to sneak out of town. Whatever he was up to, it was dangerous.

"And somehow Rosana do Rio got mixed up in it. I found Dion, Rui, Tiago and a couple of other Rock Run men outside Ric's den. They looked ready to tear him apart with their bare hands."

"His den? What the fuck?"

She explained how Rosana had apparently been kidnapped from outside Adric's den.

Jace swore. "They don't think it was Ric?"

"No. But it looks like it might've been Luc. His scent was all over Ric's backyard."

"Hell." Jace's tone matched the sinking sensation in the pit of her stomach. "So Lady B's a part of this? But what the fuck would she want with Rosana?"

"Good question. But Cleia traced Rosana to southern Maryland. I'm on 95 south of Baltimore, along with Dion and his men. Fane's with me."

"On my way." The sound of drilling faded as he made his way to the surface.

"I'll keep you updated on our location, but figure on going to Virginia. And Jace? Call Zuri, tell him what's up. Until he hears otherwise, he's in charge."

"Cat's balls, Jani. Give me the hard job, why don't you? Zuri's going to be royally pissed if we leave him in Baltimore."

"He'll just have to deal," she returned in a hard voice. "He's chief of security. With Adric and me both out of the city, he's in charge. And if the night fae catch Adric, we'll be at war—he'll have more than enough to keep busy. And Jace? No secrets." The clan had had their fill of that during the Darktime, and even since. "Tell Zuri to let everyone know what's up. Ric's going in there for me. Every den needs to decide once and for all if they're with the two of us—or against us. If not, they should leave now, or I will personally kick their asses out of Baltimore."

"Understood."

Fane leaned forward to mutter in Marjani's ear. "Tell him to send Evie and Kyle to Baltimore. They're not safe in Grace Harbor alone."

Marjani nodded. She relayed Fane's message, adding. "If she asks why, tell her the healers will need her."

It was the one argument guaranteed to get Evie back to Baltimore. If it came to war, the healers would be stretched to their limits, and Evie's ability to add her energy to theirs would be desperately needed.

"Already planning on it. Horace is with me—he'll make sure they get there okay. You heard that?" he asked the cougar fada.

When Horace said yes, Jace instructed him to shut down the mine and send everyone back to Baltimore, ASAP.

Marjani heard the rumble of Jace's motorcycle coming to life. "I'm right behind you," he told her, and ended the call.

The city fell away. The highway was lined with trees, giving the impression they were in the country, but she knew it was an illusion. This section of the East Coast was a string of towns one after another, with a continuous stream of traffic traveling the I-95 corridor.

"Don't worry." Fane squeezed her waist. "Adric will be okay. Your brother's bloody hard to kill."

She growled. "He shouldn't have gone without me."

"Mm." Her mate wisely refrained from pointing out that she'd gone to Iceland without Adric for the very same reason—to protect him.

She heaved a breath and cast Fane an apologetic smile over her shoulder. "Thanks for coming."

He shrugged. "I know the court better than any of you. Besides, I spent sixty turns of the sun with the fae. I might even be able to help. Envoy, remember? I was one of the ice fae's top negotiators."

"You're right. I'm sorry."

He wrapped his arms more securely around her waist, his hard-muscled body warm against her back. Despite her worry, her cat gave a little purr of contentment.

Fane brought his face as close to her as their helmets allowed. "You need to remember something, love."

"What's that?"

"You're not alone anymore."

～

DION WENT with his gut and aimed straight for New Moon.

Three hours later, they entered the forest surrounding the night fae court. They slowed their motorcycles to a crawl. A *look-away* spell pressed at them, but he drew on his internal GPS to keep moving forward, even when the pressure grew so strong it was like slogging through invisible quicksand.

Rui somehow picked up Rosana's scent. "This way." He jerked his chin at a narrow gravel road.

They bumped down the rutted lane until they reached a clearing. Rui engaged his kickstand and swung off his bike. He crouched, nostrils flared, to scrutinize the prints in the moist earth.

"Rosana was here," he said without raising his head. "Along with the wolf and Adric. And a night fae—a mixed blood, I think. Lady B?" He glanced up at Dion.

Neither of them had met Lady Blaer, although they knew from Dion's brother Nic that she was a night fae/ice fae mix.

Dion inhaled. "That's my guess." Beside him, Tiago grunted assent.

Marjani pushed her way through the other men to his side, her mate following. She drew a slow breath. "That's Lady B, all right. I'll never forget her scent. And the other two are definitely Adric and Luc."

Rui circled the clearing, still in a partial crouch, gathering further scraps of data. "Adric's trail leads out of here—I believe he was following the wolf." He pointed down the narrow road. "But Rosana's scent ends here, along with the fae."

Dion's stomach constricted, the small hope that they'd reach his sister in time crushed. "So she teleported out of here with Rosana."

"To New Moon," Marjani added.

"That's what I believe, *sim*. But if she's behind their wards, we can't know for sure."

"*I* know." The cougar fada's hand went to where her quartz rested beneath her leather jacket. "At least, I'm sure Adric's there."

"You can't contact him?"

She hesitated, shook her head.

He took a step forward. "What aren't you telling us?"

"He cut off contact with me. But I could still feel him, up until a couple of hours ago. Then—nothing."

"And that means?"

"He's behind a ward or—" She compressed her mouth.

"Or what?" he demanded.

"Dead."

Morningstar scowled at Dion and wrapped a lanky arm around his mate's shoulders. "So best guess is, Adric's inside the court along with Rosana. That's good news, right? She's not alone —and neither is he. Because if there's one thing I know about the night fae, two people together can fight their emotional assaults better than any one person alone."

Marjani nodded, firmed her chin. "What now?" she asked with a penetrating glance around at the dense forest.

"I'm going to contact my mate." Dion stared into the trees, his gaze unfocused. "Cleia, *minha reina*? Can you join us?" To them, he said, "She's on her way."

While they waited for the queen to arrive, he told Marjani, "Rui is going to track Adric and Luc to their last known location."

She nodded. "I contacted Jace Jones, too. He'll be here in an hour or so." To Rui, she said, "Fane and I will go with you."

"I can show you the approximate location of New Moon," Morningstar offered.

"Thanks, but we know," Rui replied. "I've been inside the court myself. But don't tell the prince." Rui's smile was thin. "He wasn't aware he had a fada guest."

The shark fada had taken the form of a smaller fish and entered the compound through a stream.

Morningstar flicked up a single dark brow. "I see."

Rui turned his hard green eyes on Marjani. "Ready?"

"As soon as I shift." Returning to her bike, she removed her clothes and shoved them into a saddlebag, and then shifted to a sleek cougar with startling turquoise eyes.

Before they could leave, Cleia 'ported into the clearing. One glance around and her full mouth compressed. "You tracked Rosana this close to New Moon?"

He jerked his chin in assent. "It appears she was kidnapped by an earth fada under a *geas*. We have to assume she's inside the court."

Her beautiful face set. "It appears I need to have talk with Prince Langdon."

osana pulled Adric closer, angling her body to take him even further inside.

He was hot, lithe, powerful. He fucked her with slow strokes that shot sparks up her spine, out to her fingers and toes.

Her pleasure built. She instinctively tightened her inner muscles around him and discovered that made it even better.

He liked that, too. His whole body went taut, and he muttered, "God's cat, you feel good," and thrust harder.

"Yes," she gasped. "So good."

His mouth captured hers, sinking his tongue deep, kissing her breathless. When he released her, he curved his body to kiss his way down her throat. His tongue rasped over each of her nipples in turn. She moaned and pressed against him, and he gave each a hard suck.

She hissed and clenched around him. It was like he'd pulled a string leading straight to her clit.

He continued moving. Deliberate, sensuous strokes that were a language in themselves.

I love you.

And I love you.

Between her breasts, the amethyst heated until it felt like another heart.

He pulled out, tapped the side of her hip. "Turn over."

She took a deep breath and then flipped onto her stomach.

"Lift your hips." He positioned himself behind her.

Yes... She immediately obeyed. Her ass was canted up, her breasts pressed into their shirts.

He grasped her hips and resumed thrusting into her. Filling her in a way she hadn't known she needed.

She'd told Adric she didn't know him, but she knew all the important things. That he was strong, confident, scary smart. A natural leader who didn't follow any rules but his own. Ruthless and ambitious, but not for himself. What drove him was bettering his clan.

Beneath that bad-boy façade, the man cared.

He twined his fingers in her hair and gave it a tug, gently urging her to lift up on all fours, her back arched. Kisses seared the side of her throat while his other hand slid between her legs to do magical things. Stroking, rubbing, circling until she was sobbing with need and want and wonder.

He released her hair to grasp her hip so he could piston into her hard and fast.

The two of us together.

Yes. Always.

They climaxed at the same time. She dropped to her forearms, moaning his name into their shirts. Behind her, he growled lowly and stilled, spurting into her, hot and urgent.

For a few seconds, he hung over her, lungs working, and then he disengaged from her and came down on the clothes, bringing her with him.

She curled into his chest. "Guess you're feeling better."

"Mm." He ran a palm down her spine. In the silence that fell, this time it was his stomach that rumbled. "And hungry," he added wryly. "But maybe no food is good news. Could mean they're not planning to keep us down here long."

"Maybe." She scooted closer. "The prince—he kept trying to get me to eat his food."

Adric's hand on her back stilled. Beneath her, his body locked up like a fighter's. "He wants you to stay, then."

"He knows I'm a Seer. He offered to help train me."

He swore. "I knew you'd be like catnip to that prick. But you told him no." It wasn't a question.

She thought uneasily about how tempted she'd been. "Oh, yeah."

"Good." He resumed caressing her. "So. Any ideas about getting out of here?"

She shook her head. "They took your dagger and the door's locked up tight. It doesn't even have a handle on the inside. The only thing they left us was your quartz."

"And that's low in energy right now. I drew heavily on it to heal myself. I probably couldn't even shift right now."

"You can't use my amethyst for energy?"

A shake of his head. "I have a magical bond with my own quartz. In an emergency, I can draw any quartz, but the energy doesn't have the same quality. I couldn't use it for something so tricky. But—" He fingered her pendant.

"What?"

"It's warm. And I can hear the crystals singing, louder than I'd expect."

"And that means?"

His brows squashed together. "I'm not sure, but... I think you've bonded with it. Not like an earth fada, but you've formed a weak connection. Don't ask me how, because I've never heard of anything like it. The good news is that if we get separated, I can use it to find you."

She gripped his wrist. "We have to stay together," she said fiercely.

He cupped her nape. "I'll do my best, okay?" He stopped there, but she heard the *but*. If it came down to it, he intended to sacrifice himself for her.

She set her jaw. *Not if I can help it.*

"I can tell you one thing," he added. "They won't take my quartz from me, not at first."

"Why not?"

He shrugged a powerful shoulder. "They're not stupid. They know it hurts like hell to have my quartz touched. They'll use it to torture me."

"*Deus*," she muttered, then brightened. "Can't you use it to call for help?"

"The wards would block it. But"—he jerked upright—"Marjani's close."

"How do you know?"

"I just know. As alpha, I'm connected to everyone in the clan through their quartz, but with her, it's even stronger. Fuck." He scrubbed his hands over his face. "This is bad."

"It is?" Rosana sat up as well. "She's here to rescue you, isn't she?"

"Gods." He drew a harsh breath. "She *knows* not to come anywhere near him."

"But why? I don't understand."

"Because. It's her the prince really wants. Not me."

She opened her mouth to ask why, but he shook his head. "I can't say any more, but take my word for it. He'd love to get his long, cold fingers on her."

And suddenly, Rosana *knew*.

Marjani had killed Langdon's son, not Adric—and Langdon had somehow found out. No wonder Adric had been so determined to assassinate the prince.

She grabbed his arm. "Tyrus," she mouthed. "It was her. And he knows it. That's why you came alone."

An infinitesimal nod. He set a hand on her mouth, warning her not to say more.

She dipped her chin, telling him she understood, and he lifted his fingers. "So that's why you wouldn't listen to me," she whispered.

"I told you not to come. But you just wouldn't listen."

"Maybe because I'm supposed to be here."

He made a small sound, half laughter, half groan. "Know something? I'm starting to believe you."

She watched as he rose to his feet and crossed to the metal trough. He took a drink and then used handfuls of water to rinse the rest of the powder off.

Adric was here to save his sister.

He wasn't here only for his clan. He was here for Marjani.

This changed everything.

She washed up herself, and they took turns using the toilet. She pulled on her clothes and sat on the bench, mind working.

Yeah, her gut told her she was supposed to be here, but why? She was a Seer, not a warrior. Until today, she'd never even seen combat. And without an iron weapon, she was helpless against the night fae. Even with their iron, the prince had fought off both her and Adric.

Adric got dressed as well and prowled around the small space, clearly unhappy at being confined. At least he was better. Seeing him so battered had hurt at a primal level, like she'd shared his pain—and she'd known the instant he'd come back to consciousness.

Which was strange, come to think of it. She furrowed her brow, unconsciously massaging her breastbone.

The realization hit her like a fist to the heart. The mate bond had formed on her side. Not just a few threads, but a shining ribbon of sea-colored light. She *felt* it, stretching from her to him. But before it reached his chest, it slammed up against something bright and hard, as if he'd thrown up a shield.

Blood roared in her ears. She gulped, the breath literally knocked out of her.

Adric fingered his quartz and slid her a look. But he didn't say anything.

The bond had formed, but he was blocking it from his side.

He's doing it to protect you.

It still hurt, but she understood—until she recalled he'd started blocking it even before he'd left Baltimore. Which meant he'd come to Virginia expecting to die.

The last piece of the puzzle thunked into place with an awful, stomach-dropping sound.

He'd told her himself, right before they'd fallen asleep: *Because, damn it, I don't care about me.*

This was a suicide mission. His life for Marjani's.

If Rosana hadn't been at New Moon, he might already be dead.

She moved her head slowly from side to side. "You...no. There has to be another way."

He didn't pretend not to understand. "Rosana." He sat next to her, took her hand. "I didn't want this to happen."

"But it has."

"No, it hasn't. The bond—it's not complete. I'm still hoping I can take down this bastard and escape, but.... At least this way, you'll be able to find another mate."

"That's up to me, isn't it?"

His glance was a brilliant mix of bronze and blue. "I need to know you have the chance, at least." He took her hand between both of his. "Promise me something. If you get another chance to leave, you'll take it."

"No." She jerked her hand free. "Don't even ask."

"Please, Rosana. You say you love me. Do it for me if you won't do it for yourself."

She growled. "That's not fair. If you were me, would you leave?"

He exhaled. "No. But this is my fight, not yours."

She just shook her head and stared out at the room.

Adric eyed her. She *felt* his will beating at hers, demanding she give in. Her body tightened.

It wasn't easy to refuse him, not when she sensed how much it meant to him. How much *she* meant to him.

The tension in the cell ratcheted up until she could've

screamed, and then he said something low and vicious and resumed his restless pacing.

"There's one thing I'd give a big fat diamond to know. How in Hades did the prince know I was here?"

She slumped against the wall, relieved he'd given up—for now, anyway. "I was there when Olivier—the butler—told him Luc was in the foyer. He knew then that you were with Luc."

"He did?" He shook his head in disgust.

"What was that invisible thing you did, anyway? I thought only wayfarers can disappear like that, but you're a tracker, aren't you?

"I have another, secondary Gift that I can use like a cloaking spell. The prince shouldn't have known I was there."

"I told you, he has the farsight. Maybe he Saw you before you entered the court."

"I was cloaking myself on and off. I mean, come on—the man can't be watching all the time, can he?"

"No. He has to sleep, eat, go about his business. And he can't hear you—just watch."

Adric swiped a hand down his face. "Gods, I made it easy for him. He just had to wait for me to arrive like a spider with a stupid-ass fly."

"He couldn't have Seen exactly what you had planned. Seers almost never See their own futures. I had no clue Luc was outside your den."

She raised her hands, palms up, and swallowed. Twice.

Adric crouched before her. "What?"

"My visions—I have to touch someone to See their future. And in the last week, I've had my hands all over you. My *bare* hands. But it hasn't set off my Sight."

"So?"

She brought her hands down, met his eyes. "So a Seer can't foretell her own future. That's why I can touch you without setting off my Sight—my fate is tangled up with yours now."

A hesitant *tap-tap* on the bedroom door dragged Langdon from a sound sleep. Pushing himself up on his forearms, he bit back a groan. By the dark gods, he hurt. Even with his powerful blood, it was going to take a day or two to completely heal.

He could almost admire Adric and that river fada female of his. They'd fought hard and well. Not that the alpha wouldn't pay for attacking him.

Another apologetic *tap-tap*.

"What?" he growled.

The door opened. Jessica, Olivier's new assistant, peeked into the darkened room, her anxiousness palpable. A recent human hire, she regarded Langdon as a cross between a monster and a god.

At all that delicious dread, his mood improved. He pushed himself up on his forearms. "Come in."

She took a single step and halted, her slender body framed in the light from the hallway. Just for fun, he nudged her fear up a notch and then sipped at the luscious, panicky emanations.

Her dark eyes rounded. She wrung her narrow hands. "I beg

your pardon, my lord. I know you gave orders not to be disturbed, but this can't wait."

He shoved off the duvet and strode naked across the floor. Sensing movement, a handful of fae lights glowed on, casting a deep aubergine light over the bedroom.

Jessica froze and blinked rapidly, her gaze jumping from his half-hard cock to his bare chest and back again before settling on his face. He caught a spark of arousal mixed with the fear. Interesting...

"Speak," he commanded softly.

"Yes, my lord." Her head bobbed up and down several times.

A pause as he waited for her to enlighten him. When she remained silent, fingers tangling nervously in front of her body, he stifled a sigh. Olivier was going to have to hire another assistant. Although she had possibilities as a toy...

"Jessica. What is so important that you disturbed my sleep?"

She started. "I beg your pardon, my lord." She licked soft, coral-colored lips and finally got it out. "The sun fae queen is here. She wishes to speak to you."

"Cleia? She's *here*?"

"Yes, my lord. Uh...not here, exactly. She's outside the wards, of course, but..." She shifted from foot to foot and added in a rush, "She's demanding to see you, my lord. Captain Quade tried to put her off, but she refuses to leave without seeing you."

His mouth pulled down. He'd expected Cleia, of course—the queen had an inexplicable fondness for her mate's young sister—just not so quickly.

"My clothes," he said. "Now."

"Yes, my lord."

Jessica scurried to obey, rushing into his walk-in closet and reappearing with a shirt and pants in a shimmering blue-black fabric. Meanwhile, he sent a message to Quade, agreeing to meet the queen in a pine grove outside the compound. Cleia might be young for a fae, but she was too powerful to allow within his wards.

That done, he selected a few pieces of jewelry—a glittering diamond pendant the size of a walnut, a couple of hand-worked platinum-and-diamond rings, a platinum watch. Jessica returned with a pair of Italian leather shoes and knelt on the floor so he could step into them.

He touched her curly brown hair. "Thank you, my dear."

"My pleasure, my lord." Her head bobbed in a way that had his mind picturing lurid acts.

He set them aside—for now—to head for the portal nearest the pine grove.

Cleia hadn't come alone. Quade and his warriors relieved her fada companions of their weapons before permitting Langdon to step through the portal. Langdon allowed it, but he couldn't help being amused; the queen was infinitely more dangerous than all the fada put together.

Time ran differently in a fae court. Inside his wards, it was early afternoon, but outside, a new day had dawned. As he stepped into the forest, the rising sun sifted pale gold through the pine branches. He donned a pair of sunglasses and took in his visitors.

The queen had planted herself in a shaft of sunlight, her statuesque body clad in a snug yellow T-shirt and bronze moto pants, her bright hair braided into a single over-the-shoulder plait. Lord Dion stood close beside her, his black hair in a ponytail, his eyes like silver flints, his broad shoulders straining at his leather jacket. A barbarian in human clothing. The fae world had been appalled when Cleia took a fada mate, but the Rock Run alpha had a certain primitive appeal. A pity the queen wasn't into threesomes.

Rui do Mar, Dion's second, stood a step behind along with Dion's brother Tiago. Next to them were a slim woman with short dark hair and large, catlike eyes, and a lean blond mixed-blood whom Langdon recognized as one of Sindre's former envoys.

There were other fada present, too, all men, but his gaze lingered on the woman.

Welcome, my pretty little cat.

He inclined his head to Cleia. "Your highness, you honor my court." He touched a hand to his chest in a gesture of respect. "Peace to you and yours."

He nodded at Dion and his stone-faced second-in-command, and then turned his gaze back to the Savonett female. This time, he let his mouth curve.

"Marjani Savonett. What a pleasure to meet you at last."

The blond male—Farr? Fern? Finn?—set a protective hand on her back and glared at Langdon.

Marjani stared back unblinking. She appeared unaffected, but he sensed the cauldron of fear and anger roiling inside her. It touched off an answering darkness in him. For a few seconds, the temptation to feed was almost irresistible, but he reined it in.

"Peace." Cleia's curt greeting made it clear she was unhappy with him. "I believe you have my mate's sister. A misunderstanding, I'm sure."

His brow lifted. She'd gone straight to the point, skipping over several pages of the polite thrust-and-parry that every fae learned at their mother's knee.

The queen wasn't just unhappy, she was furious.

"A misunderstanding?" He steepled his fingers and tapped them against his mouth. "No, my lady. Rosana do Rio is a guest."

Lord Dion made a sharp, angry movement. Cleia set a calming hand on his arm. "Then invite me into your court," she said.

Langdon considered that. But no, the queen too powerful to risk it.

He shook his head. "I'm afraid that's not possible."

With a growl, Dion lunged at him. Langdon simply faded into the shadows while Quade and the other guards surged forward. It took three of them to subdue the enraged river alpha. Meanwhile, do Mar, Marjani, and the other fada rushed to his aid.

Cleia raised her hands to the rising sun. A white-hot flame flared to life at the center of each palm. The queen didn't produce fae balls, she simply drew on solar energy to reduce an enemy to ashes.

"Let my mate go," she said in a low, terrible voice.

Langdon's guards flinched at the bright light, even Quade, the oldest and most powerful. This was getting out of hand.

Langdon emerged from the shadows. "Then tell him to control his temper."

The queen's tawny eyes slit.

Fane—Langdon had recalled his name—cleared his throat. "My lady. My lords." He glanced around at Cleia, Dion and Langdon. "If I may speak?"

Langdon inclined his head. "Go ahead."

The sun fae queen waited until Dion gave a curt nod and stopped struggling against the guards' hold. The flames winked out, and she brought her hands to her sides.

"We'll listen," she said. "After you release Lord Dion."

Langdon gestured at Quade to release the big fada. "But I'll have your word—all of you—that you'll respect this negotiation. Attack again, and this meeting is over."

When everyone had assented to Langdon's terms, Fane slid his hands into his pockets and gave Langdon an easy smile. "If I heard you right, Rosana is a guest at your court."

"Yes."

"So as a guest, she's free to go, yes?"

"She is."

Fane gave Dion a significant look.

The river fada alpha regarded Langdon skeptically. "My sister is free to leave New Moon?"

"She is."

"Say the words," he growled.

"Your sister, Rosana do Rio, is free to leave my court whenever she wishes."

Dion briefly closed his eyes. Then he gave a short nod. "See that you inform her."

"However," Langdon continued, "she has requested to remain."

"What? You lying *filho da puta*." The big river fada stepped forward, murder in his eyes. Wicked black claws sprouted from his fingertips.

"*Dion.*" Cleia gripped his bulging bicep. "You know the fae can't lie. Explain," she snapped at Langdon.

"I simply granted her request. Lord Adric was being conveyed to a cell, and the young lady wished to remain with him. I was happy to oblige."

Marjani gave a muted hiss, and Langdon's nape prickled warily. The cougar fada might be small, almost delicate in appearance, but he hadn't forgotten who'd killed Tyrus. He raised a challenging brow, daring her to break her word and give him grounds to capture her.

But she remained where she was, slender body strung tight, hands balled at her sides.

"Let Rosana go," Cleia told him. "And Lord Adric, too. You have no right to keep either of them against their will."

"No? Lord Adric attacked me in my own home. That gives me the right to exact any justice I choose. And the do Rio female is with him at her own request. Not a prisoner, but a guest."

The queen's eyes sparked dangerously. "You dare hold my mate's sister? A woman under my court's protection?"

He spread his hands. "I'm not an unreasonable man. For the right incentive, I could be persuaded to expel her from my court."

"Name your price," Dion said.

Langdon permitted himself a small smile. He jerked his head at Quade. "Leave us. All of you."

The captain's brows shot up, but he duly ordered the other warriors back through the portal. "I'll be waiting on the other side," he said with a warning glance at Cleia and Dion before following them.

Langdon drew the shadows around them like a thick cloak. What he was about to say was for no one else's ears.

"You have my granddaughter at Rock Run. She's not, in fact, dead as you and Lord Adric would like me to believe."

Dion's head jerked back. Beside him, do Mar's fists slowly opened and closed. The two men exchanged a look.

"She's alive," the Rock Run alpha admitted.

At last. Langdon's heart sped up. He slipped his hands into the pockets of his duster, kept his face impassive. "It's time she take her place at my court."

"No." That was do Mar. "Absolutely not."

Langdon eyed him. "She's not even of your blood. Why do you care what happens to her?"

"She's my daughter," was the terse reply.

Langdon scowled. He'd never understand the fada and their primitive ways. "She's *my* granddaughter, the blood of my blood. At New Moon, she'll be treated as the princess she is."

Another man stepped forward, the earth fada lieutenant who was Merry's uncle. "She's my blood relation, and I say no as well."

"Those are my terms. Rosana do Rio for my granddaughter."

"No," Dion bit out.

Fane cocked his head. "You said yourself that Rosana is free to leave. Why should we bargain with you for something you've already granted?"

A wise man didn't bargain when he held the upper hand. "As you say," Langdon returned. "Peace, my lady. My lord."

With a nod at the queen and her mate, he moved back, retreating into the shadows layer by layer until only his face was visible, a pale glimmer.

"You son of a bitch." Dion stalked forward, matching him step for step. "I demand to see my sister. *Now.*"

"She's made her choice."

Dion swore and tried to grab him, but his fingers slashed impotently through the gray mist.

"Wait!" Marjani sprang forward. "What about my brother?"

"That," Langdon said, "is not negotiable. His execution is set for the night of the new moon."

Her honey-colored skin went ashen. "For trespassing?"

"He didn't just trespass. He was here to kill me."

"But—"

"More than that, the death of my son requires an equal sacrifice."

"No! We were only defending ourselves. Tyrus came into *our* territory, stirring up trouble. Sent assassins after our people."

"Invaded my den," growled Jace Jones. "And kidnapped me and my mate."

Langdon kept his gaze on the cougar fada. "The sentence hasn't been finalized. You can still take your brother's place."

When she opened her mouth, he knew he had her—until her blond mate slapped a hand over her lips. "No!" he whispered urgently. "At least give us time to find another way."

She hissed and twisted out of his grip.

"Marjani," her mate said. "I'm begging you. Wait. You don't have to decide right now."

She gave him an agonized look. "I'm sorry, Fane. But I can't—"

"Enough!" The white-hot flame flared in the queen's palms again. "The earth fada speak the truth. Our own investigations have confirmed that your son attacked the Baltimore fada. His death is no one's fault but his own. And in the months since, you've been seen multiple times in Baltimore. If Lord Adric attacked you, it was because you provoked him into it. Self-defense is not a crime. Moreover, you have no grounds to hold Rosana do Rio."

He sneered. "I should've known you'd take the fada's side," he said with a knowing glance at Dion.

The flame in Cleia's palms burned brighter. Even with the sunglasses, he had to squint to protect his sensitive eyes. He receded deeper into the shadows.

"I'm warning you," she said in a soft, dangerous voice. "Keep Adric and Rosana, and it will mean war."

He let his mouth curve. "But to us, my lady, war is food."

35

Adric's stomach dropped. He sprang to his feet. "You—no." He paced away, then back again. "You could be wrong. Everyone knows the Sight is unpredictable."

Rosana spread her hands. "I'm not sure," she admitted, "but my Gift is strong, and I've touched you over and over in the last few days without even a glimmer—except for this gut feeling that if you came here alone, you'd die."

He stared down at her, lungs jerking. This wasn't how it was supposed to go down. If he died, Rosana was supposed to be safely back at Rock Run, free to mate with some other male.

My fate is tangled up in yours now.

He'd learned control in a hard school. But for the first time in a long time, rage got the upper hand. Rage at his uncle. Rage at Langdon and his thrice-damned son, Tyrus. Rage at the river fada who'd raped his sister, and at the members of Adric's own clan who'd set the whole thing up.

But most of all, rage at the world that wouldn't let him have the woman he wanted more than life itself.

He turned, slammed the side of his fist against the stone wall. Rosana flinched.

He exhaled, forced himself to speak calmly. "We can't bond. Not yet. I—you know why."

She jumped up as well. "I'm not asking you to choose me over Marjani," she said in a subvocal voice. "I'd never ask that. But what if you're wrong? What if the mate bond is the only thing that can save you? And don't forget what I Saw—you could set off another Darktime." She quoted her own words: "*The prince will destroy your clan from the inside out.*"

"Not if I kill the motherfucker first," he snarled.

"Don't you see?" She grabbed his arms. "It could mean *you*, not him. That you dying is what sets it off. You're the glue holding your clan together. If they lose you, the Darktime will rise again."

He stared at her, arrested. Could she be right? But if she was, where did that leave his sister?

He shook her off and backed away. "Marjani could lead in my place."

"Could she? Or would there be another series of challenges? Your clan is finally getting its shit together. Do you want to risk that? All I'm asking is that you stop fighting the mate bond. Maybe this is meant to be. Together, the two of us are stronger than either of us alone."

"Damn it, Rosana. This isn't your fight, it's mine."

"It's mine now."

He growled and dropped onto the bench. He leaned forward, head clutched in his hands.

She sat beside him. Her hand came to his nape, stroking in that way that made his cat want to lay its head on her lap and purr. He stiffened his spine against the temptation.

"I love you for so many reasons," she murmured.

"But?" There was always a *but*.

"No *but*. That you love your sister so much..." She rested her cheek against his. "It just makes me love you even more. I want you to know that."

He squeezed his eyes shut. Inside, the mate bond battered invisible fists against the barrier he'd erected.

He slid down the bench, away from her and that petting hand. "He came to me, you know. Your brother."

"Dion?"

"Yeah."

Her brows snapped down. "When?"

"The other night. After we went to Lewes."

He distinctly heard her teeth grind together. "What did he say?"

"That you and me just wouldn't work—and not only because you're his sister and my clan would never accept you. But because you're a river fada. You need water. Clean, fresh water to swim in as your dolphin."

A slash of her hand. "You think I don't know that? We could figure it out."

"You'd move to Baltimore? Leave your family, your clan? Because I sure as hell can't move to Rock Run."

She raised her chin. "Yes."

He shook his head.

"It could work," she insisted. "If we both want it to. Baltimore has fresh water—Herring Run, Jones Falls."

"They're filled with trash. And when it rains, there's run-off from the pavement. Raw sewage, when it rains hard."

"Then I'll go north every few days. I wouldn't have to go all the way up to Grace Harbor. I can swim in the Chesapeake north of Baltimore."

He ran some options in his mind. If he survived the next few days—and that was a big if—maybe they could work it out. There was still his clan, of course, although Marjani seemed to think they'd fall in line.

He wrapped his fingers around his quartz. It had warmed, the crystals humming an eager, yearning song.

Inside, the cougar snarled and scratched.

Mate. Our *mate.*

He released the quartz. "Tell you what. We'll talk, okay? When all this is over."

Her smile was wide. "Okay. Sure."

He could've left it at that. She was happy. He'd all but agreed to mate-claim her. At least if he died, she'd know he'd really wanted her. But somehow his mouth was moving again.

"You wanted to know why I didn't challenge my uncle for alpha."

"No." She squeezed his hand. "I know you, Adric. If you didn't challenge him, then you had a good reason."

He glanced at her. Tempted to agree, and then drop it. He didn't explain himself to anyone, even Marjani. But he wanted Rosana to know the truth.

"Yeah," he said with a bitter laugh. "I had a good reason."

He stared out at the shadowed room, his fingers intertwined in hers. The silence thickened. When he spoke, it was with a low rasp.

"My dad was the first. After Leron killed him, he sent my mom to fight in South America in some stupid war between two fae. And then he took me and Marjani in, and we were supposed to obey him. Like we didn't know what the fuck was going on. When I fought back, he beat me."

She sucked in a breath. "Marjani?"

"He never touched her—which is why he lived as long as he did. But he treated her like shit. Both of us. By then, I think he'd realized I was alpha material." His jaw set. "We never had enough food. We had to stay out all night spying on his so-called enemies. No schooling except what we picked up on our own. He even went after my friends. Fuck, I was counting the days until I was strong enough to challenge him. Then"—he swallowed hard—"he came to Jani, ordered her to whore for his second."

"Holy mother," she breathed.

"Yeah. His own niece."

"Did—?"

He shook his head. "She'd have killed herself first."

"Thank *Deus* she had you."

He grunted. "It was the only thing that kept us going—that we had each other. You know what that S.O.B. did? Invited the night fae into Baltimore. He let them feed on us so he could stay in power. What kind of monster does that?"

He was gripping her fingers too tightly, but he couldn't let go. He stared at their two hands, unseeing, caught in the nightmare of the Darktime.

His throat closed up. He pushed the words past it. "I was the only one strong enough to take him down."

Her swallow was audible.

"I live with it every single fucking day. The Darktime. The friends I lost. My mom and dad. But killing my uncle Leron?" His lips twisted. "I haven't lost a single minute of sleep over it."

She didn't speak, didn't try to tell him he'd done the right thing. Just opened her arms.

His breath shuddered out. Then his hands clamped on her. He dragged her onto his lap and buried his face in her hair.

"I love you, all right? I fucking love you. May the Goddess help us both."

36

---

*B*laer watched Langdon's maneuverings with interest. The Rock Run alpha and the Baltimore alpha had both come to him. And now the sun fae queen herself was involved, along with the powerful Lady Olivia and most of Rock Run and Baltimore's top people.

The prince was a master schemer. A woman could learn from him. Maybe she'd allow him to live—for now. For one thing, she was curious to know what his endgame was.

Her gaze turned to Luc, in his wolf form as he'd been ever since he'd brought his alpha to the prince. Her secret weapon. The prince knew Luc was under her *geas*—that was impossible to hide from other fae. But no one, not even Jon and Krysten, knew she could control the wolf fada through his quartz.

If she ordered Luc to kill Langdon, he would.

She wondered if Adric knew she'd learned the secret from his own cousin, Corban. Not that it mattered—Corban was dead. The fool had sought to control *her*.

Her lip curled.

She and Luc were alone in her new living room, she on a red velvet chair, the wolf fada on a rug before the hearth. A real fire burned in the fireplace. She'd learned to appreciate such things while shut up in her solitary tower in Iceland.

The solitary tower to which Langdon had helped banish her.

Luc's eyes opened. They stared into hers, an inhuman yellow-orange. The sheer hate on his furred face made her draw back. She covered her instinctive response by shifting her body on the velvet chair.

Luc had proved hard to tame. He'd lost weight, become increasingly resistant to her commands. She'd expected him to surrender to her more powerful will by now, but she was beginning to think he'd break first.

That...hurt.

She frowned. Fada were lower forms of life. Weaker than the fae, slaves to their emotions. To be used and then discarded when their purpose was served.

Why should she care what happened to Luc?

She rose to her feet. "Shift," she ordered. "And dress in the clothes I've provided, not those stinking rags you seem to prefer. We'll dine at the great hall tonight."

Luc immediately obeyed. It took longer than normal, and she wondered if she'd been wise to demand it. The stubborn ass was wasting away before her eyes.

At last, he stood before her, proudly naked. Too thin, yes, but with broad shoulders and sculpted muscles covered by smooth brown skin. By fae standards, his face was just this side of ugly: rugged and roughly formed, with a dark scruff on his jaw and bushy eyebrows jutting over deep-set eyes.

A wolf in a man's body. Wild, dangerous.

And Goddess, she craved him.

She moistened her lips. His gaze went to them, lingered, and his mouth twisted. The hate was there again, this time on a human face.

Instinct made her want to step back. So instead, she moved forward.

They were nearly the same height, with him just an inch or

two taller. She was close enough that she could feel his breath on her mouth. Her lips tingled hungrily.

She ran her fingers over the black stubble on his jaw, traced a hard pectoral. "I know you want me."

His cock twitched. He stared back, his face a mask of disdain. "I'd rather fuck a viper."

Hurt twisted through her, followed by fury. She whirled away before he could see either.

"Get dressed. And Luc? You *will* eat, if I have to force-feed you myself."

His voice was expressionless. "Yes, my lady."

37

$\mathcal{D}$ion and Rui set up a temporary ops center along with Marjani and the Baltimore fada at the motel where Adric had taken a room.

Neither Langdon nor his guards had been seen since that first afternoon, but that didn't mean their little group wasn't being watched. Every single one of them had felt ice creep up their spine, sensed eyes and ears on them. To keep the night fae at bay, Cleia conjured up fae lights for each of their rooms. They left them on low all night, shedding light on the treacherous shadows.

Marjani and Jace spent the nights as their cats, and they all took turns at watch, aware that if the night fae attacked, it would be in the hours between midnight and dawn. But Langdon refrained from attacking, clearly believing he had the upper hand as long as he remained behind his wards.

He was right. As things stood, they couldn't touch the man—or get to Rosana and Adric.

They all took a shot at breaking into the night fae compound. Cleia brought in her cousin Olivia to help shatter the wards. The two worked long hours, but each time they thought they'd done it, they hit a new barrier. At least Olivia had neutralized the *look-away* spell so they weren't constantly fighting it.

But he worried about them both. It was winter, when the sun fae were weakest. Cleia and her cousin should be home, curled up under a shaft of sunlight, not pushing themselves to the limit in this dank, cold forest.

Meanwhile, the fada tried to sneak into New Moon as their animals. Rui and Tiago changed to fish to try to enter the court through a stream, but the night fae had strengthened their wards to keep out anything larger than a minnow. And while fada could adjust their body size to a certain extent, they simply couldn't compress a man-size amount of matter into that tiny of a body.

Jace Jones didn't even get that far. He spent hours as his black panther, sniffing around the court's perimeter. But the wards repelled him with increasingly violent results. When he'd returned from his last foray with his fur singed, Marjani had drawn him aside and, after a heated argument, extracted his promise not to try again.

As for Marjani herself, she grew edgier with each day that passed. Dion kept a wary eye on her, afraid she'd slip off to exchange herself for Adric. It was what he'd do if he were her.

But where would that leave Rosana?

Sunday arrived with heavy clouds and snow flurries. They'd been in Virginia four days already. Five days until Friday and the new moon.

Dion spent the day prowling the forest around New Moon along with Tiago and Rui, daring the night fae to confront them. But the court remained maddeningly silent, concealed behind an opaque white fog.

Late that afternoon, he returned to the motel to find Marjani alone in the parking lot, gazing at the trees where they'd found her brother's keycard.

He left Tiago and Rui to approach her. "Walk with me?"

She nodded and fell into step with him. "Something wrong, my lord?"

"Please. Call me Dion."

She shoved her hands into the back pockets of her cargo pants. "Dion, then. What's up?"

The sun was low in the sky, but it was still daylight. Still, he waited until they reached the center of the lot, far from any shadows where the night fae could lurk.

"I'm asking you to be patient. Give us a little more time to work this out."

She bristled. "What do you mean?"

In the few days they'd been in Virginia, he'd learned Marjani was a Gifted strategist. Even afraid as she must be for her brother, she coolly examined a problem from all sides. Now he chose his words with care, knowing his only hope was to appeal to the strategist.

Because the sister knew that if she didn't do something soon, her brother would be executed.

"As it stands, we're even, more or less; the prince has Adric and Rosana, but we have you and Merry. So I'm asking you not to do anything on your own. We *will* bring them both home. That's a promise."

The cougar fada's gaze slid sideways. So he'd guessed right— she was planning to barter herself to save Adric.

"If they capture you," he added, "Merry will be our only bargaining chip, and I swore never to turn her over to the night fae."

"So you'll have nothing the prince wants bad enough to trade for Rosana." Marjani stared up at the darkening sky. The moon hadn't risen yet, but each night, the shadows took another bite out of it. "Even if he takes me in exchange for Adric, he'll still have her. Gods, you don't ask much, do you?"

He squeezed his nape, hating the bleak look he'd put on her fine-boned face. They both knew if things went south, her brother was dead.

"I have no choice. The night before Rosana was kidnapped, Merry Jones told Rui that she believes the prince has been watching her. Apparently, he has the farsight."

"He knows she's alive then."

"*Sim.* We think he's just waiting for his chance."

Marjani's head dropped. Her whole body hunched in on itself. The silence stretched, and then she blew out a noisy breath.

"Fine. I'll hold off for now. But only because I know if it was up to Adric, he'd sacrifice himself for Rosana in a heartbeat." She must have seen something in Dion's expression, because she snarled, low and mean. "You don't believe me? You think my brother would leave her with those sadistic S.O.B.s? And that goes double for Merry."

Dion hesitated. "I believe he'd willingly give his life for Merry, or any pup."

Adric might be a ruthless S.O.B., a man Dion didn't particularly like or trust, but he had to admit the other alpha was a good leader, one who put children and elders first. Everything he did, he did for his people.

But Rosana wasn't a member of his clan.

"You just don't get it, do you?" Marjani said. "He loves Rosana. He only kept his hands off her because he believes he's no good for her, that bringing her home to Baltimore would be a step down for her. If she didn't mean so much to him, he'd have taken her years ago."

"Maybe," he shot back. "But we both know your clan would never accept her. What kind of life is that—a pariah in her own mate's clan?"

"Merry has made a life in your clan, and she's not just half earth fada, she's a quarter fae. What makes you think we'd be any different? My own mate is a quarter fae, and Adric accepted him into the clan. He'd make damn sure Rosana was treated with respect."

He snorted. "Your brother can't even control his own people. *Mãe de Deus,* the very first night Rosana spent in Baltimore, she was kidnapped."

"That had nothing to do with Adric. That wolf—Luc—was working for the fae and you know it." Marjani leaned in. "You think you're so much better than us, but you're wrong. I've seen how my brother hurts, wanting Rosana, *loving* her—and not being able to claim her because he's too fucking noble to come between the two of you."

"She would never have him."

Then he recalled the note Rosana had left and scraped a hand over his hair.

I'm with Adric. I'm tired of hiding it. I love him, and he loves me...

Marjani gave Dion the look women reserve for clueless men. "What d'you think she was doing in Lewes last week?"

Dion rocked back on his heels. "What do you mean?"

A jerk of her shoulder. "Forget it."

"You're saying she was with Adric?"

When Marjani dipped her chin in assent, his jaw hardened. So that Tuesday night in Baltimore hadn't been the first time. In fact, that talk he'd had with Adric at the Full Moon Saloon? Apparently he'd already been too late—and the devious son of a bitch had neglected to inform Dion of that little detail.

"How long have they been meeting?"

"Overnight? That was the first time." She eyed him warily. "Look, forget I said anything. But I wanted you to know that Adric would do anything for Rosana. That's why I'm so worried about him." Her voice hitched on the last few words.

"No. You were right to tell me."

His claws pricked his fingertips. Adric, it always came back to Adric. He should've taken the *cabrão* out years ago.

But Dion didn't kill for no reason. And while Adric might be a cocky pain-in-the-ass, he'd also done things that had left Dion in his debt—like rescuing Tiago's mate from a pair of rogue river fada. Plus, he was ten times the alpha Leron Savonett had been. Take Adric out of the equation, and the situation in Baltimore would only get worse, and before you knew it, Rock Run could be dragged in.

If Dion was honest, this wasn't about Adric, it was about Rosana.

Shame squeezed his chest. That his own sister believed she had to sneak around to be with the man she loved rather than tell him, Dion, straight out.

So he can't want me for myself? she'd asked, and he'd brushed her question aside.

He withdrew his claws, stared unseeingly into the trees.

"Hey." Marjani touched his back. "She'll be all right. You'll see. Adric will make sure of it."

He jerked his chin in acknowledgement. "It's dark. We should go in."

WEDNESDAY MORNING DAWNED. Dion woke from a restless sleep with a sense of dread. Time was running out. The new moon was just two days away.

Cleia had spent the night at Rising Sun with Brisa while Dion bunked down with Tiago, both of them tossing and turning for those hours they weren't on watch, their worry for Rosana a constant, clawing thing.

He glanced at where his brother lay staring at the ceiling and threw off the sheet. "I'm going for a swim."

Tiago rose as well. "I'll come."

When they exited their room, Rui was waiting. They left Jaxon and Ed on watch at the motel and headed for the Potomac. Dion and Tiago swam as their dolphins, with Rui joining them as his bull shark. When they returned, Dion sent Jaxon and Ed for a swim while Tiago opted to make another attempt at slipping through New Moon's wards by water. Meanwhile, Rui held a convo with Marjani and Fane to determine if there was anything they were missing.

Dion took up a position in the forest near the court. The temperatures remained just above freezing, with a chilly wind rattling the bare branches. He paced a path through the trees, straining for a glimpse of Rosana, but the unnatural fog prevented him from seeing more than a few yards.

A black rage filled his head. That his sister was trapped underground in one of those cryptlike lairs. Upset, afraid, unable to shift.

With those perverted bastards enjoying her fear.

His claws pricked out. He dropped his head back, fangs bared. His animal wanted to slash and burn, to tear out Langdon's heart and feed on it.

The air nearby shimmered and then twisted as Cleia 'ported onto the grass between the woods and the court. She walked to him, a pretty peach-colored dress whipping around her long legs, her bright hair in a businesslike braid. Her only concession to the January cold was a soft cashmere shawl.

"My love." She touched his unshaven cheek. "You have to eat. Starving yourself isn't helping Rosana. And when was the last time you slept?"

Dion raked a hand through his hair. He hadn't tied it back for days, and his only clothing was a T-shirt and the leather pants he'd been wearing when Rosana had gone missing. His animal was too close to the surface to accept such human restrictions as shoes or a coat.

"I slept last night." For an hour or two. "And I'm not hungry. How's my Brisa?"

"She's good. She misses her *papai*, of course, and Rosana."

He ran a hand down Cleia's silky braid, needing to touch her. "Tell Brisa I miss her, too. With all my heart. And that I'll be home as soon as I can—with Rosana." He glared at the night fae compound.

"I already did." Cleia 'ported in a thick ham-and-cheese sandwich and a cup of coffee, and thrust them both into his hands. "But you still need to eat, and sleep more than a few hours a night."

When he just stared at the food, she sighed. "Dion. I'm as worried as you are. But you can't give up hope. We *will* get her back. And meanwhile, she's with Adric. From what the prince said, that was a condition of her remaining at the court. Adric won't let them hurt her."

Anger fisted in his chest. He hadn't forgotten that Rosana had been sneaking off to see the Baltimore alpha right beneath his nose. Even Tiago had known, or at least suspected. The sensible part of him knew his anger was misplaced, that it was just that he was so damn afraid for his sister, but he didn't care.

"If it wasn't for him," he growled, "she'd never have been there in the first place."

"You don't really believe that."

"No?"

Her lush mouth set. She started to argue further, but he shook his head.

"*Querida*. Not now. *Por favor*?"

She expelled a breath. "You're right. When they're safely back home, then we'll argue about whether they're mates or not."

"*Mates?*" That fist of anger tightened around his heart. "Who said anything about them being mates? It would never work. She can't live in Baltimore—I told Adric myself."

"Did you now?"

"And he agreed."

"Ah." Cleia opened her mouth, closed it.

"Go ahead. Say it."

"We made it work when no one—even you—thought we could. A sun fae and a river fada."

He just shook his head. He was still holding the food. He took a bite of the sandwich and followed it with a gulp of coffee.

"You *are* hungry," she said, and to please her, he kept eating until it was gone.

As he was finishing up, Lady Olivia 'ported in. They turned to her hopefully. She strode toward them, her long, fire-colored dress draped like liquid flame over her slender body, her penny-bright hair twined in a coronet around her head.

"Peace to you and yours," she said, and then gave a rueful

shake of her head. "I'm afraid I haven't made any progress on the wards."

"By the Goddess," Cleia bit out. "How is he keeping us out? You're the best spell-breaker we have."

Dion briefly closed his eyes.

Olivia touched his arm for the first time ever, as far as he could recall. "I'm sorry, Dion. I've tried everything I can think of."

"I know. And I thank you for it."

"We *will* break through," she said. "And when we do, I've prepared a few helpful...aids, shall we say?"

"Oh?" murmured Cleia.

"One moment." Olivia conjured up a blazing fae light. A nearby shadow made a small sound of pain and hurriedly withdrew. With a little half-smile, she held the glowing orb higher so they stood within a shaft of light.

Dion narrowed his eyes. He didn't have the sun fae's love of bright lights, but he accepted the need for it.

"You have the protection charm?" Olivia asked him.

He wordlessly held up his wrist. The delicate silver bracelet encircled it.

"Good," she said. "Get that back to Rosana as soon as possible. It won't block a fae as powerful as the prince forever, but it will buy her time." She handed Cleia a small silk bag. "I made a charm for the Savonett female as well."

Cleia frowned. "That's good of you, but you've expended so much energy trying to break the wards. Are you sure this wasn't too much for you?"

The other woman raised a fine sable eyebrow. "I know my limits."

Which didn't really answer the question.

Dion eyed the fae lady. Her narrow, pointed face looked gaunt. Magic at the level she'd been wielding it sucked life-energy right out of you.

Cleia sighed and pursed her lips. She might be queen, but

Olivia was her top adviser, their relationship one of near-equals. "Just remember we'll need you when we do break through."

Olivia inclined her head.

"What if he's convinced Rosana to accept his *geas*?" Cleia voiced Dion's deepest fear.

A chill prickled his skin. He was fairly certain his sister wouldn't accept Langdon's *geas* for herself, no matter what the prince offered her. But she might accept it to save Adric.

"Then we'll have to encourage him to break it," Olivia replied.

"How?" Dion demanded. "A *geas* is almost impossible to break."

"By the person who accepted it, yes," Olivia said. "But not by the fae who set the terms."

Dion's mouth twisted. "Why would he break it? He'd love to have a Seer in his power for the next ten turns of the sun."

Olivia moved a slim shoulder. "Then we'll offer him something he wants more." She pulled a gleaming iron dagger from a hidden pocket in her dress. "Meanwhile, I had one of our smiths make you this. It's bespelled."

Dion set down the coffee cup and took it by the ebony handle. Energy shivered up his hand. "A powerful spell."

Olivia inclined her head. "It will slice through any spell the prince casts at you."

He slipped it into his back pocket. "Thank you, my lady."

Dion pulled Cleia closer, and the three of them gazed at the fog-covered court.

His fingers tightened on Cleia's waist. A sun fae's metabolism burned hot, and *Deus* knew, he needed heat right now. He was chilled to the bone.

"Tell me she's getting enough to eat," he rasped. "Tell me he's allowing her to shift to her dolphin." According to Rui and Fane, New Moon was crisscrossed by creeks and streams. There was even a pond big enough for Rosana to swim.

"Of course, he is," Cleia said. "He knows a water fada will die if she's kept from the water."

Olivia made a small sound of dissent.

"What?" asked Dion.

"He may not consider that to a fada, time in a fae court can pass differently."

Cleia's gold-touched skin paled. "It depends on the fada."

Olivia inclined her pointed chin in that cool manner she had, but Dion had seen her with his sister. In her own way, the fae lady loved Rosana. "Some adjust to our time, but others find it difficult."

"She's fine," Cleia stated firmly. "He wouldn't dare harm her."

Dion's growl came from the darkest, primal heart of him. "I hope you're right," he said in a carrying voice. "Because if Langdon hurts her, he's dead."

38

In the never-ending twilight of the cell, day and night blended together. Adric had no idea how much time had passed—one day? three days?—before the night fae finally 'ported them some food.

He fell on it, his starving body needing calories, and watched, worried, as Rosana just picked at hers. But after that, meals came on a regular basis: fish chowder for her, steak for him, fresh fruit and vegetables, crusty homemade bread.

They slept, woke, plotted. He paced the cell, nerves stretched taut at their continuing confinement in the small, dark space.

His quartz had completely recharged—another clue that in the outside world, more time had passed than they knew. He gave Rosana what healing energy he could, but it was her life-energy that was fading, and he wasn't healer enough to fix that.

She grew weaker, edgier. She took to pacing the cell along with him, and when they curled up to rest, she felt warm, which was all wrong for a river fada.

And when was the last time she'd eaten?

Then the day came when she didn't get up at all, just lay curled up next to the water trough, fingers playing in the meager trickle, her breath so light, it was almost inaudible.

He bent to stroke her cheek. It was dry, feverish. Even though he'd blocked the bond, he *felt* her receding from him.

"Angel," he said brokenly.

"*Amo-te,*" she whispered. *Love you.*

He briefly closed his eyes—and then rose to his feet.

"Prince Langdon!" He stood in the center of the cell, spine erect, hands clenched at his sides. Prepared to do anything, even accept the bastard's *geas*, in exchange for Rosana's life. "Come to me—please. I'm begging you."

Rosana lifted her head to hiss, "No, Rick!"

He ignored her to loudly repeat the prince's name. "Langdon! Are you there?"

A whiff of metal and decay.

Adric scanned the cell.

There. In the corner to his left, a shadow coalesced into a man-shape.

He whipped around. Hot, angry words crowded his throat, but he forced himself to speak calmly. "Prince Langdon?"

A whisper from the shadows. "You called me."

"Yes. Rosana"—his voice broke—"she's sick. She needs her river. You have to release her."

"So you're ready to negotiate?"

A muscle in Adric's cheek worked. Inside, his cat crouched, ears back, tail swishing angrily.

"As long as you let her out of here. She has to get in the water. Even that pond outside would work."

A dark chuckle. "Soon." The shadows settled again.

"No! Wait, you thrice-damned bastard!" He pounded his fists against the stones. "She needs out, *now.*" But Langdon was gone.

Adric flung himself at the door. "Somebody, please!" He hammered on the wood between the iron straps. "Let Rosana out. She's going to die in here."

When no one came, he threw his whole body against the door, slamming into it again and again, uncaring of the iron straps. But the heavy wood withstood his battering, and when it was over, all he had to show for it were several burns on his arms and hands.

And he was still alone in the cell with Rosana.

He bit out a vicious curse and stood there, hands fisted on his hips, head hanging.

Rosana moved restlessly. "I'm so thirsty..."

"I'm here, baby." He rinsed the burns in the cold water and then sat down, easing her head onto his lap. "It's going to be all right, you'll see. Just hold on a little longer. Here, drink."

Dipping the cup in the trough, he brought it to her dry, cracked lips. She murmured something unintelligible and sucked at the cup's lip like a baby, tiny sips that had half the water trickling down her jaw.

But he heard her swallow.

"That's it. Drink some more." He urged water on her until she shut her mouth and turned her head.

ROSANA DREAMED she was a small girl again, floating in Rock Run Creek. Water flowed around her, cool and silky. She sensed her mama and *papai* on either side of her, but her eyes were glued shut.

And she was so dry, like she'd swallowed a desert.

"Shift," her *papai* said in Portuguese. "You can do it, *minha pequena*."

My little one.

Nostalgia cramped her stomach. How long had it been since anyone called her that?

And then something twisted and she was an adult again, watching her younger self play with her parents in the creek. Her father, big and black-haired like her brothers, his strong, proud face marked by the jagged white scar he'd received from a fae. Her mother, fine-boned and creamy skinned, with a heart-shaped face and blue eyes that always seemed to be smiling.

Rosana's throat burned. "I miss you, Mama," she whispered—and just like that, she was back in her little girl's body again.

"You can do it," Ula encouraged in her lilting Irish accent. "Shift, Rosie darling."

She whimpered. "I'm thirsty."

"I know. But I can help," her mama replied. "Just open your eyes."

But instead, Rosana opened her mouth to gulp down the river's fresh, clear water. It didn't help—she was drier than ever.

Her heart sank. "This is just a dream," she said sadly. "Because I need to shift and I can't."

Her dad faded away and now she only sensed Ula.

"It is a dream," she agreed. "But I'm really here. Now open your eyes, *alanna*."

"Mama?" In the dream-river, Rosana's eyes popped open. To her surprise, it was nighttime. The water flowed silver around her. On the nearby bank, bare trees scratched at the rising moon.

But her parents were nowhere to be seen.

Don't leave me. Please, don't leave me.

Hot tears clogged her throat. She squeezed her eyes shut, willing them not to spill out.

Gentle fingers brushed her face. "Not those eyes, *alanna*. The eyes you use to See."

"Go away." Rosana shook off her mother's hand. "You're not really here. This is just some night-fae trick."

"Oh, Rosie. You still haven't learned the most necessary lesson."

"Oh, yeah? And what's that?"

"Trust," Ula whispered.

"I do trust him. He loves me." Her mouth curved. "He told me."

"Ah, sweetheart. That's wonderful. Trust between mates is a beautiful, necessary thing. But you also must trust yourself, trust your Gift."

Rosana's brows snapped together. "You sound like Colm.

'*Believe in yourself. If you don't believe you can do it, then you can't.*' But what good can my Gift do? It isn't a weapon."

"Oh, but it is. Touch *him*."

She turned her head away. "*Touch* him? But I can't See anything when I touch him. And how would it help anyway when we're locked in this freaking cell?"

Hopelessness settled over her like a dark veil.

Ula moved uneasily. "I have to go now—I shouldn't even be talking to you. But remember, Rosie. When you wake up, remember these words: *Touch him*."

Then she was gone, and when Rosana forced her eyes open, she was in the cell with Adric pleading for her to drink.

To please him, she took a couple of sips. But she was so tired.

She closed her eyes, telling herself she'd only rest a minute... and slipped back into the dream-river.

39

———

*D*ion spent another almost sleepless night. Tossing and turning. Staring at the ceiling. Listening to his brother do the same.

By morning, he'd decided to trade himself for Rosana, to hell with the consequences.

The instant the sun peeped above the horizon, he was out of bed. He pulled on his clothes, sliding Olivia's bespelled dagger into his pocket.

Tiago raised his head to peer dully at him.

"Go back to sleep," he said and his brother dropped his head back on the pillow.

Overnight, the wind had dropped and heavy clouds had moved in. A storm was coming, rain this time. A daylong downpour from the air's scent and feel.

His mouth curved dangerously. Water was his element, the more the better.

This time, he didn't hide in the forest. Instead, he stalked back and forth on the grass in full view of the fog-covered court.

Daring Prince Langdon to make a move.

A movement behind him made him spin on his heel.

Rui strode out of the forest, scowling. "What the fuck do you think you're doing?" he demanded in Portuguese.

"Go away," Dion snarled in the same language. "That's an order from your alpha."

"Not when he's acting like a crazy man." Rui folded his arms over his chest, a rock-faced, stubborn-as-hell statue.

Dion ground his teeth. He knew Rui. If the shark fada had decided Dion needed him, an army wouldn't move him.

"Then don't interfere," he bit out.

Rui shook his head. "This all started when I brought Merry back to Rock Run."

Dion growled. "When are you going to stop beating yourself up about Merry's father? You took that job with my blessing. The clan needed Lord Tyrus's diamonds. You think I don't ask myself why I didn't dig a little deeper before letting him hire you? But unless you can turn back time, we both have to live with it. Merry is clan now. The night fae go after her, they go after all of us."

Rui drew a breath. "With all respect, I'd take Merry, Valeria and the girls and run before I'd let her anywhere near those dark bastards. That doesn't change the fact that this all comes back to me. I'll go to the prince. Offer myself for Rosana."

"No." Dion clamped a hand on his shoulder. "You, Tiago, Jaxon, Ed—I know every single one of you would trade yourself for Rosana. But that's not the way."

Rui regarded him through hooded green eyes. "Then why are you out here all alone?"

Dion simply looked back at him. But Rui knew him too well.

"Exactly. If you go to the prince, I go at your side. I demand this not only as your second, but as your friend."

Dion exhaled.

"I'll go." Tiago stepped out of the trees, jaw set, hands balled at his side. "As alpha, you're not expendable, and neither are you, Rui. I am."

Before Dion could draw a breath to argue with him, Marjani, Fane and Jace were there as well. They took up a stance next to

Tiago. Jace was in his black panther form. He fixed emerald eyes on Dion, while Marjani folded her arms over her chest, a shorter, wiry imitation of Rui.

"This concerns us too," Fane said.

Dion shook his head. "It appears we have a mutiny," he muttered.

"I'm going with you," Marjani said in a tone that brooked no argument. "The new moon is two nights away. If Adric is executed, the clan goes down, too. He's the only one who can hold us together. And we won't survive another Darktime. You don't have the right to ask that, even to save your sister."

"You're right. I don't." His heart clenched for Rosana, but he made himself continue. "I apologize, I should've come to you first. I'm not...thinking too clearly these days. What do you want to do?"

She blinked, taken aback, but quickly recovered. "Not here," she said with a glance around. "Back at the motel."

As Dion nodded, the air shimmered and Cleia 'ported in. "By the Sun Goddess." Her amber gaze raked over the six of them. "I hope you're not planning what I think you are. Because the prince would like nothing better for you all to go charging in there. If he captures even a few of you, he wins. He won't even have to negotiate with us."

Marjani growled lowly.

Cleia took her hands. "I know, my dear. It's your brother's life on the line. But don't forget, he has Dion and Tiago's sister—this is personal for everyone here." She released Marjani to speak to all of them. "I've talked things over with Olivia and a couple of my top warriors. They agree with me that the prince is playing a deep game, manipulating us so he gets what he wants. And we all know what he really wants."

"Merry Jones," whispered Marjani.

Jace's tail whipped back and forth.

"Yes. And I agree, it's an impossible choice. But I promise you"—Cleia's beautiful face was fierce—"I won't let him execute

Adric. Now, let's all go back to the motel. I have news for you. Good news. We've got some planning to do."

Marjani, Jace and Fane exchanged looks, and then the cougar fada lowered her chin in assent. "We'll listen. But I'm not making any promises."

40

$\mathcal{A}$ key scraped in the lock. Adric lurched into action, snatching up Rosana and scrambling to his feet.

He waited with bated breath as the door swung open to reveal a tall silhouette with a pair of gleaming eyes. The shadows arranged themselves into a night fae female in a warrior's trim black uniform, her jet hair slicked back in a perfect ponytail.

He shoved past her, Rosana cradled to his chest. "She needs to get in the water. *Now.*"

Two more warriors, both males, waited in the hall.

"The prince has granted your request," the female said. "If you'll follow me..."

"I know the fucking way." His inner GPS would get him to the surface.

"As you wish." The men flanked him, and she followed behind.

A few twists and turns, and he was at the stairs leading up to the black marble foyer. He took them at a run. In the foyer, the tall door once again opened as he approached. He jogged up the steps leading to the outside and sprinted the fifty yards to the pond, the long-legged warriors loping alongside him.

Dusk had spread its gloomy fingers over the compound. A few night fae had already emerged from their lairs, but although he caught them eyeing him and Rosana with interest, they stayed out of his way.

He lowered Rosana to the grass beside the pond and stripped off her clothes. The three warriors hovered over him until he snarled at them to back off. "She's not going anywhere." Shifters were used to being naked in front of one another, but he was damned if he'd let these cold-eyed fae ogle his mate's naked body.

The female inclined her head, and they all moved a few steps back.

Dragging off his own clothes, he picked up Rosana again and strode into the icy pond. When it reached his waist, he lowered her into the water.

She shrieked and flung out her arms like a startled infant. One hand latched onto his shoulder in a death grip.

He frowned. "Easy now. It's okay. You're in the water now. You can shift." He bent his knees, submerging her to the chest.

"No!" She shook her head wildly. Both hands clamped around his neck.

"Shift, angel." He lowered her a little deeper, but she clawed at him, climbing his body like he was trying to drown her.

What the fuck—?

"Rosana." He gave her a shake. "Shift. Change to your dolphin."

Her eyes popped open—and looked right through him. "Go away," she hissed. "You're not really here."

Panic coated his throat. He lifted her out of the water and brought his face close to hers. "Rosana! Look at me."

"*No...*" She squeezed her eyes shut. "Why won't you leave me alone?"

"Because," he growled, "if you don't shift, you'll die." But he had the bad feeling she didn't hear him.

As he lowered her back into the pond, she flailed her arms and legs, frantically trying to escape. Her breath came fast and hard. He heard the frenzied beating of her heart, saw the frightened flutter of the pulse at the base of her throat. Worse, he *felt* her blind, unreasoning fear.

He stood it as long as he could, and then rose back to his feet with her. In her weakened condition, she could die of sheer terror.

He cuddled her to his chest. "It's okay, baby. It's okay."

At the pond's edge, the three night fae warriors gathered like a flock of tall black vultures. Watching and waiting.

He snarled over his shoulder at them. They stared back, blank faced. The eyes of the male on the left flickered red; he was eager to feed. But he didn't, no doubt under orders from his superiors.

Rosana locked her arms around his neck and burrowed her head into his throat. Like she was trying to crawl right inside him.

In desperation, he tried to pulse life-energy through the mate bond. But he was blocked by the shield he himself had erected between them.

He dropped back his head to stare up at the darkening sky. If he were a wolf, he'd have howled in anguish. Rosana was dying, and taking his heart with him.

Her breasts pressed against his chest. By some odd coincidence, their pendants had lined up side by side, his quartz touching her chest, her amethyst against his breastbone. He felt her reaching out to him—mate to mate—and knew what he had to do.

He'd rejected the bond to protect her. Now he had to accept it.

In the end, it was easy. He simply let the shield drop.

The shining strands leapt toward each other, his blue intertwining with her sea-green.

Rosana jerked. Mumbled something.

His stomach dropped. Her thread was so thin and weak. A shimmer so fragile, it hurt him to see it—and yet also incredibly beautiful, glowing with Rosana's very essence.

He poured his love into that fragile green strand. Willing her to feel how much he cared.

Willing her to *live*.

To his astonishment, a new thread shimmered into being, a

gossamer gold that belonged to both of them. Together, they twined into single bright cord.

Rosana's breath shuddered in.

Hope leapt in him. He pressed kisses to her face. "That's it, love. Come back to me."

Her eyes opened. As she focused on him, a wondering look spread over her face.

She touched his cheek. "Ric. You—we—"

"Hey there, angel." Rubbing his lips over hers, he pulsed life-energy into her. This time, it worked, moving right to the deepest parts of her, healing her from the inside out.

She heaved a breath. They remained like that for a long minute.

When her lips curved in a smile, he felt it clear to his soul. "We're mate-bonded. But—" She frowned, shook her head. "I don't understand."

"I'll explain later. Can you stand now?"

When she nodded, he set her on her feet in the pond. She blinked around her. "We're outside. In the water."

"It's a pond at New Moon. Big enough for your dolphin."

"Oh. How—?"

"Go ahead." He gave her an encouraging squeeze. "Shift."

She blinked again—and then released him to sink beneath the surface.

She barely had enough juice to shift, but he remained connected to her, urging her on. That and sheer grit got her through. The dark waters glittered, and then she was a river dolphin with a long beak and charcoal gray body.

He watched tensely while she lolled in the water, sucking air through her blowhole, until she revived enough to give him a feeble nudge with her beak.

His whole body sagged in relief. He set his cheek against her smooth gray face. "Go. Swim. Catch some fish for me."

She cast him a worried look, clucked a question. Somehow he understood.

What about you?

"It's okay. You can find me later." He pressed a kiss to the edge of her beak. "I love you."

She hesitated, but she must have seen the wisdom of that because her body brushed against his and she was off.

The last thing he heard was a short series of clicks. *I love you, too.*

He watched until she was across the pond. Already she seemed stronger. She was going to be all right.

He turned and walked out of the pond.

The night fae warriors surrounded him. A fiery purple fae ball glowed in one of the male's hands, but he didn't need it.

Adric knew that if he didn't cooperate, Rosana would be back in that cell so fast his head would spin.

"Here." The other male tossed Adric his T-shirt and pants.

"The prince is waiting," added the female.

As soon as Adric was dressed, the three warriors marched him back to the prince's lair. Just before he walked down the steps, he caught a glimpse of Luc watching from a stand of trees, his too-thin face unreadable.

Adric expected to be taken to the prince, but instead the warriors took him back underground. He resigned himself to being locked in the cell again, but they kept going, navigating through a series of long, twisting corridors.

He gazed around, awed in spite of himself. The earth fada were considered master miners, but this beat anything he'd ever seen. The buildings aboveground were the tip of the iceberg. The night fae had an entire city down here. It must have taken centuries to carve out.

And still, they fucked with his clan, sucked its resources.

He shook his head, disgusted.

At last, they exited in an immense, windowless hall with soaring Gothic arches. Fanciful columns shaped like giant palm trees supported the ceiling with curved stone fronds. The only lighting was a handful of darkly shimmering fae lights ranging from purple to forest green.

Adric strode barefoot to the hall's center, the warriors on his heels.

"Well?" he demanded of the shadows. "I'm here, Prince Langdon. Now what?"

Olivier appeared in a nearby archway clad in his butler's uniform of black pants and crisp white shirt. His bow tie this time was lavender dotted with tiny white skulls.

"My lord. If you'll follow me."

He turned to go back the way he'd come, but Adric leapt forward and grabbed his arm. "Where's the prince?"

The guards clamped cold fingers on him, yanking him away with superhuman strength. Furious, he fought against their hold, but the two men dragged his arms behind his back.

An iron dagger flashed in the woman's hand.

He glared at her. "I demand to see Prince Langdon."

"Be still, fada." The blade hissed across his T-shirt, slicing through the material to his chest.

He jerked. It felt like she'd drawn a line of acid on his skin.

Her dark eyes flashed an unholy red. "I can bring you to the prince whole," she said, "or I can bring you carved. Your choice."

Adric narrowed his eyes. "Bite me."

"If I may, Neoma?" Olivier stepped between them, forcing her back a step. To Adric's surprise, she allowed it. He clucked his tongue at Adric. "My lord, there's no need for this. My orders are to make you comfortable, provide you with dinner. The prince will see you tonight."

Neoma sheathed the knife. The corners of her mouth turned up in a way that sent icy water down Adric's spine. "Yes. Tonight."

"Fuck that," he snapped back. "I want to see the prince now."

The warriors released him. Adric's neck tingled. He spun around.

Langdon stood a few feet away, dressed in a simple black outfit much like his warriors wore, his only jewelry the diamonds glittering in his eyebrows and ears. On his narrow feet were supple leather sandals.

He inclined his head. "My lord Adric."

"Lord Langdon," he returned. He about choked on the next words, but if kissing ass helped Rosana, then he'd kiss away. "My thanks for allowing Rosana to swim as her dolphin."

"She's a guest. I don't wish to see her harmed."

Then why the fuck keep her underground all this time?

But Adric knew the answer. The prince had used Rosana to break him. To save her, he'd promise the bastard anything.

His stomach clenched. He was more afraid for Rosana than ever. They were mated now. He wasn't fighting just for himself or even Marjani.

He was fighting for her.

If he accepted Langdon's *geas*, Rosana might have to do the same. A *geas* was typically for a fae year-and-a-day, or ten years in the human world. Mates couldn't live apart for that long. She might literally pine away, and it wouldn't do him any good, either.

But to Hades with that. He wanted her far, far from here.

"You have me," he said in a hard voice. "Let Rosana go."

The fae lights wafted lower to circle the two of them, the lustrous purple and green gliding like an oil slick over his skin. Or maybe it was just that standing this close to Langdon made him feel like he was covered in something foul and greasy.

Langdon spoke. "Senhorita do Rio is here at her own request."

Adric swallowed sickly. That was the truth—she'd said so herself.

"As for you, you've broken a number of our laws. Your punishment is set for the night of the new moon."

Adric's chin jerked up. "What are the charges?"

"Trespassing, attempted murder. And let's not forget your part in Lord Tyrus's death."

Adric's heartbeat thundered in his ears.

Oh, Rosana.

He could guess what his punishment would be—execution. Or

if Langdon was feeling lenient, he might invite Adric to accept his *geas* instead—and not for the fae year-and-a-day. This would be a life sentence.

He'd accepted the mate bond to save Rosana's life. But in doing so, had he condemned her to spend the rest of that life alone?

He moistened his lips. "And Marjani?"

"She'll be punished for her own part in the death of my line."

"Your own fucking son ended your line," he growled back. "He ordered Silver's death, and he got within inches of killing Merry, too. Then he went after Jace just because he's Merry's uncle. Tyrus would be alive today if he hadn't attacked us."

"So you say." Langdon's lids lowered, concealing his thoughts. "Now go with Olivier or I'll allow Neoma to play with you."

The warriors tried to grab Adric again, but he was ready this time. He side-stepped, circled to the prince's other side.

"What about Rosana?"

"She must choose her own path. But you have my word she won't be harmed."

The fae lights darkened. Shadows danced over the room. Langdon didn't seem to move, but suddenly, he blended with them, part man, part wraith.

Adric leapt after him, but Langdon just...flowed away. This time, the guards didn't even try to stop Adric. They knew he couldn't touch the prince.

"The night of the new moon," Langdon said. "In our time, that's tonight at midnight. Tomorrow at dusk in the outside world."

"To Hades with your charges," Adric bit out. "Everything I did was in response to acts of war—on myself, my clan, or my... woman." He barely stopped himself from saying *mate*. It would just give Langdon another weapon to use against them. "You might be able to kill me, but my clan won't rest until you're dead."

"That's their prerogative, of course. However, they'll find I'm not an easy man to kill." Langdon receded deeper into the shadows. "As for Rosana, New Moon could use a Seer of her power."

Fury flooded Adric, hot and red. His fangs pricked his gums, his cat quivering with the urge to tear Langdon into bloody pieces.

The three warriors surrounded Adric. Fae balls burned in the men's palms.

"You're insane," he growled. "She'll never agree to that."

"No? When you've lived as long as I have, you find that everyone has their breaking point." The prince smiled. "Don't they, Lord Adric?" And he was gone.

Adric snarled and spat on the marble floor. "Stand and fight like a man, you thrice-damned prick."

The guards raised the fae balls threateningly. Neoma fingered her dagger.

From the archway, Olivier spoke. "If you'll follow me, my lord."

Rosana swam.

For a time, there was nothing but her and the dark, life-giving water. She glided through it, instinctively mapping the pond's dimensions with echolocation so that within a few passes, she knew it and its aquatic inhabitants intimately. The school of minnows that scattered at her approach. The fat, whiskered catfish and the bluegills and carp. The snails, crayfish and leeches. The turtles hibernating in the soft black mud, and the frog slowly swimming in the deep water at the center.

She understood she'd almost died. Her body needed time to heal.

But her heart was singing—no, *shouting*—with joy, its every beat an ecstatic cacophony.

Adric had mate-bonded with her.

He loves me. He loves me. He loves me.

His amethyst hung around her neck, the cord a little too tight with her dolphin's thicker proportions—she'd have to fix that— but there, warm, comforting.

An hour passed, maybe more. She swam and healed, healed and swam.

As her energy returned, she became aware that Adric wasn't on the bank waiting. She surged out of the water in a long arc, scanning for him.

It was a murky, moonless night. Her eyes went night-glow as she anxiously searched the bank. He was gone, replaced by two night fae warriors, their eyes shining in the dark. She raced for the shore—and shifted without thinking of the cost. Her body could barely handle it. As depleted as she'd been, she shouldn't have tried to shift for another twenty-four hours.

For an awful, stomach-churning moment, she wavered between forms. She grit her teeth and powered through it. The next thing she knew, she was on all fours in the shallow water. She came up on her knees and bent forward, hands on her thighs, lungs working.

The night fae moved closer—one man, one woman, neither of whom she'd seen before. The female had Rosana's clothes.

Rosana pushed herself to standing and walked out of the pond, wobbly-kneed but determined. "Where's Lord Adric?" she demanded as she got dressed. "What have you done with him?"

"Jessica will explain."

"Who?"

They herded Rosana forward without speaking, and she allowed it, because it was clear she wouldn't learn anything from them.

It was the first time she'd been outside since arriving with Blaer. The compound was exactly as she'd Seen it: the large pond, the pebbled paths, the vine-covered lairs. The dark forest towering over cryptlike buildings.

The night fae drag Adric to a clearing in the woods and stake him, spread-eagled, to the ground.

A black-haired priestess in a silver dress steps forward, a gleaming knife in her hand...

She inhaled sharply, gave herself a shake.

The night fae walked her down a short flight of granite stairs, then led her deeper. But she balked as they approached the hall leading to the cell in which she and Adric had been imprisoned.

"I won't go back in there."

"Hello." A young woman in the same uniform as Olivier—white shirt, black pants and a bow tie—stepped forward. She gave a tentative smile. "I'm Jessica, Olivier's assistant."

Rosana blinked. "You're human." Of course, Olivier had been human, too, but Jessica was young to be living at a fae court.

"That's right, Senhorita." The woman gave another nervous smile. "Come with me, please. I promise you're not going back into a cell."

She led Rosana down another hallway and then opened the door to a roomy apartment with dark Art Nouveau furniture and large, brooding paintings. "This way."

She ushered Rosana into a bedroom with more beautiful furniture and a hand-woven rug so plush Rosana's bare feet left footprints. The black lamps on either side of the bed were in the shape of a naked woman holding a glowing moon above her head, and an intricate design of lilies and vines was carved on the mahogany headboard.

Laid out on the blood-red comforter was a sleeveless party dress in a shimmering purple so dark it was almost black. She fingered the short pleated skirt. The dress was clearly fae-made, with invisible stitches and a magic fabric that would fit itself perfectly to her body. Next to it were a bra and panties in a cobweb-fine lace, and on a rug were matching purple heels in a butter-soft leather.

If the outfit was from anyone but Langdon, she'd have been thrilled to wear it. Instead, she wanted to stuff it in a trash can.

"I'll order your dinner," Jessica said. "Meanwhile, the prince thought you might like to take a bath and change into clean clothes." She turned to go, but Rosana put out a hand, stopping her.

"Where's Lord Adric?" He was near, she sensed that much through the bond.

The human glanced uneasily at the room's darkest corner. "He's fine."

"Say the words. Tell me Adric's unhurt."

"Adric is unhurt." Her scent held the purity of truth. "Like you, he's being fed, made comfortable."

Rosana's shoulders sagged in relief.

"I'm to come for you a half hour before midnight."

Her head jerked up. "Why? What happens at midnight?"

"The new moon's tonight," Jessica said. "You'll be at the ritual. That's all I know."

A ritual. On a dark, moonless night.

A black-haired priestess steps forward, a gleaming knife in her hand...

Shaken, Rosana sank onto the edge of the bed.

Jessica edged toward the door.

"Wait!" Rosana sprang to her feet. "Please. Take me to Adric. Nobody has to know. I just need to see him for myself."

The human looked down at her feet. "I can't. But he's fine. For now," she added in a small voice.

"What do you mean, for now?"

Jessica shook her head.

Rosana dropped her voice. "Can you get a message to Lord Dion? He'll pay you—anything you ask."

"I'm sorry," the human whispered as she backed out of the room. In a louder voice, she said, "Your dinner will be in the kitchen. I'll be back for you in a few hours."

41

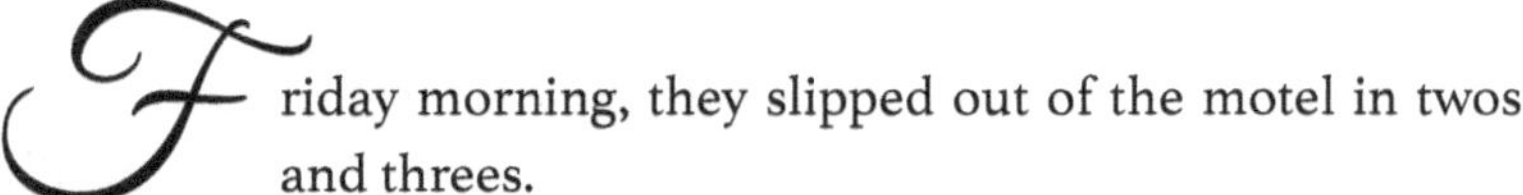

riday morning, they slipped out of the motel in twos and threes.

The meeting place was a little-used portal Fane had discovered on New Moon's west side. The plan was to go in at noon, when most of the night fae would be fast asleep. Olivia and Cleia would hit the portal with a one-two punch: first, Olivia would weaken the portal with a counterspell she'd concocted, and then Cleia would draw on the sun's energy to jab a hole through it.

Once inside, some of their group, including Marjani, Jace and Fane, would spread out to find Rosana and Adric. Meanwhile others, including Cleia, Dion and a cohort of sun fae warriors armed with fae balls, would mount a direct attack on the night fae.

Marjani, Jace and Fane reached the portal first. The *look-away* spell was powerful here, even with the counterspell cast by Olivia.

Look away. Danger. Runrunrun...

Rubbing her prickling nape, Marjani glanced away. But when it pressed her to leave, she set her teeth and pushed back.

The Rock Run men arrived and hid in a nearby marsh, while Marjani and Jace took positions high in the forest canopy. Fane simply used his wayfaring Gift to blend into the trees.

Marjani hunkered down in the branches of a maple to wait for noon. Her stomach was a tangle of nerves, her cougar edgy. For Rosana's sake, she'd kept her promise to Dion, but with every day that passed, her fear for Adric increased.

Her brother had sacrificed everything for her, even his honor. And now he was going to lose his life. Because of her.

She was *damned* if she'd let that happen.

A clot of silver-gray clouds shrouded the sun. She scowled at the shadows that raced across the forest.

Zuri arrived, along with several of the clan's top soldiers, all wolves. He'd demanded to come, pointing out that for now, the action wasn't in Baltimore, but in Virginia.

Marjani had hesitated and then given her okay. If they lost this battle, the clan might not survive anyway.

The last to arrive were the sun fae warriors, a dozen long-limbed, beautiful men and women. Marjani eyed them skeptically. In her experience, Cleia's people were the fae's version of Hollywood A-listers: all about the fun and glitter. This group looked like sexy models playing at war in their combat boots and camo gear, knit caps pulled low over their bright hair. But they silently disappeared into the surrounding forest.

Marjani glanced back at the portal. The ever-present fog made it impossible to see into New Moon. Were the night fae waiting on the other side?

She fingered Lady Olivia's protection charm, strung on the leather cord along with Fane's mate gift and her quartz. The silver charm was shaped like a prowling cougar. She'd been surprised—and touched—that the sun fae lady had bothered to make her a charm.

Her hand went to the sheathed iron dagger also hanging from her neck. Another two iron knives were tucked into her boots and her front pocket held a switchblade.

The protection charm had been a kind gesture, but Marjani wasn't here to be protected.

She was here to kill.

A STEADY DRIZZLE had begun to fall by the time Cleia and Olivia 'ported in, both in long-sleeved tees and camo pants, their hair in French braids.

Marjani swung off her branch and dropped the twenty-five feet to the ground. Fane and Jace trotted up as she tucked her leather jacket into a crook of the tree, leaving her in a slim-fitting, easy-to-fight-in turtleneck. The men shed their jackets as well.

Dion, Rui and Tiago appeared from the marshes, also dressed for a fight.

Dion kissed Cleia. "Are you sure about this?" he murmured, a frown creasing his forehead.

Sun fae were strongest at noon on the summer solstice—and this was the middle of winter. Night fae, on the other hand, were at their most powerful once each month when the new moon ruled the sky.

Which would be tonight.

Cleia cupped his cheek. "I'll be fine, love. Stop worrying." Her pointed chin went up. "It's time the prince learned he's not the only powerful fae on the East Coast."

Together, they formed a semi-circle around the portal. Behind them, Zuri and the other wolves formed a second row along with the sun fae.

Olivia glanced around. "Ready?"

At their nods, she faced the portal. The forest fell silent except for the steady *drip-drip* of the rain.

Raising her arms, Olivia took three deep breaths and spoke a phrase in an ancient fae language. Her palms shimmered. She traced a circle in the air and the portal became visible, a round door into the New Moon Court.

On the other side, fog snaked through the trees. Marjani

gulped to see that inside, it was already night. How much time did they have before midnight?

"We'll find him," Fane murmured. "I promise."

She nodded and pulled a dagger from her boot. Around her, knives appeared in the other fada's hands as well. Dion gripped the bespelled dagger by its carved black handle. Even Fane had armed himself, and the man never carried a knife.

The barrier thinned slowly, almost imperceptibly. Olivia's face grew taut with strain. Her arms began to shake, but the shimmering light never wavered.

"*Now*," she said.

Cleia raised her own arms, calling on the sun's power. Her palms glowed. She chanted an incantation, over and over. The heat intensified and fire danced over her body.

"Holy cat," muttered Jace.

Mesmerized, Marjani stared into the unearthly fire along with everyone else. A warm breeze blew through the trees, tugging at their clothes, ruffling their hair.

Cleia gathered the fire, shaping it into a white-hot ball and flinging it at the portal. The ball stuck in the center as if it had been captured in a net.

"Fuck," whispered one of the sun fae men.

Marjani clenched the dagger.

"Steady." Dion set a hand on the small of Cleia's back. "You can do it." The fire danced over him as well, as he somehow aided her to control the energy.

"Yes," Cleia whispered. The ball brightened until the light was unbearable to look at.

Marjani averted her gaze. A sizzle and a pop, and suddenly, the light was gone.

Cleia lowered her hands, chest working.

Dion rubbed her back. "You're okay?" he asked anxiously.

"Go," Olivia hissed. "Before they realize we're here."

"Yes." Cleia gave Dion a small push. "Go. Olivia can only hold the portal open for an hour, maybe less."

He glanced from his mate to the opening, clearly torn, and then sprang after Rui and Tiago, who had already slipped into the night fae compound.

Lurching into motion, Marjani followed him through the portal along with Jace and Fane.

42

———

The hours until midnight passed with agonizing slowness.

Olivier showed Adric to a large, comfortable apartment, but refused to answer any questions before locking him inside.

By then he was lightheaded from the iron poisoning his blood. He found salt in the kitchen, peeled off his shirt and cleansed the wounds as best as he could. The burns on his hands and arms had almost healed, but the knife wound on his chest seared like a red-hot brand. The salt solution burned almost as much as the iron itself, but he grit his teeth and rinsed the cut flesh repeatedly, then pulsed healing energy into it until the wound scabbed over.

He paced into the living room and sank onto a pricey antique couch.

Thrice-damned, fucking fae.

Langdon's sick bastard of a son had pushed Adric until he had no choice but to fight back—and the prince had the balls to blame him?

Worse, Marjani wasn't any safer from Langdon than she'd been before this all started, and now Rosana was enmeshed in this fucked-up mess, too.

His *mate*.

His claws pricked out. With a snarl, he slashed them through the couch's blue velvet cushions, sending stuffing flying around him.

Kill, hissed the cat.

Destroy.

Protect the mate.

He jumped to his feet and prowled feverishly from room to room, searching for a way out. The apartment was windowless, and the only exit wasn't just locked, it was warded, because when he tried the door handle, it buzzed warningly in his hand.

He was trapped again. Just in a larger cage.

With a low growl, he took a gilded chair from the dining room and smashed it against the heavy wood door, again and again, until it lay in broken shards at his feet.

He stared down at the pieces, chest heaving, and then resumed his restless pacing, half-cat, half-man.

Burning up from the iron poisoning. Furious at being confined. Terrified for Rosana.

A half hour passed, maybe more, with him only half aware of his surroundings.

When he surfaced again, he was in the opulent black marble bathroom.

He set his hands on the counter. In the large round mirror, his cougar's fiery blue eyes stared back. His fangs had lengthened, his claws fully extended to their two-inch-plus length. At some point he'd ripped off his shirt, and his pants were unbuttoned as if he'd started to remove them as well.

He hadn't come this close to losing control of his animal since his dad had been executed by Leron.

He drew a breath and then shrank his fangs, retracted the claws. His eyes changed back to bronze with just a few slivers of blue.

At least he hadn't reopened the wound on his chest. But his face was flushed with fever, his breath coming in rapid pants.

Sticking his head under the faucet, he took a long drink to

flush the iron from his system. Then he got in the shower, scrubbing off the stench of the cell. He ignored the razor on the ledge with the shampoo and soap. Let Langdon see the rough-edged, dangerous animal he was dicking around with.

By the time he got out, his fever had receded. He felt weak but clear-headed again.

He dressed in the clean clothes he found laid out in the master bedroom and began a methodical search for a weapon. But the apartment held nothing that would damage a fae.

Food appeared in the dining room. A fat, juicy hamburger. Thick-sliced fries. Spicy coleslaw and a frosty glass of beer.

His skin creeped. How did they know his favorite meal? But he ate, even though it galled him to accept food from Langdon. He'd need fuel for the coming confrontation.

Belly full, he resumed his restless pacing, increasingly anxious to see Rosana. At least he sensed through the bond that she was healing, growing stronger.

He *would* break them both out of here. He was damned if he'd submit tamely to whatever Langdon had planned.

But without a weapon, it was up to his cougar.

Yes... hissed the cat.

His claws slid out again. He stared down at the wicked curved nails. Maybe he couldn't kill Langdon, but he could do some serious damage. That should buy him enough time to grab Rosana and then cloak them both so he could spirit her out of New Moon.

Langdon might be able to sense Adric's location with those Spidey-senses of his, but Adric would bet his entire collection of quartz that the prince couldn't actually see him. Get Rosana away from Langdon, and the two of them would have a fighting chance at escape.

If the wards let us out.

Adric had always known he might not get out of New Moon alive, but it had been a chance he was willing to take. Now, though, he had Rosana to consider.

His mate.

His jaw set. Failure was not an option. He *would* extricate her from this mess, or die trying.

That decided, he curled up onto the undamaged couch to wait for midnight. Not sleeping, but resting in the way of his cat with ears wide open.

The moment he heard footsteps in the hall outside, he was up and springing across the room. He kicked the remains of the chair out of the way and waited impatiently for the lock to disengage before jerking the door open.

Olivier took in the damage with a pained look and then gestured for Adric to follow him. "If you'll come with me, my lord."

Adric grabbed his arm. "Where's Rosana?"

"Right here, my lord." The butler led him around a corner before opening another door.

Rosana stood there, legs braced apart, claws out. At the sight of Adric, she broke into a smile and retracted the claws.

He shoved past Olivier to pull her into his arms. "You're okay?" He ran his hands over her. "How do you feel? Should you be out of the water?"

"I'm fine." She touched his cheek. "What about you?"

"I'm good." His hands trembled as he cupped her face. "But I was worried. About you. I—" His throat worked.

Worried was too tame a word for how he'd felt, but Rosana seemed to understand. She rose on her toes to brush her lips over his. "I'm okay. Really."

She was. He could see it, scent it. He breathed a prayer of thanks to the gods and pressed kisses to her eyes, her cheeks, her throat.

He'd almost lost her.

He had to touch her. Taste her. Assure himself she was really okay.

Olivier coughed.

Adric growled without lifting his head.

Oliver cleared his throat. "The prince—"

"Can fucking wait."

Adric pressed a last kiss to Rosana's soft mouth and released her. This time, he registered the sassy little purple dress. He swallowed hard. "Damn. You look beautiful."

The short, sleeveless design showed off her toned arms and legs, and dipped low over her full breasts. Her hair had been braided into a single inky plait, and like him, she was barefoot.

His mouth quirked. That was his Rosana, ready for anything.

Mate, the cat whispered in satisfaction.

"They took my other clothes," she said with a shrug.

He fingered her amethyst pendant. It was warm, the crystals humming a contented tune. And the sea-green thread was back in his own quartz.

Mate.

This time, he didn't even try to fight it. No, he welcomed it.

He snaked an arm around her waist. "You're beautiful—and you're mine. Don't forget that for a fucking minute."

"I think that's the key," she whispered in his ear. "You and me, together." She inclined her head at Olivier like the alpha's sister she was. "You may take us to the prince now."

They followed the butler down another corridor and into a hall of ornate black mirrors half-covered by the lush ivy which snaked over the walls.

Rosana glanced at her reflection and jerked.

Adric halted. "What?"

"I see Dion and your sister," she said in an excited whisper. "And Cleia, and Merry's uncle, Jace. In the woods."

His brows shot up. "Together?"

"Yes." She pointed to a point on the black glass. "And there—I can see night fae lairs through the trees. They must be here—in Virginia."

Olivier spoke directly behind them. "I believe they've been in negotiations with the prince."

Adric's stomach dipped. "Marjani, too?"

"So I hear," the butler replied. "However, I haven't been privy to the discussions."

Adric glared at the mirror, but all he saw were their three reflections. "She wasn't supposed to get anywhere near the prince," he growled.

"Come," Olivier said impatiently.

"Think, Adric," Rosana murmured as they followed the butler. "Your sister and Jace aren't here alone. She's with Cleia and my brothers. *You're* not alone. You have all of us fighting on your side. This changes everything."

"It's too dangerous," he bit back. "She knows it's her the prince really wants."

"Oh, Adric. Do you think that matters to her? How do you think she'd feel if you died because of her?"

He shook his head, still trying to wrap his mind around the fact that Marjani was right outside New Moon. The prince must be rubbing his hands in glee.

But a part of him couldn't help be warmed that she and Jace had come after him. And probably Fane—the man wouldn't allow Marjani to get this close to Langdon without him. Hell, there were probably some other Baltimore fada skulking around in the woods, too.

His step hitched. Every hair on his body raised. Even his scalp lifted.

Rosana had been right all along.

Her being here changed everything.

As they followed Olivier up the last flight of stairs to the outside, Rosana took Adric's hand. The fae-tailored clothes—a deep green button-up shirt and black pants—outlined every muscle on his hard body. His face was stubbled with night-beard, his eyes a flat bronze.

Mated.

Despite the danger they were in, a delicious shiver went up Rosana's spine. This beautiful, dangerous man was *hers*.

She took his hand, grateful for once to be a Seer. She'd *felt* hope surge in him when he'd realized they had a chance of rescue.

Outside, a soft rain was falling over the foggy grounds. A couple of fae lights wafted near, shimmering like opals in the mist.

Adric brought his mouth to her ear. "Be ready to run."

She squeezed his hand. "Together."

"Together," he agreed as a half-dozen guards emerged from the fog, a tall female at their head. Olivier nodded at them and headed back underground.

Adric stiffened at the sight of the woman. He moved to put himself between her and Rosana. "Neoma." The word was a growl.

Clearly, he'd encountered her before—and it hadn't been a happy encounter.

"Lord Adric." Neoma inclined her sleek black head. The guards surrounded them. Two grabbed Rosana, jerking her away from Adric.

Adric snarled and went clawed, but a fae ball appeared in the hand of a third warrior. He brought it close to Rosana's face. She swallowed, trying not to flinch from the dark fire.

Adric froze.

"Your quartz." Neoma held a silk pouch out to him. A cruel smile curled her lips. "Just in case you had any idea of trying to escape the prince's justice."

"No!" Rosana whispered.

Adric hissed, his eyes pure blue flame. But he immediately dragged the chunky gray-and-orange pendant over his head and dropped it into the silk pouch.

"Wise choice," Neoma said. "Now, get going." She jerked her chin at a path of smooth white pebbles.

The warriors released Rosana, but kept her separated from Adric.

The trail wound through the trees and past the pond before plunging into a garden that was, impossibly, blooming in the dead of winter. A moon garden of lush white flowers: creamy azaleas, snowy peonies, roses of pale ivory. Even when they passed back into the woods, lilies of the valley carpeted the forest floor like living pearls, and the smooth pebbles beneath their bare feet were as warm as if it was a balmy summer night.

In the distance, they heard shouting, saw bursts of light above the trees. There was a crack like thunder and the entire sky lit up.

Rosana's heart leapt. "They're here!" she said in subvocal tones.

In front of her, Adric nodded without looking back.

"Keep going." The guards herded them forward.

The path ended in a clearing. A frisson slid over Rosana's skin as they entered, indicating they'd passed through a ward.

The sights and sounds of the battle were instantly erased. Instead, shadows reigned, dark, menacing. Even the rain stopped, the ground beneath their bare feet cold but dry. Neck prickling, Rosana edged closer to Adric.

One by one, a circle of night fae emerged out of the gloom, each more beautiful than the previous—but in a cold, untouchable way, like perfect, polished statues. Their faces first, gleaming palely like the ivory sheen of the moon behind a cloud, even the darker skinned among them. Next to appear were their spare, elongated bodies: three females in short silver dresses and eight males all in black.

At the circle's apex, Langdon shimmered into sight on a solid silver throne topped by a triple moon: a full moon flanked by two crescent moons. Like the other men, he was dressed in unrelieved black except for the circlet of diamond-studded platinum leaves vined around his head.

Standing at his side was the thirteenth member of the circle, a woman with ebony hair and Blaer's fine-boned face, but older, harder. Diamonds glittered in her pointed ears and on the platinum bands twined around her upper arms. A single black star hung from a heavy platinum chain around her neck.

A priestess.

Rosana's lungs locked. She dug her bare heels into the soil, tugging them both to a halt.

"Adric. *No.*"

He pressed her fingers. "It's okay."

"No, it's not." She shook her head frantically. "It's *her*. The woman in my vision. They're going to kill you."

"Come." Langdon beckoned them with a single pale hand.

"Be ready to run," Adric muttered. He released Rosana's hand and strode forward. "Well?" With a sneer, he folded his arms over his chest. "I'm here."

Rosana looked frantically around for Neoma. At least if Adric had his quartz, he could shift—or cloak himself and escape the circle. But Neoma and the other warriors who'd brought them had disappeared.

She moved up beside Adric. But he put out an arm and moved her behind him without taking his gaze from Langdon.

Still trying to protect her when they were face to face with one of the darkest, most powerful fae on the planet.

Her heart clenched. "*Amo-te,*" she whispered. *I love you.*

She remained where he'd put her. Guarding his back.

Langdon eyed them without speaking. The circle of night fae went motionless along with him, their eyes gleaming darkly like a pack of wolves.

Rosana gulped, and then pulled back her shoulders. They might sense her fear, but she wouldn't give them the satisfaction of showing it.

Adric's scent was hot with fury. He stared back at Langdon, cat-quiet.

As the tension stretched, the priestess drew the tip of her tongue over her full lower lip like she could taste their fear and anger.

Langdon broke the silence first. "Lord Adric. Senhorita do Rio. Welcome to my court. Peace to you and yours."

"Fuck your peace," Adric snarled. "We're here against our will. I demand you release us."

"It was you who trespassed," the prince returned in silky tones. "As for Senhorita do Rio, I merely granted her request to remain with you."

Adric raised a brow. "Did I trespass? Or was I brought here by Lady Blaer? It was the wolf under her *geas* who brought me through the wards."

Langdon frowned. "She told me you forced the wolf to let you into the court."

"True. But the wolf led me straight to your lair, and no one stopped us—almost as if you wanted me here. Or was it actually Lady Blaer who wanted me here?"

Rosana made a small sound. Adric had practically accused Blaer of manipulating things so he could assassinate Langdon. Viewed from a certain angle, it made sense.

Langdon turned to the head priestess. "Fleur?"

Her pale throat worked. She moistened her lips. "This is speculation, your highness. The fevered imaginings of a desperate man. Surely you don't think my daughter is working with this *fada*." She shot a dark look at Adric.

"No," Langdon replied, "I don't think Blaer is working *with* him. That doesn't mean she's not using him to cover her pretty ass."

The circle of night fae rustled in agitation.

"However," the prince continued, "none of this matters. The facts stand. My son is dead—"

"Because he attacked my people," Adric said between set teeth.

Rosana set a hand on the small of his back, willing him to remain calm.

"As you say." Langdon inclined his head. "But that's not the issue. It's not even important whether you killed Tyrus yourself, or whether it was your sister. The issue is restitution."

"What restitution? I can't bring your goddamned son back from the dead."

"No. But you owe me, Adric Savonett." The night fae rose from his silver throne, prowled toward them.

Beneath Rosana's hand, Adric's body quivered like a stallion itching to attack. "I owe you *nothing*. Your son got what was coming to him. Your clan has persecuted mine for years. My own parents died to feed your taste for darkness."

"Your alpha—your *uncle*—invited us in."

"Fuck that. Yeah, my uncle Leron was a sick S.O.B., but he would never have stayed in power for so long if not for you."

"And Lord Tyrus was in Baltimore at your cousin Corban's invitation," Langdon added as if Adric hadn't spoken.

"And that was his mistake." Adric stood toe-to-toe with the prince. "Unlike my uncle, Corban was *not* the alpha, and Tyrus didn't have my permission to be in Baltimore. I owe you *nothing* for his death—and every fada in the world will back me up on that."

"You still think I want your sister, don't you?"

Adric's chin jerked up. "Then what's this about?"

"I'll admit I desired your sister's blood. 'An eye for an eye. A tooth for a tooth. A life for a life.' Those ancient humans had it right. Harsh, but effective. However, I've reconsidered. Perhaps we can resolve this to everyone's satisfaction. A bargain."

Adric's eyes narrowed. "What kind of bargain?"

"Due to your sister, I lost a son. In fact, all three of my sons are dead."

Another rustle went around the circle. The night fae muttered among themselves.

Langdon ignored them to say, "I had a third son by a human woman." A muscle flexed in his jaw. "I should've brought him up in the court. But instead, I hid—" He shook his head.

"Had, my lord?" murmured Fleur.

The prince gave a tight nod. "As I said, all my sons are dead. But my youngest son left a daughter."

Rosana's blood chunked with ice. Her mouth formed a soundless *no*.

Adric's face hardened. "No fucking way."

"Yes." Langdon's eyes were gleaming pools of midnight. "*A life for a life.* Have your clan bring Merry Jones to me and you'll go free. In fact, I'm feeling generous tonight. Bring my granddaughter to me, and I'll free not just you, but Rosana."

43

---

*B*laer was livid at being excluded from the new moon ritual. She stood at the living room window, staring out at the rain.

Luc's nape crawled. The fae lady was at her most dangerous when completely still.

A quarter mile distant, a pitched battle was being fought, but she seemed unaware of the light and noise. This wasn't just fada. From the bright bursts of color, the sun fae had joined the battle.

For the first time in days—no, weeks—hope sparked in Luc. Not for him, but for Adric. Maybe the alpha would get out of this alive, after all.

He flashed on Rosana's bewildered young face and swallowed, shame a hot stone in his belly. Just when he'd thought he couldn't go lower, he had. He'd given a woman—a girl barely out of her teens—to the night fae.

Adric had been right to be furious. He should've just slit Luc's throat and been done with it.

At least Marjani was safe. Luc didn't know what he'd have done if the prince had gotten his hands on her.

Blaer turned her dark eyes on him. Sensing his distress in that spooky way night fae had.

"Your alpha and the do Rio woman are at the ritual."

"What?" Luc scrubbed a hand over his face. Why would Langdon invite Adric to a private ritual?

And then he *knew*. His stomach lurched.

Blaer prowled across the marble floor. Her dress today was an ice-blue scrap of material that barely covered her ass. Sapphires and diamonds dripped from her throat and glittered on the pointed ears peeking through her platinum hair.

"The fada attacked the prince in his own lair. You didn't think he'd let them off with just a slap on the wrist, did you?"

Luc grabbed her bare arm. "Why are you telling me this?"

She tilted her head. "Why do you think?"

He narrowed his eyes. "You want me to get you inside tonight's circle. But why?"

"Can you?"

He knew when he was being used. But who the fuck cared? Adric needed him. Luc had no compunction using Blaer right back.

He released her. "Take me to the circle. I'll get us inside."

Passing through the portal turned out to be the easy part. Marjani had only gone a few steps into the woods on the other side when she realized the shadows had deepened to pitch-black. Her eyes went night-glow, but she still couldn't see more than a couple of yards in any direction.

She tightened her grip on her dagger and peered around, growling lowly.

"It's okay," Fane murmured. "It's a different time of day in here, that's all."

She nodded tightly. The mechanics of fae vs. human time always made her dizzy. You could spend a few days in a fae court and go home to find a whole month had passed.

What made her heart falter was the realization that in here, the new moon might be just an hour, not five hours away.

"You feel Ric yet?" That was Jace.

"No," she admitted. She'd hoped that her quartz would relink to Adric's as soon as they passed through the portal, but it hadn't. She couldn't even say for sure if he was still alive.

"Me, neither," Jace said.

"He's here." She picked up the pace. "I know he is."

That's when the skies opened up. Rain sluiced down as if someone had turned a fire hose on them. Her black turtleneck was instantly plastered to her body. Within seconds, she'd lost sight of everyone but Jace and Fane.

She dashed the water out of her eyes and kept moving.

The deeper they went into the woods, the thicker the shadows grew. With the rain sheeting down, it was like fighting your way through a waterfall. They were soaking wet, and beneath their feet, the forest floor had turned into a gluey black mud.

The shadows grew thick enough to touch. The nearest one began to slowly spiral.

They all froze.

Marjani put out a hand to see if it was as real as it looked. The shadow—or whatever it was—tried to curl around her, but recoiled from the protection charm.

"Careful!" Fane jerked her back. "It's some kind of dark magic."

The three of them eased around the mini black cyclone, but all the shadows were swirling now.

"What the fuck?" Jace snarled, his eyes the bright green of his jaguar.

The shadows spun faster, coalescing into hairy vines that slapped at their faces, dragged at their clothes.

Marjani dodged between two vines. As before, Olivia's charm repelled them. But a third vine twined around Jace's legs and threw him to the muddy ground. In the next breath, he was being dragged through the forest, his body slamming into trees and bouncing off rocks.

"Jace!" She and Fane sprinted after him.

He managed to snag an arm around a tree trunk. With the other, he hacked at the vine with his iron dagger. As they caught up to him, the vine disintegrated into ashes.

She dropped to her knees, brushing the ashes off him. "You okay?"

Jace's chest heaved. He gingerly tested his arms and legs. "Yeah."

"Here." Fane held out a hand, pulling him to his feet.

"God's cat." The jaguar shifter swiped a hand over his face. "What the fuck are those vines?"

"Hell if I know," said Fane. "Some kind of ward? Or maybe even an illusion?"

"It was no illusion," was the grim reply. "I've got the bruises to prove it."

Fane shook his head. "With the night fae, it's hard to tell what's real, what's not."

"Look out!" Marjani slashed at a vine snaking at them from around a nearby tree. As before, it crumbled into ashes.

She took a second dagger from her boot so she had one in each hand. "Whatever it is, we have to get out of here. Stick next to me. The charm seems to repel them."

The men nodded, mouths set, as three more vines dropped around them. Together, they hacked their way forward for several endless minutes.

Just when she wondered if they'd ever get out of the woods, there was an intense flash, followed by two more in rapid succession. Through the trees, they glimpsed a group of sun fae hurling fae balls at the vines, forcing a large patch of shadows around them into retreat.

Fane swore and slashed through yet another encroaching vine. "The bloody things are multiplying faster than we can fight them."

"The sun fae." She stabbed a vine right before it wrapped around Jace's neck from behind. "They're our only chance."

The three of them continued slogging through the mud,

dodging the shadow-vines when they could, and fighting them off when they couldn't, but the sun fae warriors kept moving, too. They couldn't seem to reach them.

They fought doggedly on. First Fane, then Jace were thrown to the ground. She helped cut the vines off them, and they continued forward, but they were all tiring. On top of that, they were soaked to the skin, and if there was anything Marjani's cat detested, it was being cold and wet.

Then they lost sight of the sun fae. Although they could still hear sounds of the battle, it was impossible to tell exactly where it was coming from.

"Fuck." Marjani turned in a circle, hopelessly lost. The shadows had somehow messed with her internal GPS. "Where'd they go?"

"I have no idea," Jace muttered, while Fane just shook his head.

The shadows seemed to sense their confusion. The vines twisted around them. Not trying to touch them now, just weaving an inky cage.

Marjani hissed and shrank back against Fane. It was like the vines *knew* she was terrified of being caged—any fada was, but her own recent experience with Blaer's cages had amped the fear up to near-panic level.

Her chest compressed. She snarled, her animal brain telling her to run like hell. She sprang forward. But the vines caught her, throwing her back against Jace and Fane.

Her terror ratcheted. "The charm isn't working anymore," she croaked.

Jace gave a low growl. She scented his own fear of being trapped, and it amped up hers.

"Easy, love." Fane squeezed her shoulders from behind. "Try focusing the charm on one section."

Yes. She gripped the charm, shoved it at the vines in front of her. To her relief, they parted. She moved the charm in a circle until she'd cleared a large enough opening in the vine-cage for her to pass through, then squeezed through sideways, unable to wait any longer.

Fane and Jace were right behind her—which gave her an idea.

"Form a single line behind me," she said and moved forward, the charm held out in front of her. Fane hooked his fingers through her waistband, and she heard him direct Jace to keep touching him.

As before, the vines parted to let her through, and Fane and Jace were able to pass through as well before they closed again. She increased her pace, and the vines and trees merged into each other, twining into a narrow passage with walls of a dank, murky fog that was nevertheless too solid for them to pass through.

She was growling continuously now.

"Keep moving," Fane ordered. "Don't stop, whatever you do."

They continued to what looked like the end of the passage, but wasn't. The shadows had formed a maze, forcing them to turn first right, then left, then another left and a right, and so on, in a seemingly random pattern.

Marjani lost all sense of direction and time. All she knew was that somewhere nearby, her brother awaited his execution—and she was trapped in this thrice-damned forest with its living shadows.

She was running now, her feet beating out a frenzied rhythm.

Hurry, hurry, hurry.

At last the walls of the maze thinned so they could see the trees again. Marjani checked, unsure which way to go.

Another explosion lit the night.

The three of them sprinted toward it—and exited the trees at last.

44

———

ive Merry to Langdon?

Rosana didn't even have to look at Adric to know what his answer was.

"No," she growled. "We don't accept."

The prince turned to Adric. "And you?"

Adric's eyes were that flat bronze that was somehow more scary than the blue of his cougar. "You heard her. We refuse. In fact," he said, slowly and precisely, "you can take your bargain and shove it where the sun don't shine."

Langdon's mouth tightened. "Then you die. You've been informed of the charges against you."

"Which I don't accept," Adric shot back.

Langdon continued as if Adric hadn't even spoke. "I could demand you accept my *geas*, but as long as you're alive, your clan will plague me. I'll be fighting off assassination attempts every time I leave New Moon."

The other night fae murmured agreement. It was the simplest way to break a *geas*—kill the fae who'd set it.

"No," the prince decided. "Better to execute you."

A flick of his fingers, and Neoma and three other warriors appeared out of the shadows to grab Adric.

Rosana's lungs squeezed. It was her vision, her nightmare, come to life. Her feet seemed stuck to the ground. She watched, frozen, as they dragged Adric's arms behind his back and forced him to his knees.

Fleur stepped forward, the knife gleaming in her hand.

And Adric allowed it. He didn't even try to fight them off.

She understood why when he glared up at Langdon. "Kill me, then. But I'm begging you, let Rosana leave unharmed." To her, he mouthed a single sentence: *I love you.*

"No," she rasped.

"I have no interest in harming her," the prince replied. "But neither am I inclined to let her leave without receiving something in return. My offer stands: my granddaughter for your lives. Although Senhorita do Rio may, of course, bargain to live that life out as a Seer at my court."

Fleur stiffened and shot a dark look at Rosana, while the other night fae eyed her with renewed interest. She could almost see them rubbing their hands in glee at having a fada Seer to play with.

Langdon leaned toward Adric, his voice darkly persuasive. "Think, my lord. Without you, your clan will fall to us. Fleur has Seen it. Is one mixed-breed's life worth so much to you? I promise, the girl will be well treated at my court. Raised as the princess she was born to be."

The prince will destroy your clan from the inside out.

Ice trickled down Rosana's spine.

No. Adric *couldn't* die. Not only because she wouldn't survive his death, but because his clan wouldn't.

Adric glowered up at the prince. "Go. To. Hades."

Together, her brain shouted.

Instinctively, she reached out to Adric through the bond. The bond was still so new that she was shocked when he reached back. The connection between them hummed and sparked, and her amethyst warmed.

It was like he'd enfolded her in a full-body hug. "Together," he murmured—and slammed his head back into the night fae directly behind him while he twisted away from the others in a single lithe move. He leapt for Langdon, bearing him to the ground.

Rosana's mouth dropped open. Then her feet unstuck themselves from the ground. The guards were already moving. She threw herself in front of the nearest one, felling him with a couple of down-and-dirty blows. When your life was at stake, you went for the balls.

Her claws sprouted. She scratched them across another warrior's face. He swore and clapped his hands over his face.

Adric had his fingers wrapped around Langdon's throat. The prince's eyes bulged as he desperately sought to throw him off.

"Run!" Adric rapped out at her. "I'm right behind you."

But the night fae had surrounded her. Fae balls burned in two of the guards' hands.

She stepped back—and fingers latched onto her hair from behind, jerked back her head. An iron blade hovered over her throat. "Don't move," a voice gritted next to her ear. "Not a single muscle."

She froze.

"Release the prince," her captor barked at Adric. "Or your woman dies."

He glanced up, snarling—and stilled.

"*Now*," snapped the warrior holding Rosana. "Or I'll slice her fucking throat."

"Okay, okay." Adric rose to his feet. "I'm off, see?" He raised his hands, palms out. "Just let her go."

The warriors surrounded him and shoved him back to his knees. Neoma slammed her dagger hilt into Adric's solar plexus. He grunted and doubled over, chest heaving.

Rosana's lungs closed. Her mate was hurt. She felt his pain like it was her own. Her heart sped up and bile rose in her throat.

She dug her claws into her captor's arm, uncaring of the sharp blade an inch from her jugular vein. Just knowing she had to get to Adric.

"Be still!" the night fae hissed in her ear.

Langdon pushed up on his knees, gasping for breath. "Let her go," he ordered as two men helped him to his feet.

"My lord?" Neoma said. "Are you sure?"

"*Now*," was Langdon's reply.

"Try anything else," Rosana's captor hissed in her ear, "and I'll slit your pretty throat. Is that clear?"

"Yes," she said without hesitation. Anything so she could go to Adric.

"Listen well, then. You're going to kneel beside the earth fada. No touching him. No talking. Is that understood?"

"Yes, yes."

"Go, then." The fae released her, and she flew the few yards to Adric and lowered herself to her knees beside him. He was still bent over, chest working. She yearned to touch him, to reassure herself he was all right, but kept her hands at her sides as ordered.

Adric managed to straighten. He even gave her a reassuring smile. "You okay, angel?"

She nodded and summoned an answering smile.

Meanwhile, Langdon was already almost back to normal, his powerful fae blood healing any damage Adric had done.

As he turned toward Adric and Rosana, a warrior stopped him. "Begging your pardon, my lord, but Captain Quade has sent a messenger."

"Let him in."

The messenger bowed and drew Langdon aside. The two murmured, low-voiced, while Rosana strained to listen.

The snatches she heard made her heart leap. "The sun fae have breached the wards" and "we've suffered several casualties."

She exchanged a hopeful look with Adric.

"Withdraw underground, then," Langdon said more loudly. "And seal off all the entrances. Even if the queen finds her way inside, she'd spend days trying to find you, and she can't be away from the sunlight for that long. As for the circle, she'll never breach these wards—not during the most sacred hour of the most sacred night of the month."

The warrior looked doubtful. "The queen's powerful, my lord, and she brought a dozen sun fae warriors with her. And what about the fada?" He shot Adric and Rosana a look of dislike. "They're...devious."

"Let them run around in the darkness all they want. They won't find their way here unless I allow it."

"But—"

"Go," the prince commanded. "Before the hour of our Goddess is past."

"As you wish." The warrior inclined his head and exited the clearing.

Fleur walked to the center of the circle. "Start the moon fire."

A wide, burnished metal bowl appeared on a low stand. A night fae priest stepped forward, a silver triple-moon pendant around his neck. He pointed a finger at the bowl and a purple flame sprang up in the center.

The guards latched onto Adric's arms and legs, forcing him onto his back. He fought back, twisting and kicking in their grip, until Neoma took his quartz from the silk bag and wrapped her fingers around it.

"Be still, fada."

He jerked and let out an agonized groan.

Rosana glanced frantically around for rescue. *Where was everyone?*

The night fae formed a circle around her and Adric. Fleur raised her shiny iron knife to the moonless sky. "We are reborn with this New Moon."

"We are reborn with this New Moon," the circle chanted.

Rosana's stomach bottomed out. *No.*

It couldn't happen like this. Not when they were so close to being rescued.

Her mom's cryptic words flitted across her mind. *Touch him.*

She stared helplessly down at her hands. What good would touching Adric do? Even if she did See something, it would be his death.

Everybody leaves. That hurt, abandoned part of her dropped back its head and shrieked a primal *no* at the midnight sky.

If they took Adric from her, she might as well let them stick a knife in her heart, too. Because this was one loss she wouldn't survive.

The prince raised his hands. "May the Dark Goddess bless our circle tonight."

She glared up at him, her whole being consumed with a dark, burning hatred. She should've killed him the library when she'd had the chance. If only she still had her stiletto, she'd plunge it into his iceberg of a heart. Her fingertips literally tingled with the desire to kill the man.

She curled them into her palms—and suddenly, she *knew*, with a Seer's gut instinct. Her mom hadn't meant Adric, she'd meant Langdon.

And everything *wasn't* happening exactly as in her vision. Because she, Rosana, was present.

She was the key.

"Wait, your highness!" She scrambled to her feet. "Perhaps we can make a bargain after all."

"Quiet." A priest loomed over her, his impossibly beautiful face set in cold lines. "Or the Goddess will gain another sacrifice."

But Langdon beckoned her forward. "Let her speak."

She pushed past the priest. "You want a Seer," she told the prince, "you've got one. But execute Lord Adric, and you lose me, too."

Adric groaned. "Rosana, no!"

She turned her face so she wouldn't have to look at him. She *knew* this was the right thing to do. But she couldn't risk even a whispered "Trust me," to Adric.

"We're mates," she told the prince. "Kill Adric, and I won't live for more than a few days after him."

"Mates?" Langdon glanced at Adric. "An earth fada and a river fada?"

She raised her chin. "That's right. And I'm willing to join your court as a Seer. But Lord Adric lives—or we both die."

Fleur sneered. "You lie, fada. You won't die along with your mate. I've seen fada live for years after."

"Truth," Rosana snarled back. She touched her hand to her heart, sealing the vow. "Kill my mate and I'll *will* myself to die."

Adric let out a blood-curdling growl and fought like a wild man to get away from his captors, but they had him stretched out now, their hands clamped around his wrists and ankles.

He rasped her name beseechingly, his torment vibrating down the mate bond. "Don't do this, Rosana. *Please.*"

She swayed on her feet, his pain nearly dropping her to the ground.

Langdon scrutinized her. "She's not lying," he said, almost to himself.

She wiped her sweaty palms on her pleated skirt. What if she'd imagined that whole scene with Ula? It could've been some kind of fever-induced dream.

Trust your Gift.

She straightened her spine and held out her hands to Langdon. "Well, my lord? Do we have a deal?"

45

Marjani, Fane and Jace were on a hill, the compound's grounds spread out before them, the low, vine-covered buildings barely visible through the pouring rain.

Up until now, the shadows had been doing all the fighting. Now, Marjani saw night fae warriors for the first time, engaged in a fierce battle with the sun fae, Cleia at their center. Fiery explosions of silver, copper and gold vied with bursts of dark purple, green and blue as the two sides hurled fae balls at each other.

The sun fae were holding their own, but they were outmatched, four or five night fae for every one of them. Shadows surrounded the sun fae's circular formation, creeping closer with every second.

Dion, Rui and Tiago were nowhere to be seen, no doubt searching for Rosana, but she glimpsed Zuri and his wolves slipping in and out of the trees, harrying the night fae.

But no Adric.

She closed her eyes and went deep into her quartz. She didn't have an alpha's ability to locate a clan member through their quartz, but Adric was family—her only brother.

But the darkness swallowed the connection like a stone dropping into a black bog. Her chest closed up. She'd been so sure she'd be able to find Adric once she got inside the wards.

She gripped Jace's arm. "Where is he? Can you feel him?"

A muscle worked in his jaw. He shook his head. "I'm sorry, Jani."

"Let's try the prince's lair." Fane pointed to the building nearest to the pond.

They started down the hill at a jog. The heavy rain had turned the grass into a muddy, slippery mess. If Marjani hadn't been a cat, she'd have face-planted halfway down.

As they neared the warring fae, Cleia raised her arms. The black sky lit with a burst of gold. Bright sparks streamed out from the center as if she'd set off a firework. The night fae screamed and slapped their hands to their faces, shrinking back into the shadows.

Marjani, Jace and Fane were temporarily blinded. Fane grabbed her hand and Jace glued himself to her other side. Together, they felt their way forward, skirting the battling warriors.

"Holy Mother," Jace muttered as another bright burst lit the night.

"Yeah," said Fane. "The queen's a one-woman war machine."

They were back in the shadows again. No obstacles this time, just a deep, unrelenting black. There was a hunger to the gloom now that reminded Marjani of the Darktime. A chill slid over her like a snake brushing past her skin.

Fane squeezed her fingers. "Use the charm." A pulse of love came through their bond.

She nodded, and with a whispered *fuck you*, lifted the charm and ran directly into the shadows' dark heart. As before, they parted seemingly at random, forcing her into a zigzag run. She soon lost track of the prince's lair.

She kept going because halting wasn't an option—that's how the night fae won. If she stopped, she'd lose first hope, then the motivation to keep moving...and then despair would set in.

Minutes passed. Her heart was in her throat. Was it midnight yet?

Hurry, hurry, hurry.

She darted left, then right. Cold and miserable from the monsoon-like rain, but determined to find her brother or die in the attempt.

Hurry, hurry, hurry.

Miraculously, a path opened before her, its white pebbles gleaming.

She couldn't sense Adric, and yet she *knew* this was the right direction. She pelted down the path.

Heart pounding, mind chanting: *Hurry, hurry, hurryhurryhurry...*

She slammed into a ward. Pain jolted through her. She reeled backward into a tree and leaned against it, sucking oxygen.

Her quartz twanged, the crystals humming with joy at reconnecting to the alpha's quartz.

Adric.

She'd found him, and he was still alive—but she was trapped on the wrong side of this fucking ward.

The air in front of her shimmered, and right before her eyes, a portal opened. A Marjani-size portal.

The hair on her nape lifted. She eyed it suspiciously. Still, what choice did she have? She pulled the dagger from the sheath around her neck and inched forward.

Footsteps pounded up behind her. She raised a hand, signaling Fane and Jace to halt as she peered through the opening.

What she saw there made her entire body ice.

Adric was on the ground in front of Prince Langdon. Several black-garbed night fae had pinned him down while others loomed nightmarishly over him. Rosana do Rio had her back to Marjani, her hands stretched out to Langdon. Nearby, a dark fire flickered.

Marjani shot a glance over her shoulder and then gulped as her brain caught up to what her nose had already told her. Fane and Jace were no longer behind her. Somehow, in her mad dash to reach Adric, she'd lost them—and picked up Lady Blaer and Luc instead.

Luc grabbed her arm. "Play along," he muttered, and stepped forward with her through the portal. "Your highness. Here's the fada that murdered your son."

46

———

*A*dric had resigned himself to dying. He'd never surrender Merry in return for his own life.

But gods, it hurt to die leaving Rosana still trapped at New Moon. He had to believe that her brothers and Cleia would get her away from the prince.

Then Rosana made her offer. Let Adric live, and she'd join Langdon's court as a Seer.

No. Fucking. Way.

Adric's muscles bunched. If only he had his quartz... But without it, he couldn't shift—or cloak himself.

Langdon's gaze went past Rosana to a point behind Adric. His smile made Adric's insides ice.

"Marjani Savonett." The prince deliberately spoke her full name in an attempt to establish power over her. "Welcome to my court."

Adric flung a look over his shoulder in time to see his sister enter the circle along with Luc and Blaer. And instead of helping her, Luc gripped her arm, urging her forward.

"No, Jani!" he said in a low, urgent voice. "Get the fuck out of here."

Blaer came up on Marjani's other side. A chill slipped up

Adric's spine. This woman knew the secret incantation. If she shared it with Langdon, his clan was well-and-truly fucked. With Blaer's knowledge and Langdon's resources, the night fae could enslave every single member.

Horror gripped him as he recalled Rosana's prophecy.

The Darktime isn't over. The prince will destroy your clan from the inside out.

"Peace to you and yours, my lord." The tall blond fae lady bowed to Langdon. "I apologize for interrupting the ritual, but I believe you've been looking for this woman."

No.

Adric bucked wildly, fighting to get free of the night fae pinning him down.

Neoma tightened her grip on his pendant. The pain was almost unbearable, but he gritted his teeth and kept fighting. He had to get free. Had to somehow stop this.

The prince jerked his head at Marjani. "Take her," he commanded.

Twisting away from Luc, Marjani dropped into a crouch, a dagger in each hand. Two warriors broke from the circle to approach her, their own blades out, but she slashed about her, keeping them at bay.

At the same time, Luc saw Adric pinned down in the center of the circle. He growled and started forward.

"No." Blaer slapped a hand on his chest.

Luc halted. He sent a shamed look at Adric. At his sides, his fingers flexed and unflexed.

Then Rosana grabbed Langdon's hands. As her fingers closed around his, her body jolted and her braid lifted. The tie wrapped around the end slid off and the plait unwound itself to twist around her face in a sinuous black cloud.

"The old ways are no more," she said in a low, eerie voice. "Change is coming."

Everyone in the clearing froze, even the warriors attempting to capture Marjani.

Rosana moistened her lips. "Merry," she said in a scratchy voice.

"Yes?" Langdon turned his hands so he was gripping her. "What do you See?"

"Merry's a princess." She faltered. "I See a crown."

"Go on," he urged.

"Your granddaughter will rule. But not in darkness. In light."

The prince's diamond-studded brows snapped together.

Rosana's slender body shook. Adric could hardly bear to watch her, but she'd drawn everyone's attention. Even the men trying to corral Marjani were distracted.

Now was his chance to get his quartz back.

"And you," she told the prince. "Your life is a fine-spun web. Tear the wrong thread and you're dead. *Deus*, no." Her breath sobbed in.

Langdon's handsome face hardened. "What?"

Rosana shook her head and tried to pull her hands away, but he tightened his grip on her. "Tell me, damn you!"

"Death," Rosana whispered. "Death to your line...at the new ruler's hand."

"What new ruler?"

Rosana snatched her hands from the prince's, backed away. He reached for her and then checked as if she'd burned him.

Her body shimmered as if lit from inside by starlight. The night fae shrank from her. She swung around, pointed.

"Her. Lady Blaer."

Blaer straightened. "You lie," she hissed. "You'd do anything to escape." She motioned Luc forward. "Kill her. Kill the river fada."

Luc's hands fisted but he didn't move.

Blaer grabbed his quartz, squeezed. "I said, *Kill her*."

Luc growled, eyes wild. The man was near the breaking point —and Blaer either didn't know or didn't care.

The night fae pinning Adric down were still intent on the drama. He forced his body to relax completely, and as he'd hoped, their grip on him loosened.

Now.

Jerking out of their hold, Adric lunged at Neoma, ripping the pendant from her hand and dropping it over his head. His body shuddered with relief at having his quartz back. As the guards dove for him, he drew on its power with everything he had, leaping straight up so they passed beneath him—and shifted while he was still in mid-air.

He lost precious seconds during the change. When he came back to himself, he was a cougar, his clothes in shreds around him. The warriors tried again to grab him, but with a slash of his claws, he was free.

Luc had apparently started for Rosana at Blaer's command, but Marjani had put herself between them. The two men who'd been trying to capture her were on the ground, bleeding from multiple wounds.

"No, Luc. You can't! She's his mate."

"Get out of the way," Luc said in a dull voice.

"No." Marjani took a fighting stance, daggers at the ready. "You want to kill her, you'll have to go through me."

Adric went invisible. The three warriors circling him swore. One of them shot a fae ball at the spot where he'd been standing, but he'd already slipped between two of them. He reached Rosana right as she came out of her trance.

She glanced around, blinking. "Adric?" she asked on a rising note of fear—and collapsed to the ground.

In an instant, he was standing over her, ready to protect her at all costs.

He nuzzled Rosana's neck, sending reassurance through their bond. To his relief, her eyelids fluttered and then opened.

"You're here," she whispered, sinking her fingers into his fur.

He rumbled in response.

"What—?" Her gaze went past him and Marjani to Luc. She sucked in a breath and tried to stand but could only manage to bring herself to sitting. She leaned against Adric, lungs working, face as drawn as if she'd run a marathon.

Luc's claws slid out. "Don't make me hurt you," he told Marjani in flat, emotionless tones. "Just get the fuck out of the way."

"*No.*" She jabbed a dagger at him, forcing him to back off. "I won't let you do this."

Langdon stalked toward Blaer. Adric could almost see the prince recalling his earlier insinuation—that Blaer had manipulated events so Adric could assassinate him.

"A Seer in the grip of a vision doesn't lie," Langdon stated. He seemed to grow taller, darker as he spoke.

Blaer licked her lips. "She's a fada Seer," she said with a scornful glance at Rosana. "Who knows what she can do?" She looked at Luc. "I gave you an order—kill Rosana do Rio. If the Savonett woman is in the way, then kill her, too."

Luc's irises turned pure wolf, twin orange embers in the dark clearing. He glanced from Blaer to Marjani, and then he withdrew his claws and turned away. "No."

Blaer cast him an incredulous look. "What did you say?"

"No," Luc repeated.

Blaer lunged. "I said, *Kill them both.* Now!" She squeezed Luc's quartz, her lips moving, adding the power of the incantation to the *geas*.

Luc jolted and dropped to his knees, his body a man, his scent all wolf. He was seconds from going feral, and Blaer either didn't know, or she just didn't care. He dropped his head back and howled at the sky, a sad, lost song that had even the night fae tensing.

Blaer bent with him, tightening her grip on his quartz. "Kill. Them. Both."

It was a fatal mistake. Luc had accepted the *geas* to save Marjani's life. By ordering him to kill Marjani, the fae lady had broken their bargain, releasing Luc from the *geas*.

Luc tore off his clothes and shifted. Blaer went stick-still as the brown wolf's fierce, half-mad growls filled the clearing. She threw up her hands and began to call on some other kind of magic, but it was too late. Luc sprang, slamming her to the ground.

With a muttered incantation, the prince raised a long-fingered hand. The leaves and twigs scattered around the clearing levitated off the ground and streamed toward Luc and Blaer.

The other night fae edged to the clearing's outskirts, giving the prince a wide berth.

Marjani inched back to stand by Rosana. A brief caress of Adric's back told him that she knew he was there, too, but her gaze was glued on Luc and Blaer and the debris swirling around them.

"What the fuck?" she breathed.

A twig formed itself into a wolf that knocked Luc off Blaer, tossing him three yards away before falling back to the ground, a twig again. Langdon rotated his wrist and the other leaves spiraled around Blaer, faster and faster, before morphing into ravens that flew around her in tight circles.

Blaer scrambled to her feet, but it was too late. She was enclosed inside a living cage of ravens.

Luc got off the ground and gave himself a shake. He bounded back to Blaer, lips peeled in a furious snarl—and then stopped short. He prowled around the circling birds, searching for a way to get at Blaer.

She locked gazes with Langdon. "You want a fight, my lord?" Her chin jutted. "You forget I'm half ice fae."

"No," was the prince's reply. "I haven't forgotten."

The ravens' harsh caws filled the clearing.

Blaer raised her hands. Frost crept up Langdon's shoes.

He flicked a finger and the birds dove, pecking at her eyes and face. She shrieked and dropped to her knees, arms flung up to protect herself.

At a murmur from Langdon, the ravens backed off but continued to twine around Blaer so she was forced to remain crouched on the ground.

Luc crept closer, eyes burning.

She tossed her head, the cuts on her face already healing. "Go," she told him bitterly. "The *geas* is broken. You have your freedom."

But he didn't leave. Instead, he paced a circle around her, not attacking the ravens, but clearly guarding her.

Adric frowned at that—and then set it from his mind, because the prince had turned back to Rosana and Marjani.

Adric changed back to man but remained invisible. He rose to his feet, drawing Rosana up with him. Marjani shoved a dagger in his general direction, and he took it with a murmured thanks as she retrieved another dagger from the sheath around her neck.

Neoma conjured up a fae ball and aimed it at Marjani. "Stand down, fada."

Adric sprang at Neoma, slashed her forearm. The fae ball winked out of existence as she hissed and twisted away.

Meanwhile, Marjani had slipped Rosana the third dagger. The two of them stood back to back. Rosana blinked down at the iron blade, still shaky from her vision.

Adric's heart clenched. She needed food, rest.

He moved up beside her. "Leave," he whispered. "We'll cover you."

She tightened her grip on the dagger and lunged at a night fae approaching from her other side, slashing it across his knife arm. "Together," she growled as the warrior danced backward.

"Nice," murmured Marjani.

"Thanks," Rosana returned.

Adric's mouth twitched. "Together," he agreed. "Jani. What's the plan?"

"Get the fuck out of this warded circle. There's help on the other side."

He nodded. "You two go first. I'll keep them busy until you're out. The night fae might be able to sense me, but they can't be sure exactly where I am, especially if I keep moving."

"Works," said Marjani.

Rosana was more suspicious. "Promise you'll come with us."

He touched her cheek. "You have my word," he said, and then sprinted across the clearing to kick over the fire pit. The dark fire blinked out as it hit the ground.

The night fae hissed and snarled. Fae balls appeared in more warriors' hands. Adric slashed at the nearest one's arm and darted away.

The two women edged toward the portal while Adric bedeviled the night fae, dashing from one side of the clearing to the other, slashing at arms, legs, faces—anything to draw attention from Rosana and Marjani.

A crack of lightning split the night. Wind whipped through the clearing, but the wards—or whatever was protecting the circle—kept out the rain.

"Capture him!" the prince commanded. "You can't see him, but he's bleeding emotion. Focus on that."

The shadows deepened. Tendrils snaked through the night, seeking Adric. He instinctively froze. A glance over his shoulder told him that Rosana and Marjani had almost reached the portal.

He doggedly continued to zigzag through the night fae. But he was moving slower now, his limbs strangely heavy, as if the shadows had somehow taken on weight and were tugging on him.

Another bolt of lightning forced the shadows to retreat. Or maybe it wasn't lightning, but the sun fae.

Hope surged in Adric. He slipped around a couple of night fae warriors to join Marjani and Rosana, but the prince had realized the two were about to escape.

He flung up a hand. "Marjani Savonett and Rosana do Rio!" he commanded in a voice thick with power. "Halt!"

Rosana checked, but Marjani spun around, one hand on a silver charm that hung from her quartz. For the first time, he realized she was wearing a protection charm.

A warrior started forward, fae ball in hand.

Adric rushed back to Rosana and his sister. "I can cloak all three of us," he said. "Get ready to run like hell." He slipped an arm around each of their shoulders.

The portal wavered.

"Hurry!" he said. "Before it closes."

The shadows surrounded them. Tendrils snaked toward them.

Marjani shoved the protection charm at them and they retreated. But the portal had closed.

"Fuck," she muttered.

Then the sky lit like someone had torn back a curtain to let in the noon sun. As the night fae hissed in pain, the wards broke with an audible crack, sending a surge of energy that forced the three of them to stagger back.

Rain sluiced down.

"Go!" Adric urged the two women forward again.

More bolts of light slashed through the night. Queen Cleia strode into the clearing, her body a sunlit column, bolts of gold shooting from her fingertips.

For a few seconds, everyone—even Prince Langdon—stared at her, mouths ajar. Then the night fae snapped to life.

But more people poured into the clearing behind the queen.

Sun fae. River fada. And Jace, Fane, and a pack of Baltimore wolves with Zuri at the head.

"Now these kind of odds I can live with," his sister said.

Adric dropped the cloak so the three of them were visible again. The earth fada surrounded them, and they prepared to fight as fae on each side armed themselves with fiery balls of light.

Cleia planted herself at the center. With a wave of her hand, a fireball exploded at Langdon's feet. "I warned you to set the fada free, my lord. Now I'm here to demand their release. And think before you answer. I have two hundred more warriors itching for a fight."

Langdon conjured up a seething mass of shadows and doused the fireball.

"Shadows blot out the sun," he returned. "It's the night of the new moon. Do you think you can beat me?"

Cleia raised her hands. Behind her, Dion placed his hands on her shoulders. Something flashed between the two of them. Twin suns sparked to life in her hands.

"But sunlight chases away the shadows." The glowing balls in her hands grew brighter.

Langdon recovered first. He took two steps forward, face pale and eyebrows glittering. Two black-clad warriors flanked him, fae balls glowing in their palms.

Cleia raised her hands higher. An unearthly flame danced in her palms, lighting her gold, silver and copper hair so that it shone like living fire.

"Tell your guards to stand down," she gritted, "or I'll turn them into ashes."

"Try it." Langdon pointed a finger at Cleia, but the rest of them had had time to shrug off whatever spell he'd cast.

Dion leapt to block him. In his hand was a dagger shimmering with magic.

Langdon flicked his fingers at the dagger, trying to change it to something else, but the bespelled dagger remained just that—a dagger.

Dion lashed out at Langdon, fada-fast. The prince only just managed to leap clear of the slashing blade.

Dion stalked after him, his eyes pure, molten silver.

The prince conjured up a whirling wall of twigs and leaves, but Dion slashed his way through them.

Meanwhile, the priests and priestesses had melted into the shadows so that only their eyes were visible.

Two wolves came at Langdon from either direction, but he evaded them by sinking into the shadows himself. More twigs and leaves swirled around Cleia, but before they could turn into anything, she incinerated them with another bolt.

A second, more powerful explosion ripped the night fae from the shadows. This time, Langdon was ready. He threw up a shade of leaves and other debris to protect him and his people from the worst of the light.

But Adric and the other fada had engaged them, he and Marjani fighting neck-and-neck with Rui and Tiago, while nearby, Zuri and the other wolves took down another couple of night fae.

Adric could see the moment Langdon realized that even if he

survived, he was going to take heavy casualties, including losing most of the court's priests and priestesses.

He threw up his arms and a powerful wind blasted everyone except Cleia to the opposite side of the circle. But when they jumped to their feet, he ordered his own people to stand down, and then turned to Cleia.

"Peace, my lady." He kept his hands by his sides, palms out, in a proudly open posture. "Rosana do Rio is yours. I ask only one thing in return—that you grant me the rights I'm owed as a grandfather."

Dion moved next to Cleia. "A grandfather?"

"Yes. I demand the right to know the daughter of my youngest son. You and your clan have no right to keep me from the blood of my blood."

"Fuck your rights." Adric shoved his way next to Dion. "You'll have to go through me and every member of my clan first," he spat.

But Dion nodded as if he was considering it. "You'll release my sister without obligation?" While he was speaking, Dion undid the silver bracelet around his wrist and tossed it to Rosana, who quickly clasped it around her own wrist.

Adric shot him a furious look, but something in the other alpha's expression made him hold back.

"Yes," Langdon said. "She's given me an invaluable piece of information. I consider any debt between us paid in full. That is," he said to Rosana. "If I can't persuade you to remain as court Seer?"

Rosana couldn't conceal a shudder. "No," she said curtly. "But I refuse to leave without Marjani and Adric."

"Rosana," Dion said with a scowl.

Her jaw set. "He's my mate."

Cleia spoke. "You owe the fada a boon, Prince Langdon."

"My sister's life," Adric said.

"And Lord Adric's," Rosana quickly added. "We'll accept nothing else."

"Come," Cleia said. "That seems reasonable. After all, this was started by your own son."

Langdon eyed Adric coldly. Adric had a sudden insight—the prince was searching for a way to save face in front of his people. But more than that, he truly wanted to get to know Merry.

And it *was* Merry's birthright. She had the right to make her own decision.

"As for your granddaughter," Adric added, "as far as I'm concerned, the choice is hers. Not yours, and not Lord Dion's."

Rui do Mar made a sharp movement, but Dion nodded at Adric. "Go on."

Adric dropped his voice so that only Langdon, Cleia, Rui, Dion and Rosana could hear.

"When Merry comes of age, then you'll invite her to visit the court. I'm sure Lord Dion will agree that the choice at that point will be hers. But for now, leave her where she is. She's safe, happy. The river fada have done a good job of protecting her, and the queen keeps an eye on her as well. Too many people are interested in her."

A muscle in the prince's cheek worked. His gaze slid to the nearby night fae, straining to hear the low-voiced conversation.

"Very well," he said. "If you and Lord Dion both swear that when my granddaughter comes of age, the choice is hers."

"No tricks or coercion," Adric said. "She must be given a true choice."

Dion waited for Rui to nod, and then said, "That's acceptable to us."

Langdon inclined his head. "You have my promise."

"And my promise as well," first Adric, then Dion said.

Langdon hesitated. "I would like the chance to get to know her, though. Perhaps a meeting or two a year."

"That's up to her father," Dion said.

Rui crossed his arms over his broad chest. "No."

"And that goes double for me," said Jace from behind Adric's shoulder. "You had your chance to get to know her when she was on the run from Tyrus. Now, she stays with us."

The prince's mouth tightened. "Very well. But perhaps you can ask if she wishes to meet me. I promise, I want only to become acquainted with her."

Rui's dark brows lowered. "We'll see," was all he'd say.

"Thank you." Langdon stepped back. "Let them leave unharmed," he told his warriors. He bowed to the queen. "Peace to you and yours, Cleia."

"And to yours," she returned with a gracious bow of her own.

Adric and Marjani exchanged an incredulous glance. But that was the fae. Polite even as they slipped a knife into your rib cage.

In the exodus that followed, Adric sidled up to Langdon. "Just so you know," he murmured, "if you take Merry, I'll know. Every earth fada in the clan is connected to my quartz."

"I see." Langdon's eyes dropped to Adric's pendant.

Adric fingered it just to make sure his point was taken. "You can hide her, but eventually, I'll find her. And I wouldn't advise looking for a way to break the connection. It might work—or you might kill her. We're not the enemy," he added. "Your own people are."

Langdon's gaze flicked at a priest setting the metal bowl back on its stand. Others had faded back into the shadows, so that only their faces were visible. Watching. Waiting.

"I'm aware of that," the prince said, and striding back to his throne, settled onto it with his legs sprawled in front of him as if he hadn't a care in the world.

Adric's chest heaved. It was over.

He reached for Rosana, but she was already there. She took his head between her hands and gave him a smacking kiss, uncaring that her brothers, Cleia and the upper hierarchy of both their clans were watching. Or maybe, that was the point.

"You did it!"

"No, we did it," he corrected, enfolding her in his arms. "I love you, you know that?"

"Right back at you." She buried her face in his neck and they stood there, arms tight around each other, rocking back and forth. "I was so scared," she muttered.

"I'm sorry, angel."

She pulled back. "You should be," she said with a crooked grin. "Now take me home."

He glanced at where Marjani was crouched next to Luc, speaking in a low voice. The wolf growled and shook his head.

"You go," he told Rosana. "I'll be right with you."

Her gaze had followed his own. "Of course." She hugged him again and then turned to Dion, who was waiting to wrap her in a hug of his own.

Marjani looked up at Adric, biting her lip. "He won't leave. I think he's bonded to her somehow."

Adric scowled down at Luc. He'd thought the next time he saw the wolf, he'd rip off his face for what he'd put Rosana through, but now he just felt sorry for him. Besides, if he knew Luc, the wolf would punish himself more harshly than anything Adric could do.

He set a hand on Luc's head. The wolf pushed into his palm, taking his alpha's scent on himself.

"Luc. Come with us. The clan misses you. I miss you."

The wolf turned his head to look up at Adric. His eyes had lost their madness. He gave Adric a decided nudge toward the exit. *Go.*

Adric's throat tightened. He wanted to argue further, but almost everyone had left now. Besides him and Marjani, only Fane, Cleia and a couple of sun fae warriors waited, and it wasn't fair to ask them to stay in this nightmare of a court any longer than they had to.

"Okay. If you're sure that's how you want it." He rubbed his cheek against Luc's. "But when you return, your place in the clan will be there. That's a promise."

Luc dipped his head in acknowledgment.

There was still one thing left to do. Keeping a wary eye on the circling ravens, Adric thrust his quartz toward at the woman trapped within. "Lady Blaer," he commanded. "Look at my quartz."

She glanced up and dully shook her head.

He let the fire flare inside. "Lady Blaer," he repeated in a hard voice. "Look at my quartz."

This time, her gaze caught on the quartz. Held.

Maybe it was because he was so determined, or maybe it was because she'd been weakened by her fight with Langdon, but when he said, "You *will* forget the secret words. You'll even forget they exist," she gave a jerky nod.

"Say it," he ordered.

"I will forget the secret words. As if they never existed."

"And you'll never use them against a fada again," he added.

"And I'll never use them against a fada again."

"Good." He bared his fangs at her. "Because if you do, the next time we meet, I'll carve your fucking liver out."

He rose back up.

A tear ran down Marjani's mud-streaked cheek. She touched Luc's shoulder, then turned and stumbled toward the portal, where Fane wrapped an arm around her shoulders. Together, she, Fane and Adric exited the clearing, Cleia and her men behind them.

Dion and Tiago waited on the other side of the portal, along with Rosana, who had an arm around each of them.

"You came." She was laughing and crying at the same time. "*You came.*"

"Of course, we did," Dion growled and handed her off to Cleia for a hug.

"You were awesome," Rosana told her. "Totally kickass."

The queen grinned—and swayed on her feet. Her skin was pale under its dusting of gold. Dion was instantly there, sweeping her into his arms.

"Let's get the fuck out of here," he said.

Together, he, Tiago, and Rui hurried the two women through the forest. Rosana cast an apologetic look over her shoulder at

Adric, but allowed it. But when she stepped through the second portal, she halted to wait for Adric.

He immediately set an arm around her waist. Staking his claim in front of her brothers.

Dion cast Adric a dark look. "You really mated with this *filho da puta*?"

"I was dying." Rosana moved closer to Adric. "He saved my life. We're bonded now. You can't undo it."

"But we would like your blessing," Adric added.

Tiago sneered. "What about your clan?"

"They'll treat my mate with respect, or they'll find a new clan." Adric touched his quartz. "I swear on my mother's grave."

Beside him, Marjani and Jace nodded agreement.

Dion gave curt nod. "I'll hold you to that."

Rosana beamed. "It will work," she assured her brothers. "You'll see."

As they started forward again, she lifted her face to a ray of sunshine. With a shock, Adric realized it was morning, the sun rising in a winter-blue sky.

His lungs expanded. Inside, his cat gave a luxurious stretch.

A dizzying exhilaration filled him. This was happiness, he realized. This light-as-air feeling.

The night fae had been defeated—for now, at least. His sister was free of the death sentence hanging over her, and he'd neutralized Lady Blaer. They'd even bought Merry some time before she'd have to deal with Prince Langdon.

And not only had he survived, he'd somehow won this smart, beautiful, caring woman as his mate.

Rosana turned to look at him. Curious at first, and then she broke into a wondering smile.

"You're happy. I feel it. Here." She pressed her fingers to her breastbone.

"Hell, yeah." He touched his lips to hers, taking that smile inside him. "Let's go home."

"Yes," she murmured against his mouth. "Let's go home."

47

The mate ball was held at the Court of the Rising Sun.

Queen Cleia had offered, and Rosana had been so thrilled that Adric had agreed, even though he'd assumed they'd hold the ceremony out of his den. Still, at the end of the night, she'd be going home with him, and that was all he cared about.

The ritual was scheduled for sunset on the spring equinox. Adric slid a finger under the collar of his bronze button-up shirt as he waited for Rosana in the crowded, flower-filled tent. A fae light drifted by, a soft pink dotted with lazily spiraling bits of gold. More fae lights cast a hazy rose hue on the assembled clans—his, hers, and a sizable number of sun fae.

At his side were Zuri and Jace, and nearby were Rosana's attendants, Merry and Jenny. Dion and Marjani were joint officiants.

Dion was imposing in a deep blue shirt and dark slacks, his long hair flowing over his shoulders, his big feet bare. His pint-sized daughter was cuddled in one arm, her bright eyes taking in everything.

"Savonett." The other alpha nodded, unsmiling. "All the best on your mate-day."

He nodded back. "Thank you."

He turned to Marjani, stunning in an African wax-print dress with cheerful red poppies splashed on a green background. It was still a shock to see his sister in something besides brown, gray or camo-green.

"Jani." He embraced her. "You look—"

"Gorgeous?" She hugged him back. "Glowing?"

He grinned. "Yeah. All that." He stepped back to scan the meadow for Rosana again, but she was closeted with Cleia and her former nurse Isa in the queen's fanciful, four-tiered white mansion.

After they'd left Virginia, Dion had taken Rosana back to Rock Run to rest and prepare for the mating celebration. She'd visited Adric every few days, but at his request, it had been a week now since he'd last seen her. He'd spent the time making his den ready for her.

But damn, he ached for her. And not just his cock, which had been half-hard all day. No, it was his heart that ached. It *hurt* to be separated from his mate.

He shoved his hands into his pockets and scanned the tent again. This mating stuff was for the birds. It made you weak, vulnerable—and he wouldn't trade places with another man in this tent for any amount of riches.

The sun was painting the sky a spectacular peach and purple when Rosana and her entourage finally emerged from Cleia's mansion. An excited murmur rippled through the crowd as Tiago and the queen escorted her across the meadow to the tent, with Isa following, a proud smile on her elderly face.

Adric craned his neck, but after a brief glimpse, all he saw was the top of her black head as she wended her way through the crowd, greeting and being greeted.

It seemed like hours before Rosana finally came into view—and stole the breath right out of his chest.

She was gorgeous in a calf-length gown of ivory and gold that clung to her upper body, showing off her high, firm breasts and nipped-in waist before widening to an airy froth around long, sleek-muscled legs. Her only jewelry was his amethyst pendant, the charm bracelet, and a pair of dangling earrings, and she wore short lace gloves on her hands.

But what made him grin were the red kitten-heel boots on her feet.

"Breathe, Ric." Marjani slanted him a teasing smile.

Breathe. Right.

Adric sucked in a loud inhale that had everyone nearby chuckling.

Tiago took his place with the other men, and Cleia took little Brisa from Dion before joining the other women.

Zuri stepped forward to take Rosana's hands and thank her before everyone for saving Adric's life. Marjani and Adric had made sure everyone knew what Rosana had done at New Moon, starting with how she'd refused to leave him alone at the court after he'd been badly injured. It had gone a long way to reducing the clan's antagonism against her.

It didn't hurt that they had a healthy respect for Rosana's Gift. Some of them were even a little afraid of her, which was a good start. Fada respected strength.

True acceptance would take longer, of course. But he had a feeling Rosana would win them over. She'd already won over Zuri, and he wasn't an easy sell.

As for the hardliners, the ones who muttered their alpha shouldn't mate with the enemy?

Adric had made sure they knew that Rosana was his mate— period—and they'd treat her with courtesy, or find another clan. He'd only had to shove a few of the more dominant up against a wall to make his point.

Now, he stepped forward and extricated her from Zuri.

"Ready?"

She took his hands. "You know I am."

The ceremony passed in a blur. All he could see was Rosana, blue eyes smiling, a constant smile on her lips. Crazy in love, and unashamed to show it.

He no longer wondered if she'd ever learn to protect her heart.

Instead, he thanked the gods that she'd given it to him. It was a gift he intended to treasure the rest of his life.

He spoke his vows to her loud and clear, proudly claiming her as his before everyone present. She accepted his claim in the same clear tones.

His mate gift to her was a three-strand bracelet of semi-precious stones—amethyst, lapis and green jasper—with a silver cougar and dolphin intertwined at the center.

Her mouth rounded in a soft *Oh* as he clasped it around her wrist next to the charm bracelet. "I love it," she said, leaning in for a kiss.

But he stopped her, removing his quartz. "Take off your gloves."

When she did, he wrapped her bare hands around the chunk of gray and orange. The earth fada sucked in a breath, understanding the symbolism.

Rosana was truly his mate.

Taking back the quartz, he cupped her face and kissed her as Dion and Marjani pronounced the last few words of the ceremony, asking for their mating to be blessed by the gods and goddesses, the sun and moon, and everyone present.

When he released her, her eyes were a deep, saturated blue.

"I love you," he said, and they turned to accept the congratulations of their clans.

Hours later, Dion and Adric ended up side-by-side, watching the dancers. Their two clans had managed to get through dinner and the dancing that followed without any incidents. They were even intermingling. Zuri was currently charming a sexy older river fada, and Davi was dancing with Suha.

A tall, golden-haired sun fae spun Rosana in a circle and then bent her back over his arm. She laughed up at him and pivoted away, the skirt swirling around her slim legs.

An almost noiseless growl escaped Adric at seeing her so close to another male.

Mine.

It was primal, primitive—and he didn't give a damn. He was a newly mated fada male, and he wanted his woman all to himself. But he folded his arms over his chest and stayed where he was, because he also wanted his woman to be happy, and Rosana was clearly enjoying herself.

Dion's look was knowing. "It isn't easy watching your mate with another man."

He scowled and shrugged.

"You kept her alive. I owe you my thanks."

Adric snorted. "Like hell you do. I almost got her bound to the prince in a *geas*."

"You did what you had to do. I know the whole story—how she went to Baltimore, tried to get you to take her with you. And then when she had a chance to leave, she refused."

Adric met his eyes. "If this is the part where you say be good to my sister or I'll bust your balls, don't worry. I know I don't deserve her—but I love her. I'd burn down the fucking world for her."

A short nod. "I know you would. Do I trust you? You still have to earn that. But in this, I do—you won't hurt her because it would hurt you too much."

Adric moved uncomfortably on his feet. "She's my mate," he muttered. "Don't make me into some kind of hero."

Dion grunted. "Believe me, I'm not. I'm a mated man myself, remember? I know how it is." A feral grin. "And if you did hurt Rosana, I wouldn't have to do a damn thing. She'd bust your balls for me."

Adric gave a bark of laughter, watching as Rosana danced by with another man—Jace, this time. "You're right."

"But I have a proposition for you. I want to see my sister more than once every couple of weeks, and I know you're never going to be satisfied until you have more land for your clan."

"Go on."

"Here's the deal. You need a place for your people to run free as their animals. Rock Run might be able to help you there."

Adric's heart sped up. "Yeah?"

"I'll rent your clan the portion of our territory farthest from the base. I'll give you a line that you'll tell your people not to cross, but you'll still have a few hundred acres of forest to run in. Maybe down the road, you can buy up some of the nearby land, expand. When that Factory of yours finally gets off the ground, you'll have some extra cash."

"I see."

"Well? You interested?"

"Very," he returned with a cool nod, although inside, he was leaping for joy.

"We'll have to work out the details," Dion said, "but I'd say we have ourselves a deal." He brought his fist to his heart, and then offered his hand to Adric.

Adric touched his heart as well, and the two of them shook on it.

"Thank you," he said. "You won't be sorry."

"See that I'm not."

Adric nodded—and then grinned. "But for the record, I'm not done being a pain in your ass."

Dion smiled back. A white-toothed, frankly evil smile. "You just took on my sister. I figure we're about even."

48

———

At midnight the celebration was still going strong. That was the sun fae for you; they'd still be partying until midnight tomorrow. Not that the fada looked ready to go home anytime soon, either.

But Adric had had enough.

He found Rosana near the dance floor with Jenny, their dark heads together, chuckling about something.

"Time to go." He put a hand on the small of Rosana's back.

"Already?" She glanced at him, surprised. Whatever she saw in his face had her sharing a grin with Jenny. "Guess we're leaving."

The two women hugged. "Don't be a stranger," Jenny said.

"I won't, I promise," said Rosana. "And you can come see me. Right?" She cast Adric an uncertain look.

He frowned. A Rock Run fada's mate in his den? The very idea raised his fur.

But that was the old Adric, the one who'd had to be suspicious of everyone and everything to survive.

So he smiled at Jenny. "You're welcome anytime."

The human's dark eyes lit. "Thank you, my lord."

"Please. Call me Ric."

"Ric," she said, her smile increasing.

He turned to Rosana. "Ready? I have a surprise for you."

Jenny smirked, and he winked at her as he took Rosana's hand. "Not that kind of surprise," he said.

Rosana's mouth twitched as they walked around the tent to thank Cleia and Dion for the party. "No? Now I'm curious."

He patted her round bottom. "Be good."

She nipped his earlobe. "But you like me bad," she murmured —and smiled at her brother and Cleia, leaving him to hide his erection. "This has been the best day of my life," she told them.

He set his mouth to her ear. "You'll pay for that," he promised in an equally low voice, and added his thanks to hers.

THEY RODE BACK to Baltimore on Adric's motorcycle. Rosana wrapped her arms around his lean waist, still in her dress and red boots.

She slipped her hands under his leather jacket, toying with his ridged abs beneath the soft bronze shirt. "Did I tell you how good you looked today?"

"Mm." He took her hand, bringing it to his lips before setting it back on his waist again. "You were the hottest woman there."

She leaned her cheek against his jacket and slipped her fingers lower to the ridge beneath his zipper. "Keep talking, and you might get lucky tonight."

A wicked chuckle. "I'm counting on it, mate."

Her dress came off as soon as they walked in the door. Her only underclothes were a wispy white bra and panties.

Adric shrugged out of his jacket. "The boots stay on," he said as he pulled her into his arms.

Her whole body thrilled at the low command.

He filled his hands with her ass and lowered his mouth to hers, tasting her with slow, knee-weakening sweeps of his tongue. She pressed against him.

He was still cold from the ride, the shirt soft and cool against her bare skin, his pants slightly abrasive. He pushed his thigh between her legs as he kissed her, rubbing against her sex through the flimsy panties.

She moaned and sucked his tongue deeper.

He eased up on the kiss and rested his forehead against hers. "It's been too damn long."

"A week."

"It felt like a year. Ten years." Suddenly, her feet were swept out from beneath her. She squeaked and looped an arm around his neck as he headed down the hall with her in his arms. "But first, your surprise. Close your eyes."

She obediently shut them. "What is it?"

He nipped her throat. "If I told you, it wouldn't be a surprise. No, don't open them yet." He set her on the floor and covered her eyes with his hands, nudging her through a doorway.

She gripped his wrists. Was that water she heard?

He took his fingers away. "Go ahead. Look."

"Oh, Adric." She clapped her hands to her mouth.

Amber quartz sconces lit a stone grotto twice the size of Adric's living room. A waterfall fed the pool in the center—a pool large enough for her dolphin with a few yards to spare—and a narrow stream exited from the opposite end, providing further room to swim.

"It's beautiful," she breathed.

He caressed her shoulders from behind. "There are crystals set in the walls of the pool to purify the water, but it comes from an underground spring, which is about as pure as Baltimore water gets."

She turned in his arms. "I love it. I—" She shook her head, throat too tight to speak. "How—?"

A shrug. "We worked around the clock—me and three other stoneworkers. We didn't carve it all by hand. I blasted out the main cavity, then we went from there."

"It's incredible. I can't believe you did this—and so fast."

"You're my mate. I want you to be happy."

She took his face between her hands and kissed him on the lips. "I love it, and I love you. Thank you." She knelt to trail a hand in the water.

It was cool, clean-smelling. Perfect.

He smiled down at her. "Go ahead. Take a swim."

"I will." Rising to her feet, she set a hand on his chest and walked him backward until he was against the wall. She started undoing his shirt buttons. "Later. First, I have to thank my mate properly."

A slow grin. "I think I'm going to like this."

She helped him out of the shirt and dropped it on the stone floor. Removing her bra and panties, she sank to her knees before him.

His breath rasped in. "In the red boots? You know this is my fantasy, right?"

"Yeah?" She eased his zipper down over his erection and freed him from his boxers. "Tell me more." She licked her way around the rim, delicate, teasing touches.

His cock jerked beneath her touch.

Adric fisted his hands. His hips strained toward her.

She gripped one hip with her hand and wrapped the other around his hard stalk. It was so thick, her fingers barely made it around. She swiped her tongue over the smooth head, and he groaned.

His hands threaded into her hair, holding her in place as he stroked into her mouth.

"In my fantasy," he said, "you come to me, wet from the water, wearing those fuck-me boots and nothing else. I order you to get on your knees and take me, and you do. Because you like it as much as me."

The hot, dark words sent a jolt of excitement to her already soaked sex.

"You say you like my taste. My scent."

"Mm." She moaned around him. "I do."

"You say, *I See a lot of sex in your future.*"

She chuckled, causing him to jerk.

"Gods. When you laugh, I feel it vibrating clear to my balls." He pressed deeper into her mouth. "Take me, Rosana. Take me all the way."

She eagerly sucked on him, loving the salty-sea taste. He fell silent, his face taut with desire. Letting her pleasure him.

Even better, she could *feel* his enjoyment through the mate bond.

She slid a hand between his thighs, cupping and caressing his balls. They were drawn up tight.

He groaned and rasped, "And then, you say you love me. Tell me, Rosana. Tell me you love me."

But when she opened her mouth to obey, he lifted her from her knees, turning with her still in his arms and pressing her up the wall.

His tongue slipped into her mouth. "I can taste myself," he muttered. "And you. You and me, together. Now say it."

She wrapped her arms and legs around him. "I love you. I love you. I love you."

He started to press in, and then halted. "Condom," he muttered.

She dug her heels into his taut buttocks, keeping him where he was. "It's okay. If it happens, it happens. I want a big family like my mom and dad had."

"Yeah?" His eyes were a gleaming mix of bronze and blue. "That sounds pretty good to me."

He stroked in the rest of the way, and for a long while, the only sounds in the cavern were the waterfall's musical trickle—and an earth fada and a river fada making love.

Together.

Need more Fada Shapeshifters? See all the books in series order here —>https://rebeccarivard.com/shapeshifters/

ALSO BY REBECCA RIVARD

THE FADA SHAPESHIFTERS

Stealing Ula: A Fada Shapeshifter Prequel (Nisio & Ula, set in Ireland)

The Rock Run River Fada

Seducing the Sun Fae (Dion & Cleia)

Claiming Valeria (Rui & Valeria)

Tempting the Dryad (Tiago & Alesia)

Sea Dragon's Hunger (Cassidy & Nic)

The Baltimore Earth Fada (The Darktime Trilogy)

Saving Jace (Jace & Evie)

Charming Marjani (Marjani & Fane)

Adric's Heart (Adric & Rosana)

Fada Shapeshifter Short Reads

Lir's Lady (#3.5—Lir & Isleen)

Shifter's Valentine (#3.6—Jenny & Chico)

Find out more and read exclusive excerpts: https://rebeccarivard.com/shapeshifters/

The Vampire Syndicate Romances

Pursued (Gabriel)

Craved (Rafael)

Taken (Zaquiel)

The Vampire Blood Courtesans

Ensnared: Star

Compelled: Cerise

Find out more: https://rebeccarivard.com/vampires/

Join **Rebecca Rivard's newsletter** to stay informed and be eligible for giveaways and sneak peeks. As a thank you, Rebecca will gift you with a steamy short story!

Sign up at rebeccarivard.com or go to this link: Rebecca's newsletter

ABOUT THE AUTHOR

USA Today bestselling author Rebecca Rivard read way too many romances as a teenager, little realizing she was actually preparing for a career. She now spends her days with dark shifters, sexy fae and other magical creatures—which has to be the best job ever. When she's not writing, she walks, bikes and kayaks in the Chesapeake Bay area with her guitar-playing, storytelling husband.

Five of her novels have been awarded the coveted Crowned Heart Review from *InD'Tale Magazine* and the FADA SHAPESHIFTER SERIES was voted Best Shifter Series in the Paranormal Romance Guild Reviewer's Choice Awards.

Her books have also won the prestigious PRISM Award (*Charming Marjani*) and the PRG Reviewer's Choice Award (*Saving Jace*), and have finaled in both the RONE and the HOLT Medallion.